THE RIVER STYX

MICHAEL BLACKETT

JUPITER4PRESS

Copyright © 2006 by Michael R Blackett
All rights reserved.

Cover Art and Text Copyright © 2006 by Michael R Blackett
All rights reserved.
This book, or parts thereof, may not be used or reproduced in any form whatsoever, electronically or mechanically, without written permission of the publisher and author.

JUPITER4PRESS

The contents of this book are a work of fiction. Any and all references to medical situations and conditions are not intended to be factual or portray situations past or present, but are constructed from the author's imagination. Similarities or resemblances to names, characters, persons living or dead, places and/or incidents are purely coincidental and again only the result of the author's imagination.

Published by Jupiter4Press in cooperation and by arrangement with the author.
Jupiter4press
P.O. Box 334
Schererville, Indiana 46375

If you purchase this book without a cover you should be aware that this book may have been stolen property and reported as "unsold and destroyed" to the publisher. In such case neither the author nor the publisher has received any payment for this stripped book.

*To my wife Mary
and my daughters
Michelle and Marie*

ACKNOWLEDGMENTS

There is no story without the people behind the scenes, for it is not solely generated by the writer. The idea may come from the author's mind but many minds become involved. I would like to take this opportunity to thank a number of gracious and extremely helpful people who gave selflessly to aid me in this publication.

Encouragement may only come from one source, but in my case I was blessed. It was my two daughters, Marie and Michelle who convinced me to write this story. Equipped with their enthusiastic support and many ideas, I found a great deal of confidence to proceed. I must thank them for their faith that I could accomplish this undertaking.

There is one person without whom I could not have accomplished this task. My deepest thanks and appreciation go to my wife, Mary, who spent endless hours proof reading my early ramblings. Her suggestions helped me build what I hope has become a good story. Her critiquing also helped me find better paths. I must also thank my mother, Doris, for the time she spent critiquing and offering her opinion and suggestions.

My dear friend and editor, Ceil Dahlen, was my savior who came to my rescue at the last moment. She gave her time fearlessly, God bless her, and tenaciously ploughed through hundreds of pages of script, even taking it on vacation with her. Her ideas, suggestions and constructive criticism were invaluable. Thank you, Ceil, for all you have given to me.

A policeman's lot is a burdensome one, for he lives the job twenty-four hours a day. They are the good Samaritans to the public as well as their scapegoats and they are praised and condemned in the same breath. Little consideration is extended to these dedicated men and women for the situations they must face on the front line in the time of crisis, and in the heat of the moment, when their lives are on the line. This story, in part, is about them…their frustrations, disappointments, hardships and triumphs.

Because this tale is set in a very specific place, it was important to me that certain technical aspects of the plot be reasonably accurate. Despite the fact that the story is fiction, the plot had to be convincing. I was, therefore, obliged to seek a source of information that would allow me to attain that goal. I must thank Jim Hollandsworth, retired Commander – Chicago Police Department for his time and patience in answering my many questions regarding the CPD.

Last but certainly not least, I must express gratitude to my very good friends in Write-On Hoosiers for their patience, help and critiquing over the last year and a half. I put them through rather torturous agony while they sat and listened to what seemed like the endless saga of 'The River Styx'. Their feedback was invaluable.

AUTHOR'S NOTE

Tale of One City

This is a story of fiction in which all of the incidents and characters are figments of the imagination. However, the location where the action occurs is not. The place is quite real, for it is the City of Chicago. The City of Chicago was born out of the small military settlement of Fort Dearborn. In 1833 it had a population large enough to be incorporated as a village. From that moment, the small hamlet of 150 souls set out on a bumpy road of progress fraught with turmoil, tragedy, hardship and success to emerge as one of the finest cities in the country and the world.

Today, Chicago is a city to behold with some of the most unique and magnificent architecture found anywhere. Located on the shores of Lake Michigan, it presents one of the most picturesque skylines and at night, if viewed from the lake, it is a virtual fairyland. The scenes and locations in the story were chosen very carefully. The Field Museum, founded in 1893, is one of many grand and fascinating buildings in a city rich with such structures. Northwestern Memorial Hospital offers some of the finest medical services in the country and has done so since 1865. A huge complex affiliated with Northwestern University, it is a pulsating hive of nurses, doctors, practitioners and students alike, all dutifully working to heal those in need. And then there is Lake Shore Drive. I have seen few places around the world that can compare with the beauty found along this scenic bustling thoroughfare.

Chicago is well known worldwide for its infamous history of gangsters, territorial crime wars and illegal liquor peddling. If any city has been immortalized due to its association with crime, it is Chicago. But there is so much more to this great conurbation. Today it is a thriving commercial center that is still growing and guarded passionately by dedicated men and women of the Chicago Police Department. It is one of the finest police forces in the country that works daily keeping law and order in a city so famous for its outlaws.

This is Chicago. And because it has so much character, it is one of the many reasons I chose it as the backdrop for this tale. Chicagoans are proud of what they have and rightly so. There is a certain charm about this grand old lady of concrete and steel. But what makes this city is, without question, its people. Their warmth and friendliness is almost unique. Chicago is a city that never sleeps, a pulsating metropolis full of life and character. It is a city to fall in love with and fall in love in and should be seen and experienced at least once in a lifetime and more often if possible.

Michael Blackett
2006

35 I have seen a wicked man
    overbearing,
  and towering like a cedar of
    Lebanon.
36 Again I passed by, and lo, he was
    no more;
  though I sought him, he could not
    be found.

37 Mark the blameless man and behold
    the upright,
  for there is posterity for the man
    of peace.
38 But transgressors shall be altogether
    destroyed;
  the posterity of the wicked shall
    be cut off.

Psalm 37

THE RIVER STYX

MICHAEL BLACKETT

-Episode 1-

Comes The Devil

DÉ-JÀ-VU

▼▼▼▼▼ 1

Out of the darkness a hand grabbed her cloak and held her fast. Sally fought desperately to escape, but her assailant struck her, knocking her to the ground. She struggled to her feet and slipped on the frozen ground but managed to remain upright. Before she could run, he was on her again. There was a flash, then excruciating pain as the blade he wielded sliced into her flesh once more. Then Sally seized an opportunity and lashed at her attacker.

Her hand struck him on the chin then fell upon something metallic about his neck. The blow sent her attacker staggering backward. As he slipped and fell, his weapon pierced his right shoulder. A scream of pain erupted from his throat. At that instant the world about her was churned into chaos by the howling wind. Her assailant vanished in a vortex of white. Sally's feet were ripped from beneath her and she was thrown, turning and tumbling into the air. In a shudder of agony she came to rest in a snow bank still clutching the object. With the knowledge that death was on her heels, Sally scrambled to her feet.

The lone pathetic figure now staggered and groped her way along the dark and deserted street engulfed in a churning mass of white that obscured everything beyond her fingertips. Sally had two companions...fear that relentlessly tore her from within and winter's breath that tore at her from without. She rushed from the terror that was trying to steal her life; her destination was of no importance at that moment.

Sally screamed into the howling wind. "Stay away from me! Leave me alone! Why are you doing this?" No answer was forthcoming except the sirens of the dead. "I will not submit to you!" A street lamp, a solitary beacon on the corner, cast the only light. As close as it was, it was but a blur through the blinding blizzard.

Her outstretched hand found the wall of an adjacent building. For a fleeting moment, as if gathering some hidden strength from the brick and stone monolith, this half-frozen, wounded woman loitered. Then once more, driven by fear, she commenced her flight through the angry night. As she cried, her tears froze on her cheeks. Again she wailed to her invisible assailant. "Go away! Leave me be!" But Sally knew he was behind her, closing the distance between them, preparing to strike her down at any moment.

Without pausing she glanced over her shoulder but saw no one. As she approached the street lamp, a long shadow slithered silently over the snow-covered walk shrinking with each step as it crept upon its owner. Then for an instant it vanished before it slipped out in front of the pathetic figure leading her back into the blackness to the next beacon. The wind clawed at Sally's tattered cloak. Strips of torn cloth slapped angrily at the air. There was no reprieve from the bitter cold, no shelter offering a warm fire; it was a night only for the dead. Tormented by demons pursuing her from the darkened crevices of every invisible alley, she staggered.

Then the air was filled with an inhuman sound. Terrified, she paused to listen. It roared and ground its way through the darkness. As suddenly as it began, it ceased and only the cry of the wind remained. Exhausted, breathing heavily, the ice-cold air ripped at her lungs with every breath. Her body was wracked with pain and her life's liquid flowed from her wounds but she continued. She wanted to sleep. Yet the need to live, to survive, drove her blindly forward through the frozen streets of the city she knew so well yet did not recognize.

The orgy of weather pushed her before its tenacious charge, buffeting her fragile body. If she stopped she knew it could mean certain death...death dealt from the elements and the loss of life's precious liquid, or death from the demon that hunted her. But death no matter how it came would be the victor. Wounded though it might be, the monster would not rest until he held her lifeless body in his grip. The sound came again. It was alien, unfamiliar but close, a deep roar, like that of a tiger. Panic gripped her. She tried to run.

"Stay away from me you murderer!" She screamed into the night. She knew that mindless ogre that had ripped her body apart like a chicken in a slaughterhouse was out there not far away. It was not human of that she was certain. It fed on death by taking life without remorse. It prowled the alleys and hovels of the city forever searching for a new victim to satisfy its cravings.

What she had ripped from her assailant she did not know, but she continued to clutch it in her viselike grip. It was her only link to reality. It dug deep into her flesh. The pain kept her mind focused. Then she questioned. Was her escape a reprieve or was it his way of deceiving her? Was he playing with her like a mouse in this cruel and inhumane fashion? His tenacity was unfaltering. He was the devil incarnate. He would have her soul. Sally saw the next street lamp ahead.

That alien sound enveloped her once more, that grinding, roaring sound like the demons of hell clawing their way out of the earth. The ground shook beneath her feet.

Once more a scream erupted from her throat. "No, no, do not do this! I do not want to die! Please...I do not want to die!" Her voice trailed off into anguished silence. In a muted voice, she pleaded. "Please let me be. Leave me in peace. Let me live." In desperation she forced her body to respond to her commands refusing to die there on the walk. The fluid that gave her life marked her passage through the virgin snow. She stumbled on trying to ward off the dizziness. Like some unearthly being, the street lamp passed overhead. She was back in the dark praying for help.

Suddenly her foot ploughed into a deep drift and Sally almost fell. In a desperate attempt to save herself, she grasped at the air. She regained her balance but to her horror lunged straight into the arms of a large shadowy figure. She screamed and began flaying her arms, fighting the predator that would inevitably steal her life.

"Let me go! I will not submit…"

In the midst of her screams came a soft voice. "It's okay, I'll help you. Just calm down."

But in mindless panic she fought on. "I will not let you take my life! Go back to hell for I will not go with you!" She sensed death was upon her. Her energy was exhausted and her mind failed her. In an instant the violent world around her faded. She felt herself floating. A vision of a kind but unfamiliar face appeared. Then her world turned black.

Sally woke in warm, comfortable surroundings bathed in brilliant white light. *At last I am safe. Death was not so difficult. Now I can rest, as I will have peace for all eternity. I am beyond the demon's reach.* Her battle over, her body exhausted, Sally closed her eyes and slept.

2

January 17, 2006

As the phone rang, it tore Detective Paul Salvatore from a deep sleep. He rolled slowly onto his back. In the darkness he stared at the ceiling trying to will himself awake. The phone continued to ring annoyingly in his ear. He turned his head and looked at the luminescent numerals of the clock on the nightstand…*5:40.* He cursed. He had only been asleep for an hour and a half. Frustrated, he threw the covers aside, raised himself on one elbow and reached for the phone.

"Whoever this is, you're fired," he mumbled. He immediately recognized the voice on the other end.

"Paul, Mario." Detective Mario Quinones, Paul's partner, sounded troubled.

"Quinones, you know what time it is?"

"Yes. We've got another body, Paul." Immediately he was fully awake, adrenalin rushing through his veins.

He rubbed his eyes and tried to focus. "Where?"

Quinones' voice was strained, not a surprise to Paul. They had been playing games with this killer since New Year's Day or, more to the point; it was the other way around. "This one's on New Orleans Street."

Paul flopped back on the pillow feeling despondent. He feared this nightmare would never end. "Same MO?"

"Same MO."

His face contorted in frustrated anguish, he cursed out loud. "Damn! This is the fifth fricking victim. For crying out loud, doesn't this guy ever quit? Is Perry there yet?"

"Yes, she's been here for the last 15 minutes."

"What's her prognosis?"

"She's as frustrated as we are."

"She find anything?"

"Nothing as yet."

"I'll be there in 20 minutes." Paul hung up. He slid his feet off the bed, sat up and rubbed his eyes. He cursed once more, stood, stretched and headed for the bathroom. As he showered he contemplated the events of the past few weeks. It began on January 1, 2006 and since then, like clockwork, a victim appeared every four days. He shivered beneath the scalding water as the chilling hand of fear touched him. A sudden foreboding slithered down his spine. Paul dressed quickly and left his apartment.

He drove south, turned onto Michigan Avenue then right onto Grand heading for Orleans Street. It was a bitterly cold, snowy morning with low hanging clouds obscuring the tops of the buildings. Even though the heater was on high, Paul was still freezing. He'd lived in Chicago most of his life, but he hated the winters.

▼▼▼▼▼ 3

As he reached Orleans, Paul turned south. Ahead were the flashing lights of squad cars, ambulances, and fire trucks. He pulled up to the yellow police tape, turned off the engine and got out of his black 2004 Dodge Intrepid. He spotted his partner approaching.

Mario greeted him in his usual cheerful manner. "Good morning, Paul."

"Yeah, right. I'm here and that's about it. Damn, I hate this weather," Paul grumbled.

"You get out the wrong side of the bed?"

"I had barely climbed in when you called. So what've we got?" Paul ducked under the tape.

"Like I said on the phone, exactly the same MO."

"Anyone else here?"

"Apart from Sam? No."

"Lucky SOB's are probably still asleep. Call them."

Mario sounded surprised. "Call them?"

"Yeah, why should we be the only ones trudging about in this freezing weather? Call them!" Paul's tone was one of frustration. As they approached the bundle on the sidewalk, Mario called the other two detectives. Medical Examiner, Dr. Samantha Perry, was checking the body. She looked up.

"Morning, Paul."

"Morning, Sam. So, what don't we know that you can't tell us?"

"I like that...subtle. Nothing has changed. The scene is the same, the clothes and shoes are the..."

"Okay, okay spare me the explanation, I get the idea." Paul tried to maintain his composure, but he was in a pressure cooker ready to explode.

"This is another massive dose of dé-jà-vu. Time of death was between two and four. No trauma or signs of a struggle, no indication of the cause of death. Same old story, Paul."

"Encouraging." Paul and Mario squatted beside Perry and looked at the body. It was an uncanny sight.

"I'm sorry, Paul, but there is nothing new here." She looked at Paul with her dark penetrating eyes. What he saw didn't make him feel any better. He stared at the body. The shoulder length blond hair, height about five feet one or two inches, the same dark burgundy evening gown and black shoes, and wrapped in the same Persian style rug. Her hands were crossed right over left on her stomach. *Whoever gave this case the name 'Mannequin Murders' had a warped sense of humor,* Paul thought to himself. He shook his head, stood and paced again.

"Paul, before you go running off you might be interested in two things we did find." Paul froze. Samantha Perry stood, removed her surgical gloves, and stared at him over the rim of her glasses realizing she probably should have told him immediately.

He glared at her. "You're now telling me you *do* have something?"

She wasn't intimidated. "As a matter of fact, yes."

Paul was well aware of Samantha Perry's reputation as a medical examiner and her curt bluntness. Justin Davenport had trained her well but his cautiousness had not rubbed off. "Look, Sam, I'm in no mood for games. Either you have evidence or you don't. Which is it?"

She stared at him in defiance. "There's a possibility we have something."

Paul grunted. "Then spill it."

"Hey, you want this job?" she retorted, then continued. "We found this button hidden in the bodice of her dress." She handed Paul a small plastic zip lock evidence bag. Paul studied the contents.

"You didn't think this was important enough to mention earlier?" He wasn't angry just annoyed so she let it pass. The bag contained a brass button possibly from a military jacket. The small crest looked familiar but he couldn't place it. "Interesting. What do you make of it?"

"Can't say for certain but it doesn't belong to her."

"You think?" Paul's cynicism was evident. "And the other evidence?"

"The two guys from forensics over there found a shoeprint. Could be the killer's." Intrigued by this news, he joined the two forensic team members.

"Detective Salvatore...Ed Biker, Forensics." They shook hands.

Paul pointed at the ground in front of him. "Pleased to meet you Ed... killer's shoeprint?"

"Could be, Detective, we'll know soon enough."

"Let's hope so."

"It's a clean print. There's another impression here." Biker pointed to a small indentation beside the shoeprint.

"Part of another shoeprint?"

"No, too small. Not too sure, but it could have been made by a cane. We'll check it out."

"Right."

"If this shoeprint belongs to the killer, it will tell us a great deal."

"I can't wait…Thanks Ed." Paul turned to rejoin Mario and Sam Perry.

"You know, Paul, this guy is becoming really boring."

"He's a pain in the ass is what he is, Mario. I want him off the damn streets and that can't happen soon enough."

Mario tried to sound optimistic. "We could have a break with that shoeprint."

Paul glanced at the body once more. Sam Perry had said dé-jà-vu, yet it was far more than that. Paul felt he had been cursed with this case. The woman that lay pale and lifeless offered up no clues. It was as if she dropped from the sky. He shook his head, turned and started toward his car.

"You leaving, Paul?"

"I'm heading back to District HQ, Mario. Nothing else we can do here. Sam, call me with your findings. Even if you find a zit on her ass, I want to know immediately but damn it, call me with something."

"Will do, Paul."

"Mario, I'll see you back at the district HQ. Do me a favor. Give this to Forensics and have them check it out. I would be interested to know its origin. Oh, and one other thing. Call Carrie and Yoshi and tell them not to bother coming out here." He tossed the plastic evidence bag to Mario then strode to his car.

▼▼▼▼▼ **4**

Paul slid behind the steering wheel, closed the door and started the engine. He sat for a while to let the heater warm the interior. There was so much going on yet nothing was happening. Each crime was devoid of clues, identities, and witnesses. The killer was eluding the police and carrying out his crime with great precision and with very little contact. Paul knew if they didn't get a break soon, solving the case could take years, for as each day passed the trail grew colder. As he felt the warmth soak into his body, he sighed and shifted the car into drive. As the flashing lights disappeared in his rear view mirror, Paul wondered if that was how this case would end. His cell phone rang.

"Salvatore."

The River Styx

"Detective, you don't know me, but I thought it was time we became acquainted."

"Who is this?"

"I am the one you're looking for." The voice was confident and arrogant. Paul went cold. Could this be the killer or just another crackpot?

"How did you get this number?"

"You guys think you're untouchable; well never mind that, we have to talk."

"What do you want?" *Cranks make calls like this every day of the week when a high profile case is being worked. But this guy sounds completely sane; normal would be a good word. Then again, what's normal? There's always some nut case trying to get his name in the news, but there's something sinister about this guy.* Paul waited for a response.

"Funny you should ask, Detective. You and your team are making little or no progress in solving this case. Am I right?" He didn't wait for Paul to reply but went on. "You have ignored my letters, so it's time for a changing of the guard. I like a challenge and all you are doing is wasting all my talent. I'm playing to a blind audience here; I need a lot more."

Paul was no longer surprised but he was now growing impatient. "You got to be out of your mind. Who do..."

"Shut up Salvatore and listen. I suggest you get the great detective, who is able to solve any case, to help you out."

"And who might that be?"

"Come on, Detective, you don't have to play games with me, we both know to whom I'm referring."

"Sorry but you have me at a disadvantage."

"Wake up, Detective, you're smarter than that, or are you just playing dumb?"

Paul wondered where this was leading, but he had had enough. "Look, I have no idea who you're talking about, or who you are. This conversation has gone on long enough..."

"Don't hang up before I've given you some advice."

"I don't need your..."

"Super cop, Graham Farlon..." There was a long silence. Paul was taken back for it was the last name he expected to hear. Although it had been his intention to try and find the old detective, over the last few days he had forgotten about Gray Farlon. Why, all of a sudden, had this crazy guy, claiming to be the Mannequin murderer, called with that one name?

It was now his intention to try and draw the killer out. "What's he got to do with this?"

The voice turned ice cold. "Let me put it to you a little more bluntly. Get Farlon on this case now. Do you understand?"

"Why Farlon? Why do you particularly want him on this case?"

"That's between me and him."

"Sounds personal."

"Don't you worry about that, just get him. You got that?"

"You're in no position to make demands. If..."

He immediately cut Paul off. "You want the body count to keep going up, because I can certainly oblige. Do what I'm requesting and maybe the body count will stop."

"You've made no request, you've demanded. No you've threatened, and I don't take kindly to threats."

"Interpret it how you wish Detective, the end result is on your head." The line went dead.

Paul was left with a churning in his gut. There was no doubt it was the killer. The only people who were aware of the existence of the two letters were the investigation team. He wondered what kind of mind game this guy was playing.

They needed help, of that he was well aware. He had spotted Farlon at the third crime scene. The man looked a wreck, a derelict draped in ragged clothes; hair long, gray and disheveled and he hadn't shaved in at least a year. The important thing was that he was alive, a situation many questioned. That very day he had put the word out he was looking for the old man. Paul was well aware that if there was anyone out there who might bring this case to a close, it was Farlon. One thing of which he was certain, they had to stop the terror that now plagued the streets of the city and Farlon was the solution.

Graham Farlon had been his mentor and friend. One year after he joined the Chicago Police Department, Paul had been assigned to Farlon's investigation team. It was the best thing that had ever happened to him. Farlon was a prodigy, his crime solving abilities a legend. He could weed out and predict every move a killer made with unprecedented accuracy. The criminal had little chance. Farlon had been called a psychic, which he denied. Nevertheless he solved every case he'd ever worked on. Paul turned west onto Belmont Avenue.

He had learned quickly that Farlon despised tyrannical leadership. He was a man of high moral principles and totally dedicated to the law. He led and taught by example. He never asked anyone to do something he would not do himself. He never belittled anyone. Members of his team were made to think for themselves. It was the way he imparted his knowledge.

Paul knew that without the training and sound direction he had received during his years under Farlon, he would not have been able to deal with all he had encountered recently. But what confronted him at that moment was unlike anything he had ever encountered, and now the elusive killer had made personal contact, if it was the killer. Paul realized he had to find Farlon and convince him to return to the Force. He approached District 3 Police HQ and pulled into the parking lot.

▼▼▼▼▼ 5

Graham Farlon had to get a grip on his life. He had turned his back on it and let it slip into the gutter. Now he groveled in the filth of alleys, back streets, and cold, lonely underpasses, sleeping where he could. He was destitute, a man without an identity. Dreams for the future were dashed against the rocks. His interest in life had vanished. He was not living...he was barely existing. Life was full of injustices, but was that an excuse to throw in the towel? What had happened in the past was forever lost in it.

This day began as the day before...dreary, bitterly cold and overcast. Old cardboard boxes and newspapers were no protection from winter's anger. A stinking pile of garbage on one side and an overflowing dumpster on the other were his only protection against the biting winds that rushed through the city.

Graham Farlon lay in an inebriated stupor, his head reeling and his sixty-three-year-old body wracked with aches and pains. The penetrating cold settled deep in his bones. Cardboard was no substitute for a soft mattress, something he had not experienced in a long while. *But whose fault was that?* He asked himself. *I can blame no one else for my foolishness. Why am I thinking 63 is old? Sixty-three isn't old. Hell, you're only as old as you feel. Why do I feel so damn old?*

He started to move but decided against it and remained where he was a while longer. His muscles felt like jelly refusing to cooperate. There was little energy left in the frail body he carried around with him day after day. Cheap liquor could only suppress the haunting memories. The escape was only temporary, and then they rushed back like thundering waves against rocky cliffs. Days were spent recovering from previous nights. It was a routine to which he had foolishly surrendered. He despised himself.

Life had been good. There had been a family who loved him and he was happy and content. Then it all faded like ink on old parchment. All that remained were shadows of that life. Now he was just another pathetic example of humanity's failures. Once he walked proud, tall and confident, but time had ripped that away. His gaunt, feeble frame was but a reflection of what had been. Like an aged tree, he also had withered. The look of forlorn failure and despair were the masks that now curtained a once jovial face. The outer façade reflected the pain within. All the strength, joy, confidence and dignity had been washed away. Like that proud giant tree that takes centuries to grow and is destroyed with one foul deed, so it was with his life.

He rolled onto his back and stared up between the towering buildings at the strip of murky gray sky far above. *It's going to snow soon; I should find better shelter, but shelter from what? Is it really worth the effort? No one needs me any longer. All the knowledge I have in my head is worthless, outdated. Griffith had been right: I am a has-been, no longer useful. Fresher, younger blood has replaced me. But many of them will, someday, end up just like me. It is a perpetual circle of life discarding life. Why the hell did Griffith's name roll into my head? He's the last person on earth I need or even want to think about.*

He reflected on his career and the life he'd spent fighting crime and pursuing right, truth and justice but that had also vanished. Thirty-six years on the Force and they gave him a gold wristwatch, a $5,000 retirement bonus and a party at Pete's Place, a small bar and grill three blocks from the district HQ. He pawned the watch. The five grand he'd blown on booze and Pete's Place had long since closed. The only things he owned from his past were the wedding ring he still wore and a crumpled, grimy, dog-eared, but very precious picture of Gwynne and Julia.

Gwynne, his wife of 29 years, died of cancer at the age of 48. Nothing, no one in the world, meant more to him than Gwynne. She'd known him better than anyone, she had been his strength, and always supported him knowing what his job meant to him. She tolerated the long, sleepless nights wondering if he would come home. Then she gave him Julia, the most precious thing to enter their lives. Years later when Gwynne died, Julia never understood and partially held him responsible. She believed the stress her mother endured was the cause of the deadly disease.

Julia had left home at 25. With her degree in Journalism she moved to New York to pursue a career perhaps with one of the newspapers. He didn't know if she was still there. It had been almost seven years since he'd heard from her. That was when life lost all its meaning and he started drinking. He realized that was no excuse, but he had not been prepared. If a stray bullet had snuffed out his life or he had died on some city street...he could have accepted that. Gwynne dying of cancer was not acceptable. It tore him apart, ripped his heart to shreds and turned him away from the God who gave him life.

He felt the zip lock plastic bag in his pocket containing the photo of Gwynne and Julia. It had been his mainstay over the past years. He withdrew it and in dawn's dim light stared at it, his only link to reality. He cried like a baby as he lay in that filthy alley. The pain in his heart ached like an old wound in the damp of winter. At that moment he faced reality. He promised himself he would not go on living like this, feeling sorry for himself. He had wallowed in his own self-pity long enough. Somehow he would get to New York and find Julia. That would be his goal. He carefully slipped the photo back into his pocket. In anger he tossed the cardboard and newspaper aside.

As Gray struggled to his feet, he almost lost his balance. His head spun. He placed a hand on the wall to steady himself. The alley rolled and pitched like the deck of a storm tossed ship. His head continued to spin. Where would he go and what would this new day bring? Would he get through it? Would he survive? Would the effort be worth it? Why didn't he just curl up and fade away instead of prolonging the agony and the inevitable? *No damn it, I refuse to continue thinking that way.*

Gray staggered from the alley, his senses more alert, and his mind more focused. He headed for the Salvation Army Shelter three blocks away anticipating his first meal of the day. Deep in thought, his brow knitted together. He ignored the cold and walked with his mind set on his new goal. How to achieve it was not in question, for he knew he would. His fingers slowly wrapped around a single dollar bill and a few coins...a fortune but not enough. *I must find a job. It's going to work...it has to work.* He crossed the street and entered the shelter. He welcomed the warmth.

Although the aroma of food was no different than the day or week before, eagerly he filled his plate, found a table in a secluded corner and made himself comfortable. As he ate, plans for the future churned through his mind. If Julia were still in New York, he would find the newspaper that employed her. A peace settled over him. He was going to see Julia. If she welcomed him back that would be great, if not he would have to accept it. To see her and speak to her, to know she was all right would have to suffice. He finished his meal and left the shelter in search of a newsstand.

▼▼▼▼▼ **6**

At that moment four *Mannequin* victims lay in the morgue. Justin Davenport, Chief Medical Examiner, was about to meet the fifth. He was not enamored, having had little time to address the first victim before the rest began arriving. He was on his way to a meeting at police headquarters. Not only did he not wish to attend the meeting, but he really did not have time for it. He glanced at his watch. If he was late it was too bad, he had more pressing issues. He headed for the morgue where he found Medical Examiner Samantha Perry busy with the new victim.

"Good morning Samantha." He tried to sound cheerful.

"Morning Justin, come meet Jane Doe number five."

"I heard you brought her in. Anything new?"

She stopped and raised her face shield. "Nothing."

"Damn, is there no reprieve from this maniac?"

"Doesn't appear to be. Not yet anyway. I'm telling you this is weird. Where the hell is he finding these victims? They're all so much alike."

"Anything I can do to help?" He was hoping she would say yes giving him an excuse not to go downtown.

"No I'm fine. I could do it in my sleep it is so routine. This guy is punching victims out of the same mold. This one has a nasty scar here at her waist, and a small one on her left calf. Aside from that, it's business as usual." Justin sensed Sam's frustration.

"When is this going to stop?"

"Soon I hope. I found the same note." Sam picked it up and handed it to Davenport. He had seen it before but read it again out of habit.

*"Non sum qua-lis eram,
Charon"*

"Any ideas on this?" he said handing it back.

"According to Detective Simpson the rough translation is *'I am not what I used to be,'* or *'I am not the same as I was'*, or something to that effect."

"What's that supposed to mean? Well never mind. If you don't need me I'm going. If you find anything out of the ordinary, call me."

"There is one thing that's rather strange."

"What's that?"

"Not one of these victims has ever had an inoculation against any of the common diseases. In actual fact their blood is telling us a great number of things that are rather strange."

"Such as?"

"The absence of antibodies. The presence of unusual toxins that we don't normally find. The list goes on. Justin, there are so many pieces of the puzzle that are missing. I suspect these women are foreigners."

"Well they came from somewhere."

"True, the question is where?"

Justin Davenport started for the door. "Send me your report. I'm out of here"

"Fine. I'll see you later." Davenport was about to leave and Sam return to her work when she stopped him.

"Oh, before you go there is something else." Davenport stopped. "Remember the small blisters we found on the other victims?"

"Yes."

"She has them also. Brian informed me yesterday they are not blisters but small puss sacs just under the skin, loads of them."

"Ideas?"

"None that I can offer at present."

"Okay, call me."

"Will do, Justin." Sam pulled the face shield down and picked up a saw. She was about to open the chest cavity of the corpse when Brian, the lab technician, walked into the room.

"Sam, I think you had better have a look at this."

"Brian, you can see I'm busy. Can't it wait?"

"I don't think so."

Perry sighed. "Okay." She laid the saw down and lifted her visor. She reached for the chart, glanced at it and was about to hand it back when she saw something that shocked her.

"Oh my God…"

"Told you that you'd be interested."

She looked up at the technician and gasped. "Are you serious? Is this correct?"

"Certain. I ran four separate tests and got the same result. So I had Chuck run it. He reached the same conclusion."

"It can't be. This is impossible Brian."

"Impossible or not it's there."

"But... Oxytyosis." Sam Perry slowly removed her gloves and tossed them in the trashcan. The face shield she placed on the cart and as she walked to her desk, she sat down and stared at the clipboard. Finally, she put it down and looked up.

"Damn it, Brian, something has to be wrong. This condition cannot occur in a gravity environment."

"You know that, I know that, but the results don't lie, Sam."

"But only an...hell, this is getting creepy. Only astronauts in cryogenic sleep in zero gravity get this. Logical scientific reasoning states this is impossible. All five have the same condition?"

"All five." Sam shook her head. In her entire career she had never come across a situation where she was forced to question a scientific fact. Now she was confronted with something she knew was impossible, something that was contrary to all she had been taught and believed.

"Why didn't we catch this earlier?"

"Come on, Sam, we've never run an Olympus Hemoglobin test. We had absolutely no reason to run it. Besides if someone asked you, wouldn't you wonder why or question their sanity?"

"Of course. But what made you run it?"

"With each test I kept getting this spike. I had the others look at it and no one could explain it. I went back and ran my tests again and bingo, there was the spike. I checked my control and it was good. It was Chuck who suggested I run the OH test. I told him he was out of his mind. He didn't argue, just took the samples and ran them himself. Those are his results."

Sam Perry was stunned. "This is unbelievable. How do we explain this one?"

"Hey Doc, that's your department, I just work here."

"You're a lot of help." Sam shook her head. "Oxytyosis. My God, what the hell is going on?"

◆◆◆◆◆ 7

At *9:30 A.M.*, Paul, carrying two pieces of interesting news, was on his way to the War Room for the morning briefing. He had also invited the Chief Medical Examiner to attend. As he entered, he stepped directly to the opposite side of the room with his first piece of information, a new picture, which he pinned on an already cluttered crime board. The other four members of the team were seated at the table.

"Victim number five?" someone asked.

"No, this is our new recruit." Everyone got to their feet and gathered, curious as to who it was.

"Who the hell is that?" several asked in unison.

"New recruit! The guy's old enough to be my grandfather."

"Possibly, Yoshi, but we're in need of his help," Paul said.

"We are?" Detective Carrie Simpson questioned.

"Yes, and let's hope we find him. Okay folks, let's get started." The small group drifted back to their seats. Paul leaned on his chair, glanced around the table then took his seat.

On his immediate right was his partner, Mario Quinones, 37; an energetic and dedicated detective who had been with the Force for nine years and on the case from day one. Next to Mario was Detective Carrie Simpson, an attractive, rather petite 29-year-old African American with razor-sharp intelligence and a love for the law. After graduating with a degree in Criminology seven years earlier, she immediately joined the Force. She also joined the team at its inception.

Across the table from Carrie sat Pat Yoshi, 35, a transplant from the San Francisco Police Department two years earlier. He had only just joined the team. Next to Yoshi was Sergeant Patrick O'Malley, 25. Only on the Force three years, O'Malley had been recruited to the task force because of his expertise with computers.

Paul Salvatore, 41, was born in Allentown, Pennsylvania in 1965. He graduated with a degree in Criminology and went on to gain a Master's. His first position was with the Philadelphia Police Department. Then in 1992 after five years in Philadelphia, he was offered and accepted a post in Chicago. In his fifth year with the CPD he was assigned to a task force headed by renowned super-cop, Graham Farlon. After joining Farlon's team, Paul never looked back. He admired and highly respected the man they called the 'Super Sleuth'. Because of that past association, he was more determined than ever to find Farlon and secure his help and expertise.

"Paul, you think by bringing this old guy back we'll solve this case?"

"I didn't say that, Carrie. I'm hoping with Farlon's knowledge and investigative experience we will have a far better chance."

"Farlon, the guy they called the Super Sleuth…that's who we're talking about here, right?"

"That's correct, Yoshi."

"I thought he was dead."

"So did many others, but not so."

"And he is going to join us?"

"Yes he is, Carrie…well, maybe."

"Maybe? You seemed certain a moment ago. What happened?"

"I haven't spoken to him yet. In fact, we need to find him first. He's out there and he's definitely not dead."

"If you believe he's the answer, Paul, I hope you do find him."

"Me too. Okay, moving on, anyone know where Davenport is?"

"Haven't seen him. Why?"

"I asked him to be here for this..." At that moment the door to the War Room opened. "Morning, Justin... good of you to come."

The Chief Medical Examiner entered and took a seat next to Yoshi. "Sorry I'm late Paul but I got hung up at the morgue. Damn place gets busier by the day."

"Sounds like a personal problem," Paul quipped then continued. "Now that we're all here, let's get started. As you're all aware, yesterday we found the fifth victim and this time, I believe, we got lucky. I'm hoping what Justin has, gives us our first big break. But before we hear from Justin I believe we should recap. I received an interesting phone call early this morning. It was either a well informed crack pot, or our killer."

"What did he have to say, Paul?" Everyone leaned closer, eager to hear what Paul had to report.

"Get Farlon on the case."

"That's it? Get Farlon on the case."

"That was all, Carrie, except he mentioned the letters..."

"But we're the only ones who are aware of the existence of those letters."

"Right, Yoshi, and that's what has me concerned. If this isn't our killer, he seems to know things he shouldn't."

"But, Paul, this is a deviation from the letters that only brag about his ability to remain at large and that we will never get our hands on him."

"That's true, Carrie, but I believe if he is who he says he is, he's throwing out a challenge."

"You mean he knows Gary Farlon?"

"Everyone knows Gray Farlon, Mario, at least everyone who has lived in this city since 1985 when he solved his first big case."

"One of the creeps he put away?"

"I don't know, Carrie. But he was emphatic that Farlon be brought into the case. Enough speculation, what do we have so far?"

"Two letters, five identical notes, five victims that remain nameless, and a killer that we are unable to catch," Mario said.

"A number of strange, unexplainable conditions related to the victims and no idea how they died," Carrie added.

Justin Davenport interrupted them. "I believe I can ease at least part of your dilemma."

"Then why don't you go ahead, Justin."

Justin Davenport squirmed nervously in his chair, glanced around at everyone then began. "Although the cause of death remains a mystery, yesterday, as Paul mentioned, we did get a break."

"You've discovered what killed them?" Mario said hopefully.

"Not exactly. But we have reduced the odds, though at this point it's only a theory."

"I hate to throw cold water on your enthusiasm, Justin, but do you think theories are going to solve this case? We need facts."

"I understand, Paul, but if you'll let me finish you may just learn something." The battle of words between Salvatore and Davenport was old and ongoing. Despite their respect for one another, they seldom saw eye-to-eye. Paul had little patience for Davenport's long windedness.

"Then get on with it."

"As I was about to say, our theory may now put the cause of death well within our reach. We have whittled the suspect list down to three possibilities...a common compound called *Potassium Chloride* that can be fatal and is untraceable; a not so common compound *Succinylcholine*, or SUX, again fatal and is undetectable. Finally, an elusive and little known compound, not only impossible to detect but almost as difficult to find, *ChloroPheno-Dexatrone* or CPD. CPD is not fatal but just as deadly. It renders the victim immobile by shutting down selective muscles. The victim remains alive but is unable to react to outside influences.

"We believe this compound, possibly used in conjunction with one of the other two, is how the killer dispatches his victims. One of our technicians found a minute blemish on the right eyeball of one victim. At first he thought little of it. But being suspicious, he double-checked. He discovered the same blemish on all the victims. We believe the killer inserts a fine needle through the eye and injects the fatal compound into the brain cavity..." Carrie gasped in horror.

"Dear God, why?"

"And it's this CPD stuff the killer uses?" Paul was pleased to think they were getting closer to the truth.

"No."

Paul sighed. This was his frustration with the ME. "No! But you have just told us that..."

"What I said was, what was injected into the brain cavity is possibly what killed them, and that would have either been SUX or potassium chloride."

"Then how do you know it is what killed them?"

"We don't. It is just..."

Paul couldn't restrain his sarcasm. "Excuse me, Justin, but am I missing something here? If these substances are, as you say, untraceable, how do you know they're what we are looking for?"

"That's why we know."

Paul threw his arms up in frustration and leaned back in his chair. He'd about had enough of Davenport's double talk. "Am I dense?" He looked around the table at the team. "Are any of you getting this? I must be dense...*'that's why you know?*" he retorted.

"Detective, when we could not identify a single traceable substance, we turned to substances difficult if not impossible to trace. After exhaustive tests, we settled on these three possibilities."

"And?" Paul said, raising his eyebrows.

"And, therefore, these are all we have."

"Are you sure it's one of these compounds?"

"We are about 90 percent certain, yes."

"What about the other ten percent?"

"We may never know, Paul."

"Never!" Salvatore reached boiling point. "Damn it, that's just not acceptable. We need to be beyond that shadow. I want nothing less than 99 percent, otherwise we're toast and we lose this case."

"That's just not possible Paul. We have nothing..."

Salvatore slammed his hand on the table causing everyone to jump. "I don't give a rat's ass what you have! We have a killer out there. Until we nail the bastard, he goes on killing. That's not going to happen. Do you understand? I want this psycho put away where he'll never see the light of day again. You got that Mr. ME?" Justin looked a little bull-whipped but his rebuttal was just as angry. He rose from his chair, leaned halfway over the table and glared at Paul responding in a controlled but quivering voice.

"Get this into your head. First of all you're not the only game in town, Detective. The Mannequin Murders is not the only source of bodies coming into my morgue. In case you don't realize it, Detective, we have other cases we're working on so stand in line. Secondly, I will give you what I have when I have it. Finally, don't start making demands of my department like that because I won't stand for it."

"Listen I..."

"No...you listen, Detective. My team has worked day and night to learn the truth behind this killer's methods. We have given you all the time we can afford and we've made great progress, but we're still obliged to theorize and draw some rash conclusions. If you don't like it, that's too damn bad because it's all we can offer." Davenport, his face flushed, dropped back into his chair.

Paul raised his hand almost in submission to the onslaught. "Okay, okay, then give us what you do have and let's get on with this case."

▼▼▼▼▼ *8*

The War Room immediately grew uncomfortably quiet. No one wished to be the next to speak. Carrie looked at Justin; her brow furrowed with concern and broke the tension. "Justin, you're saying this madman injects SUX through the victim's eyeballs?"

In nervous agitation Justin straightened his tie, rested his arms on the table and responded. "It's a theory in part reinforced by the blemishes we found. We believe he's using SUX in conjunction with CPD. Because CPD can be administered orally as well as intravenously, it makes it easy to use."

Paul leaned forward and placed his elbows on the table. "Then tell us, Justin, what exactly does this CPD stuff do?"

"It selectively disables certain areas of the body rendering the victim incapable of movement. They are able to breathe, the heart continues to beat and the brain is alert but they are unable to react to any action taken against them in any way. They can't even blink."

Carrie gasped, a look of horror and disbelief on her face. "My God, Doctor, you're saying these women were unable to fight back in any capacity?"

"Correct."

"What kind of demented animal are we dealing with?"

"By all accounts, Carrie, the worst."

Paul gave a deep sigh. "It appears the Devil's come to town."

"That's not funny, Paul."

"No...but it appears to be the truth, Mario." Paul turned his attention back to the medical examiner. "Please go on, Justin."

O'Malley cut in with a question. "These compounds are all difficult to obtain?"

"Not all. Potassium chloride is quite easy to come by. SUX is not so easy. CPD is another issue."

"Why is that?" Mario asked.

"It's made up of three compounds; two that are difficult to acquire and a third only found in the jungles of Borneo. It's difficult to extract, easy to make but requires specific storage methods. The plant is impossible to find unless you are familiar with it. Its identity is a closely guarded secret by the natives of the region.

Mario frowned. "If it's that hard to obtain and store, then surely it should be fairly easy to trace."

"You would think so, but no. People in third world countries are eager to make a buck. Anyone willing to pay can get as much as they want. The authorities can seldom find a still."

"So, it's hard to find, very difficult to trace, can be made in a garage, how *do* we find the source of this devil juice?"

"Could take years, Paul. The fact that it is produced in a remote Asian jungle you may never find the source. Manufacturing it is illegal, but when the authorities raid the villages they find nothing. When they leave, the natives start up again."

"That easy to make?" Carrie sounded surprised.

"It's a small garage operation. A hot plate, hot water, glass jars and a reliable refrigerator and you have it. Like many drugs, once you have the ingredients and the correct formula, it is a cinch."

"When you say plant, is it something like marijuana?" Carrie asked.

"No. It's actually extracted from the root."

"Found only in Asia?" she said.

"Yes."

Mario looked around at his colleagues. "Convenient. Well that sucks."

"Nowhere else like…say…the Amazon jungle?" Carrie pressed.

"No, Detective. Only in the jungles of Borneo, no place else."

Carrie released a deep sigh. "Damn, this is complicated."

"Not half as complicated as finding the answer."

Paul scratched his head. "Is it the answer, Justin?"

"We'll never be absolutely sure unless you find the killer and he confesses."

"Are there no tests to detect this crap?" Paul's hopes were again dashed against the rocks.

"None."

Paul sipped his coffee. "So we're still on first base."

Mario straightened in his chair. "Justin, what about the Center for Disease Control? Could they run tests for this CPD?"

"They have no more at their disposal than we do, Detective."

"Great. Some damn concoction brewed up in a primitive jungle lab in Asia and we can't even find it," Mario responded.

"I'm sorry but that's all I can offer."

"Are you ever going to be able to offer more?" Paul's sarcasm was seldom far from the surface.

"Somehow I don't believe so."

Paul continued. "Well, don't that beat all. Is there any other uplifting news you have for us?" The phone in the corner rang. Carrie answered it.

"Justin, it's for you, it's Samantha." Justin took the call. He listened intently with an expression of deep concern on his face. He then replaced the receiver and returned to his seat.

"That was Perry with some very disturbing information. This is truly baffling."

"Oh joy. Then lay it on us Doc. Baffling situations seem to be the norm these days," Paul said curtly.

"Discovered yesterday and confirmed a few moments ago it is a condition called Oxytyosis. The baffling part is…" he paused, not certain he should continue. "…it only occurs in astronauts."

"What!" Paul almost screamed. He had had it with all Justin's mumbo jumbo. "You're not trying to tell us these women were in space, because if you are this meeting is over. This case is complicated enough without adding a load of crap about a space disease..."

Justin gritted his teeth. "Excuse me Paul, but if you would allow me to continue you'll understand. To begin with this is not a disease. Also we're not suggesting anything closely resembling space travel. May I go on?"

Paul took a deep breath and tried to relax. He reached into his pocket, removed a pack of antacid tablets and popped three into his mouth. Then he closed his eyes and waved his hand at Justin.

"Proceed." At that point Carrie sat forward as shocked as Paul.

"I don't wish to take further issue with this, Justin, but...astronauts? How the hell do we go from serial killer to astronaut?"

Justin took a deep breath. "Oxytyosis occurs when astronauts are subjected to prolonged periods of weightlessness while in cryogenic sleep. If the condition did not occur, the astronaut would die."

"Wow, that's a mouthful. So these women had a space disease," Yoshi said. Justin grew more agitated.

"Would you people listen to me. This is not a damn disease. It's a condition. Not only is its existence impossible in a gravity environment, it is not even life threatening..."

"You're saying its presence is impossible?" Yoshi said.

"Yes, impossible. I have..."

Paul opened his eyes and stared at the ME. "It appears, Justin, that has suddenly changed."

Davenport calmed down. "Yes, Paul, it does and that's why I'm completely taken aback by it."

Paul was at the end of his rope. "So where is all this leading us?"

"I have no idea. At this point you now know as much as we do."

"You have no idea what caused the condition?" Yoshi asked.

"No idea at all."

"But, Doctor, you must have some inkling," Carrie said.

"None."

"None?"

"Absolutely none."

Paul buried his face in his hands in frustration. Then as he looked up, he grumbled. "For God's sake, Justin, don't you guys know anything? You have no idea how these women died and no idea how they contracted this condition. Do you have any idea what's going on here?"

"I'm sorry, but no. Let me explain a little more and just maybe you'll see our dilemma."

"No, no spare us. What you have said so far is more than sufficient. You've spilled enough crap this morning, we don't need any more."

Justin was annoyed. "Suit yourself."

"Well Paul, I for one would like to hear more."

"Then, Carrie, get with him afterwards. Anything else we need to know, Justin?"

Carrie interjected. "Excuse me, Doctor, I have one other question. Could these two conditions together have resulted in death?"

"Can't say. Though under any normal situation I very much doubt it."

In a state of agitation, Paul got out of his seat and paced about the room. "From where I sit, Doctor, we don't have anything resembling a normal situation."

"No we don't."

"So now what?"

"We keep testing."

Yoshi looked up from his notes. "You think you'll find anything further to substantiate your suspicions?"

"My honest opinion...I don't know."

▼▼▼▼▼ 9

Although at peace within himself, the memories buried deep in Gray Farlon's subconscious surfaced regularly. He had a job working three days a week for his old friend Mr. Yu, though the Chinaman had no idea who he was. He could now accumulate enough money to make the trip to New York. His dream of seeing Julia would be realized. Yet he could not sleep peacefully. As difficult as it had been, he tried to put the past behind him. But now the phantoms were back, persistently pursuing through his dreams. He had seen a great deal during his years on the Force, more than any man should. But despite all those memories, terrors and demons rushing back, it was no excuse to give up.

Why it had happened he did not know. That ominous shadow of death stalked him once again. Lifeless eyes of unrecognizable corpses stared from out of the darkness. These were the victims. Then there were the demented minds of killers. Gray had always been reluctant to climb into killers' minds, but it was his only way to know them, to bring them to justice. Through all those years he never let these events bother him. But now, like reruns of old movies, the horrors played back in his head. Sleep was no longer a release.

His mind drifted uncontrollably. In the darkness, woven between a half-waking, half-sleeping world, the memories rushed in like waves upon the shore. Some he bathed in, wishing them to remain. Most he tried to shun for they carried great pain. Lying on a cot in the back room of the shelter, Gray once again drifted reluctantly into troubled sleep.

As the sounds of the night faded, the sounds of his dreams took over. He walked dark passages seeing only shadows. Voices he recognized floated about him like feathers on the breeze. Ghostly figures passed unrecognized, calling his name, beckoning him to follow. But to where he did not know. A door opened then closed. Sleep had overtaken him.

Graham Farlon, known to his friends as Gray, was a conscientious and dedicated police officer. He was born in Malahide, in the county of Dublin, Ireland, in August of 1943. Then four years later his family moved to Chicago. Graham had two older sisters, Deidre and Colleen. He grew up on Chicago's south side and came to love his adopted city. He was a good student, planning to study architecture. During his years in high school, his sisters always talked about returning home.

Then, in 1960, Graham's dreams of college were dashed when his father passed away. His mother with only a part time job was unable to make ends meet. Deidre and Colleen both had jobs, but it was still difficult for the four of them. Gray felt obligated to change his plans. He found a fulltime job with a local grocery store where he worked hard and made enough money to help pay the bills. Then, in 1964, Graham joined the Chicago Police Department. It was a decision he never regretted.

A year later, in September, he met Gwynne Riley. Born in Callan, in Kilkenny County, Ireland in 1945, her family moved to Chicago in 1957. The two began dating and soon his family realized they were quite serious and that a wedding was in the wind. But once more tragedy struck the Farlon family. In January of 1968, five months before Gray and Gwynne were due to get married, Gray's mother passed away. After that bittersweet day Gray's two sisters moved back to Ireland.

With his life now established, Gray was a very happy man. Like most in his position he had seen his share of trouble, bad guys and the low life that infested the city. Life had been good to him and he had no complaints. His predicament at that moment was the fault of no one but himself. He could have done it differently but he had lost too much, or had it been an excuse to give up. What would Gwynne have said? Would she have thought that he was not strong enough to fight it?

▼▼▼▼▼ *10*

There was a great deal bothering Paul. Though he was convinced there had to be a simple explanation for everything that was happening, he wondered if they would ever find answers. As he walked across the lobby to meet Carrie, he felt confident, despite the fact that they were about to undertake a task that did not excite either of them. Their destination was the police archives. Located in the basement of the building, it was a dark, dusty, endless maze of floor to ceiling storage racks filled to capacity with file boxes of old cases. It was the one place in the building seldom visited. Its only positive feature was that it was warm. Behind a wooden desk, in front of the elevator, sat an old man in his late sixties who looked bored to tears. *Hell, I suppose I would look like that if I had to sit in this hole every day for eight hours at a time.* Paul thought and sympathized.

He and Carrie stepped up to the desk. "Detective Paul Salvatore and Detective Carrie Simpson. We need to review some old records."

"ID's?" the man snapped. Paul and Carrie showed their ID's.

"What year?" The bluntness and grumpiness of the old man was understandable.

"I have no idea. We are going to pick a year then work from there."

"I need a year," he snapped again in a monotone voice.

"Oh for crying out loud. All right 1900."

"Is that a confirmation or just a guess?"

"Damn it all, if I knew exactly what I was looking for I would give you a solid date; in the meantime humor me."

"Very well, sign here." They both signed the book then entered the vast enclosure.

"What *are* we looking for Paul?"

"Truthfully, Carrie, I'm not sure. A thought crossed my mind the other day that led me here."

"So 1900 was a guess?"

"Not a guess, just a number."

"That's a big help. How do we even know where to begin looking then?"

"1890," Paul said. Carrie smiled and gave him a cynical glance shaking her head. They walked along the narrow canyons of towering racks; their footsteps were muffled by the expanse of boxes and packages stacked one upon the other as far as they could see. Now and again they were forced to squeeze around a rolling staircase parked in the aisle.

The rows were a chart indicating the years and dates of items stored there. Paul had no idea where to begin but 1890 seemed a good guess. He found what he was looking for.

"Okay here we are."

"Fine, now would you mind telling me what we're looking for?"

Paul started down the aisle. "A crime that resembles the Mannequin Murders."

Carrie followed closely. "So you're looking for a copycat killer?"

"Maybe. I have this gut feeling our guy obtained his ideas from history. It's only a hunch based on what we have so far."

"Like what?"

"The gown in which the victims are dressed. The old fashioned way they're dressed. The note, written in Latin; no one uses Latin any more. And the button from the police uniform that is over 100 years old. I have a feeling our killer is using an old crime as a blueprint."

"That would answer a lot of questions."

Paul stopped and looked up at the third shelf. He then retrieved a rolling stairway and pushed it back to where he wished to begin his search. He started up the stairs. "1890 is a good place to begin."

"Whatever you say, Paul. Pass me a box and I'll get started." Paul handed the box labeled *'1890-July thru December'* to Carrie. By the time they reached the 1870 files it was *4:30P.M.* and both detectives were exhausted. Having stared at page after page of poorly written, fading reports, statements and old photos, they were ready to quit.

"I've about had enough for one day, Paul, how about you?"

Paul looked at his watch. "I agree. Tell you what, there are fewer boxes in the 1860's. Let's get through them then call it a day."

"Okay, but then you owe me dinner."

Paul retrieved two more boxes. "Deal."

After 20 minutes an excited exclamation erupted from Carrie. "Paul, I think I have something!" She waved a sheet of paper in the air. "It's a memo dated August 27, 1867. It mentions a series of unsolved murders that occurred during 1865." Paul stopped and stepped to Carrie's side. He took the paper and began reading.

...There has been no progress on the investigation of the seven women killed in the city last year. To date Pinkerton has offered nothing of any consequence. It is my opinion whoever might have been the perpetrator of those terrible crimes has since either died or departed the city. As my resources are limited I am unable to continue this investigation. Therefore, I reluctantly close this case, unsolved.'

The Police Commissioner, a gentleman by the name of Claude Marshall, had signed the document. Paul looked at Carrie in excited anticipation then immediately scurried up the steps and retrieved the boxes from the previous year.

"Carrie, does that memo mention any other dates?"

Carrie shuffled through the stack of papers. "No."

At that moment the clerk appeared. "Excuse me but how much longer are you two going to be? I want to go home and have my dinner then catch the Sox game. I don't intend to miss it."

"Sox fan, huh?" Carrie said

The man's eyes brightened. "Yes, you?"

"Absolutely. Look, can't we stay? We can lock up."

"Can't do that. I'm responsible. I must lock up. So how much longer are you going to be?"

"Give us another, say half hour?"

"Are you sure?"

"Yes," Paul said convincingly.

"Fine." The clerk turned and disappeared behind the shelves.

"I guess we've outstayed our welcome. Who are they playing?"

Paul looked up at the boxes in front of him. "What was that?"

"The Sox, who are they playing?"

"Not sure, Yankees I believe."

"Hell the Sox will win. Okay, where were we? Oh yes, 1865, file by file."

"Right, file by file. Damn. Well there are only two boxes." Paul pulled them down handing one to Carrie and he took the other. In anxious anticipation they shuffled through the files.

Then Paul let out a yell of triumph. "Got it." Picking up the file he walked over to Carrie. "Look here. A note in the margin of this letter says;

...these seven killings are a mystery. As yet no progress in solving this crime...

This has to be it, Carrie. The letter is dated May 12, 1865. A Pinkerton Detective named Sheldon, Barry Sheldon, wrote it. It looks as if the Pinkerton Detective Agency got involved in this case."

"But it says nothing of the crime itself."

"No. Let me get the rest of the papers." Paul retrieved the remaining bundle of files. "Hell, there's a lot of stuff here." He dropped it on another shelf then he and Carrie eagerly paged through each sheet.

"Boy they had their problems in those days. Listen to this:

> *A woman disappeared from a bordello last evening. As yet a body has not been found. Owner of the bordello, Madam Francine, said someone was pursuing the woman who dashed from the building into the snow.'*

He chuckled. "Hope she was wearing clothes."

"Here's something, Paul, January 28, 1865:

> *'The disappearance of Victoria Baxter has yet to be explained. I conversed with her husband, William Baxter, yesterday but he was unable to shed any light on the case. As the two men are business partners, and closely associated, I decided to interview Claude Marshall, the owner of the exclusive men's club The Eastern'.*

"Wait a second. Wasn't this Claude Marshall guy Police Commissioner in one of the last things we read?

Paul looked back through the papers. "Yes, here it is. You're right, Carrie. Hell he must have moved along in the political world. He owned a men's club. Why would he want to be Police Commissioner?"

"I wonder. It goes on:

> *'...Claude Marshall. As it was with Baxter, Marshall was of no assistance. He did mention he had seen Mrs. Baxter on a number of occasions when in town but offered nothing further. I do not think either man is involved in Baxter's disappearance.'*

"This doesn't look like it's related even though it's signed by that Sheldon fellow."

"Maybe some other case, Carrie, but look at this. A report dated four days earlier on January 21, 1865 regarding another murder:

> *'Victim number six was found this day at 5:50A.M. It is uncanny to see crimes perpetrated in an identical manner and each victim having almost identical physical descriptions. I am perplexed as to what drives this madman to commit such heinous atrocities.'*

Paul and Carrie stared at each other. Paul immediately looked back four more days and came up with murder number five, then four, until he had the reports of all six victims laid out in order on the floor in the aisle. Standing shoulder-to-shoulder, Carrie and Paul scanned the files in total disbelief.

"I'll be damned. I guess we have ourselves a copycat killer. He followed this crime in detail, leaving nothing out. The rest of the team is going to love this." Then Carrie scooped up seven small sheets of paper and leafed through them in shock. She turned to Paul.

"What is it Carrie?"

"Look at these. Here's one thing that is definitely the same. This killer also left a note but the message was different. This one says:

> *'In death they go two by two, twin sisters*
> *hand in hand. A mirror of the fate to come,*
> *repeated, in time again.'*

"Not much of a poet. What the hell could it mean?"

"Beats me Paul, but I guarantee there's a message buried here just as there is in the note our killer is leaving."

"But what is it? What is our killer trying to say, and what was this guy's message?"

Carrie looked at the note in her hand. "Whatever it was, it's not much use to us now."

"True, but what we have to do is solve the riddle left by our guy."

Carrie then picked up an envelope. "What's this?" She opened it and removed a stack of old photos. "Looks like the seven victims, Paul. My God, this is eerie. Look at them; they could pass as our victims. They look so much alike."

"Okay Carrie, let's take them and the rest of this stuff and get out of here."

She waved her hand at the files lying on the floor. "You want all these files?"

"Definitely. I'll have O'Malley go through them and see if there is any other useful information." They gathered everything they needed, replaced what they did not, and returned to the clerk's desk.

"We're done. Now you can go watch the game."

"Thanks. You taking that box with you?"

"Yes."

"Gotta sign the book. Can't let nothing out of here without signing the book."

"No problem." Paul signed and the two detectives headed for the elevator. The doors slid open and Carrie and Paul stepped into the car. As he pressed the button for the lobby, Paul called to the clerk.

"Thanks for waiting. Enjoy the game." The elevator door slid closed.

▼▼▼▼▼ *11*

Paul's efforts to find Farlon were about to pay off. The morning after he and Carrie had spent time in the archives, Paul received a call from a woman working as a cook at the Salvation Army Shelter on the west side.

"This is Detective Salvatore."

"Good morning, Detective, this is Mary Parkson. I am the cook here at the shelter. A policeman was in here a few days ago looking for someone. I spoke with him and he showed me a picture of a man…"

The River Styx

Paul became excited. Had this woman seen Farlon? "Have you seen him?"

"I'm not sure Detective. The photo was not very clear but the man here looks very similar, only he has a beard and long hair."

"But you think it might be him?"

"It could be. He's here now having breakfast, that's why I'm calling."

Then Paul had an idea. "Can you try to keep him there. I'm leaving right away."

"I can try, Detective, but if he wants to leave, how can I stop him?"

"I don't know, but please, do what you can. I'll get there as fast as I can."

"I will do my best, Detective."

"Very good. Thank you very much, you have no idea how much I appreciate this."

"You're welcome." Paul hung up and rushed out of his office. As he raced toward the shelter, he turned on his siren and light.

Paul burst from the car, dashed up the steps and through the front door. Inside, he went directly to the row of food tables. An elderly woman serving a street person looked up startled as he dashed up to her waving his badge.

"Detective Salvatore. I'm looking for Mary Parkson."

"Of course, Detective, through that door."

"Thank you." Paul stepped around the table through the swing door and found himself in the kitchen. He saw a woman in her mid-sixties rinsing a large cooking pot in the sink.

"Mary Parkson?"

"Yes, Detective." She turned off the tap and placed the pot in the sink. As she walked toward him she wiped her hands on the soiled apron around her waist.

"I came as fast as I could. Is he still here?"

"I'm sorry Detective, I could not delay him any longer. He said something about going to New York and had to find a job to get the money. He seemed nervous and left immediately after we spoke. I'm sorry."

"Not to worry, Mary, we'll find him I'm sure. You wouldn't happen to know where he was headed?"

"Afraid not."

"No you wouldn't."

"Has he done something wrong, Detective?"

"No, we just want a word with him. I won't keep you, but should he come back please call me immediately." Paul handed her his card. "Thank you again, Mary."

"You are quite welcome, Detective." A little disappointed, he drove back to Headquarters. If Farlon intended to go to New York, Paul had to move quickly. Back in his office he was about to make a phone call when Yoshi walked in.

"Morning, Paul, what's new?"

"Nothing much. I have just come from the Salvation Army Shelter on Maxwell…"

"Yeah, I know the place. What's going on over there?"

"Farlon. One of the women there called me. She said she saw him. He was gone by the time I arrived."

"Now you know where he hangs out."

"Apparently he may be heading for New York."

"What's in New York?"

Paul threw his mind into high gear. "No idea, unless…"

"Unless what?"

"His daughter. He's going to see his daughter. She works for one of the newspapers there." Paul thought for a moment then snapped his fingers. "Yu! That's it."

"Me! What the hell did I do?"

"No Yoshi, not you, Mr. Yu, an old store keeper in Chinatown, knows Farlon well. They were close friends. Farlon got the old guy out of a nasty situation. I'm betting that's where he'll go. That's where I'm going. Want to come along?"

"To meet a legend, damn right."

"I wouldn't count on it, although I hope you do because that will mean I get the chance to talk him into coming back."

"You think he will?"

"I can't say for sure Yoshi. He got a bum wrap from the department before he retired. He may still hold that against them. Let's go and see what we can find."

▼▼▼▼▼ *12*

They headed south on Halsted Street then turned east onto Cermak Road and drove into Chinatown. Paul then turned off of Cermak heading toward 23rd Street. The streets were narrow and the cars and trucks parked on both sides made it difficult to navigate. As they traveled along West 23rd Street, Paul saw an empty space and pulled to the curb. As both men emerged from the car, Paul spotted the small shop in the middle of the block on the opposite side of the street.

As the two detectives entered the shop, a small brass bell above their heads announced their arrival. The pungent aroma of spices mingled with the smell of burning incense, filled the air. There was little natural light; most came from three naked bulbs. The shop had an almost eerie atmosphere reminding Paul of old Charlie Chan movies. Both men stood for a moment to allow their eyes to grow accustomed to the gloom. Then out of the shadows, at the rear of the shop, shuffled a small figure.

The Chinaman approached Paul and Yoshi, then stopped, scrutinizing them for a few moments. He appeared to be making up his mind if he should stay or not. Then he asked in a quiet but blunt tone.

"You cops?" He did not move or change his expression.

"Yes. This is Detective Pat Yoshi and I am Detective Salvatore."

"So what you want?" He squinted as he pointed a crooked finger at Paul.

"You are Mr. Yu."

"How you know that?" he snapped.

"It's my job to know things."

"True. So what you want?" he asked again.

"We are looking for a friend of ours. You know him very well. We need to find him." Paul shifted his weight and glanced at Yoshi.

The Chinaman was still wearing a deadpan expression staring fixedly at Paul. "I cannot tell you I know your friend if you not tell me his name."

Paul chuckled. "Oh, I'm sorry, it's Graham Farlon."

The old Chinaman seemed to relax a little. "Why do you look here? I not see him for over six year."

"Graham Farlon retired about six years ago, Mr. Yu. We have not seen him since then either. We have reason to believe he might be here."

"Then you must speak to my helper. He say he speak to Detective Farlon last week. The detective send him here for a job. He's velly good man Detective Farlon. I owe him much for his help in my bad times."

"Yes, I understand, Mr. Yu. But as I said, Detective Farlon does not work for the police any longer. The man working for you could be Graham Farlon."

He shook his head emphatically. "Cannot," he said. "I know Detective velly well, this man not him. This man velly old, sure not cop." The Chinaman was most confident. So much so, Paul felt he might be wrong.

"Is he here today?"

"Yes, he working in back. Follow me, you speak with him." The Chinaman moved for the first time since he planted himself in front of Paul and Yoshi. They followed into the ever-darkening gloom.

"Mr. Gray, there is gentlemen here to see you," A moment later a shadowy figure emerged from the storeroom. There was no doubt it was Graham Farlon, but he looked like hell. He wore tattered old clothes and his hair was a long tangled mess of gray. He had not shaved in months and he looked years older.

"Graham Farlon, well I'll be damned. What the hell are you doing here?" It took Farlon by complete surprise. Shielding his eyes against the light bulb above Paul's head, he stared at Paul.

"My name is not Graham Farlon. It's..." The voice was so familiar. Paul interrupted not wanting Farlon to degrade himself further.

"Gray, I would like a moment of your time. Can we talk?"

"Why would you wish to speak to me?"

"Let's just say I have a proposition."

"What sort of proposition?"

Paul turned and retraced his steps. "Mind if we go back into the shop where it's not quite so cramped?" Yoshi, the Chinaman and a reluctant Farlon followed. Back in the shop, Paul addressed Farlon.

"Gray, give me ten minutes."

Gray Farlon was silent, his gaze fixed on Paul. It was obvious he had not been prepared for this encounter.

"Gray, are you listening, I need to speak to you."

Then the old man spoke. "If you're here to try to get me to come back, you're wasting your time."

"Gray, please, would you just…"

"Forget it." He turned to leave.

"Wait, hear me out, then kick me out if you like."

He turned, fixed his eyes on Paul again then said bluntly. "You've got five minutes."

Paul wasted no time. "Yes I'm here to ask you to come back. But before you turn me down consider the facts. The Board has changed, things are a lot better and you won't have to do any leg work."

"Are you suggesting I'm unable to do leg work?"

"Yes…no…no…oh shit, bad start…" Paul cursed.

"Damn right." Farlon folded his arms across his chest in a gesture of defiant rejection.

"Gray, we have a problem."

"Why is everything with you a problem?"

Paul ignored him and went on. "We're working on a very complex case. We have five murders and no clues. We don't…"

"Paul, cut the crap and get to the point."

"We need your expertise. I have…"

"No deal."

"Why?"

"Not interested."

"That's bullshit and you know it."

"I don't have to stand here and take your abuse."

"For crying out loud this is not abuse. I…"

"Do me a favor."

"What's that?"

"Just leave and leave me alone."

"No. I want you to hear me out. Besides, my five minutes is not up."

"I would say it's been good seeing you, Paul, but I'd be lying."

Paul avoided Gray's ploy to change the subject. "Gray, we have a damn killer on the loose in this city…"

"I may be old but I'm not blind; I can still read so what's your point?"

"Damn it you stubborn bastard, would you just listen to me for a moment?" Gray looked up at the clock over the counter.

"That's about all the time you have left, your time's almost up."

Paul had had enough of Gray sidestepping the issue. "For Christ's sake, Gray, listen. I want you back. We all want you back. It doesn't have to be permanent but at least give it a chance. There are…" Suddenly the Chinaman who had been standing open-mouthed staring at Farlon interrupted their conversation.

"You really Detective Farlon? Man you look like shit."

Farlon turned to Mr. Yu. "Thanks, Mr. Yu. I am sorry I lied to you."

The Chinaman looked hurt. "You not trust me, Detective?"

"I trusted you, Mr. Yu, but it wasn't about trust, it was...well it was..."

"That's okay, Detective, I just sorry you are no more a policeman."

"I'm sorry too. It was important I get to see my daughter in New York. I needed a job."

"You were best man on Force, Detective. Always help the little people like me. No your life not over yet. Now you go help Mr. Italian and solve these bad crimes." The Chinaman took Graham by the arm. "Go catch that killer."

"It's a little more complicated than that, Mr. Yu."

Paul immediately jumped in. "You're the one who's making it complicated Gray."

Gray ignored the comment confronting him with a question. "What the hell are...why are you here, Paul?"

"I have already told you why..."

"Right, but why are you here?"

"We need help and you're it. We're in a corner with no way out..."

Gray responded bluntly. "There's always a way out."

"You're not going to make this easy, are you?"

"Why should I? I'm not changing my mind."

"We'll see about that." Paul realized he had to change his tactics.

"You're wasting your time, Paul. Go solve your crime and just..."

Paul then threw fate to the wind. "You're afraid. You're afraid you won't meet expectations. You're afraid to face the truth even if the truth tells you you're still as good as you were. You..."

"Now hold on one damn minute." Gray grew agitated. For five minutes the two fenced back and forth each making their point, neither getting anywhere. Finally, Yoshi tried to interrupt but he barely got in a full sentence before Gray cut him off.

"What is it with you people? Where the hell did you find this guy? You trained him, Paul, because he talks just like you. Damn, I don't believe you two. Look, this is not debatable. Please leave me alone...go back to your jobs...go catch that killer. I'm finished with that life...I'm washed up." Farlon turned on his heels and walked away, but Paul was not ready to give up.

"That's bullshit and you know it! You're just looking for excuses to avoid making a decision." Gray immediately spun around and stepped close to Paul, the fire of anger burning in his eyes, something Paul had never seen in Farlon. He addressed Paul under his breath.

"I like you son, you're a good policeman and a great friend, but don't you dare presume to know what I am trying to do, so drop it." But Paul was not through. He took Gray by the arm and stepped toward the rear of the shop. For another five minutes Paul pressured the older man. Exhausted, Gray finally backed down.

With a deep sigh, his shoulders dropped in submission. "Paul, face facts, times have changed. I would be a dark horse. I'm not sure I want that. I respect your opinion but you're wrong in your statement. Both you and Yoshi are wrong. Do me a favor, since you haven't approached the Board, drop it. Get into that crime son and solve it." Then Farlon pushed past Paul, picked up his coat and headed for the door. Paul followed.

"Where the hell are you going?"

"I'm leaving."

"You can't do that."

"I certainly can and I am." He opened the door, then paused and addressed the three men. "Sorry gentlemen, but I am not up to it any longer. Have faith in your own abilities, Paul; you can do it. Yoshi, it was a pleasure meeting you. Mr. Yu, I hope I still have the job."

"Yes, Detective, job still yours." Farlon closed the door and was gone.

"Damn it!" Paul yelled as he slapped his hip. "We had him. For one brief moment we had him. He was about ready to come back. Damn that Board, they're the cause of this mess. That's it I guess. We may as well head back, Yoshi. Mr. Yu, thanks for your help."

"I do nothing, only watch."

"You gave Gray Farlon a job and that helped us find him."

"He come back to Force, Mr. Italian. I talk to Buddha with joss sticks. Detective Farlon see wisdom."

"That sounds great. Thanks, Mr. Yu." Paul and Yoshi left the store.

Forgotten Memories

▼▼▼▼▼ *1*

January 18, 2006

Seated at a corner table in the Salvation Army Shelter, Gray had just finished his evening meal. Paul Salvatore was seated across from him. They were in deep conversation with Paul doing most of the talking. Gray knew Salvatore would not give up now that he had caught up with him once again. He also knew trying to avoid the man was futile. Gray had made up his mind but did not intend to let his friend off the hook easily. After more than two hours of listening to Paul's begging and pleading, to the delight of the younger detective, he accepted the offer.

The drive to Paul's apartment was made in silence. Gray was deep in thought as he pondered the decision he had made, as Paul was reminiscing over the times he had spent learning his trade under the guidance of this great and compassionate individual.

"Okay, here we are. You remember the place...I believe you've been here before?" Paul said as he opened the door to his apartment. Gray followed Paul. Like leaves cascading from a tree in fall, memories tumbled into his mind. Gray felt the pangs of remorse. Once more he wished the clock could be turned back to have a second chance to set things right. So much had gone wrong. There had been so many mistakes. Life was unrelenting. But time would not stop let alone turn back.

"Sure, Paul, I remember the place. I remember you had one hell of a party for...I can't remember the name of that beautiful girl."

"Cindy, Cindy Palmer."

"Cindy, that was it. You had a going away party for her. Wasn't she leaving for some exotic place, like Australia?"

"I'd forgotten about that. Yes, she was a knockout, wasn't she?"

"I was certain you two would get hitched. I remember...you came to the house for dinner with Gwynne and me. Julia was in college at the time. You said you had proposed but she needed time to think. I guess she thought about it."

"You've got a good memory, Gray."

"Gwynne died about 18 months after that."

"Now, there was a wonderful woman, Gray...the best. You were a lucky man."

"Yes I was, wasn't I? Couldn't have found anyone who would have put up with my antics as she did. Damn, I miss her Paul. I miss her so much. I was so wrong putting the job before her and Julia. They deserved far better. It was my fault she went the way she did. I should have known…I should…"

"Gray, don't beat yourself up over it. It was not your fault. Life has its ups and downs; they are uncontrollable. There are those mysteries in life that will always remain mysteries, that is why life is so great. Cherish the memories. Hell, if we knew what was around the corner, there would be no excitement, no joy, like Christmas knowing everything under the tree. Life would become flat, uninteresting and meaningless. It would have no purpose. No, getting up in the morning and not knowing what lies ahead is a joy, it's exciting. Besides Gwynne knew what she was getting when she married you. She knew how dedicated you were to the Force and she wouldn't have had it another way. No, Gray, you were not to blame for anything. It was the way life was supposed to be. It was the path you were destined to follow."

"I suppose you're right."

"You know I'm right," Paul said with a smile. They fell silent for a while then Gray looked at Paul.

"So the little lady went to Australia. Ever see her again Paul?"

"Never did. She went and I don't think she ever came back. Probably married some kangaroo farmer and now lives in the outback. She was the outdoors type."

"No regrets?"

"No regrets. She was a great kid, full of life and much better off without me. Hell I couldn't go mountain climbing or winter backpacking or polar bear watching. I don't even like the damn cold weather. She loved it. She loved life. We lived on different planes. We seldom communicated on the same wavelength. I didn't want to see it at the time, but I realized it after she left. She knew it though. She's happy now, at least I hope she is, and I'm happy."

"No one else then?" Gray said.

"There are a number of prospective candidates."

"Good. Need to find a good wife and settle down. At your age it seems less important than it does at mine. When you reach my age, things become very empty, very lonely without a partner."

"Well I guess you're right, but I would have to be absolutely certain before I tied the knot," Paul said.

"So you decided to stay put and not move?"

"Yes. I like this place Gray, it's quiet and comfortable and you can't beat the view. I've been here over ten years now."

"That long? Damn it only seems like yesterday that you moved in." Paul gave Gray the tour, showing him where everything was.

"Just make yourself at home. Take the second bedroom." They walked down a short hall past two closed doors.

"That's my room and that's the third bedroom. At the moment it's full of junk. You can have this room," Paul opened the door into a spacious bedroom with a king-sized bed, dresser with a high mirror and an armoire. "There's a full bath and plenty of closet space," Paul said sliding open the doors to a large walk-in closet. "Those clothes you have on, just throw on the floor in the bathroom. I will have the maid dump them. These are some clothes that belonged to my brother. They have been here since he passed away."

"Your brother passed away? Oh Paul, I'm so sorry, I had no idea."

"It was a year after you retired. He had a massive heart attack while playing racquetball. Never recovered. Clare was a mess for months. Finally she left Saint Louis, took the two kids and went home to her folks in Seattle. I have only seen her and the boys once since then. I miss Jack. He used to spend at least a week out of the month here when he was in town. That's why he kept clothes around."

"I'm so sorry Paul."

"Yeah, well, you never know, do you? Nothing's forever, that's when it really hits home...okay, everything you need is in here. Make yourself at home. Should you need anything else just holler. You can stay until you decide what you are going to do. In the bathroom you'll find toiletries that Jack left behind. I never got around to tossing them so I think you'll find everything you need. If not let me know; I have extras." Paul left Gray standing in the middle of the bedroom a little bewildered.

He felt lost. At that moment, he did not know quite what to do next. He had been on the streets too long. The claustrophobic sensation that flowed over him scared him. He was unsure of himself for the first time in his life. But as uncomfortable as he was, it felt good. It made him realize he was fragile, human and alive. Then he glanced at the pathetic figure in the long mirror, threw his shoulders back, straightened himself up and pushed the long hair out of his face. He quickly looked away. Shaving was the first order of the day or rather the night, then he would shower. Dealing with his hair would have to come later. Things were going to be different from now on. He could feel it.

Reaching into his inside coat pocket, he withdrew the plastic bag containing the picture of Gwynne and Julia. Gray stood and stared at it for a long while. *I'm changing my life, Gwynne. I made you a promise and I intend to keep it. Paul has given me a second chance. I guess you had a hand in that. Anyway, things are looking better. I will see Julia soon. I hope she will speak to me. Of course, if you have anything to do with it, she will.* He removed the photo from the bag, placed it carefully on the bureau then walked into the bathroom. Gray stripped off the old rags, tossed them into the corner and proceeded to shave. As soon as he finished, he turned on the shower. Within minutes the room was full of steam. Adjusting the temperature to a tolerable level, he stepped into the stall and closed the door.

Gray stood still for a long time as he relished the feel of hot water cascading over him. He finally picked up the soap and a cloth and began to wash away the grime and filth of three years on the streets. After he had scrubbed, he again stood soaking up the luxury of the moment, allowing the almost scalding water to pound against his tired flesh. The feeling was exhilarating and the world around him was taking on a new and fresh appearance.

After an hour of ablutions he was clean in body, clean-shaven except for a narrow gray beard and mustache. Dressed in a fresh set of clothes, his hair pulled back in a ponytail, Gray walked into the living room. He felt a little self-conscious but rejuvenated. A man renewed.

"My God, Gray, you don't look like the same person. I would never have recognized you."

"Paul, you have no idea how much I appreciate this. You know you didn't have to do this."

"I know but if I didn't, I would kick myself for the rest of my life. Besides, I don't want you sneaking away again. I have battled hard enough to get you this far, now you're going the rest of the way."

"I won't change my mind now, believe me."

"I do."

▼▼▼▼▼ 2

In the shadows stood a figure, silent and still. From his vantage point he patiently waited and watched the empty street. His blood flowed through his veins as slow as treacle and as cold as the night air. He was prepared to wait through the night, if necessary, though he knew it would not be that long.

From the restaurant across the street he saw a woman emerge with her escort. He watched intently. His quarry was now in the open and as soon as he was prepared, he would strike. The unsuspecting couple strolled along the street and entered an underground parking garage. It was time.

The shadowy figure slipped from his hiding place, crossed the street and entered the garage. He could not see the couple but could hear the sounds of laughter and high-heeled shoes on concrete. With cunning and stealth he stalked his prey. At the bottom of the incline he paused. Cautiously, he peered around the corner to see the two walking toward their car. Moving away from his cover he stepped across the apron, slipped behind a car and moved quickly and silently in the direction of his target.

With cold calculating precision he was upon his prey before either she or her companion could react. The needle passed through the woman's coat and into her arm. Instantly, the woman went limp. He scooped her up and disappeared into the darkness. The man barely took three steps when he realized he had no chance of saving his companion. In an instant she and her abductor were gone.

In a state of panic he fumbled for his cell phone and dialed 911 realizing neither he nor his partner or the attacker had uttered a sound. Suddenly the voice of the operator exploded in his ear.

"This is 911…what is your emergency?"

"Yes...oh God I want to...there has been an attack on my girl friend. Some weird looking guy has just abducted her."

"Please try to remain calm, sir. What is your name?"

"Charles, Charles Layton, my girlfriend is Tracy Sullivan."

"What is your location?"

"A parking garage on the corner of West Huron and North Franklin, half a block from Benici's Restaurant. I'm on the first level. Please send someone quickly before it's too late...he took my girlfriend and I don't know where he went... please hurry."

"Sir, a car is on its way, just wait there."

"Where the hell do you think I'm going?" The man turned off his cell phone and paced agitatedly back and forth waiting for the police to show. Then he heard a car enter the garage. A police cruiser appeared down the ramp and stopped beside him. Two police officers emerged.

"Mr. Charles Layton?" one of the officers asked as he walked around the squad car.

"Yes."

"You called in a report that your girlfriend has been kidnapped?"

"Yes."

"What time did this take place?"

"Not ten minutes ago."

"Did you get a look at the attacker?"

"Hardly, I had my back to Tracy ready to open the car door. I couldn't find my keys and by the time I found them it was too late. That was when I heard a strange noise."

"What sort of noise Mr. Layton?"

"Like someone being hit in the stomach. I turned to see this guy turning the corner over there carrying Tracy. I ran after them. When I got to the street level...nothing, they had disappeared. It happened so fast." The first officer continued questioning Layton while the second walked around Layton's 1967 Dodge Charger with a flashlight.

"What's your girlfriend's name?"

"Tracy, Tracy Sullivan."

"What does she look like?"

"She's five foot three, has blue eyes, shoulder length blond hair and is wearing a long black fur coat and black leather gloves. She was also carrying one of those small clutch purses."

"Does she have any identifying marks?"

"She has a small tattoo of a butterfly on her left ankle. There is also a birthmark on her inner thigh. It's irregular like a splatter of paint, light brown in color. Oh, she also has a mole on the back of her right shoulder about the size of a pencil eraser...can't you go look for her. That guy could be miles away from here by now."

"Sir, we're already on it. We'll do everything we can to find her. Do you know her address?"

"Yes, of course…it's 633 Braxton Towers, Apartment 23 in Oakbrook."
"Who is your employer, Mr. Layton?"
"I work for GHB Electronics in Oakbrook."
"And your girlfriend. Where does she work?"
"Trinities…it's a fashion boutique in Oakbrook Mall." The officer was diligently making notes in a small spiral-bound notebook. At that moment more police cars arrived. The area quickly became a hive of activity.

As the officer scribbled away, without looking up, he asked. "Did you see a car?"

"No. The only thing I saw was the red glow of tail lights reflecting off something in the alley across the street."

"A red glow, that's it?"
"Yes."
"Nothing else?"
"No."

The officer took Layton by the arm. "Well, I'm going to have to ask you to come to the station Mr. Layton. It's just a formality, there is more information we are going to need."

Layton was nervous. "Are you arresting me?"

"No Sir, but we need more details." The officer called to his partner who was in conversation with another officer and two other men. "Hey Joe, you ready to leave?"

"Give me one second while I finish with the guys from Forensics."

"Whenever you're done." Layton and the officer walked over to the police cruiser. The officer opened the rear door. He then guided Layton in when the second officer approached.

"Okay, Frank, let's go. Forensics will deal with the rest. I filled them in on everything." The two got into their car and left the parking garage.

▼▼▼▼▼ 3

On the night of January 20, shortly before Gray rejoined the Force, the investigating team had been on an all night stakeout. The result of that effort turned out to be futile, for, although they encountered someone, they never managed to apprehend the individual. At 6:45 on the morning of January 21, Paul received a call informing him that a body had been found in the general vicinity of the other murders. Having barely recovered from the stakeout, he and Mario drove over to investigate.

Paul scratched the back of his neck. He watched Samantha Perry examine the body. This was not what he had expected. At that moment, Carrie walked up to the two detectives. She surveyed the scene.

"Doesn't look like one of ours, Paul."

"No it doesn't but there are a number of similarities. The way she's laying, her hair spread out around her head, her hands on her stomach…"

"Agreed, but she's wearing a raincoat, and that's all she's wearing," Perry said.

Paul paced around the corpse. "Someone may be copycatting our killer."

"That could be." Sam Perry stood. "Also, I see no cause of death. There is some fresh bruising on her wrists, thigh and temple, a first if she is an MM victim. There are also scuffmarks on her heels indicating she was dragged to this spot. And one other thing, you have an eye witness on this one."

Paul's interest was immediately heightened. "We do? Where Sam?"

"The police sergeant over there." Leaving Perry to her work, Paul walked to where the police sergeant was standing talking to an old woman.

"You witnessed this, Sergeant?"

"Not me, Detective, she did." He pointed to a short, bedraggled woman standing beside him.

She quickly responded. "I didn't actually sees 'im. I sees 'im lights a cigarette."

"He lit a cigarette?"

"Yes."

"But you didn't see him?"

"No just an outline, a shadow like."

"So you can't give us a description?"

"Like I says, I only sees this shadow. That's when I waves down the garbage truck." Paul's elation was suddenly swept away. Thanking the woman, he walked back to where Carrie and Sam were standing.

"Anything?" Carrie asked.

"No. Only a killer with a bad habit."

"Pity."

Paul, feeling agitated, started pacing about. He was frustrated to have come close to a witness then lose one. Then he stopped pacing and addressed the ME. "How long has she been out here, Sam?"

"Two, maybe three hours."

Mario looked up from the body. "That's not possible Sam."

"Why not?"

"Our stakeout team was here until *5:15A.M*. This place was crawling with police up until then. Besides, this is a busy street, someone would have called this in before six."

"Mario's right Sam. She could not have been here that long."

"She has been dead for about four to five hours, guys. She's been exposed to the elements for at least two. I have…"

Paul squatted next to the body. He rolled it on its side and looked beneath the raincoat. "The pavement under her is soaked Sam. It has been snowing since around five. She was placed on snow, not dry pavement."

"Be that as it may, she has been out in the elements for far longer than an hour Paul."

"Maybe she was somewhere else then moved here, indicated by the scuff marks," Mario suggested.

Samantha bent and examined the body further. "That's possible. Aside from all that, she's Hispanic, around five-feet seven inches tall, black hair and roughly 120 to 130 pounds. She definitely doesn't fall into the same MO as the other victims. If this is the work of your killer…"

"You're right, Sam, but why here? Also, it has been exactly four days since the last murder and the layout of the crime scene is similar." Paul tried to make some sense of it.

"I think we'll know a lot more when we get her back to the morgue. I can't give you much right now. But you're right, this could be a copycat."

"Was there a note?"

"No, Carrie. The pockets of the coat are also empty. No note, no ID and, so far, no cause of death."

Paul stared at the dead woman. Something troubled him. He had a strong sense of recognition; her face looked hauntingly familiar. He stood and began to pace again…then he walked back, stooped next to the body and studied her face closely. "I've seen this woman somewhere."

"That's possible, Paul. You see a lot of people during the course of a day. She may have been downtown or in court."

"True, but it's not that sort of recognition. This is deeper…someone out of the past. An old acquaintance, a face out of place, an old high school friend, it's that sort of recognition. One thing is certain, she is no hooker."

"How can you say that?"

"A gut feeling, Carrie."

"Are you sure?"

"Yes, Mario, I'm positive. She's no hooker. Damn, I know her but just can't place her."

"Don't lose sleep over it, Paul, because I have a feeling you're wrong."

"I hope so Sam. I would hate to think she was someone I knew."

"Well if you guys are through, I will get her out of here."

"That'll be fine Sam. I'm heading back myself." Paul, still troubled, walked back to his car and drove back to District 3.

▼▼▼▼▼ 4

Paul Salvatore stared in disgust at days of accumulated paperwork piled on his desk. He loved his job but despised the paperwork. In disgust, he lifted the top sheet. He had just finished reading the third paper when Yoshi stepped into his office.

He leaned against the doorframe and folded his arms. "I thought you'd left."

The River Styx

Paul looked up waving his hand over the foot high pike before him. "Are you out of your mind, look at this lot. They keep dumping this damn stuff on my desk and I'm supposed to have it back the next day. I thought computers were supposed to eliminate this mess. With the case taking all my time, how in the name of hell am I supposed to get through this mess?"

"Hey Paul, I have my own stack of problems. I have been reading over my notes on the sixth victim. The facts, or lack thereof, really bother me."

"Just on the sixth victim?"

"No, they all bother me, but if you look at the time the sixth victim's body was discovered then work back, it could not have been there for more than half an hour, an hour at best. Certainly not two or three hours."

"That's what I was trying to explain to Perry. Her timing doesn't tie in with the conditions. It was already snowing when the body was placed there."

"And the garbage truck driver's statement…" The phone on Paul's desk interrupted their conversation. He reached for it.

"Salvatore."

"Detective? This is Kerry Pollard, Personal Assistant to the Mayor."

"Yes, Kerry, what can I do for you?"

"The Mayor would like a word with you. If you will hold a moment, I'll connect you."

"Salvatore?" The voice boomed through the phone.

"Good afternoon, Mr. Mayor, what can I do for you?"

"What the hell is going on down there, Detective?" he barked.

"Regarding what, Sir?"

"You know damn well what I'm referring to, Detective. What is happening with this serial killer business? Where are we? Are we making any damn progress at all?" Paul listened; contemplating what he was going to say once the Mayor finished ranting.

"We are moving forward Sir, but we need more help."

"Then get it. If it will get this case solved, get more help. If you need the damn National Guard get them. I want to see results, Detective, and I want to see them now, not six weeks or six months from now, you understand? This city is in the grips of panic and it has to stop. Am I making myself clear?"

"Yes, Mr. Mayor, crystal. But as I mentioned we need…"

"Damn it, Detective…"

"No, Sir, I mean we need one specific individual, but I'm certain I'll meet resistance when I propose…"

"Look, Detective, I don't give a rat's ass who it is you need. I want this case solved now."

"Very well, Sir. I need to reinstate Graham Farlon." There was a moment of uneasy silence.

"Hell, is the man still alive? I thought he died years ago." The Mayor sounded shocked.

"Oh he's very much alive, Mr. Mayor. But I'm sure I will meet resistance from…"

"From no one. You go ahead with your plans, Detective; tell the Board you have my full approval. If they question it, have them call me. If you think Farlon is your answer, bring him back for as long as you need him. I'll talk to the Commissioner in the morning and let him know you have the go ahead. But I had better see results, Salvatore, or I'll have your job."

"You will, Mr. Mayor, you will see results. Thank you Sir."

"Don't thank me, Detective. Just get that murdering bastard off my streets."

"Very good, Sir, I will do that."

He snapped back. "Good. See that it happens." From his bluntness it was obvious the Mayor was in no mood to hold a discussion.

"Yes, Sir, I..." But the Mayor had hung up.

"Sounds a little ominous," Yoshi said flatly.

Paul put the receiver down. "Not at all, Yoshi. We can bring Farlon back without question. And that's straight from the horse's mouth."

"That is great news."

"You're right because I already have him at my place."

"So you did catch up with him?"

"Yes. Took a while to talk him round but I finally succeeded. Now we can breathe more freely. Where were we before we were interrupted?"

Yoshi got out of his chair. "Paul, I have to move. It's good to know Farlon's back."

"You're right. See you later, Yoshi." Reluctantly, Paul returned to his paperwork. Taking the next document from the top of the pile, he began reading but his mind was not on the contents. He tried to follow a little advice given to him years back by Graham Farlon. *'Get into the killer's head and learn what he's thinking.'* Paul had no idea how to accomplish that let alone where to begin. *How the hell do you get into the mind of a killer when you don't even know the identity of the bastard? Farlon must have been able to otherwise he would never have been able to solve all those crimes.* Paul shook his head in frustration. His thoughts were interrupted by another knock on his door. Paul looked up to see O'Malley.

"Excuse me, Paul, but this came for you this morning." He handed Paul a large envelope. Paul looked at it suspiciously. His name was the only thing scribbled on the outside.

"Thanks, Patrick. Do you know who sent it?"

"No. It came by courier and was left at the front desk. It wasn't marked urgent so no one said anything until a few moments ago."

"Okay, thanks." As O'Malley left, Paul leaned back in his chair and stared at the envelope. He never liked mail that contained secrets and this obviously was one of those. He reached for the letter opener and slit the envelope. It contained a 20-page document. Attached to the first sheet was a post-it note.

Paul,
When you receive this call me.
Davenport

As he reached for the phone, he called the morgue.

"Davenport." Justin's voice crackled through the phone.

"Justin, Paul."

"Paul. You received the papers?"

"Yes. What's this all about?"

"You sound a little depressed."

"No, it's nothing, just a little frustrated."

"I don't blame you. I feel that way myself. I've about had it with this guy. I wish you'd either catch the bastard or he move on."

"I'd prefer to see him behind bars. Better still, hang the bastard by his balls."

"He's one sick son of a bitch. I suggest that he find a better way of breaking up with his girlfriends, something less extreme or permanent."

"No kidding. How do you stop someone like this?"

"That's your department Paul."

"Well I'm beginning to wish it belonged to someone else."

"I'll say this for him, he's got the mechanics of this crime down to a fine art. But then again I guess he's had a lot of practice."

"What are you driving at?"

"You might want to look at the contents of that envelope. Believe me, it's pretty damn interesting. If I'm right, this guy's been real busy."

"Are you serious? You're saying the killings here aren't his first?"

"Not if what's in those papers is what I think it is." There was a long silence.

Paul stared at the document before him stunned. "Where?"

"New York."

"City?"

"Yes."

"How long ago?"

"Six victims over three years. Started back in '97. Last one was in '99. A real strange case."

"It was?"

"How he spaced out his victims is really weird. Wait till you read it; believe me, it'll blow your mind." There was another long silence.

Paul stared at the document. "Where did this come from?"

"Trent Gillespie, one of our ME's. He's from New York and worked for the Medical Examiner's Office on the case. As soon as we found the third victim, he recalled the incident and produced that document. Look, Paul, I've got to go. Enjoy reading. I'll talk to you later."

"Hey, Justin, thanks."

"Anytime. Hope it helps."

"I'll let you know." Paul hung up and stared at the papers in mild disbelief. As he began to read, his interest was fueled by the almost unbelievable contents of each page.

5

On January 23, Gray Farlon walked into the District 3 Headquarters building for the first time in over six years. The feeling in the pit of his stomach was like a schoolboy starting ninth grade. So many things were familiar, so many weren't; the smells, the sounds, the bustle of activity, policemen hurrying, going about their daily business. He paused in the lobby for a moment taking it all in trying to slow his heart and relax. He was nervous.

"Gray." Over the noise a familiar voice reached his ears. He turned to see Paul approaching.

"Paul, good morning."

"So, how do you feel?"

"A little like a kid on his first day in kindergarten. It's all the same yet, it's all so different."

"Yes, I know what you mean. Let's go upstairs." Paul approached the elevator as the doors slid open. They got out on the third floor.

"Seems like a lifetime."

"I bet. This way." They walked along a brightly lit corridor and stopped in front of a closed door.

Paul waved at the door. "Your office."

"I don't need an office, Paul."

"Sure you do. Can't communicate well without an address." Paul opened the door and the two men entered the spacious room. It was furnished with a large old wooden desk behind which was a new high-backed, black leather chair. On the floor was an almost room-sized rug covering the wooden floor. In front of the desk were two arm chairs and against one wall a rather well used sofa. Two filing cabinets sat side by side in one corner. Two thirds of the wall behind the desk was a window overlooking the city.

"This is not an office, Paul, it's a damn ballroom. I don't need anything this big."

"Hey, call it home for it's all there is."

"I really appreciate this, but it was unnecessary."

"No problem. Look I have something I need to do right away. Get yourself a cup of coffee and I'll be with you in about 20 minutes. If there is anything you need, call extension 4635; that's O'Malley, he'll make sure you're accommodated." Paul walked over to the desk on top of which were three stacks of files. "This is information on the first three victims. I thought you might want to get yourself familiar with what's been going on."

"Great, that will be really helpful."

"Okay I'm out of here. Anything else?"

The River Styx

He patted the stack of files. "No, I'll be fine. I have plenty to do. And, Paul, thanks again for all your help."

"Hey, don't mention it. You're quite welcome." Paul left. Gray sat down, reached for a file and began to read.

Then a voice interrupted his concentration. "Excuse me, Detective, would you like some coffee?" Gray looked up to see a young sergeant standing in the doorway. "My name is…"

"O'Malley, yes, Detective Salvatore mentioned you." O'Malley stepped into the office as if he were stepping into the throne room of royalty.

"Would you like coffee, Detective?"

"Yes, please, black." O'Malley dashed out and was back in less than a minute carrying a mug.

"Here you are, Sir."

"Thanks, Patrick. Don't mind if I call you Patrick, do you? I see it on the investigation roster in these files."

"Not at all, Sir, Patrick is fine."

"So is Detective. Better still, call me Gray, like everyone else. Forget the sir. What do you do around here, Sergeant?"

"I work the computers for the team. Sort of a whiz at it, at least that's what they all say."

"Yes, Detective Salvatore mentioned it. It's good to meet you, Patrick."

"Likewise, Detective." He appeared reluctant to leave, hovering in the doorway as if he wanted to say something else. Just then Paul walked back in.

"I see you met our resident computer guru."

"Yes. He was taking care of me."

"Good. Thanks, Patrick." Patrick disappeared down the hall.

"Pleasant young fellow."

Paul slipped into one of the armchairs. "Yes, he is damn good on the computer too. By the way I brought you this." Paul handed Gray a manila envelope. "Thought you should have a look at what we're dealing with."

"What is this?"

"Our murderous friend has been getting a great deal of practice. According to that information he was busy in New York in the late 90's carrying out similar murders. From what I have read it could very well be our guy."

"So this is not his first stop?"

"Maybe not. We are also convinced he's a copycat working off a crime back in the mid-1800's."

"That could prove useful."

"It could since everything he's doing shadows the old crime. Next thing, I have a meeting with the team in five minutes, like to join in?"

"Absolutely. Where, in your office?"

"No, we operate out of a War Room on the fourth floor." Paul and Gray left the office.

6

On the morning of his second day back reality set in. Gray was not prepared for the devastating and heart-breaking shock he was about to face. As he entered the elevator on his way to his office, Paul intercepted him.

"Gray, I have just received a call from the coroner. I'm heading up there now. Would you care to join me?"

"Sure, I need a break from all those files. Anything new, Paul?"

"Not sure, the ME can be elusive when he wants to be. I think it may have something to do with the sixth victim."

"I was getting ready to read that one." Arriving at the garage the two detectives climbed into Paul's car and headed uptown.

Davenport was in conversation with a lab tech when they entered the morgue. As he finished he turned his attention to Gray and Paul.

"Gentlemen, good morning." He walked over to Gray and shook his hand vigorously. "My God, Gray, it is good to see you. It's been a while. What…it's four years since you left?" Paul glanced at Farlon and raised his eyebrows.

"Actually, it's just on six years."

"Six years. That long? How time flies."

"How have you been, Justin? I'm surprised you're still here."

"Got no place else to go. Who's going to hire a washed up ME?"

"Washed up…no way. You're the best in the business, I can attest to that."

"Thanks for those kind words. You're looking good Gray. What's with the pony tail?" he smiled.

"Changed my style."

"Looks good on you. Sort of distinguished."

Paul interrupted the flow of conversation. "Are you two done? Justin, what's so important we had to rush up here?"

"Rush! Who said anything about rushing? Actually it's good you both came." Davenport walked over to an autopsy table where the outline of a woman's body was visible beneath a white sheet. Paul leaned close to Gray's ear.

"Never seen him so damned cheerful. Hell, you had to be his happy pill for the day." Davenport stepped around the table and pulled the sheet down. The woman was Hispanic, pale in death but still beautiful. The ME laid the sheet back to the dead woman's shoulders.

Gray stared at the face, his mind exploding with grief and remorse. Pain shot through his head like a shaft of ice cold steel and that empty, hollow feeling settled in his stomach. His face grew pale. Tears crested his eyelids. His chest tightened. He wanted to run from this place, find a dark corner and sob.

Memories rushed into his mind like a spring flood. *You shouldn't be lying here. Why? How did this happen? O God, Juanita, who is responsible for this? I failed you. I swore so long ago I would protect you and I failed. I am so sorry, Juanita, so very sorry. I will find who did this and make them pay. Oh God...* The pictures, memories, and familiar scenes flowed like a living scrapbook. His thoughts were interrupted as he felt a hand on his shoulder. He looked up and saw Paul staring at him perplexed.

"Sorry Paul. It came as a great shock."

"Gray, are you okay? For God's sake what's the matter, you look as if you have seen a ghost."

"No, not a ghost Paul, but..." He choked back the sorrow. He stood silently staring at the dead woman.

"Gray, are you sure you're okay? You really don't look good."

Gray found his voice. "I'm fine. Just give me a moment." Davenport went to replace the sheet.

"No leave it." The room fell silent. Gray looked down at Juanita. His mind traveled back...back to youth when this woman had been a child in pigtails...back to better times...times of peace, joy, happiness, times of innocence. Then he looked up at Paul and broke the silence.

"When did you find her?"

"Morning of the 21st."

"A victim of the serial killer?"

"Yes," Justin said.

Gray closed his eyes, then opened them and looked at the ME. "Give me the story, Justin."

"She's definitely a Mannequin victim; most of the characteristics are the same, but not all. It was those differences that caused us to doubt at first."

"Doubts?" Gray did not look up.

"Yes. We first thought she was a copycat victim. She was not killed in exactly the same manner. A syringe was used but in her case it was inserted behind her ear. The others never put up a fight, she did. The bruises and lacerations indicate that."

He lifted the sheet. "There's a bruise on both wrists from the killer gripping her very tightly." Davenport laid her arm down. "She has a large bruise on her hip and one heavy bruise on the side of her head. This one possibly rendered her unconscious. There are numerous other bruises, contusions and abrasions to her legs, arms and torso.

The skin on the heels is heavily scuffed indicating she was dragged across black top, confirmed by the material we removed. Lastly, her little finger on her right hand is broken. She did not die instantly." Davenport paused. He looked up at Gray who was staring at the woman. Silence spread through the room once more; like death's smothering blanket, it screamed in Gray's ears. He almost put his hands up to cover them.

He looked away. "Damn. Why? Why her, Paul?"

"You know this woman?" There was a long pause.

Then he broke the news. "It's Juanita Rodriguez."

"Who...?" Paul almost yelled. "Oh my God!" He stared at the body, "I knew it. The moment I saw her I recognized her. I just couldn't place her; it's been so long. Her face has been haunting me. I told Mario I recognized her. Now I...Damn it Gray, I'm so sorry," Paul said, his tone reflecting his own grief.

"Why? What did she do to deserve this? She was a good kid with a big heart." Anger and frustration boiled up in him. "The bastard has to pay. Damn it. He's not getting away with this," Gray said under his breath, fresh tears rolling down his cheeks.

"Who's Juanita Rodriguez?" Davenport asked in a sympathetic tone.

"She is...was the daughter of my old partner, Juan Rodriguez. You may remember him, Justin."

"Yes. A really nice fellow, shot during a hostage situation in a nightclub, as I recall."

"Yes, and she was only six at the time. I swore then I would take care of her and his family. Hell, I couldn't even take care of myself." He turned and left the room. He grieved for having broken a promise.

"Excuse me for a moment Doctor. I'm sure we will be right back."

▼▼▼▼▼ 7

Paul stepped out of the room, walked over and stood beside Farlon. For a long time both men stared out the large window, not speaking. The sun had found strength to break through the heavy overcast. Shards of light pierced the gray bringing brilliance to a frozen city. It was like a sign, a sign of respect for the dead, as if God opened passages of light for the troubled souls to find their way to a better place.

Gray tried not to remember, but his mind was on one thing; find the monster responsible for this. He must find the crazed maniac that walked the streets of his city, unhindered, invisible and unknown. It was a pollutant, a malignancy that had to be neutralized before it struck again. It was a virus he had to wipe from the face of the earth. He made a silent promise with vigorous determination then turned and spoke to Paul.

"I'm going to nail this one. The son of a bitch is not going to get away with this. No, damn it, he has just made his biggest mistake. He's made this personal." Paul saw the anger in Gray's eyes.

"As I live and breathe, he's going down. Why, Paul? Why Juanita? What the hell is this bastard playing at? If he thinks he can get away with this, he's mistaken."

"They were all just kids Gray, all so young."

"This is the last straw. I'll bring the son of a bitch to his knees. I will have him begging for his own miserable life before I'm finished. I'll cut out his ice cold heart and stuff it down his throat." Gwynne dying had been God's will. This was different. A killer, an animal, worse than an animal, had messed with someone close to him. Paul placed a comforting, reassuring hand on his shoulder.

"Don't worry Gray, we will get him."

"Damn right. We will send the murdering bastard straight to hell." He calmed his voice, "I wonder if the family knows yet?"

"I have my doubts. I don't recall seeing a missing person's report. I would have recognized the name immediately."

"I think I should go pay my respects. I must let them know before they hear some other way. This is going to destroy Anita, her mother. What am I going to say, Paul? First her husband, now her daughter; what do I tell her?"

Paul squeezed his shoulder. "You will find a way to handle it, Gray. You always have. They know you'll bring the son of a bitch to justice. That will be of some comfort to them."

"I hope you're right. Thank God Juan is not alive to see this." He turned from the window and re-entered the morgue with Paul right behind him.

"Let's see if Davenport has anything else for us." Anita played on his mind. He was troubled.

"Are you sure you're okay? You don't have to do this, you know. I can finish up here."

"Quit mothering me, I can handle it. It was the initial shock of seeing her lying there on that table. I was not prepared for it."

"I'm sorry, Gray. If only I had..." Gray put his hand up to silence Paul.

"Paul, it's okay," he said quietly. Gray walked up to the table, the outline of Juanita's body still hauntingly visible beneath the white sheet. "Got anything else for us, Justin?"

"No, Gray, that's it. As soon as something new comes up, I'll call you."

"Before I get out of your hair, a question. In your last report you mentioned you were targeting Chloro... whatever the name of that compound is, as the method the killer used to dispatch his victims."

"*ChloroPheno-Drexatone,* CPD. As I explained to the guys at the district HQ, it's not the CPD that killed these women, but most likely the compound called SUX. It's also untraceable."

"How can you target a poison if there is no trace of it?"

"A great deal is based on gut instinct and a process of elimination. But when there is nothing in the blood we focus on those substances that are untraceable. In part we then have to play a guessing game. But at this point, I would stake my reputation on CPD and SUX."

"Then we have a smoking gun."

"Not quite, Gray, but we can, with utmost confidence, say one or both of these two compounds were used."

"You also mentioned that the CPD could be taken orally."

"Yes, and it has virtually the same effect but takes longer to react. The killer may place it in drink, or mix it with food. It's tasteless, impossible to detect."

"I'm not so sure that is going to be of any help to us, Justin, but thanks anyway."

"Sure thing, Gray." Gray, deep in thought, left with Paul on his heels.

Finally Paul invaded his thoughts. "You sure you're okay, Gray?"

"For God's sake Paul, I'm fine. Just drop it. I appreciate your concern but, yes, I'm fine. Let's get out of here and go catch ourselves a killer."

8

Gray was strong, he always had been. Death was nothing new to him; he had seen enough in his lifetime. But the death of a dear friend was different. His insides ached with grief, but he was also burning with anger, an anger that he knew would not subside until he had his hands on the killer's throat. As he and Paul rode back to the office he said nothing, there was nothing to be said. Paul had tried to console him but it was not consolation he needed. His feelings did not surprise him; he was human and he wanted revenge. As they entered the building they ran into Yoshi and Carrie.

"Hey, Paul, we've put a name to the dead woman found on the 21st."

"Juanita Rodriguez," Paul responded.

"How did you know?"

"Just come from the morgue. We saw the body, Gray recognized her immediately. She was the daughter of his old partner."

"Oh God, Gray. Damn, I'm so sorry. I had no idea," Carrie said sympathetically.

"Gray, I'm so sorry to hear that," Yoshi offered.

"Thanks, guys, but don't worry. All I can say is we had better find this bastard soon." Gray took a deep breath fighting back his emotions. "We'll peel this city apart layer by layer until we find in which cesspool he's hiding. We will play his game and bring him down. We need to find out who he is, learn his habits, where he comes from, where he goes, what he eats, where he eats, who his acquaintances are, and their relationships. Find out how many times he goes to the bathroom, his brand of aftershave and his tailor. We need to know everything about this guy. But we must find him...now."

"Anything new from the ME?"

"Nothing, Carrie."

"I have something, Gray. I did some checking on those expensive shoes and coat. There was nothing much on the coat; the brand is not sold in here. I had more success on the shoes. Marshall Field's and 'Suave – The Gentleman's Outfitters', both carry Galano's. I spoke to Suave; they were unable to offer anything related to past sales. On the other hand, Field's keeps records of their big customers. I paid them a visit. Though they were a little reluctant, they supplied the list. It's basically a list of who's who of prominent figures. Folks like the Mayor; real estate tycoon Mathew L. Grant; Clive W. Maitland, the antiquities guru; Illinois Senator, Eugene Chapman; Parlos, the Sox baseball player and, get this one, Sonny 'pan face' Molino. Anyway the list goes on."

"That's great, Yoshi. Drop the Mayor off the list. As far as the rest, go through the list and check on each name. Any that look the least bit suspicious, categorize them and we'll look at them closer. I think we can also rule out Parlos and the Senator. But just as a precautionary measure you can check their itinerary for the last few months."

"What about other locations?"

"Stay local for now. If nothing turns up here, we'll look farther afield. It's a process of elimination, which will take some time but we must do this quickly. If you need any help, say so."

"A quick question, Gray. Aren't we sticking our necks out a little digging into the lives of all these wealthy people?"

"I suppose we are, Carrie, but the birth of a killer is not confined to any particular social group. They come from all walks of life. The street bum to the banker, a janitor to a king there's no distinction. Any human being can turn killer in a heartbeat."

"I guess you're right but, as we already know, on that list are names like Sonny Molino. As Carrie said these people won't appreciate us digging into their private lives."

Gray pressed the elevator call button. "Yoshi, we do whatever it takes to close this case."

"Okay, Gray."

"I understand your concern, Yoshi, but we're under the gun."

"You think our killer's on that list of names?"

"Who's to say? Look back in history. See where some of the most infamous killers originated. Many were very well educated, came from good lineage and were wealthy," Paul said as they entered the elevator.

"So, we ruffle some feathers, that's the breaks, Yoshi. First condense the list then if there are any names left, we'll get together and review them."

"Right, Gray, I'm on it."

▼▼▼▼▼ **9**

As Paul and Gray walked into Paul's office, the phone rang.

"Salvatore."

"Am I speaking with the Detective in charge of the Mannequin Murder investigation?" A soft-spoken, honey smooth rather seductive voice poured from the phone. Paul recognized it immediately. Suddenly he was sweating.

He stuttered over his response. "Ah…yes…ah yes you are."

"Paul?"

"Yes?" He pulled himself together.

The woman on the other end chuckled. "Well hello Paul. We've been playing phone tag for the past few days. Are you avoiding me?"

"No."

"You were supposed to call me last, as I recall." Paul felt his face flush.

"You could be right."

"I am. So where do we stand?"

"I'm not sure I understand the question."

"Come now, don't be so evasive. You're being awfully formal, is someone with you?"

"Yes."

"Ah, my father?"

"Correct. So how may I help you?"

She laughed. "Wow, this could be a lot of fun but I'll let you off the hook this time. I'm coming to Chicago to do an article on the murders. I was…"

Paul almost panicked. "Excuse me, would you hold a second, I have to take another call."

"No problem." Salvatore put the woman on hold then looked up at Gray pointing to the phone.

"This is Julia."

Gray gave Paul a blank look. "Julia? You mean my Julia?"

"Yes."

It was Gray's turn to become agitated. "How…what…what does she want?"

"She's coming out here to do an article on the murders."

Now Gray was in a panic. "Oh God. You're kidding."

"Not at all. She's with the New York Daily…"

"I know who she works for. Damn!" Gray had not counted on this, at least not this early.

"Do you want to talk to her Gray?"

"No. No damn it…no. I'm…I'm not ready."

"You sure? I would say it's as good a time as any."

"I said no," Gray snapped.

"Okay, Gray, it's your call." Paul pressed the hold button. "Ms. Farlon, sorry to keep you. What can I do for you?"

"Ms. Farlon? Aren't you spreading it a little thick, Paul? What happened to 'Julia'?" Paul tried to ignore her.

"We can discuss that when you arrive. When do you arrive?"

"I arrive in Chicago around *7:30P.M.* on Friday, February 3."

"And what is it you want from us?"

"Come on, Paul, quit playing games. I need a story. Give me some time, please."

"I'll see what I can arrange."

"What! Are you hedging? Oh, I get it, you haven't told my father about us, have you?"

"No."

"Great. You spineless wimp…are you going to tell him?"

"I'm not sure. Maybe you could."

"I knew it, you are spineless. You don't have the balls to tell him."

"I think it would be better if we covered that when you arrive."

"We'll do that." Her anger rattled through the phone.

"Very well, I will see you then."

"Count on it." She hung up.

"What was that all about?"

"She wants a story Gray. I told her we would have to discuss it."

"She gets nothing."

"What! Why?"

"She's a reporter. Besides, this story is not being splashed all over the front page of every paper in the country."

"This is not every paper, Gray."

"Paul, to break this case we need an edge. Our only edge is not to let the killer know what we know."

"But we don't know anything."

"The killer doesn't know that."

"Wait a second, Gray. You think she is going to fly out here and accept the fact that she gets nothing?"

"She may be my daughter, but she's also a member of the school."

"School! What school? What the hell are you talking about?"

"The school of barracudas."

"Gray, for crying out loud. Can't you…"

"I wouldn't give a damn if she were Cleopatra Queen of the damn Nile, she's not getting a story."

"You're not going to give her anything?"

"No, and neither will you."

"I don't believe…"

"Paul, what's going on?"

Paul gave Gray a rather puppyish look. "I don't understand."

"Look, pal, don't play games. We have known each other and worked together too long. I know you. What's going on between you and Julia? Is there some kind of a conspiracy?"

"Gray, honest, nothing is *'going on'* as you put it and there's no conspiracy. Damn it, I was just trying to be helpful. This is the opportunity you've been waiting for. You wanted to go to New York, now…"

"We're on a crucial case, we're not running counseling sessions. If I felt I needed your help I would have asked, so quit meddling." Gray was trying not to raise his voice.

"Oh, for crying out loud, you stubborn old bastard. Gray, I'm not meddling. I'm only trying to be a friend or are you too blind to notice?"

"Then don't, at least not in that area, so drop it."

"Gray, you told me the day you decided to return to the Force that all you wanted to do was mend the wounds between you and Julia. Now she's coming here. Take the opportunity or she will come and go and you'll lose your chance. She's not going to bite your head off. Gray, see her, talk to her. How bad could it be?" Gray had calmed down. He looked at Paul and saw a good friend.

"You're right, of course."

"Of course, I'm right."

"But is this the right time?"

"Right time? Come on, Gray."

"I'm not sure I really don't know."

"There is no right time, only the moment. Take it, you have nothing to lose and everything to gain. You *will* lose if you don't talk to her."

"Okay, Mr. Psychologist. What do I say?"

"That's up to you. Be the person she wants to see."

"Okay, I'll speak to her."

"Good."

"But no story."

"Then what?"

"She gets what everyone else gets, nothing more."

"But Gray you…"

"That's final Paul, you got it?"

"All right. She gets the basics only."

"Agreed." For the first time in his life Gray was having a massive panic attack. His heart raced and he could feel the perspiration running down his back. At that moment Carrie stepped into the office.

"Am I interrupting?"

"Not at all, Carrie, come in."

"You two look very intense."

Gray got up from his chair. "Heavy discussion. Anyway, I've got to go, I have something I must do."

"So we give her a line?"

"I said we give her the same as everyone else." Gray turned and solemnly walked out of the office.

"He's a man with a lot of pain," Carrie said as she watched him leave.

"He's also a man with a lot of heart, Carrie."

"That, also."

▼▼▼▼▼ *10*

It was on the bitterly cold and blustery morning of January 25 when the seventh victim was discovered. The MO was the same, everything was the same, except that the body was not within the Red Zone but in the parking lot of the Merchandise Mart. This one deviation didn't concern Gray, but what did concern him was, like Juanita, this woman was no hooker. She had class and came from money. It was that fact alone that bothered him. It planted a fresh and troubling question in his mind. Had the killer moved into higher circles among the unsuspecting and vulnerable rich?

At *7:50A.M.* Gray, Paul, Carrie and Mario walked across the wind swept area toward the spot where Sam Perry was inspecting the corpse.

"Morning, folks."

Gray squatted beside Sam. "Morning, Sam. What have we got?"

"Same MO...different location. There are some subtle differences but nothing striking. This woman, as with number six, is no hooker. In fact, I would go so far as to say she is from money. With well-manicured nails and clear skin I'd say she's been pampered. One huge difference though, she is wearing what might just be a wedding ring."

Gray gasped. "She's what?"

"She's wearing a wedding ring." Sam showed Gray her left hand.

Gray looked closely at the ring. "Beautiful, fancy and expensive too I bet. So she was possibly married. Any ID?"

"None...only the ring. From what I can see, and I'm no expert, the ring's old. Possibly an heirloom."

Paul took a look at the ring. "This could be our big break."

"Don't get too excited, Paul. It could also be a red herring."

Carrie, crouched across from Gray and Sam, took the victim's hand and inspected the ring. "Maybe, Gray, but I don't think so."

"Why's that?"

"She's had this ring on for a long time."

"Carrie's right, Gray," Sam said.

"If she's married, we should have little trouble tracing her," Mario said.

"Right. Mario, let's check missing persons. Look local and national. Put her photo out. Also, get a photo of that ring. Hopefully we'll get a quick response."

Carrie glanced about. "Why here, Gray?"

"I was wondering the same thing."

Paul stood. "When he makes one change he has to make others. Not a hooker, a different location, and different clothes. But it appears he wants to stay close to the four-block area."

Paul looked at the ground in the immediate area. "No fresh tire tracks. That's strange."

"No, Paul, he carried her here. After midnight this place is black as pitch."

"Then that's a problem because the only footprints were around the body. None leading to this spot or away from it."

"Are you sure Sam?"

"I've seen enough of these cases, Paul, to know what I'm looking for."

"I'm not doubting you, Sam, I'm just a little shocked. No footprints at all?"

"Not one fresh one, Gray."

"Hey, guys. The damn ground is as hard as a diamond. How could there be a footprint?"

"You're right, Carrie, but fractured ice, scuffs and cracks would be visible."

"Okay, so how did she get here?"

"We need to find that out, Mario."

"Seven damn victims and all we get are more mysteries."

"Live with it, Paul, and let's find some answers."

Sam stood and removed her gloves. "There is a witness."

"Another one? We might get lucky this time?"

"A delivery truck driver crossing the bridge on Orleans said he saw the guy standing out here smoking."

"How would he know that from that distance?"

"Apparently he saw the guy light up."

"Our killer certainly has a bad habit. That's the second time. He seems to enjoy a cigarette after he kills."

"But Paul, that makes no sense. Why would he draw attention to himself in such a blatant way, especially out here in the open?"

"The thrill of it, Carrie. He is obviously very sure of himself."

"Cocky is more to the point," Sam elaborated.

"It's a challenge. Here I am, now try to catch me. He's goading us, trying to get us to make mistakes. Well, guess what…we'll not play his game. We will play ours. We need a strategy that forces *him* to make mistakes."

"How do we do that, Gray?"

"At the moment, I have no idea. But we'll come up with something."

▼▼▼▼▼ 11

After an hour plus spent at the crime scene, Paul, Gray, Mario and Carrie were seated in the warmth of the cafeteria each with a steaming cup of coffee. Gray was deep in thought, his mind a million miles away. He stared despondently at the black liquid in the white styrofoam cup trying to stay focused. He couldn't put his finger on why he could not probe the mind of the killer. Almost every night he ventured into the darkness of his dreams where there were demons, phantoms and unimaginable evil. The voice of his adversary was ever present, but he could never see him and that made little sense. The truth was hidden from him, which disturbed him. Gray was frustrated and confused. Had he lost his ability to solve crimes? Suddenly a startling thought crossed his mind. He looked around at everyone.

"What if they were not missing?" They all looked at him.

Carrie looked at him quizzically. "Who?"

"Juanita, the seventh victim. What if they were not knowingly missing?"

"Explain, Gray."

"Suppose for a moment the victim plans a vacation. She leaves and everyone assumes she is enjoying relief from all the stresses of the daily grind on some sunny beach in paradise. No one's expecting to see her until she returns a week or so later. Therefore she's not yet missing. Not a very good illustration, but do you see what I'm getting at?"

"To a degree, yes Gray. But how could she tell everyone she's going on vacation when she's already dead?"

"No Paul, she's not dead. The killer marks his target, makes contact then plays her. She becomes vulnerable as she slowly weakens. Finally the killer weaves in the vacation idea. She bites and it's all over. He can then carry out his intentions with plenty of time to spare."

Paul sipped at his coffee. "That would certainly work, Gray. But women talk. Don't you think they would tell their friends about this guy?"

Gray sat back a little despondent. "That would be the big drawback to the idea."

"Unless of course he makes sure no one else sees him." Carrie suggested.

"She has a good point, Gray. He could quite easily remain somewhat incognito so as not to be suspected."

Gray sat forward eagerly. "Mario, get in touch with Juanita's old employer. Find out why they never contacted her family or anyone when she failed to show up for work." Mario got up and left the cafeteria.

"Gray, what about this seventh victim. You seem so sure she wasn't a hooker."

"Too well manicured, Carrie. Her hands were soft as were the soles of her feet. Nails were painted and there was no soil under them. The same with her toe nails. Also her hair was groomed, clean and perfumed. Her skin, generally, was not that of a woman of the street."

"So you're putting your money on the assumption that she is, as you have put it, not yet missing."

"Yes, Paul. Besides it's the only logical explanation for never receiving a missing persons report."

"What about the hookers?"

"All I can suggest there is they're from out of town, Carrie."

Mario returned and slid into his seat. They looked at him expectantly as he drank his coffee.

Gray became impatient. "Well?"

"She was on a two week vacation."

"I knew it. Our killer plans his escapades very well. He's also very selective with his victims. All single with possibly very few ties. He is not going to be easy to bring in."

"Gray, you said all single. What about the ring on the seventh victim?"

"That ring does not constitute marriage, Paul."

"True, but it's a pretty strong indicator."

"Possibly, but we'll have to wait and see on that one."

"One I'm certain of, Gray. Someone has to know this guy. Someone had to have seen Juanita with him, either at a restaurant, a bar or some place."

"Right, Paul, and we need to turn this city upside down until we find one or more of those individuals."

12

For the next three days, while waiting news from the ME and Forensics, everyone worked diligently trying to build a plan that would trap the killer. Everyone was troubled by the fact that no one had filed a missing persons report on the seventh victim. Her full physical description, along with her photo and a photo of the ring, had been splashed across the country, yet there hadn't been a murmur. As each day passed with no response to that publicity, Gray grew more concerned. He believed that if she had possibly been married or engaged, it should have brought something, but the airwaves remained silent.

Then something even more disturbing occurred, or rather did not occur. On the morning of Monday, January 29 nothing happened. By noon that day there had been no phone call, no report of a body being found in what had become known as the Red Zone. Nothing. Everyone held their breath and waited.

Monday rolled into Tuesday and still nothing. Gray became convinced something drastic had happened. Questions were popping up everywhere. The first one was why? Why had the killings suddenly stopped? Speculation was rampant. The killer had died. He had been killed in an accident. He had left the area…on and on they went. Gray was certain the killings had not stopped. Postponed, yes, but not stopped. The killer was still out there, ready to strike down another victim.

13

Carrie handed Paul a newspaper clipping. "Do you recall three weeks ago a woman disappeared down town, as the eye witness put it, 'in the blink of an eye,' and there has been no trace of her since?"

"Yes, from a department store, as I recall."

"Well, it's happened again, this time in an underground parking garage on Huron. Read it." Carrie pointed to the article. Paul read it.

"What the hell is going on? Women go missing and don't show up, women that show up and not declared missing, and all have virtually the same physical description. It doesn't add up."

"I agree."

"It's strange you should bring this up. O'Malley mentioned the same thing to me last week. The woman that disappeared three weeks ago was not the first. Apparently there have been others going back to 2002. He said there were a total of six. All disappeared and have never been found."

"I think we need to make another trip to the archives. I'm beginning to think there is a lot more to these cases than meets the eye. My gut tells me they're all related. I bet if we dig deeper, we'll find a lot more than we are seeing here."

Paul handed the article back to Carrie. "Then let's go see what we can find."

"I can't this afternoon, but I am available first thing in the morning."

"Why don't we give this to O'Malley? He loves this sort of thing. Look how long we spent down there last time. Granted, we uncovered a great deal of interesting stuff, but in this case we could be there a month."

"Good point and he has the computer. He could access all that information quicker than we could find the first file," Carrie suggested.

"Maybe, but only if that data has been loaded into the computer. We could ask him to try."

"If he finds nothing, then we go hunting again."

I'll see if O'Malley has time."

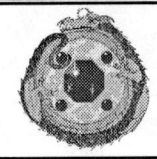

-EPISODE 2-

Encounter

No Place To Hide

▼▼▼▼▼ *1*

February 01, 2006
On the morning of February 1, Gray received a note from O'Malley asking him to call as soon as possible. Gray reached for the phone and dialed the extension. It barely rang on the other end when it was picked up.

"Hello," the voice said.

"This is Farlon. Is Pat O'Malley there by any chance?"

"Hang on a second, Detective and I'll check." Gray waited. The officer came back on the line.

"Detective, he's still in the building."

"To whom am I speaking?"

"This is Sergeant Walters, Sir."

"Sergeant, do me a favor. When he gets back, have him call me. I'll be in my office."

"Will do, Detective."

"Thanks." He hung up and went back to his reading. Five minutes later his phone rang.

"Farlon."

"Detective, this is O'Malley."

"Yes Patrick, you asked me to call you."

"Oh yes, a call came in for you about 20 minutes ago from a Dr. Rashid at Memorial. He would like you to call him."

"Did he mention what it was about?"

"No, all he said was it might be important."

"His number?" O'Malley gave Gray the number.

"Thanks, Patrick."

"You're welcome, Gray." He tripped the switch and dialed.

"Hello."

"Dr. Ben Rashid, please."

"This is he."

"This is Detective Graham Farlon, CPD."

"Thank you for calling, Detective. I am not sure if this means anything but I thought there might be a connection..."

"A connection? To what are you referring, Doctor?"

"We have a patient here who was brought in three days ago. She was found stumbling about in subzero temperatures and is fighting for her life. She was cut up to such a degree it took over five hours to stabilize her. She lost a great deal of blood and putting her back together took over 1500 stitches." Gray was shocked but unable to see the connection to which the doctor was referring.

"Excuse me for interrupting Doctor, but you've lost me. I don't understand why you're calling me on this. You say she was admitted Sunday?"

"Yes, around six in the morning. One of our doctors who had car trouble had to walk a few blocks to the hospital and almost fell over her." Gray's pulse quickened and his palms began to sweat.

"Any ID? Driver's license, social security card, library card?"

"Nothing, Detective."

"Nothing?"

"All she was wearing was one of those heavy long theater cloaks. You know the kind down to the floor with the large hood."

"Yes, I think I know."

"She also had a small pendant around her neck and is clutching something in her hand. The cloak wasn't much use to her as it had been cut to shreds."

Gray became tense. "Could you give me a physical description?"

"She is about five feet tall, has blue eyes and shoulder length blond hair..." The news was like shattering crystal. His veins were rivers of ice. The hair on the nape of his neck stood erect. "...and there's a birthmark on her left thigh in the shape of a crescent moon. Her attacker used a very sharp, very fine instrument like a very thin bladed knife, possibly a stiletto. Judging from her condition, she put up one hell of a fight."

"How is she doing at the moment, Doctor?"

"The prognosis is not good. She's extremely weak and we're keeping her heavily sedated because of her violent outbursts. What happened to her is not a pleasant sight. We've repaired the external damage, but psychologically is another story."

"She's not in a coma?"

"No."

"May I see her, Doctor?"

"By all means, but she is unable to speak. Since Sunday she has improved, but she has a very long hard road ahead of her."

"Is there nothing else you can do to save her?"

"We're doing everything possible, Detective. Most of it now is up to her. If she has the will to survive, she might make it. This is one of the worst cases I've ever seen. It was one hell of a slice and dice job believe me."

"I'll be up there first thing in the morning."

"My office is on the 14th floor, Detective. I will be here by eight. Should she pass away before then, I will have someone notify your office to save you an unnecessary trip."

"Very good, Doctor, that would be helpful but, either way, I want to see her. Thank you for calling."

"You're quite welcome, Detective. I only wish the prognosis was more favorable." He hung up the phone.

2

Gray paused to catch his breath. This news was stunning as well as encouraging. Could this be a Mannequin victim who had managed to escape? He lifted the phone to call Paul and noticed his hand was trembling. Hell, I must be getting old; need to get a hold of myself. He dialed Paul's extension.

"Paul, Gray, can you spare a few minutes? Something extremely important just came up."

"Sure, be right down."

"No, meet me in the War Room. Oh, and Paul, better bring everyone with you."

"Wow! It must be important." He hung up and headed upstairs. Anticipation tickled him. Had a solid witness, one who had come face to face with the killer, been dropped in their laps? Gray reached the War Room before everyone else.

As he took a seat, Paul walked through the door. "What has you so excited, Gray?" The rest of the team followed. Everyone stared at Gray expectantly.

Gray waved at the chairs around the table. "Folks, take a seat and hang on. We may have victim number eight." Instantly the atmosphere turned electric.

"What? Are you serious?" A murmur rippled through the group. Everyone shifted in their seats eager to hear what was to follow.

Gray sat forward feeding on their enthusiasm. "Quite serious, Yoshi."

"Where?"

"Hospital, Carrie."

"Hospital! You mean, as alive and in hospital?"

"So far, yes, Carrie."

"So far meaning?"

"Meaning, Yoshi, she's fighting for her life."

"That's too bad."

"That is too bad, Paul. This is a minute-by-minute situation, folks, for she remains in critical condition."

"Is she one of the Mannequin victims?"

"That's the big question. The description fits, Carrie – blond hair, blue eyes, just over five feet tall and about 100 pounds. And that, I would say, is not a coincidence. But before we all run off with the idea this is victim number eight, we must to get all the facts."

Mario let out a deep breath. "Damn."

Gray looked around at the team. "This could be our big break folks."

"True, and if she is victim number eight, he screwed up."

"If she is, Yoshi, he screwed up big time."

"How long before we'll be able to speak to her?"

"Not for quite a while, Mario."

"So we keep waiting?"

"Afraid so. In the morning, Paul, you and I will pay a visit to her doctor."

"She was found on Sunday morning?"

"Yes, Carrie. They had a rough time with her; it took over 1500 stitches to sew her up." A horrified gasp rippled through the group.

"Dear God in heaven...what the hell did the bastard do to her, practice his Carving 101 class?" Carrie asked.

"There are many questions arising from this, but because of the delicacy of the situation, we'll proceed on the assumption that she is a victim. Her condition and existence is being kept under wraps."

"How do we manage that, Gray?"

"We manage it, Mario. The killer must believe she's dead otherwise. We'll post security outside her room 24/7. We take no chances."

"What about the hospital staff?"

"Paul and I will take care of that in the morning."

Mario mused. "Sunday morning...the 29th."

"Exactly. She was admitted around six."

Paul interrupted. "What time in the morning, Gray?"

"I just said at six..."

"No. What time shall I meet you?"

"Oh, *7:30*, downstairs."

"Do we know who she is, Gray?"

"No. When they found her, all she was wearing was a heavy cloak and a small pendant. The pendant might tell us something. She also has something clutched in her hand. Maybe a piece of jewelry."

"Folks, this could be the break we've been waiting for. It will only pay off if she survives, so let's hope for the best."

▼▼▼▼▼ 3

They had the woman placed in Room 1409 under 24-hour police protection. Gray, Paul and Dr. Rashid entered. A small, pallid but beautiful face was all Gray could see. From just beneath her chin, bandages covered the remainder of her body. Tubes ran to each arm from two IV bottles filled with clear liquid. A third IV was dispensing fresh blood. Wires ran from various parts of her body to an electrocardiograph. The pulse of her life's engine echoed around the room as a thin green line on the dark screen skipped along in rhythm.

Gray's eyes drifted to her clenched right hand and the short length of broken silver chain hung between her fingers. He stepped close to the bed.

"May I try to see what this is, Doctor?"

"By all means, Detective."

Gray gently lifted the woman's hand and attempted to pry her fingers apart to get a better look. All he could make out were semi-circular lines resembling scales and part of what appeared to be a clawed foot grasping a red gem. He could also see the edge of a larger red stone. There was a heavy scratch across the surface. He was no expert but it looked like costume jewelry. He laid her hand back on the bed.

"Any ideas, Detective?"

"Hard to say, Doctor; it could be a pendant judging by its shape, design and the chain."

"That was my guess," Dr. Rashid said.

Gray stepped away from the bed and closer to Rashid. "And the only other items she had, you said, were the cape and a small pendant?"

"Correct, they are both downstairs."

Gray turned to Paul. "Let's get those items over to Forensics."

"Right."

Dr. Rashid then explained. "She has some areas of heavy bruising on her arms, legs, and torso. But that's minor in comparison to the multitude of cuts and stab wounds covering her body. Quite honestly, I don't know how she survived – the odds were against her. The elements, loss of blood and the wounds she sustained were more than enough to kill her."

Gray stepped to the window and leaned on the sill. He then fired questions at the doctor. "How long do you think she was out there, Doc?"

"Hard to say, but ten minutes at the most. Longer than that in her condition she would have succumbed to hypothermia."

"Frost bite?"

"Surprisingly, no."

"What sort of recovery time are we looking at?"

"It depends. Physically, six weeks, two months, could be longer."

"Exactly how bad?"

"She has 43 slash and stab wounds, some superficial, most are not. The worst is a cut that runs from her right shoulder diagonally across her chest over her breast slicing through the nipple, over her abdomen to her navel. The bastard then thrust the weapon about two inches into her navel. He also pierced her left side all the way through. There are horizontal and vertical cuts on her stomach, thighs and back. As you can see he never touched her face.

"Except for the penetrating thrust wounds, all the wounds on the front of her body were not deep…possibly made to inflict maximum pain. The wounds on her back are deep, most likely made while she was trying to escape."

"Forty-three wounds. My God." Paul shook his head in disbelief.

"The good news is that we have her stabilized. Now it's up to her."

Gray rubbed his chin and thought for a moment. "How long before you think she'll be able to speak?"

"That will depend on her recovery rate. A week, maybe less, Detective."

4

Back in Dr. Rashid's suite, the doctor continued to explain the patient's situation.

"I'm confident her physical recovery will be good. If she is a strong woman, and it appears she is, she'll pull through."

Gray and Paul sat. "The fact she survived such a vicious attack and that deadly weather says something for her," Gray said.

"Yes, it does."

"Our first intent, Doctor, is to find out who she is and where she's from. Secondly, security will be in effect until you release her."

"Very well, Detective. May I ask a question?"

"By all means."

"Is she a victim of the killer roaming the city?"

Gray hesitated. "We can't answer that, Doc. Her physical description does fit the killer's MO."

"She put up one hell of a fight," Paul said.

The doctor raised his eyebrows. "That she did, Detective."

"Regarding her being here, Doctor, I don't want a connection made to the Mannequin Murders. I can't stress that enough. Make certain those attending her fully understand."

"I will inform my staff."

"Very good." Gray got out of his chair and Paul followed suit.

"I will also let you know the moment she's able to talk."

"Thanks, Doc. Thanks for letting us see her."

"Any time, Detective."

Gray and Paul walked into the hall. "By the way, Doctor, a couple of other things. I don't want anyone going into her room other than the medical staff you assign to her. I will also need a list of those names."

"I will see that you're sent one immediately."

"I'll arrange to have her belongings picked up. Finally could you arrange to have a sample of her blood sent to the coroner?"

"I will see to it right away."

"Thank you for your time, Doctor; we will be in constant touch."

As they left the hospital, Gray's cell phone beeped. He pulled it from his jacket and flipped it open. "Farlon."

"Detective Farlon, this is Kerry Pollard at the Mayor's office."

"Yes, Kerry, to what do I owe this call?"

"The Mayor would like to meet with you. Could you be here around ten Monday morning?" Gray thought for a moment as he and Paul got into the car. Why would the Mayor want to see him? There was only one thing that important.

"I can manage that, Kerry. Tell the Mayor I will be there."

"Thank you, Detective. I will let him know." He hung up.

"The Mayor's office?" Paul asked as he started the car.

"Yeah."

Paul pulled away from the curb and eased into the traffic. "And I bet it wasn't an invitation to his morning coffee klatch."

"Hardly."

"You know what he wants, Gray, and it's not a snow job."

"I'll give him one."

Paul gave Gray a surprised glance. "A snow job? You're kidding, right? You're not kidding."

"I'm quite serious."

"That could mean trouble," Paul said as he turned the heater to full.

"He's a politician and I don't trust politicians. They may kiss a lot of babies, but they kiss a lot more asses."

"But he won't spill the beans."

"You believe that?"

"No."

Gray chuckled. "Neither do I."

"A snow job?"

"A snow job." They headed back to HQ.

▼▼▼▼▼ 5

Gray prepared himself for his encounter with Julia, but he could not shake the fear that she might reject him. As he stepped out of the elevator, he immediately smelled her perfume. It pervaded the entire floor. It was not overbearing, but a delicate and noticeable aroma. With butterflies in his stomach, he headed for his office.

The door was closed. He turned the handle and pushed it open. Julia was sitting with her back to him, her jet-black hair plaited in a French braid. Except for her peach colored blouse, she was dressed in black. Black slacks were tucked into a pair of calf high, black high-heeled boots. A black leather coat was thrown over the back of the second chair.

As Gray closed the door and walked toward his desk, she did not move. With each step he grew more nervous. The butterflies had turned to piranhas. He tried to calm himself but was having little success. As he approached his desk, Julia gave him a quick glance. He fell apart. He stopped and stared at her, unable to believe that this was his daughter. She looked so mature and so beautiful – elegant, poised, with a look of determined defiance on her face. Gray cringed. Silence still reigned and Julia's demeanor did not falter. He walked around his desk and stood looking at her.

The silence was deafening. Who was going to speak first? Gray made the effort. "Hello Julia. It's wonderful to see you. It's been so long." The silence rushed back like a tidal wave. Gray could not stand it. He continued. "Have you been waiting long?" The piranhas were working overtime. Finally she spoke.

"Hello, Daddy." She paused, then continued. "Yes, it's been a long time, but whose fault was that? You never bothered to contact me. Never attempted to find me. I could have died and you wouldn't have known. I can't say that it's good to see you because I would be lying. I have..." Gray put his hand up and interrupted her.

"Julia, please. I don't want to start this way. It was not my intent to meet so we could fight. I made this decision so I might..."

"Might what, Daddy? What is it you want to do, pick up where we left off?" The bitterness in her voice cut him deeply.

"No, please let me finish. I wanted to get together so we might at least talk. I don't intend to try to pick up where we left off for that would not be possible..."

Julia's dark eyes flashed. "Damn well got that right. I..."

"Julia, please. When I'm finished, if you wish to leave and cut the ties so be it. Just give me half an hour of your time."

Although she was angry, she was willing to listen. "Okay you've got it, but this better be good."

"Julia, first I have to express my deepest apologies for having neglected my duties as a father. I screwed up big time and I realize that. I hope that somewhere down the road, you will find it in your heart to forgive me." Gray was struggling with words for they refused to come out as he intended. He sat down and continued.

"I've had a great deal of time to think and there is so much I want to say but I don't know how." He dug deep into the archives of his mind and admitted all the wrongs he had committed before and after Gwynne died. The times he had not been there for either of them when he should have. The priority he had placed on his job that should have been placed on his family. The missed dinners, anniversaries, birthday parties and school activities. All had been pushed aside because of his work.

As he poured out his heart, Julia sat motionless. He was determined not to let anything remain unsaid. Julia seemed to be listening, but he was uncertain if he was making headway. Putting faith in her and knowing she was her mother's daughter, he pressed on.

"...so you can see why I have not been myself Julia. Honey, I never meant to abandon you just as I never wanted to end up as I did for the last three years. For all that, I am so very, very sorry. Julia, your mother was not supposed to die...it should have been me. I was the one in harm's way each day, not her..."

The River Styx

Julia interrupted. "Yes, and she sat around every night waiting for you to get home, wondering if you would or not. That stress, that constant tension, is what killed her."

"It was the cancer, Julia..."

"Yes, it was the damn cancer," she spat the words out like poison. "But you were the one who brought it on. Your damn job always came first and she supported you through it all. Why, I don't know. I remember so many times..." She fell silent, then got out of her chair and paced the room. "Hell, what does it matter now, anyway? Mom is no longer here and I have nothing more to say. I have to go." She reached for her coat.

"Julia, I've changed; I am not the person I was six years ago. Give me a chance. I want you back in my life, not for selfish reasons but to try to make amends for all the hurt I've caused."

"Daddy, you cannot wash away years of hurt overnight."

"I am not saying that. I know it will take time, but please give me a chance. Don't just walk away. I beg you, give me one more chance."

"Do you realize what you're asking me to do? You want me to forget all you did, all that happened over the years and start fresh?"

"Would your mother expect anything less?"

"That's hitting below the belt."

"No, it's not Julia. It's the truth, because you are your mother in so many ways. You also have her heart."

"You're not playing fair, Daddy."

"This is not a game, Julia; it's the truth. It broke my heart when all this happened. I was helpless. How could I stop it? It was not supposed to happen, Julia."

"You're right. You, the super cop, who could solve any crime, when it came to that moment you were lost, you were afraid and you would not face it."

"I have never felt so helpless and scared. I could do nothing but watch your Mom fade away. They said she could pull through, she believed them – damn it, I believed them. They lied, Julia, they..." Finally Gray broke down. He could not help it. All the heart-tearing, painful and tragic memories came rushing back. Tears ran down his cheeks. Julia stopped pacing and looked at him. Tears welled up in her eyes and she cried.

She swore. "Damn it, I told myself this would not happen. Look Daddy, I understand what you're saying and I believe we can work something out, but it is going to take time."

"All I'm asking is that you please give it a chance." Gray sighed and stood up. He walked around the desk and stepped up to her. Father and daughter stood staring at each other, neither sure of the other, neither knowing what to expect or do next. Gray made the first move as he wrapped his arms around Julia and held her to him. She burst into deep sobs and held him, resting her head on his shoulder.

The two stood that way for a long time...each remembering...not wanting to invade the silence...trying to dispatch the harsh, painful memories that lingered. Time seemed to stop as each gathered their thoughts and strength for what was to come. Both knew there were going to be hard times and bitter disagreements, but they also knew it would be worth the effort. Julia lifted her head, kissed him gently on the cheek, then lowered her arms and stepped back.

"All right, but don't expect much at first. I have been alone for over six years, fending for myself when I needed you the most."

"Julia, all I want is to be the father I should have been. It's not too late. If it takes time; so be it, but we have that time now."

"What about your job? You are working on this huge case. Are you going to be back in that routine of..."

"No, Julia, that will not happen again. I'm paying a debt, that is all."

"A debt?"

"Yes. Had it not been for Paul, I would still be on the streets."

"So I have Paul to thank for having my father back?"

"Yes." Gray finally realized things were better. He was now a happy man. Silently he thanked Gwynne, knowing she had a hand in the outcome. He took Julia's hands and held them.

"Will you come with me to visit Mom?"

"What?" Julia looked a little shocked.

"I visit Mom's grave every Saturday. I have, ever since you left. I find a great deal of peace sitting and talking to her."

"You sit and talk to Mom?"

"Every Saturday. We have long conversations, mostly about you. Will you come with me? Mom would love to see you there."

"But Mom is..." She stopped herself. "Yes, I'll go." Gray squeezed her hands then let them drop.

The days that followed were the most precious he had spent in many years. Getting to know his daughter once more was now a reality. He learned so much about her that he'd never known. And as their meetings became more frequent and open, his pride in her grew. Despite that, he remained guarded in one area knowing she was still a journalist. She had a story to write. He had an obligation to protect a witness.

▼▼▼▼▼ 6

By five o' clock on Monday afternoon, February 6, Gray knew he would not be heading home any time soon. With hunger gnawing at his gut, he walked to the corner deli for something to eat and drink. He preferred the food from the deli rather than the District cafeteria. Back at his desk, as he ravenously attacked his meatball sandwich, Gray continued to dig into the case, desperately searching for answers. As he glanced at the calendar, he made a mental note – nine days had passed since Jane Doe had turned up. It was this event that deeply troubled him. Who was this woman? What mysteries lay with her? Could she be the key to answering their big question? Her appearance on the scene had spurred anticipation.

Then there was the killer. What was going on in his mind? The thought of that demented maniac provoked troubled memories. Gray knew in order to solve this crime he must go where he dreaded the most – into the mind of that madman. It was time to try his age-old skills, but an underlying fear held him back. There was something out there, something terribly evil. It was mostly instinct; a gut feeling that had been gnawing at him. Though the killer's activities had stopped, Gray knew he would surface sooner or later. He also knew he would have to take that fearful step, but take it he must if they were to stop the killer.

7

Each week Gray and other members of the team paid regular visits to the hospital to watch over their most prized witness. Her periodic violent outbursts had subsided and her demeanor was calmer. Her recovery was not as rapid as they would have liked but she was improving, though she still had not spoken. Dr. Ben Rashid was pleased with her progress, but Gray was growing impatient. He and Paul were on their way to the hospital, once again, hoping for something new to emerge. As they stepped from the elevator on the 14th floor, they encountered Dr. Rashid.

"Good afternoon, Ben."

"Gray, Paul, what brings you two up here? Weren't you just here this morning?"

"Yes, but we are anxious to see how our patient is doing."

"She hasn't changed much in six hours, Gray. You must be expecting something big."

"We're hoping for something, Ben, some small piece of news."

"Well, she still hasn't spoken, if that is what interests you."

"May we see her?"

"Why not, you guys have beaten a path from the elevator to her room." Paul, Gray and Ben Rashid made their way to the woman's room. As they entered, Gray was surprised to see the bandages on her arms had been removed. The only visible bandages were the ones over her right shoulder and across the upper part of her chest. Gray thought she looked much better.

"Getting rid of the bandages, I see. That's a change since this morning."

"Her wounds are healing very well; in fact, better than I expected."

'That's great news."

"She still won't give up that thing in her hand."

"That isn't critical, Ben. What else can be done for her at this point?"

"Apart from what we're already doing, not much. Once she's able, we will get her up."

"What sort of timeframe are we talking about? When can she be released?"

"In about three weeks, might be a little longer."

"Is there a chance...?" Suddenly Gray was interrupted. Though barely a whisper, a voice brought silence to the room.

"Where am I?" her voice, hushed and mellow, floated on the air like musical notes – the tinkling of wind chimes touched by a gentle breeze. Then silence, as if the world had just lost something precious. The shock of hearing those three words stunned them. They stared in disbelief at the fragile creature. The silence seemed to last for eternity, as if willing the music to begin again. Then the woman opened her eyes and stared about her. It was apparent, from the expression on her face, that she was not only confused but terrified as well.

"Well, hello, young lady. We have been very worried about you." She stared in Ben Rashid's direction as if willing him to speak again. But her eyes never rested, darting from one object to another...constantly alert, constantly searching.

"How are you feeling?"

"There is so much pain everywhere."

"That's quite understandable. You've been through a terrible ordeal."

"Who are you?" Her voice remained hushed.

"I am Dr. Rashid."

Looking highly agitated, she stared at Rashid and asked again. "Where am I?"

"You are in Northwestern Memorial Hospital. What do you remember?" She didn't appear to hear the question.

"How long have I been in this place?"

"Almost three weeks, 20 days, to be exact."

"You said I might be able to leave in another three weeks?"

"You were awake?"

"Yes."

"You are healing well and if that keeps up, three weeks is very possible."

Gray stepped up to the bed and spoke quietly to her. "I am Detective Farlon. You are one very lucky lady to have survived such an ordeal. What is your name, child?"

The question generated visible panic. Mortified, she stared at him as her eyes widened like pools of dark blue liquid spreading over a white marble floor. She grew more agitated, her mouth quivered at the corners. Suddenly she turned away, staring off somewhere; another place, possibly a better place. Tears rolled down her cheeks. She spoke again as she choked on her words. What she said struck them like a clap of thunder. They were words no one was prepared to hear.

8

"I...do not know. I do not..." She began to sob. "I am unable to remember anything. Why am I not able to remember, Doctor? I do not know who I am. What is my name?" Panic was etched into her face. Tears tumbled from her eyes, ran down her cheeks, trickled off her chin onto the sheets. She appeared ready to leap from her bed, bolt from the room, from the hospital, to escape her nightmare. Rashid glanced at Gray who looked gravely concerned.

Doctor Rashid gently took her hand. "You're obviously suffering from temporary amnesia, but it should pass in time."

"I am unable to remember anything. My mind is empty." Her voice trembled.

"Don't be concerned. It is not uncommon for someone who has experienced what you have to suffer some level of amnesia."

"How long might it last?"

"That's hard to say. It could subside in a few days or it might take a number of weeks."

"Will I then remember everything?"

"I see no reason why not."

"But I must know who I am," she said in panic.

Gray leaned close to the terrified woman and, in a quiet, soothing voice, addressed her. "As we don't know who you are, I think we should give you a name, a name a little better than Jane Doe. What do you say?" She said nothing, only stared into space. Gray glanced at Rashid who shrugged his shoulders. "Would you like us to give you a name until we know your real one?" Again there was a long silence before she finally responded.

"Yes."

"Let's see. How does Ann sound?"

"I like that," she said timidly.

"Then Ann it is. Ann, my name is Graham Farlon. That big fellow is Paul Salvatore. We are both detectives with the Chicago Police Department. And this tall skinny fellow is Doctor..."

"I am very sorry Mr. Farlon but I am unable to see you, any of you," Again something they did not expect.

Gray turned to Ben Rashid. "Doctor?"

"She received a number of severe blows to the head. It may have caused temporary visual contravention."

"Visual what?"

"A restriction of her vision."

"How long might it last?" Gray was more troubled.

"If not severe, which it does not appear to be, perhaps a few more days."

"Let's hope it clears up quickly."

"What happened to me?"
"You were viciously attacked."
"I do not remember."
"It's just as well for now."
"Is that why I have these bandages?"
"Yes."

Ann's eyes glazed over as she stared into oblivion. Then she spoke again. "What if I should not recover my memory?"

"I don't think that is likely," Rashid said.

"Ann, over the next few weeks we will ask you questions to try to stimulate your memory."

"You wish me to answer questions?"

"Yes, but not right away. In a day or two."

"But what if I am unable to answer?"

"Don't worry; as time passes the answers will come."

Rashid looked at Gray. "I think a psychologist would be a big help here."

"I agree, Ben."

"A psychologist?"

"Yes, to help you regain your memory."

"Oh."

The two detectives and Doctor Rashid stepped away from the bed. "We'll leave you now so you can rest. Try to get some sleep. We will talk again later."

"I do not like to sleep."

"Why Ann?"

"When I sleep I see terrible things."

"That's okay, Ann, you're only having nightmares. But some of those dreams could be memories."

"I see."

"Now try to get some rest."

"You will come back?"

Gray stepped to her side, rested his hand gently on her shoulder and smiled. "Yes Ann, we will be back, maybe tomorrow." Ann was silent. The only semblance of a smile on that beautiful face was a slight creasing around her mouth, but her deep blue eyes screamed for help.

▼▼▼▼▼ *9*

Gray stood in his apartment staring over the lake, reflecting on the last few weeks, as the light of another day faded. He felt chilled. He shivered though the apartment was quite warm. Thoughts of Juanita played on his mind and he was determined to find her killer. Why had she been a victim? Was it a message? Why was the killer targeting him, and who was he? Gray had locked up many criminals. Could it be one of them? He lifted the mug of coffee and sipped it as he spoke to his nemesis.

You're out there somewhere you murdering fiend and I am only steps behind you. You can run but you can't hide for long. I am going to nail your sorry ass to the wall and stop your heinous killing spree for good. To his complete shock a voice floated back, nearly causing him to drop the mug.

"*You really believe that. Well, try as you might, you will fail, and for as long as you live I will continue to elude you, for I am far better than you.*"

Though stunned, Gray replied. "*You dare to invade my mind. Get out and don't come back. I may have failed to identify you thus far, but I will discover your secret soon enough; then I shall bring you down.*"

The voice echoed back. "*I do look forward to that day. But don't be disillusioned, for it will never come.*"

At that moment the phone on his coffee table rang startling him. Gray reached for it.

He pushed the handset to his ear. "Hello."

"You're still in the dark."

"Who is this?"

"You know Farlon."

Gray felt a chill. "That's smart, calling me at home so the call can't be traced."

"Doesn't matter if it is, you still wouldn't find me."

"Damn sure of yourself, aren't you?"

"A lot more than you are."

"What do you want?"

The monotonous, monotone voice went on. "Things are going to get a little more interesting. I am becoming bored with your incompetence. I would have thought that, by now, you would have learned something…but nothing…you have absolutely nothing. It's so pitiful."

"You're calling just to goad me?"

"Not at all. You're the great detective, so detect. As I have said, things are going to get more exciting. We need to stir the brew a little, add more spice, you know another body here or there."

Gray cringed at the thought of more dead women on the streets. "You won't get away with this."

"I already have. You are pathetic. All this time you and that bumbling fool Salvatore have been stumbling about in the dark. You have no idea what you're looking for, do you?"

"What is it you're about to do you sick, perverted freak?"

"You'll find out soon enough. Remember one thing, no matter what you do I'll know about it. You are not invincible."

"I never believed I was but you think you are."

"Oh, but I am. I've already proved it. I can hide in plain sight but time is what separates us I'm just way ahead of you in every aspect. I think so far above your head you have little chance of learning the truth."

"I'll learn it soon enough."

"Never."

"You know what they say about that."

"But in my case I'm sure."

"Let me say this you maggot. You are going to trip up and when you do I'll be right there to jump on you."

"That's where you're wrong, Farlon, because I won't be making any mistakes."

"Don't count on it. We all make mistakes."

"Yes you do, don't you. I will admit though I have made a few but I can hide them where you can't get to them. Face it, Farlon; you're too old for this. You're out of time and out of your league."

"That's your opinion. But mark my words I will get you."

"Sure you will. Well I must be going, but I'll be in touch." The phone went dead. Gray sat back in his chair sweating. Now his dreams were turning to reality. What troubled him the most was that he did not recognize the voice; it did not fit anyone he knew or could remember.

Gray walked into the kitchen as his thoughts slowly turned to Ann. He felt certain she was a critical ingredient to the case. Of course the greater secret was locked away in her head. At that moment a disturbing thought crossed his mind. If the killer knew his thoughts, then he had to be aware that Ann was still alive. How could he stop this invasion? How could he prevent the discovery of that secret?

He refilled his coffee mug, returned to the living room and dropped into the recliner with the intention to try and read. But his mind was too occupied with the case and he was unable to concentrate on anything else. *How did Ann manage to escape?* He wondered. Gray then turned his thoughts to a brighter subject. Julia.

They had resolved many differences but had she forgiven him? She had not told him so. He looked at his watch. It was after eleven. Julia was most likely asleep. As he set his mug down, he got up and retreated to the bedroom. He felt worn out. The complexity of the case was becoming a heavy burden. He wondered how much longer he could last. He knew the stress was taking its toll.

He changed into his pajamas, went into the bathroom and picked up his toothbrush. As he looked at himself in the mirror, he shuddered. His hair was still long and thick, but now silver gray. His skin sagged like wet dough, and the bags under his eyes were trunks. He looked at the worn out package he walked around in and realized it was not a pretty sight.

You're over the hill, old man, and if you were honest, you'd admit this case is way too much for you. You're out of your league and there's no way you can catch up. He interrupted his thoughts, squeezed toothpaste onto the toothbrush and proceeded to brush his teeth. This all had to end somewhere, but where? He finished, turned out the light and climbed into bed. Sleep was welcomed but how long before it was permanent?

Quit being such a damn pessimist. There are still a lot of miles left in you. Think about it. Are you ready to throw in the towel before you've even found the answer? What is the answer? Since when have you wanted it handed to you on a platter? Since when have you balked at a challenge? When have you turned your back on an opportunity such as this? It's the ideal case to put those dormant skills to use. Come on, you've got the balls to do it, now do it. That's easy for you to say.

He drifted off to sleep.

▼▼▼▼▼ 10

It never occurred to him where he might be. He was not unduly concerned that he could not find what he so diligently sought. Now here he was in the thick of it and he could not see the light.

"You came here to find me?" The voice did not come as a surprise.

"To find...who are you?" He was confused. Where was he? He thought he knew; now he was not so sure.

"You came here to find me."

"First you ask, then you answer. Who are you? Tell me that, then maybe I can answer your question."

"You don't need an answer. You fully understand. Your blind dedication brought you here. You are taciturn yet you feel you have much to say. What prevents you from moving into the unknown? Is it trepidation or are you no longer willing to take the risk?"

"I will go where I please, do as I please and don't require your coaxing. Yet you avoid my question."

"What question is that?"

"You don't wish to divulge your identity."

"You truly don't know who I am? That is your failure, not knowing or understanding yourself. You are so willing to give of yourself yet you do not know the reason why. You are selfless but do not consider your own destiny of any importance. Therefore, to reinforce your eagerness to please, you ask a question. Here, then, is your answer. I am the culmination of who you are. I am your thoughts, your actions and the essence of your mind. I am the spirit of who you are and of what you are destined to become. You should therefore be fully aware of who I am. The question is, do you know who you are? In thoughtless passion you all but destroyed yourself. You stepped away from your moral foundation and reneged on your promises. You wallowed in self-pity, a condition you so adamantly despised – Nos·ce te ip·sum."

"What the hell are you talking about?"

"Know thyself. You find fault with all that you do. You are so hard on yourself you forget who you are."

"You judge me for my actions?"

"Possibly. But would it not be more profound that you cease judging yourself?"

"I have and I have come to terms with my actions. I have repented..."

"Are you then ready?"

"For what?"

"Do you know why you came here?"

"Hell, if I knew where here was, I could answer."

"That is irrelevant. You made a choice, therefore you must now confront the issues."

"Riddles, you constantly speak to me in riddles."

"No, not riddles, I only urge you to look into yourself. You must confront those issues."

"That may be so, but I am still unaware of this place."

"Then you have failed."

"I cannot fail at something in which I am unaware of participating.

"Then you should become a participant."

"And how should I do that?"

"It is already done."

"You still speak in riddles and expect me to comprehend your meaning."

"Of course. What you seek is beyond the boundary of reality. To discover what you seek you must step beyond that barrier. You asked who I am. I am that which can guide you through the mists and depths of the unknown. I am your guide, but I am not your informer or advisor. What you seek is there in the mist. You have traveled there in the past and you are aware of the perils. Therefore you must now make a choice. You may proceed – seek your destiny or turn back and forget, but be warned. Should you turn back, this place will be closed to you forever. This is your last chance. What is your decision?"

"I'm not sure that I understand. You tell me I have been here before yet I don't remember. You say if I turn back I can never return, yet I have no idea what I'm turning from. Therefore, how can I make a conscious decision?"

"There is no conscious decision to be made. You must decide now."

"What is it that I'm supposed to be looking for?"

"Your destiny. That which has been tearing at your soul, tormenting your mind and taunting your conscience."

"Then I guess I'll proceed."

"Very well. I cannot accompany you, but can assist at any time."

"Before I go, I have a question."

"Ask your question quickly."

"Fourteen women all dressed in black pursue me, why?"

"They look to you for retribution."

"I only know of seven. I know nothing of fourteen."

"They have been captured in time. Look there for your answer."

Thanks, more riddles. Why do they single me out?"

"Because they know you are the one who will destroy the demon who stole their souls."

The River Styx

"*But I cannot be sure I can do that.*" There was no reply. "*Are you there?*"

"*I am here.*"

"*I cannot give them something of which I am not certain.*"

"*That is your problem. Now you must go.*"

"*But I need an answer.*" Silence shrouded him and he stood in the darkness seeing nothing, feeling nothing and wondering what he should expect next. What happened next he certainly never expected. Screams and cries from out of the darkness. Souls tormented by terror. His fear surfaced for the first time. Then realizing where he was, his own terror took hold.

Bitter cold snapped and tore at his flesh. The sense of bewilderment was fleeting but strong. He had come to find his adversary. He was now in that place where he'd always known he would eventually have to venture. The thought sickened him. One thing was certain and that was his courage must not fail him. Not here. Not now.

"*I know you're there,*" he said finally and forcefully. Then the voice he dreaded to hear floated back from the cauldron that was now before him. A swirling mass of filth and degradation, the accumulation of all that was soiled and despised in humanity was exposed. The sordid undesirable cesspool of the life every sane and God-fearing human wished never to see was now presented to him in all its grotesque horror.

"*You have come, Farlon. You really believe you can find me even down here?*"

"*Show yourself, you creep. Let me see the foul demented creature you are.*" The scene around him was replaced by gray mist, and in it was suspended a formless shadow. The stench was unbearable.

"*My, my aren't we bitter. It's not necessary to be nasty. I know what you have come for but you will leave without it. You think things are that easy. You will not discover the truth by just stepping into my world. You must take me for a fool.*"

"*Not a fool but a killer. A heartless, sadistic maniac who has no respect for life.*"

"*On the contrary, I have a great respect for life. But that part of it must be destroyed.*"

"*Why? Why must it be destroyed?*"

"*You wouldn't understand. You don't understand, Farlon; those women were the dregs of humanity. They fed off all who used their bodies. They were sinful and shameless. They corrupted everything they touched.*"

"*Who gives you the right to be judge, jury and executioner?*"

"*It is my responsibility to carry out the eradication of this scourge on humanity. I have been entrusted with that task.*"

"*You don't have that right and were never given it. God will strike you down and if he doesn't, I will.*"

"God? God has no power here. You are confident for a man who has no idea where he is or with whom he is dealing. Remember I do not make mistakes."

"You made a big one when you killed someone who was not, as you call it, the dregs of humanity. You have now crossed swords with me."

"Oh, you are referring to the Mexican woman, Juanita. Well she was a treat, the small diversion I needed at the time. She passed the test with high marks. It was so invigorating. She put up a hell of a fight."

"You sick bastard! I will not rest until I get you no matter how long it takes!"

"You don't have that much time."

"Why don't you show yourself, you slime ball? Or are you scared that I will bring you down that much quicker?" But there was only the shadow, shapeless and foreboding.

"It would spoil the thrill of the chase. The game is becoming so exciting and though I reluctantly say it, you are so good. This is the ultimate chess game with the two greatest players. The big question is, who will win?"

"I will, you demented son of a bitch! I will kick you back under whatever rock you crawled from."

"My, you are determined."

"You have no idea."

"Then let the game commence."

"It's already begun whoever you are, and I will destroy you!"

"Never!"

"Don't be so bold, my demented friend, for you are a dead man."

"We shall see, Farlon, we shall see. You seem to forget I have the advantage."

"Not for long. You may have changed but I will find your secret."

"You may, but it will still be a delusion and the truth will still be obscure."

"There is no place to hide and you can't escape me. One way or another, you will die. I will see to that."

"Death is but an illusion. It only happens to those who fear it. It is reality only to those who are unprepared for it. Only if you believe in it and don't fear it, is it a bridge to far better opportunities."

"Keep looking over your shoulder for I will be right behind you. Before you realize it, I will snatch you off your feet and lock you up for all eternity. Trust me, you will beg to die."

"Eternity is a frame of mind, Farlon. When the mind is free it matters little for the possibilities are limitless. We shall meet soon enough, so beware, for it's I who will destroy you. Time is always my ally...always. It is my companion and protector."

"I will be back you sick-minded bastard. We will finish this once and for all."

"It will not be that simple. It will take more than your lifetime to achieve that end. But please come back for I do so enjoy watching you try to solve the puzzle."

"Oh, believe me, I will be back."

▼▼▼▼▼ 11

Gray woke to a violent crescendo of shouts and screams, flying sheets and blankets and thrashing arms. He sat up and looked about. He expected to see the shadowy figure before him but there was only his dimly lit room. Gradually the awareness of his surroundings crept into his consciousness. The events had only been a nightmare, or had they? He had stepped into the killer's world, but not as he anticipated. It had been on the killer's terms, which should not have been the case. He got out of bed, went into the kitchen and turned on the light. The glare blinded him momentarily. As he stepped to the refrigerator, he removed a carton of orange juice. Retrieving a glass from one of the cabinets, he filled it and replaced the carton.

His mind was a jumbled yet empty mess. He sat at the table staring at the glass of orange liquid. What was happening to him? It had all appeared so real. He talked to the killer; at least he presumed it was the killer. Who else could it have been? The only discernable object in that fog had been a gigantic cauldron – the vat from hell, full of tormented screaming bodies. They thrashed and struggled in a cesspool of human feces as it bubbled and boiled, incited by the fires of Hades. He still could smell the overpowering stench of death.

His pajamas were drenched. He shivered. Why had he poured a cold drink? He needed something hot. Reluctantly, he drank the juice. It soothed him. The sweetness gradually dissolved the bitterness. He stared into nothingness, confused. How the event had unfolded troubled him. It had all been wrong. The killer should not have been aware of his presence. Gray felt fear spawned in that place deep within the subconscious where no human dared to venture – an alien fear.

He cursed his weakness, drained the glass, then got up. He switched off the light and returned to bed. The clock on the nightstand read *3:50A.M.* That was not possible, he had only just fallen asleep and now it was almost time to get up. Exhausted, he turned the clock away, slipped under the covers and gradually drifted back to sleep.

12

Gray felt his world falling apart. Day and night he ventured into the squalid environment of the killer knowing that to solve this crime it was where he had to go but nothing was forthcoming. His ability to concentrate became difficult. As he laid the paper he had been reading on the coffee table, the quiet chimes of his doorbell invaded his thoughts. He got up and opened the door to find Paul standing on the threshold clutching a bottle of scotch.

"Am I bothering you?"

"Not at all, Paul, come in. I was just reading."

"Then I will. This is not for you by the way," he said waving the bottle in the air. "Knowing you're dry with nothing in this place to drink other than milk and water, I brought my own."

"Fine, but I do have wine."

"I'm not a wine drinker," he said stepping into the apartment.

"What true Italian doesn't drink wine?"

"Me and who's complaining?"

"Glasses are…hell, you know where they are."

Paul walked toward the kitchen. "Can I get you anything, Gray?"

"No thanks, I have coffee." Paul poured his drink, returned to the living room and took the second recliner.

"Reading?"

"Yes. I've been trying to find some damn clues in this case," Gray said, motioning to the two piles of documents on the floor beside his chair.

"Anything?"

"Nothing that helps."

Paul settled deeper into the recliner. "It's all so baffling Gray. I have never seen anything like it." He raised the footrest and relaxed, then lifted his glass. "A salute," Paul said and sipped the golden liquid then rested his head against the chair.

"To be very honest, Paul, neither have I."

"What do you make of it?"

"Not sure. Clues are shrouded in a fog. You can't hold onto shadows, let alone capture them."

"I'm not following you, Gray."

"Never mind. I'll explain it to you sometime. This case is full of immense paradoxes. So many pieces are missing. It's so damned frustrating. If I could see…well it will just have to play out on its own."

"Gray, what the hell are you going on about?"

"As I said, I'll explain it to you some other time."

Paul raised the tumbler to his lips but paused half way as the ice clinked against the glass. "Gray, what part do you think Juanita played in all this?"

"I've been racking my brain over that one. I do believe she was part of his plan."

Paul sipped his drink. "Part of his plan?"

"Yes. In his mind he didn't deviate. I'm convinced she was bait. This guy doesn't do anything by accident. Every move he makes is carefully calculated. I'm becoming more convinced that it was revenge. Revenge for what, I don't know, but we'll find out. Juanita was a personal message."

"Revenge against you...a personal message? But Juanita never worked for the department; she worked in the DA's office. You have no connection to her. Her murder makes no sense."

Gray got out of his chair and went into the kitchen to pour himself another cup of coffee. "Oh there was a connection to me, Paul."

"You truly believe the killer is targeting you?" Paul dropped the footrest, sat up and placed his elbows on his knees, staring at Gray as he returned from the kitchen and sat down.

"Yes, with everything that has happened to date I believe it." Gray drank his coffee.

"Why?"

"I'm not sure, Paul, but I have my suspicions, especially since Juanita's death."

"What does Juanita have to do with it?"

Gray lay back in his chair. "Remember, Paul, her father and I were partners. Our families were very close. Still are. I believe that's the connection. She was guilty by association." He thought on it for a moment then placed his coffee mug on the table beside him.

"So you think he's targeting you indirectly?" Paul shook his head in disbelief.

"Each move he makes gets closer to me."

"One hell of a way to make a point. My God, he could start killing more people who are connected to you. The fact that this guy seems to know you is unsettling enough. What makes it even more unsettling is that you have no idea who he is."

Gray threw his arms up in frustration. "I couldn't even begin to guess who he might be, Paul. Hell, there's a long list of possibilities."

"You're right. All those slime balls you put away."

"It places folk like Anita and her family, you, Julia and God knows how many more in harm's way." Gray shivered.

"Not a pleasant thought."

"No, but I'll say this. Whoever he is, he does not intend to get caught..." Suddenly, deep in his subconscious, a light went on. "He said – *he had all the time in the world* – No, that wasn't it. What the hell was it he said...*he had plenty of time*...no. Damn it, what was...*time was his*...*t*hat's it. *Time was his ally.*"

Paul drained his glass then sat clutching it as if it were some sort of lifeline. "Gray, what are you talking about? Who said that?"

"I wish I knew, but that's what he said."

"Gray, this is nonsense."

"Paul, remember years ago I told you to understand a killer you must climb into the cesspool of his mind? Go where he goes, think as he thinks and so on?"

"Yeah, vaguely, why?"

"That's how I dig into these cases. I might as well explain it otherwise you'll think I'm nuts."

"Too late."

As he picked up his coffee mug, Gray stared off into space not quite sure where to start. "Let me put it as simply as I can. I tap into my imagination to try to see into the killer's mind...actually it's not really my imagination. I'm not quite sure how it works but it does. Anyhow, I can see things."

"You see things?" Paul sounded skeptical.

"Yes. I see people, places, and things the killer sees. He's unaware I am doing this. It's like the proverbial fly on the wall, so to speak. But in this case it's completely different. I actually hear this madman. I don't see him but his voice is as clear as yours, and he knows I'm there." Gray felt like an idiot trying to explain something to Paul when he had difficulty believing himself.

"You're there? Where the hell is there? Gray, is this your secret? You're telling me you're clairvoyant?"

"No, Paul, I am not clairvoyant. Look, I don't know how it works, but it does. In every other case I've seen the killer. I become a shadow in his world. It's like looking through a one-way mirror. But in this case I see nothing but shadows and all I hear is a voice...familiar, yet not."

Paul looked quizzically at Gray. "A voice?" Again came the skeptical tone.

"Yes, a voice. It's the killer's. But damn it, Paul, I can't place it."

"Gray, you're not making sense. Besides, you're giving me the creeps."

"Trust me, it scares the hell out of me. What bothers me the most is that he knows I'm there but he shouldn't. It's all in a fog, nothing's clear. You know what I'm trying to say?"

"The hell I do. One-way mirrors...flies on the wall...shadows, voices. Gray, I'm beginning to think you've lost your marbles."

"I'm sorry, Paul, but I don't know how else to explain it."

"You have actually spoken to this guy?"

"Not in the true sense, no, but yes."

"I don't know, Gray, this is damn freaky. You're telling me this is how you solved crimes over the years?"

"Yes. Just that simple."

"Definitely not simple. Why haven't you ever mentioned it before?"

"Would you have believed me?"

"No, and I'm not so sure that I believe you now."

"I find it hard to believe myself."

"You're weird, my friend."

"I wouldn't put it quite like that, but it's certainly strange if I say so myself." He looked at his watch. It was 11 o'clock. "I hate to throw you out but this old guy needs to sleep."

"Oh my God, I'm sorry Gray. I didn't realize the time," Paul said as he got out of his chair.

"That's okay, I'll see you in the morning. Thanks for the company." Gray walked Paul to the door.

SECRETS

1

Dr. Ben Rashid arranged for a psychologist, Dr. Sharon Fillmore, to take Ann under her wing. It was imperative that they learn the identity and background of this woman. Had she seen her attacker and could she identify him? After two weeks, and the conclusion of Ann's fifth therapy session, information began to surface. Dr. Fillmore called Gray to bring him up to date.

"I'm not sure this will mean much, Detective. There is a great deal of disjointed and meaningless information, but we believe Ann's real name could be Sally. Her last name may be Mayfield…"

"That's encouraging, Doctor. If we…"

"Don't get too excited, Detective, we can't confirm it. We can only continue probing to see what else turns up. She did mention a few other names. One is Victoria Baxter. Sally might have worked for her as a maid. Another is Madam Francine…could be a madam in a brothel, by the sound of things. Jenny is one that might be of help if we could learn her second name. It appears she was very close to Sally. One other name, a street, Payton Street, no city reference."

"I don't know of a Payton Street, not in this city anyway."

"One other piece of information for what it's worth. It appears that Victoria Baxter's husband might be your killer. It might have been Baxter who killed Sally's friend. There may not be a great deal of merit in all this, but I am probing in an effort to learn more."

"It sound's encouraging, Doctor. Please keep me up to date, especially if she mentions her attacker."

"I'll do that. Oh, one other thing, Sally may have been raised in an orphanage."

"That may help. Thanks, Doctor." Gray hung up, sat back in his chair and closed his eyes. Was this progress, he wondered, or just a jumble of meaningless information that fit nowhere?

Sally Mayfield – there have to be thousands of Mayfields. The orphanage idea might be worth investigating. If we could link a Sally Mayfield to an orphanage, we might just have our person. Gray thought they might be on to something. He left his office in search of Paul.

2

"What brings you fellows down here?" Justin Davenport greeted Gray, Paul and Mario as they entered his office.

"We were on our way back to the District and decided to stop in to see if you have anything new."

"It just so happens that I do. In fact, I was going to call you. Follow me gentlemen and I'll fill you in as we go." The four left the office. "Gray, I don't know what's going on here, but we are a little disturbed. We've been chopping away at one situation that makes absolutely no sense to any of us, but we believe we may have come up with an answer. It has been two grueling days and this morning we arrived at a conclusion. A conclusion, I might add, that is still shaky but we all seem to agree that we have made progress."

"So what is it that you've found, Justin?" Gray asked.

The Medical Examiner paused and looked at the three Detectives. "You're aware of the condition that exists in the victims."

"The enzyme and blood cell thing?"

"Yes. Well each time we dig deeper, the mystery seems to grow exponentially. We have just finished running another series of tests."

"You still don't know why the condition is present?"

"True. But that has been superceded by an even bigger mystery." The four continued along the corridor.

Gray shot him a side-glance. "It has?"

"Yes. What we found has really thrown us for a loop. Talk about muddying the waters even more." They entered the lab and crossed to the far side. On the wall in front of them were eight flat panel computer screens. The ME turned to one of the technicians.

"Pam, bring up the cell analyses on the Mannequin case." The technician typed codes on a keyboard and the screens flickered revealing a series of pictures.

"What you're seeing are enlarged photos of blood cells taken from each of your six victims..."

"I see seven pictures, and we do have seven victims."

"Patience, Gray, I'll explain. Believe me, it gets even better. First, your victim number six is completely clean. Now starting with this picture on the left, you have victim number one, then two and so on. As you move along, you will notice each has the same condition. By referring to the scale along the top and down the side of each screen, you notice the cells are almost all identical in size." The Chief Medical Examiner paused for a moment. He then continued. "Now here's the ball buster." He pointed to the seventh screen. "This is a blood cell from your eighth victim."

Gray was confused for a moment. "But we don't have an eighth..." Then it hit him. Sally. The three detectives stood gaping at the picture. Gray turned to Justin.

"You mean Sally has the same condition?"

"Yes."

"How?"

"That's it, Gray, we don't know."

"But...but she's still alive."

"Precisely. And that's what has us baffled. The condition in the other victims was acceptable... unexplainable but acceptable. But for this, and I hate to say this, there is no explanation."

Gray paced agitatedly about the lab. "What's going on, Justin?"

"I can't say, Gray. What this tells us is that the condition now appears to have nothing to do with their deaths. And what's even more confusing is the condition is more prevalent in Sally. I have spoken to the folk at the CDC. They are running tests on the samples we sent the and their results match ours. They're as baffled as we are."

"So there's no cause for it?"

"There has to be a cause but it's eluding us. Something extremely unusual has happened to these women."

Gray raised his eyebrows in mock surprise. "A new disease?"

"Not sure but we don't think so. The CDC concurs. It's too confined. If it were a disease it should have surfaced elsewhere by now. The CDC continues to run tests. If they come up with anything profound, they'll inform us immediately."

"Why doesn't victim number six have the condition?"

"Don't know. She's our proverbial wrench. At first we were convinced if we ran comparison tests, victim six would be the key to finding an answer. That was not the case. In fact the more we compared, the further apart the evidence became. There are so many variations in the sixth victim, the fact that the condition is not present does not surprise me."

Gray shook his head. "So what has..."

Justin cut him off. "This could take months, maybe years to solve. We might never get to the bottom of it. The question is, 'Is it a major issue in the case?'"

Gray leaned against the desk. "What are you driving at, Justin?"

"The condition is not life threatening. Don't get me wrong; I'm not saying we drop it. It's something that must be solved. I'm suggesting we leave it to the CDC. We have other more pressing issues. We won't let it drop and we'll continue monitoring your patient."

"It's your call, Justin. But should the situation change, I want to know immediately."

"Certainly."

"Anything else?"

"No, and I believe that's enough for one day."

"In that case, we'll get out of your hair."

▼▼▼▼▼ 3

Gray woke to the ringing of his phone. Reluctantly he got out of bed and walked into the living room. He turned on the light, sat and lifted the handset.

"Hello."

"Gray, it's Ben."

Gray looked at the clock. "Ben, it's *5:15* in the morning."

"I know, Gray, but you need to hear this. That piece of jewelry Sally had in her hand…"

"What about it? What do you mean 'had'?"

"It's gone."

Gray was stunned. "What the hell do you mean gone…gone where?"

"No idea. It's just disappeared."

"Nonsense. What does Sally have to say about it?"

"She's still asleep, Gray."

"Then wake her. Find out what she knows."

"Are you going to the hospital?"

"Hell yes, as soon as I dress."

"I'll meet you there."

"How do you know it is gone?"

"The night duty nurse called me. Sally's nurse discovered it missing…."

"Never mind, I'll see you in about half an hour. Keep the night staff there until I arrive."

"Already arranged."

"Thanks, Ben." Gray hung up. Suddenly he noticed he was sweating.

At *6:30* Gray was sitting in Ben Rashid's office questioning the nurse who was tending Sally when the alleged incident occurred. Nurse Wyncote, a small rather mousy woman, was stumbling through an explanation.

"It was *4:30* this morning. I had just finished checking Sally's vitals when I noticed her hand was open. Since we all knew the muscles in her hand were locked, I was shocked."

"What did you do next?"

"I first looked at her hand closely. It was obvious the object had been there as there were deep impressions in her palm as well as a number of areas where the skin had been broken. But there was no bleeding. I then looked around the room for the object. The officer helped me."

Gray watched the nurse closely. "And?"

"We found nothing. We looked everywhere; under her bed and between the sheets. It was not in the room. I then went to the nurses' station and reported it to the night duty nurse."

"You're sure it was not in the room?"

"Positive. There are not that many places something could get lost in a room that bare."

"That will be all for the moment, Nurse. Thank you." Gray turned to the police officer.

"You were on duty at that time?"

"Yes, Detective. It was around *4:30* when Nurse Wyncote came out of the room and told me what had happened so I went to help her. We found nothing and Nurse Wyncote left."

"What did you do then?"

"I went into the room to look again."

"You still found nothing?"

"Correct. As Nurse Wyncote mentioned, there is little clutter in those rooms."

"Apart from Nurse Wyncote, did anyone else go into Sally's room during the night?"

"No Sir."

"Thank you Officer, that'll be all for now."

"It looks like someone walked off with it, Ben. Is Sally awake?"

"Yes. We asked her about it but she has no idea what happened."

Gray stood and walked to the door. "I'll have a word with her anyway."

"By all means, Gray."

Gray and Ben left Ben's office and went to Sally's room.

"Good morning, Sally, how do you feel?"

"I am very well, thank you, Detective Farlon."

"Sally, do you have any idea what happened to the thing in your hand?"

"I am unable to tell you anything, Detective. When I awoke it was gone."

"You didn't feel it being removed?"

"No."

"You saw no one in your room during the night?"

"I was asleep, Detective. If there was someone in my room I would not have known."

"Of course. Thank you, Sally." Ben and Gray left Sally's room.

"What do you make of it, Gray?"

Gray stopped and glanced down the hall. "I have no idea, Ben. But I'll say this, things don't just disappear into thin air."

▼▼▼▼▼ *4*

A few days after the disappearance of the object from Sally's hand, the pace of the investigation picked up. Startling new information came to light. Regardless, Gray felt compelled to continue his struggle to discover the identity of the killer. He feared he was losing a battle he should not lose, but the killer's mind was closed to him, sealed behind a seemingly impenetrable barrier. He had to break that barrier. The pressure was on, his health was suffering, sleep was difficult and what he managed was not restful. Gray felt helpless.

He poured himself a cup of coffee and, on his way to his office, he ran into Carrie. "Morning Carrie."

"Good morning, Gray. Boy you look like hell." She fell in beside him.

"Thanks, Carrie, I love you too."

"No really, you don't look good. Do you feel okay?"

"Let's say I'm not at my best."

"Anything I can do to help?"

"Not unless you can identify the killer."

"Wish I could."

"Me too. Enough of my troubles, anything new this morning?"

"I'm not sure, Gray, but you might want to check with O'Malley. He's been running around looking for you. I have no idea what it's all about, but for him to get that excited, it must be good."

"I guess I should give him a call."

Carrie chuckled. "Might be a good idea before he blows a fuse."

▼▼▼▼▼ 5

Gray called the team to the War Room. O'Malley, seated next to Paul, was grinning like a Cheshire cat. The room fell silent.

Gray looked at Patrick and smiled. "Okay, Patrick, now that you have everyone's attention, let's hear it."

O'Malley squirmed nervously in his chair, looked around the table, then opened the folder in front of him. "First, we, that is Paul and I, have narrowed the wearer of the shoe, matched to the print found at the sixth crime scene, to one individual. It's a long shot but it's all we have. Our suspect is Clive W. Maitland. He is…"

Carrie gasped. "Maitland, the antiquities guru? That's impossible. I've met the man, he's a wimp, and I doubt he's ever killed a fly let alone a woman. What brought you to that conclusion?"

Paul raised himself in his chair. "He's only a suspect Carrie and even wimps can kill. One major reason we targeted him is that Maitland did not exist before 1986."

"What?" Gray exclaimed.

"Maitland has no history prior to that date."

"Nothing?" Pat Yoshi said.

"Nothing. Let me explain." Patrick continued. "And bear with me, for this gets a little complicated."

Gray interrupted him. "Is this going to take long young man?"

"I do have a great deal of information here, Gray. So, to answer your question, yes, it could take a while."

"Very well then, let's get started." The small group made themselves comfortable.

O'Malley proceeded. "Maitland's story actually begins in California in 1957..."

"But Patrick, you just said that..."

"Mario, let Patrick get on with it. We don't want to be here all night."

"Sorry Patrick, continue."

"It begins with a guy named John Winslow, a graduate of USC, who was teaching in a small private school at the time."

"In California?"

"Yes. After a series of events that I will cover later, Hal Moffitt went to California to find..."

It was Gray's turn to interrupt O'Malley in shocked surprise. "Moffitt? What the hell has Moffitt got to do with all this?"

"As most of us know, Hal Moffitt was a member of the Police Board here in Chicago until his early retirement in 1989. There were two things of which no one was aware at the time. One, he was under a doctor's care in the Bahamas and had been for three years. And second is that he was related to a guy by the name of Miles Webber. In fact, Webber was Moffitt's twin brother..." The room exploded in an uproar.

Paul quieted everyone down. "Okay folks, let me explain. What Patrick is saying is correct. Webber is, or more to the point was, Moffitt's brother..."

"But his name was Webber, not Moffitt."

"Right, Gray. While he was still living in Virginia, he changed his name. We're not sure of the reason for the change, but we believe it might have been pressure from his brother Hal, in an effort to disassociate himself from Miles and avoid embarrassment."

"Avoid embarrassment! Hell the guy was a criminal!"

"Right, but Hal was in law enforcement and wanted no part of Miles' problems. He inherited them anyway."

"But Paul, Webber was in jail for armed robbery for four years. A year after his release he was killed in a night club shooting." Instantly every other thought but one was wiped from Gray's mind. The picture of that night so long ago loomed in his head. The dim nightclub lounge, the confusion, the explosion of gunfire, the gunman lying dead in front of his hostages, Juan collapsing, fatally wounded, and Griffith standing over them with that smirk on his face as if he had saved the day. Gray shook his head trying to clear the horrors of the past caught in the cobwebs of his memory.

"That's correct, Gray, but there is a great deal of history to this. It might be better if we let Patrick finish what he has to say then we can ask questions."

Gray cleared his mind. "I agree. Patrick, I apologize, please go on."

"That's okay, Gray. Hal Moffitt's mother was Carol Henderson, a former Miss Virginia. She met Hal's father, Claude Moffitt at a gem convention in Washington. After a whirlwind affair lasting just under five months, they got married. At the time the two met, Henderson was in the throws of a nasty divorce. I told you it was complicated. Moffitt, who, by the way, was CEO of Triton Gems Limited of South Africa, took his new wife home to Johannesburg.

"Eleven months after the wedding Carol Moffitt gave birth to twins, Hal and Miles. For some reason the grandfather took to Hal, whose actual name was William Bennett Moffitt, his grandfather gave him the nickname Hal. He was the grandfather's favorite. The name stuck and Hal never used his other names except on legal documents. Triton was growing and Claude Moffitt began to reach beyond South Africa to expand the company. It was this move that may have been his downfall.

"In 1951 Claude Moffitt purchased a California company owned by Stanley and Beth Winslow, John Winslow's parents. From what we have discovered, the Winslow's ran a rather shady operation. Although the company was valued between five and six million, it was on very shaky ground. Whether this purchase caused the collapse of Triton, we don't know. What we do know is that 18 months after the acquisition, Triton was in a heap of trouble and hemorrhaging financially. Within two years the company bled to death.

"Claude Moffitt committed suicide a year later. His wife believed it was due entirely to the Winslow purchase; at least that was where she placed the blame. An extremely bitter woman, she left South Africa with her two boys and returned to Virginia. What happened next is a mystery. In 1956 the Winslow's were killed in a rather suspicious car crash in California. The investigation found nothing but many questions remained. We do know Carol Moffitt never let her sons forget who caused their father's death.

"As the boys matured, they grew very close but their careers were to take them in two separate directions. Hal went into law and married Adriana Pachinko, a Russian model who had only been in the US a few months. Miles, on the other hand, got involved in petty crimes ending up in jail a number of times. Hal had one major vice. He was a compulsive gambler unable to resist a card game. The outcome of one of those games forced him to leave his job with the Virginia Police Force, and he and his wife moved here to Chicago. He walked away from a debt of over $300,000. Not long after that, he joined the Chicago Force. Then he learned some interesting news. Miles went to him with information that John Winslow was living in California. The hatred for the Winslow family was as fierce as ever. Hal immediately flew to California with a diabolical plan formulating in his mind.

"Then things began to happen. Winslow made a sudden and unprecedented move to Chicago, taking a position with the Natural History Museum. Soon after that he was introduced to David Griffith who was..."

Gray could not help his reaction. Griffith, the man responsible for the death of his partner, the one who had single-handedly destroyed his life, was the only man, the only human being for whom Gray had any semblance of hatred and had never found the strength or will to forgive. "Good God, what have we got here...Larry, Moe and Curley? How the hell does Griffith fit into this story?"

"We're not sure he does, Gray, but his name comes up periodically. For all intents and purposes it appeared that Moffitt was assembling a master plan. He and his brother were seeking retribution against Winslow...sins of the father and all that sort of stuff. We believe his idea was to use Griffith as a scapegoat. The relationship between Moffitt, Winslow and Griffith was barely a relationship. We believe Moffitt developed his relationship with Winslow solely for money, about three quarters of a million. Winslow was Moffitt's pot of gold at the end of the rainbow.

"Moffitt's quest for revenge turned into greed. Remember, he had a debt hanging over his head that was haunting him and he wanted to be free of it. Winslow was his way out so he began to manipulate the man.

"But Winslow was no dummy. He had brains enough to realize he was in trouble. He quit his position at the museum and disappeared. Moffitt was furious. Until this moment Moffitt was on the straight and level. But suddenly his life was unraveling at the seams. Winslow had disappeared, and then he discovered his wife was having an affair with some bank manager. It was then he took the plunge. And right into the deep end believe it or not. He and his brother drew up a plan. They engineered a highly sophisticated bank robbery with the intention of eliminating one of the problems. The robbery was unsuccessful and no one walked away. During the holdup, Moffitt's wife, who was in the bank at the time, was shot, as were the robbers.

"All he had to do now was find Winslow. If this story isn't strange enough, believe me it gets worse. Moffitt found Winslow in Tennessee teaching history at a school in Knoxville. As soon as the teacher realized he'd been found, he grew nervous and once more quit his job and for another year dropped out of sight. Moffitt had to go hunting again. But in the meantime he had been busy with other things. In an effort to pull off the bank job, he needed an inside man. We are certain he bought the service of the bank security guard, one Dan Whitely. Whitely was to become the key player in Moffitt's plan."

▼▼▼▼▼ **6**

Gray pushed his chair back. "Patrick, sorry to interrupt you but I think we need a short break." Five minutes later everyone was back at the table.

"Okay let's see where all this is going," Gray said making himself comfortable.

The River Styx

Patrick continued. "Moffitt then began making trips to New York for reasons I will explain in a minute. During this time he learned that Winslow was living in Baltimore. At this point things get a little vague. We believe Moffitt went to Maryland to find Winslow.

"Winslow lived in an apartment just outside Baltimore. One night the police received calls from people hearing gunshots in Winslow's apartment. Nothing came of the ensuing investigation...no blood, no body, nothing. The apartment was locked from the inside, there were no signs of forced entry, and no one was seen arriving or leaving. Winslow was never found.

"The following year Moffitt continued with his plan. His visits to New York persisted. Then a strange thing occurred. Dan Whitely, the bank guard disappeared. His family filed a missing persons report but the guy was never found..."

"A lot of people were disappearing around Moffitt," Yoshi said.

"True, but we do have some answers. To wrap this up, I'll cover this area quickly. Moffitt was taking courses in theatrical makeup. He had also made contact with a cosmetic surgeon named Simon Chang. Chang, you may recall, was the fella who had his license revoked in California when a patient died on his operating table. He left the States but returned three years later to set up a practice in New York. Moffitt employed his services. By this time Moffitt had become a master of disguise. With this expertise he began to make trips to Hong Kong..."

"As who?" Carrie asked.

"Whomever he liked, but we believe he traveled as Maitland," Paul said.

"In the meantime our man Whitley was in New York studying as diligently as a first year med student. He was taking history and archeology, as well as theatrical makeup..."

"Whitely was taking theatrical makeup also. Why..."

"I think it was for the same reason Moffitt did. Moffitt wanted broad flexibility in his plan. Moffitt's plan was coming together. By early 1986 he was ready and he had everything in place. He made his move."

Mario rubbed his chin. "So Moffitt was never really ill?"

"No, he was in New York."

"He deceived everyone."

"And he did it well. Then Winslow's name turned up again, of all places, in New York. He applied for a name change. He claimed to have been involved in a kitchen fire and was seriously burned. The name he picked...Clive Maitland." There was a ripple of chatter among the team. Patrick went on. "Moffitt then paid a visit to Simon Chang and underwent an identity change. But he was not the only one. Whitley also went under Chang's knife and was given a new identity."

"So three characters were customers of Chang?"

"No, Carrie, only two. You see it wasn't Winslow who requested the name change, it was Whitley."

"Whitley? Then what happened to Winslow?"

"We're not sure, but Moffitt may have actually killed him. He has not surfaced in almost 20 years."

"But the guy did have a habit of disappearing regularly."

"But he always showed up sooner or later. Anyway, Moffitt's plan was complete. He only had one thing left to do and that was to pay off his gambling debt."

Gray raised his eyebrows in surprise. "He did what?"

"The guys were closing in on him and, to avoid disruptions to his plans, he paid his debt."

"Excuse me but I'm a little confused. Winslow is dead, possibly killed by Moffitt. The ex-security guard Whitley, is now Maitland. What about Griffith?"

"Griffith dropped out of the picture, Carrie. We expect he left town."

"Then somebody tell us who the hell Moffitt is," Yoshi said in frustration.

"I'm getting to that," Patrick responded.

Paul interrupted. "I might add...although Moffitt developed this very elaborate plan, he remained in the background. His protégée, Whitley, alias Maitland, was pushed into the limelight."

Mario looked at Patrick deep in thought then asked. "Is there a possibility Moffitt could be Maitland?"

"No, because two names came up in Chang's records. One was Whitley whose name always appeared along with Maitland. The other was Hal Moffitt though his name was never written in full. Only his initials appear in the books."

"I do have one question. Why the trips to Hong Kong?" Carrie asked.

"Moffitt got wind of a very rare and priceless artifact. He had to find it."

Mario twisted in his chair. "Moffitt, disguised as Maitland, made those trips?"

"We believe so, yes. At least at the outset, until Whitley completed surgery."

"Damn Patrick, complicated was an understatement. What about this artifact?"

"It was a statuette of a Buddha, Gray, along with another item."

"The Ivory Buddha of Janakpur and the 'Eye Of The Spider' Medallion." Everyone looked at Carrie.

"You know about this, Carrie?"

"Yes. History is one of my passions, especially Chinese history. For centuries it was believed 'The Ivory Buddha' was just a myth. Then suddenly five years ago Maitland presented it to the public. The medallion on the other hand *is* pure myth. It only exists as reproductions, somewhat like the sword Excalibur. I have a book that briefly explains the history behind both the Buddha and the medallion, but it reads very much like Grimm's Fairy Tales."

"So Maitland went to Hong Kong to find these items?"

"At least the Buddha, which we know he found."

The River Styx

Gray looked at Carrie. "Why was it so important Maitland find this Buddha?"

"In my opinion, Gray, Moffitt wanted credibility for Maitland. Until that moment he was a nobody in the field of antiquities. When he found the Buddha, his status multiplied tenfold."

Deep furrows formed across Gray's brow. "The Ivory Buddha of...Janakpur?"

Carrie leaned forward placing her elbows on the table. "Janakpur is a small town in northern India located high in the Himalayas. The Buddha was discovered not far from the town. But now Patrick is telling us Maitland is not Maitland but Dan Whitley, or could Maitland be Moffitt, as has been suggested?"

"We're 99 percent certain Whitley is Maitland. Remember, Moffitt wanted Winslow's money. To obtain it he had to become Winslow. Moffitt's name was always accompanied by JW, John Winslow's initials. Well that's virtually the whole story.

Carrie waved her finger in a circular motion and glanced at Gray. "Why this charade? What does it all mean?"

"That's what I was wondering. Why go to all this trouble if Winslow is already out of the picture?"

"I believe I can partially answer that, Gray. As far as who is who, I think we now have that straight. Why Moffitt took Winslow's identity was, of course, the money. The case regarding Winslow's disappearance was closed about three years ago, once the police realized he was alive and living in New York," Paul said.

"He was able to fool them to that degree?"

"Yes. He had fingerprints grafted, the lot. We're convinced he looks like Winslow, that he is Winslow and he has Winslow's money."

"The question remains, why the charade?"

"That we can't answer, Yoshi."

"Then Patrick, you're telling us that the bottom line here is that Maitland could be our killer?"

"It's a possibility Mario, but we have no proof."

Gray was suddenly overcome with curiosity. "One last question Patrick, what about Griffith?"

"Four months after you retired, Griffith was fired from his position on the board for gross insubordination."

"You're kidding?"

"No."

"I'll be. I always wondered what would happen to him. Do we know his whereabouts now?"

"No, Gray, we don't. It was rumored he was killed in that warehouse explosion five years ago, but we believe he just left town," Patrick responded.

Gray rested back in his chair. "Do you have any other mysteries in that file of yours, Patrick?"

"Yes I do. Would you like me to continue?"
"Is it something that can wait?"
"I think so."
"We have a great deal to think about for now; let's leave the rest for another day. Great work Patrick."

▼▼▼▼▼ 7

Gray rose from the table. He had spent a pleasant evening at dinner with his daughter and felt happier than he had in many years.
"Another glass of wine, honey?" he asked Julia.
"Please."
"Coming right up." Gray disappeared into the kitchen. "There's no Chardonnay left, but I do have a bottle of Pinot Grigio."
"That will do fine, thanks."
He returned with two glasses of wine and handed one to Julia. He was about to sit down when the phone rang. "This had better not be Paul. I told him it was my weekend off." He lifted the receiver.
"Hello."
"Gray? This is Ben Rashid." Ben Rashid's voice was raspy and he sounded tired.
Gray was surprised. "Yes, Ben, what can I do for you?"
"Sally's gone." His voice was barely audible.
Gray almost dropped his wine glass. "What the hell do you mean, GONE?" He felt the blood drain from his face. He turned and stared at Julia who gave him a quizzical look.
"The duty nurse called me ten minutes ago in a state of panic. She said Sally had not returned from her therapy session. That was around ten this morning..."
Gray looked at his watch. It was ten after one. "Therapy on a Sunday morning?"
"Sign of the times, Gray...it's a long story. The point is that Sally is nowhere in the building."
"It's a big building, Ben."
"I know, but I've had security cover every department. There is no sign of her."
Gray was trying to comprehend the magnitude of the situation. "What happened?"
"Knowing Sally was scheduled for therapy, the nurse didn't give it a second thought."
Gray was trying to think. "Wait...wait...wait a second. What about the officer on duty?"
"Oh, he was there. He helped the doctor lift her onto a gurney..."

"Doctor? What doctor?"

"A doctor by the name of Winslow." Gray's blood turned to ice.

"I'll be there in 20 minutes, Ben. Have your staff standing by. Also, let the officer know I'm coming."

"Very good." Gray hung up then dialed Paul's home number.

"What's wrong, Daddy?"

"Sally may have been kidnapped."

Julia scowled. "Kidnapped? How?"

"No idea..."

Paul answered the phone. "Hello."

"Paul, Gray. We have a major situation. There's a possibility Sally has been abducted."

"Oh my God. When?"

"They're not sure, sometime between ten and twelve."

"Maitland?"

"Could be. We had better move. Locate Carrie and Yoshi and have them meet us at the hospital."

"What about Mario?"

"He's out of town for the weekend."

"I'll see you in half an hour."

Gray hung up. "Julia, I must go. Please stay and make yourself at home. I'll be back." Gray grabbed his coat and gloves and dashed for the door.

"I'll go with you."

"No. No, stay here and finish your lunch. If you go back to your hotel, just close the door. Leave all this and I'll clean it up later. This is police business and I don't want you involved. Please Julia."

"All right, I'll stay here until you get back."

"Fine." Gray rushed from his apartment and drove to the hospital.

▼▼▼▼▼ 8

"Afternoon Ben," Gray said as he entered Ben Rashid's office.

"Hello, Gray, I have everyone in the conference room down the hall. Detective Yoshi has just arrived." Gray followed Ben from the office. As they walked down the hall, Carrie Simpson appeared around the corner.

"Afternoon, Carrie."

"Gray."

Gray stopped. "Carrie, this place will be swarming with our people in a few minutes. Could you bring them up to speed and I'll be with you in about half an hour."

"Will do." Gray caught up with Ben as he entered the conference room. Gray dropped his coat over the back of the chair but did not sit down.

Agitated, he began to pace the room. "We have a guard outside Sally's room. We have officers at every entrance on the ground floor, this place is crawling with our people." He turned, placed his hands on the back of the chair and stared at everyone. "How in the name of hell did some guy, posing as a doctor, manage to walk out of here with a patient?" The anger and frustration was imbedded in Gray's voice. He raised his hand. "Don't try to answer. Okay, would someone mind telling me what happened? Which one of you was on duty at the time?" He waved his finger impatiently at the two nurses.

"I was, Detective. Jill Mason, I'm the duty nurse."

"Fine, Jill, please fill me in."

"This doctor came up to the nurse's station and handed me a clipboard. I'd never seen him but that is not unusual these days with so many new staff. His nametag said Dr. Winslow. There were a number of papers on the clipboard. The one on top was a release for Sally to be taken to her therapy session. The Physiotherapy Department is located on the 12th floor. The timing was a little unusual but hospital schedules are never logical at the best of times. It was also her first session so I really didn't give it another thought. The release was in order, Doctor Rashid had signed it, so I signed it and he left."

"Isn't it a little unusual for a doctor to run those sort of errands?"

"Normally, yes, but we're so short-handed, Detective, everyone is pitching in, including the doctors."

"I can vouch for that, Gray," Rashid concurred.

Gray slipped into his seat and began scribbling notes. "Jill, can you describe the guy?"

"He was medium height, maybe five feet ten. He had blue eyes and short, light hair, not blonde but more of a sandy brown.. There was a fine scar about two inches long beside his left eye. He had a ring on his right hand. It had a blue stone in the center. I got a good look at it when he signed the papers. It looked like a college ring, but it wasn't."

"What makes you say that?"

"Where the school name normally is, there was a Greek key design. It was also antiqued."

"What was he wearing?"

"Green scrubs and a white lab coat. He had a stethoscope around his neck."

"How about his speech? Any accent? Could he have been foreign?"

"There was a slight underlying accent. It could have been foreign...hard to say though. He might have come from Europe. Sorry, Detective, that's about all I can tell you." Gray was diligently making notes.

"Beard, mustache, glasses?"

"No, he was clean shaven. No glasses."

"Not too many props, just enough to draw the right amount of attention. What time did he arrive?"

The River Styx

"It was just after nine. I remember because one of my nurses had been out sick. She called to say she would be a little late. As I looked up at the clock, this guy stepped up to the counter."

Gray scribbled more notes. Then he glanced at Nurse Mason. "Did you see him leave Jill?"

"No, I was called on an emergency. I was away from the station for half an hour or so."

"Thanks, Jill, you've been very helpful."

"May I leave I ha..."

"Yes, but I or one of my staff may want to talk to you again." Gray turned to the second nurse.

"You are Nurse...?"

"Carol Black, I'm Sally's nurse on the day shift."

"What did you see, Carol?"

"I ran into this doctor in the hall. He was rolling Sally to the elevator on a gurney. As Nurse Mason already mentioned, his nametag said Dr. Winslow. He said he would be around for three or four weeks."

"So you had a conversation with him?"

"Hardly a conversation. I asked where he was taking Sally. At that point he remembered he had forgotten his clipboard back in her room. He asked me to watch Sally while he ran to get it. When he returned, I left and I didn't see him or Sally again."

Gray laid his pen down, got out of his chair and began to pace once more. "Did he appear nervous or agitated at all?"

"No. In fact, he was very calm. He seemed a little annoyed but he was very pleasant."

"Is there anything you can add to what Nurse Mason said about his appearance?"

"No. I think she covered it all, Detective."

"Thank you Carol. I may call on you again."

"I'll be here until four, Detective." She got up and walked to the door, then paused. "Oh, one other thing I should probably mention, Detective. While this doctor went for the clipboard, Sally didn't even stir. She was sound asleep. I thought it rather strange since she was on her way to therapy."

Gray walked over and stood beside the nurse. "Did you mention it to him?"

"No, but it did seem odd."

Gray opened the door for her. "Thank you again Carol." As he closed the door, he turned back to the room.

"Yoshi, get with Security. I want a play-by-play of every vehicle that came and went over the last 48 hours." Yoshi left the room.

Gray turned to Officer Nesbit. "You were on duty when this character showed up?"

"Yes, Detective. He looked like a damned doctor to me. He had all the right..."

"It's okay, Officer, no one's blaming you, just tell me what happened."

"He showed me his papers, I checked them and everything appeared to be in order. He said he was taking Sally to therapy. Hell, Detective, who was I to say he was lying?" The police officer was agitated.

"Officer…Nesbit, relax, forget it and let's move on. If it's any consolation, I would have most likely let him in myself."

"I asked if he needed a hand. At first he said no, then he changed his mind. Asked if I could help him lift Sally onto the gurney."

"Why do you think he would do that?"

"I'm not sure I understand the question, Sir."

"Don't you think Sally could have climbed onto the gurney herself?"

"She appeared to be sleeping. Once in the room, the first thing he did was give Sally a shot."

Gray gasped. "He gave her a shot?" He glanced at Ben Rashid who shrugged his shoulders.

"Yes. He said it would help her relax."

"Did he put on surgical gloves?"

"Yes, well…no, not exactly..."

"Which is it, Officer? Either he put gloves on or he didn't."

"He was already wearing gloves, Detective."

"When he arrived he was already wearing gloves?"

"I didn't notice at first but now thinking, yes, he was wearing them when he arrived."

Gray leaned over the table, picked up his pen and wrote on his note pad. "Unusual wouldn't you say considering the reason for putting them on in the first place? Did he take them off when he was finished?"

"No, I don't think so. No, definitely not. When he left he was still wearing them."

Gray straightened and paused for a moment tapping his pen against his teeth. He then folded his arms and continued. "I don't suppose you happened to notice what was in the syringe?"

"Yes. It was a pale yellow liquid."

"What happened when he gave Sally the shot?"

"Nothing. She was asleep when we went into her room. The doctor, the guy, did not wake her. He just gave her the shot."

"Then what?"

"She woke almost immediately."

"And?"

"Nothing. She lay there quite still with her eyes wide open."

"That was rather odd, don't you think?"

"No, Sir, not really. With all the drugs they give you in hospital, who knows what they can do to you."

Gray started pacing once more. "Point taken. You said she just lay there with her eyes open. Would you say she was unconscious?"

"Possibly, it was hard to tell."

"Meaning?"

"I just found it a little funny when he closed her eyes for her."

"He did what?" Once again Gray was shocked. He stopped pacing, stepped over to where Sergeant Nesbit was sitting and slipped into the chair next to him. "Okay, tell me again. What did he do?"

"He passed his hand over her eyes and when he took it away they were closed. But..."

"He actually closed her eyes."

"Yes, you know like folk do when someone dies."

"Was she?"

"Was she what Sir?"

"Dead. Was she dead?"

"Oh no, she was alive."

"Are you absolutely sure of that?"

"Yes Sir. She was still breathing," the officer said emphatically.

"Right." Gray stood, then turned back to the Sergeant.

"You're positive she wasn't dead?"

"Positive, Detective."

"Did she move at all after he gave her the drug?"

"No."

"How quickly did the drug take effect?"

"Almost instantly. It was damn quick."

Gray gave Dr. Rashid a questioning glance. "Thoughts, Ben?"

"Could have been anything, Gray."

"To have worked that fast."

"There are a vast number of drugs that will put one into a deep sleep in seconds."

Gray continued to pace. "Then what happened, Officer?"

"Once she was on the gurney, he rolled her out of the room. I asked him how long she would be and he said about two hours. I decided to go for a walk and stretch my legs. I did comment on how potent the stuff seemed."

"What did he say?"

"Nothing."

"What time did he leave with Sally?"

"About *9:15*."

Gray returned to his seat and asked a few more questions of the officer. "When did you realize there might be a problem?"

"At about *12:40*."

"What did you do then?"

"I walked to the nurse's station to see if there *was* a problem."

"Then what happened?"

"The nurse made a couple of calls and that was when the shit hit the fan, Sir."

"What did you do?"

"I went downstairs to main Security. They said no one pushing a gurney had left the hospital."

"Okay, Nesbit, you may go."

"May I return to District, Detective?"

"Sure. There is nothing left to guard. I will want to talk to you again." The officer got up then paused.

"There was something else rather strange."

"What was that?"

"When the guy gave Sally the shot, you asked me if she was unconscious. Before he closed them, her eyes were wide open but blank like eyes of a dead person, seeing nothing, staring straight at the ceiling. I'm not sure I'm making myself very clear, Detective. It was weird to see and I can't really describe it. Sort of like dead but not dead, if you get my meaning. And like I said, her eyes were wide open, very wide until he closed them. It was spooky." Again Gray looked at Dr. Rashid who nodded in response.

"Thank you, Officer." After he left, Gray rested in his chair and closed his eyes. "What are your thoughts on all this, Ben?"

"I'm not too sure, Gray; there are a number of possible explanations."

"Hey, Ben, help me out here, throw me a bone."

"The first thing that comes to mind is a drug called Succinylcholine. It is a compound that renders the victim completely immobile but conscious. It is a neuromuscular blocking agent and kills the individual in quick time because it shuts down all muscular activity. In the hands of a killer it is a deadly substance. But if the nurse saw Sally breathing, it couldn't have been that."

"That name's familiar. I have read about it." He glanced at Paul. "Isn't that the drug Justin suggested may have been used in the killings?"

"Yes. The Medical Examiner, Justin Davenport, said the killer could have injected his victims with 'SUX' was how he referred to it..."

"That's the abbreviated name," Gray added.

"He said he might have used that. He also suggested potassium chloride. He said both are extremely difficult, almost impossible, to detect."

"He's right. Succinylcholine will kill virtually without a trace, KCl...potassium chloride...the same. There are other drugs that react similarly and won't necessarily kill the victim, at least not right away. He could have put a cocktail of drugs together; it all depends on how much this character knows. Hell, there are thousands of drugs out there that will do whatever you wish if you know what you're doing. But the majority of them can be detected. Real nice fella you have wandering about this city, Gray."

"Tell me about it. I wish we could rope him in. Well, Ben, I think we're through for the moment, but there are going to be a bunch of our guys wandering about for a while asking questions and digging around Sally's room. I apologize in advance for the inconvenience but I'm afraid it's necessary."

"I understand, Gray, although I won't like it much. Do me one favor, will you?"

"Sure, what's that?"
"Get this guy off the streets and behind bars."
"Believe me I would love nothing more, Ben. By the way, not a word of this gets out. Tell your staff to say nothing to anyone, absolutely nothing. The press will only get a short statement. You know what they're like."
"Only too well. But, Gray, they're going to want to know something, what should we tell them?" Rashid asked.
"We don't want the killer to know what we know so tell them one of your patients walked out."
"Okay, that will work; it wouldn't be the first time."
Gray glanced at his watch. "Good. Well, I'm going home to finish my lunch with my daughter, though it's more like dinner now." Reluctantly, Gray left the hospital. He wanted answers but there were none. The killer had Sally, but where had he taken her, and how had he managed to get her out of the hospital undetected?

▼▼▼▼▼ **9**

The normal daily activity in a hospital was almost overbearing. Add to it the confusion of teams of investigators floating from one area to another and the hospital was plunged into chaos. And if that wasn't enough, there were the inquisitive patients. Gray watched in apprehension, his gut telling him they were wasting their time, that all they would find would be years of accumulated hospital dust.

Gray stepped out of Sally's room into a hall filled with chaos. Police, detectives, Forensic techs, hospital staff and patients were scurrying in all directions. Down the hall Paul was talking to Yoshi. Paul called him over. "Gray, we may have something."

As Gray approached the two men, he addressed Yoshi. "You talked to Security about traffic in and out?"

"Yes, Gray. There's only one vehicle of interest. A white van from a company called *'Perfect-Pile Carpet Cleaning Service'* arrived at the main gate at *8:43A.M.*"

"Carpet cleaning service on a Sunday?"

Yoshi frowned. "Exactly."

"Did you get a description of the driver?"

"The guard said he didn't pay close attention to him. He was more interested in what was in the van."

"Figures. What time did he leave?"

"Van pulled out at *9:46.*"

"Did they check it then?"

"Yes, Gray."

"And?"

"It was empty," Yoshi said.

"Damn. In at *8:43A.M.*, took Sally from her room at *9:10* and left empty at *9:46*. He was here barely an hour. Where was he between *9:10* and *9:46*? Yoshi, let's try to find out where he was for those 36 minutes." Gray was trying desperately to fight his frustration.

Paul interrupted. "Gray, I had Security pull all the video tapes."

"Find anything?"

"I've only managed to view the one from the service entrance so far. It shows pretty much what we already know. The security camera in the elevator was out of order, so we have no idea where he went with the rug."

"Did the camera pick up the floor he went to?"

"They're not elevated enough to pick up the floor numbers."

"He was here for about 20 minutes before he showed up on this floor. That's two time gaps that must be filled." Gray's cell phone rang.

"Excuse me a moment, Paul...Farlon."

"Gray, this is Rick Shelby."

"I can't talk now, Rick, I'm in the middle of a crisis..."

"But I need to see you right away."

"Unless it's urgent, I don't have time right now."

"I believe it's urgent. I'll come up there."

"Okay, when you get here, call me and I'll meet you in the cafeteria."

"I'll see you in about half an hour." Gray hung up.

"What was that all about?" Paul asked.

"Shelby, apparently he has something that warrants our immediate attention."

"He's coming up here?"

"Yes. Okay, let's proceed. How long has the camera on the service elevator been out?" Gray strolled down the hall toward the elevator.

"Security said it failed yesterday. It's due for repair tomorrow."

Paul and Yoshi followed Gray. "That was convenient."

"Damn, this guy's been busy."

"You think he sabotaged the camera, Gray?"

"I would bet my life on it."

"The guy who carried the rug into the hospital, and the doctor who emerged on the 14th floor were not the same guys, Gray."

"Trust me, Yoshi, they were. This guy is a master of deception and disguise."

Yoshi looked at Gray, confused. "Then where did he go for that 20 minutes?"

"The cameras on each of the floors swing a 45° arc. They cover the entire floor."

"That is not quite the case, Gray."

"Explain, Yoshi." Yoshi made a quick sketch.

The River Styx

"We have found there is a ten second blind spot at every elevator every 50 seconds. It's a flaw in the system, one that's gone unnoticed until now," Paul added.

Gray stopped and ran his hand over his mouth as he mulled over what Yoshi had just said. "Okay, so our friend was able to use that ten seconds to his advantage. He must have spent some time here staking out the place."

"So where the hell did the kidnapper do his work?"

"I don't know. In the elevator?"

"No, Yoshi. An elevator tied up for that long would have been checked." Gray paced, his hands buried deep in his pockets.

"What are you thinking, Gray?"

Gray stopped in front of the elevator. "How many floors in this building?"

"Twenty-five in this wing." Yoshi snapped his fingers. "That's it and the top three floors are being renovated."

"Then that's where he had to have gone."

"But at the moment the elevators don't go to those floors, Gray."

"Not the regular elevators, Yoshi, but the service elevator does."

"You're right, and that's the one without a working camera."

"Get up there, Yoshi. See what you can find. I doubt he left any clues but you never can tell."

"I'll take a couple of guys."

"Search those floors top to bottom and check the roof. Also have someone check on that van. We have to know if it's connected to Sally's disappearance." Gray's cell phone rang again.

"Farlon."

"Gray, Rick. I'm downstairs in the cafeteria."

"Give me five minutes, Rick, and I'll be there." Just then Carrie walked up.

"Hi guys, anything new?"

"We may have a lead on where our guy went when he left this floor, Carrie."

"Yoshi, you got something to do?"

"Sure, Gray."

"Then what the hell are you standing around here for?"

"On my way."

"And Yoshi, if you find anything, I'll be in the cafeteria."

"Right."

"Okay Paul, let's go see what is on Shelby's mind. Carrie, we'll be back, hold the fort for a while."

"Sure thing, Gray."

10

Gray and Paul found Rick Shelby seated in a booth. They slipped into the seat opposite the doctor.

"So, Rick, what brings you here?" Shelby reached into his jacket pocket, withdrew a small buff colored envelope and handed it to Gray. Gray took it and stared at it for a moment thinking it looked so insignificant.

He looked up somewhat surprised. "This is it?"

"Open it Gray."

Gray flipped open the envelope and a sliver of paper floated to the table. He turned it over and was now looking at a note. He began to read.

> *This is my daughter Sally. I am leaving her with you, as I am unable to care for her. Please take care of her and make sure she finds a good h God bless you. Her name is Sally Mayfield born on September 12, 19*

When he finished, he looked at Rick. "Is this…?"

"The note from the pendant you sent us, yes."

Paul took the note from Gray and read it. "So her name is definitely Sally Mayfield."

"Maybe, maybe not."

"What are you getting at?"

"I'll get to that in a moment. As you can see, we were able to determine the month and day but not the year."

Gray glanced at the note again. "We know she is in her twenties."

Paul handed the note back to Gray. "This is great. Okay, what did you mean when you said yes and no?"

"We ran a series of carbon dating tests on the paper, the ink, and the pendant. We were unable to determine a date for either the paper or the ink. We are unsure of their age. We can't even guess."

"What are you driving at Rick?"

"The ink and paper appear to be a lot older than 25 years, Gray. We got one date result over 150. We ran 20 tests and got 20 different results. It's unheard of."

"What about the pendant?"

"The pendant is about 60 years old, possibly an heirloom."

"But nothing on the paper and the ink?"

"Sorry."

"Rick, I think we have covered enough. For the moment let's assume that our patient's name is Sally Mayfield and she was born sometime in the seventies."

"I thought carbon dating was accurate."

"Oh, it is Paul, but in this case something is completely amiss."

Paul twisted in his seat. "This may sound a little off the wall but what if the note didn't belong to Sally?"

Gray raised his eyebrows. "Paul, I think we should drop this for now. Finding Sally is foremost on our agenda. We can concern ourselves later with the age of the note and pendant."

"Fair enough, Gray."

-EPISODE 3-

Without The Pendulum

THE DARKEST HOUR

▼▼▼▼▼ *1*

March was coming to a close, Easter was just around the corner but winter was not yet ready to depart. Gray despised winter but loved this city; the idea of moving never entered his mind. Sadly, it was another year without his Gwynne, but Julia was back and he was happy.

Although his days were full with so much to do, the excitement of the work didn't flow through his veins as it once had. The only light that burned brightly was Julia; everything else was dim by comparison. She was his breath of spring. He stood before the large window in his office and gazed over the city he loved so much. Motionless, hands buried deep in his pockets, his thoughts drifted to Maitland.

Are you the one we're after? If so, we'll soon drop the net and haul you in. If you are, we know where you live. If you're the one, the devil can stand in line because your miserable life and soul are mine. You'll get enough rope to hang yourself. Rest assured that sooner or later we'll get you. You can't hide forever. No matter where you go, we'll find you. From now on I'm going to be right on your heels.

His soliloquy over, he turned from the panoramic view. As he crossed the room, the phone on his desk sprang to life. He reached for it. "Farlon."

"Gray, Paul. You may want to see what we have found on these security tapes."

"I'll be right there." He replaced the receiver and headed for the War Room.

"Gray, come in. Take a look at this." Gray crossed the room and took a seat. The 52 inch flat screen monitor at one end of the room was displaying static.

"What's so interesting?"

"The first thing we confirmed was that the guy who delivered the carpet left as the guard said and took nothing with him."

"So he's not our man?"

"I didn't say that. All I'm saying is he left empty-handed. There are other ways to disguise a body."

"No doubt. Okay let's take a look at what you have."

"If the driver and our spurious doctor are one and the same, then we have something. He enters the service elevator in the basement at *8:46A.M.* Fourteen minutes later he appears on the 14th floor. At *9:10* he's back on the elevator with Sally. The next time we see him he emerges from the service elevator at *9:44*. That's 34 minutes after he left this floor. It took him over twice as long to leave."

"I wouldn't call that too unusual since he had to get rid of Sally if he wasn't taking her out in the van."

"Sure, Gray, then where is she? He never came back for her. No gurney is pushed from an elevator during those 37 minutes. Another thing is that there was no order placed for carpets to be cleaned in the building."

"Why am I not surprised? Okay, it looks suspicious, but you're going to have to come up with a lot more than that, Paul, I'm not convinced, so convince me. What about the van? What about the morgue?"

"Still looking. The morgue saw no activity on Sunday. Here's something else that's odd. At *11:53* on the night of March 12, the day that object in Sally's hand disappeared, every security camera and almost every piece of electrical or electronic equipment was disrupted for one and one half seconds."

Gray looked unimpressed. "So they had a..."

Paul interrupted him. "That's not all. The day Sally was abducted, at precisely *9:23A.M.* and again at *9:29*, it happened again, and again it lasted one and one half seconds."

"What are you trying to tell me, Paul?"

"I have no idea, Gray. It's just that...well it's one hell of a coincidence that the interference should occur at those particular times."

"I'm sorry, Paul, but I still don't see the connection."

"Neither do I. But I believe there is one and we're going to find it."

"Good, and let me know when you do."

"You don't appear too enamored with the news."

"If I knew what it all meant I might be, but I see nothing of intrinsic value. Electrical interruptions are not uncommon."

"I agree, but just when Sally is being abducted, when..."

"Paul, tell me what you're implying and I'll listen because at the moment, I fail to see the point."

"Gray, for crying out loud, humor me. I'm just saying I believe there's a connection and we're going to find it. Look at the tapes." Paul was frustrated.

"Okay, play them through." Gray, Paul, Yoshi, Mario and Carrie all sat and watched. At the conclusion Gray looked at Paul.

"So you believe the driver and our phony doctor are the same person?"

"Yes," Paul said with confidence.

"Why?"

"Primarily because of the timing. It all fits together."

"No other reason?"

"I know it's not much, but I believe it all fits, Gray."

Gray turned to Mario. "Go back to where the driver steps out of the elevator." Mario obliged. "Now zoom in on his shoes. Closer...enhance the area around the toe." The picture kept getting larger but grainier. "Stop. Look at the toe of the shoe." Gray got out of his chair and stepped up to the large screen. "Here...he's wearing wingtips, certainly not the shoes of a delivery guy. Now go back to our illustrious doctor exiting the elevator on the 14th floor."

"You see something, Gray?"

"Possibly." Mario found the spot. "Focus on the toe of the right shoe and augment." Mario repeated the exercise.

"Well, well, well, I'll be...it's the same shoe. How the hell did you know, Gray?"

"I didn't. I assumed that if they were one and the same he might change his clothing, but not his shoes. The shoes look new and expensive, definitely not the kind of shoe a carpet cleaner or delivery person would wear."

"So I was right. I told you they were the same guy."

"Perhaps you are right, but for the wrong reasons. This proves we're dealing with the same man, but there is still nothing to say he took Sally. We need proof...we need a body."

"The guy did his work, changed, took care of Sally and whatever else he did on the 24th floor."

"Then our bogus driver/doctor is a master of disguise."

"It certainly appears that way, Carrie." Gray turned to leave.

Paul eyed him as he reached the door. "Where are you going?"

"Back to my office. When you have something more concrete, call me. What you have here is a great leap forward, but it won't put our killer behind bars." Gray walked out of the War Room.

▼▼▼▼▼ 2

They were about to take their biggest gamble. Gray and Paul drove to Maitland Manor and virtually demanded Maitland accompany them downtown. Gray knew it was a rash move but in desperation men were prone to rash decisions. Despite the lack of evidence, they had to eliminate every possibility. Gray had to determine whether or not it was Maitland.

An hour later they had Maitland in an interrogation room firing questions at him, searching for some damning evidence, but it was not forthcoming.

"Am I under arrest?"

"I have already told you, Mr. Maitland, you are not under arrest."

"Then for the record please note I'm protesting this action but am cooperating."

Gray sighed with agitation. "It's noted."

"Good, step out of line and I will sue the pants off you guys."

"We get your point. Now what were you doing in Hong Kong?" Paul asked.

"I make periodic buying trips to different parts of the world and Hong Kong happens to be one of them," Maitland responded with an air of indignation.

"Whose idea was it that you visit Hong Kong?"

"I'm not following you."

"Who suggested you make those trips?"

"No one. If I am looking for a specific item, I select the area where I might find it and make the trip."

"And what was so interesting in Hong Kong?"

"I'm an antiquities dealer and collector, Detective. I was looking for something very rare."

Paul hovered over Maitland like a vulture waiting for death. "What specifically?"

"A certain Buddha."

"What's so special about it?"

"It was an item that was believed to be non-existent. I did not believe it."

"You made six trips to Hong Kong hoping to find something that everyone believed did not exist?"

"It does exist. I just had to do the convincing, and it was only four trips."

"And all you did each time you were there was search for this Buddha?"

"That and a little sightseeing, yes."

Paul changed direction. "Where is Sally Mayfield?"

"Who?"

"The woman you abducted from the hospital. Where is she?"

"I have no idea what you're talking about."

"Bullshit! You're lying! What have you done with her? You get your rocks off killing beautiful women, Maitland?" Paul had had enough of Maitland's belligerent attitude.

"Paul, let the man talk. If he's lying, we'll soon find out."

"I'm not lying...I have nothing to hide. What the hell are you idiots driving at anyway?" Paul placed his palms on the table and leaned close, his nose only inches from Maitland's.

"We're suggesting, slime ball, that you know something about the murders taking place in this city."

"You honestly believe that? You have to be out of your minds. Don't you have something better to do than harass innocent citizens? If you're going to make accusations, I want my lawyer."

"Did I accuse you of anything?"

"Yes, you're implying I have killed someone."

"Not one...seven. We want answers, got that?" Paul straightened.

"Where were you last week?" Gray asked.

Maitland snapped back. "Right here."

"Wrong answer. Your car was in the garage but the house was as barren as an Egyptian tomb..."

"You went into my home without permission..."

"We had a search warrant." Gray knew he was skating on thin ice.

Paul jumped into the arena. "Answer the damned question! Where were you? Your own security people have no record of you leaving or returning. Unless you were fricking invisible or hiding under the rug, you were not home."

"I most certainly was. I resent you people spying on me! What I do in my home is my affair! That's invasion of privacy!"

"Privacy, hell! It all becomes public when people start dying around you!" Paul had run out of patience.

"Let's get back to Sally Mayfield. Tell us where you're keeping her." Gray watched Maitland closely but he didn't flinch, blink or react to the question.

"Look, I don't know this woman." Gray stared at Maitland. If he was lying, he was doing a great job, but he might also be telling the truth.

"Yes you do, so tell us…where is she?"

Maitland threw his hands up in despair. "You guys are unbelievable. You're both nuts. Your ineptitude is getting you nowhere so you're going to pin blame on the person who buckles under your interrogation."

"We didn't pick you out of the phonebook. We have this nice picture of you pushing a patient on a gurney." Gray thought he saw a hint of interest in Maitland's eyes, but he couldn't be sure.

Maitland laughed. "You guys *are* crazy."

"If you killed those women, Maitland, I'm going to nail your ass to the wall. I don't give a damn how rich you are or how much weight you carry. If you're guilty, you'll fry."

"What am I doing here, anyway? I've done nothing so just back off."

"We're going to get to the bottom of this, Maitland."

"You have nothing on me and you know it. I have told you all I know and it's all the truth."

"Truth! You wouldn't know the truth if it bit you in the ass!"

"Enough! You got a good memory, Maitland?" Gray asked.

"Darn sight better than yours, Farlon."

Gray stood and leaned over the table toward Maitland. "Good. Where the hell were you the night of January 21?" His voice rose to a shout.

"How the hell am I supposed to remember what I did one particular night over two months ago?"

"I don't have a problem remembering that far back."

"Well aren't you just the mastermind. You..."

Gray interrupted him "A smart guy like you, come on. You just said you have a good memory. So don't bullshit us. What were you doing January 21?" A knock at the door interrupted the interrogation. Gray opened it to see Carrie.

"Gray, sorry to interrupt, but I thought you might want to see these." She handed him five photos as he stepped out of the room and closed the door behind him. He looked at them one at a time then handed them back to Carrie.

"What are they?"

"These are photos of the medallion, the one I mentioned to you."

"Oh, the one that goes with the Buddha."

"Right, this Buddha." She held up a photo of a seated Buddha. "These were taken in Maitland's place the same night that object disappeared from Sally's hand." Gray grabbed the photos of the medallion again, this time looking at them closely. The medallion was a silver disc with a dragon encircling it. The disc had an inner and outer band. The outer band, about a quarter of an inch wide, was darker with eight clear gems spaced equidistant apart. In the inner disk were four small emeralds and set equidistant between them was four large rubies.

In the center of the medallion was a large red gem that he assumed was a ruby. Gray studied the medallion closely and realized the patterns on the dragon were identical to those on the object Sally held in her hand. He looked up at Carrie then back at the photos.

He was hesitant to commit himself. "It could be a similar piece of jewelry."

Carrie stared at him. "It's the identical piece, Gray."

"Not possible."

Carrie insisted. "The scale patterns, the deep scratch on the dragon's front leg. This is not a coincidence, Gray. It's the same medallion."

"That can't be Carrie. The time-frame contradicts that."

"That I cannot answer, but this is the exact piece Sally held in her hand. I'll stake my reputation on it."

"You may have to. Look, I have to get back in there. Let's talk about this later."

"Fine, but I know I'm right."

Gray stepped back into the interrogation room and closed the door.

Maitland looked up. "Unless you intend to arrest me, I'm leaving." He made a move to get up. Paul stepped closer and shoved him back into the chair.

"Look you sick son of a bitch, you're not going anywhere until you tell us what we want to know. Either we get some answers or I'll rearrange your face. Am I making myself clear?" Paul stepped back from the table.

"Quite, Detective. I believe you're threatening me."

Paul glared at Maitland. "Threatening? Hell, I haven't even begun. You'll know when I'm threatening. No, I'm making you a promise, you bastard..."

"I have no idea..."

"Shut the hell up. Just answer the damn questions."

"Ask and I'll see what I can do."

"You're a real smart ass, Maitland, you know that? All you've done so far is dance around the answers. Now where the hell were you on the night of January 21?" Paul growled.

"I don't know. Most likely in New York." It was an answer that took Gray and Paul a little by surprise.

Paul dropped into a chair opposite Maitland. "New York? Why New York?"

"I attend conventions and banquets periodically. I attended three in January, but I can't remember the exact dates," Maitland said smugly.

Gray bit his tongue then slammed a photo on the table, pushed it toward Maitland and barked. "Know her?"

Maitland glanced at the photo then glared at Gray "Never seen her before. Who is she?"

Paul got up and paced the room nervously, itching to get his hands on Maitland. His temper was raging. As he passed the table, he stabbed his finger at the photo and yelled at Maitland.

"That's Juanita Rodriguez, the woman you killed on January 21!"

"I've told you, I never killed anyone and I have never seen her."

"Sure you have," Gray snapped.

"Sorry."

"How did you kill her?"

"For God's sake, I keep telling you that I didn't kill anyone."

"We don't believe you," Paul smirked.

"Get this through your thick heads! Just because I do not know where I was on a particular night does not make me a killer!"

"No, but in my book it makes you a damn good suspect." Paul was having a hard time controlling his temper.

"You have absolutely nothing to pin on me, Salvatore, so why don't you go find someone else to harass."

"You're a piece of work, Maitland."

"Where did you get the medallion?"

"I have already told you."

"How did it get damaged?"

"How should I know? It was scratched when I bought it if that's what you're referring to."

"And you bought it in Hong Kong?"

"I told you I did."

"You're lying!"

Finally Maitland exploded. "That's it, I've had enough verbal abuse from you people! If you want to talk to me again, contact my lawyer! And stay away from me and my house!" Maitland threw the chair aside and made for the door.

"Mr. Maitland." Maitland stopped, turned and faced Gray.

"What?"

"Do you always wear wingtip shoes?" Maitland glanced down then back at Gray.

Without another word he turned, opened the door, slammed it behind him and stormed out of the station. The two detectives watched him leave. They knew they couldn't hold him. Paul had tried to aggravate him but failed. He was visibly upset and Gray knew if the confrontation hadn't ended then, Paul would have torn Maitland limb from limb.

"I liked the bit about the shoes. Very subtle."

"They're not unusual, Paul, but it's a coincidence worth mentioning."

"He didn't flinch. The man's a cool customer."

"Or he's simply innocent."

Paul slammed his fist on the table then, in angry frustration, pointed at the closed door. "Innocent, hell, that son of a bitch is as guilty as sin. He killed those women. I know damn well he did. He just sat there as frigid as a fricking iceberg, knowing we have absolutely nothing we can pin on him. What the hell are we to do now, Gray?"

"Paul, calm down. If he's guilty, we'll get him."

"If...if he's guilty? For crying out loud, he wreaks of guilt, Gray!"

"Maybe, but for the moment we have no proof."

"Okay, so Maitland is back on the streets. How do we stop him?"

"We don't."

"We don't?"

"No."

"We just let him go?"

"No, we're having him followed. But if he is our man, I have my doubts he will kill again soon."

"You do? Why? What makes you so sure?"

"Well, let's say, not in this city."

"What makes you say that?"

"Call it a hunch."

"We're going to let him walk on a hunch?"

"Not at all. If he's our man, we'll get him. Besides he's concerned."

"You think he's only concerned?"

"Yes. Maitland doesn't ruffle easily, as you have just observed. I'll guarantee you, if he's guilty, he'll be taking short steps while looking over his shoulder from now on."

"Then we have to find something more concrete, something that is still out there."

"We'll find it soon enough."

"I sure as hell hope so."

▼▼▼▼▼ *3*

"Damn it, we need leads." Gray was desperate and the case was moving far too slowly. "Sally is out there and if we have to, we'll tear this city apart brick by brick to find her before that maniac does her more harm."

"Gray, we're doing the best we can, but nothing has surfaced." Gray, Paul and Carrie were walking through the lobby of District 3.

"I understand, Paul, but is there nothing more to help this move quicker?"

Paul stopped. "Gray, we found the gurney, we found the toolbox, but no prints. There's the doctor's coat with the nametag. But how he got her out of the building, well..."

They continued walking. "Did he get her out?"

Carrie shot him a quizzical look. "What do you mean Gray?"

"Carrie, Sally's abduction could not have gone unnoticed. Therefore, if no one saw her being taken from the hospital, she must still be there."

Carrie stopped and faced Gray. "But where? How can you hide a body in a hospital?" They all stopped.

"Where could you hide a body in plain sight?"

"If we assume she's dead, the morgue."

Gray, agitated, was playing with his car keys. "Right. Has anyone looked there?"

"No. We're banking on her still being alive."

"That's great, Paul, but what if she's not?"

Carrie nodded. "It would be the last place anyone would look. But what if she *is* alive?"

"Let's proceed by elimination. Check the morgue."

Carrie ran her hand through her long black hair. "If that's the case, Gray, he didn't have to get her out, someone could do it for him."

"That would work. Carrie's right, Gray. It has been four days since Sally's abduction. Things have quieted down. That would give the guy every opportunity to move the body."

"I doubt it. This guy's a loner. He trusts no one. Why don't you two go to the morgue."

Carrie turned toward the elevator. "We're on it. Paul, are you coming?"

"Right behind you Carrie."

"If you find anything, call me immediately."

"Will do, Gray, but I'm hoping we don't." Carrie and Paul entered the parking garage, got into Carrie's car and drove to the morgue.

"I'm not too thrilled about this, Paul."

"Me neither. I only hope to hell Sally's not there."

"It has been twelve weeks since the killer struck. As methodical and persistent as he is, he has to be foaming at the mouth to kill again. If Sally's not dead, I would say she has little time left."

"You're probably right, Carrie."

In the morgue they headed for the autopsy room. Carrie could never get used to the smell, and besides, the place gave her the creeps.

"Okay, let's see if she's here," Paul said as he opened the door and allowed Carrie to enter first. A man with his back to them was working on a corpse. At the sound of footsteps, he turned.

"May I help you?"

"Detective Salvatore and Detective Simpson," said Paul as the two flashed their badges. "We have come to see if we could identify a body."

"Dr. Wendell Jones." He removed his visor and gloves and stepped away from the table. "We have loads of bodies, Detective, anyone in particular?"

"A woman with blond hair, blue eyes, about five feet tall, covered in scars...has a crescent shaped birthmark on her left thigh. She may have been brought in three days ago." Jones dropped his instruments on a cart and walked over to a large chart on the adjacent wall.

"Three days, you say? I'm not sure, let's see. Twenty-three bodies have come in over the last three days."

"Could be two or three days."

"Was the individual from the hospital?"

"Yes."

"Well, that narrows it to eight; three male and five female. Okay, Drawers 44, 21, 27, 10, and 17. Let's see who's here. Drawer 44." Dr. Jones walked over, took hold of the handle, opened it and pulled the sheet back. It was a woman possibly in her sixties.

"Definitely not her." They opened all five. Sally was not here.

"Is there any possibility a body could be placed in here without your or anyone else's knowledge?"

The doctor gave Paul an indignant look. "Absolutely not. We maintain excellent records, Detective."

"I'm not suggesting you don't, Doctor. I'm asking if it's possible for someone to sneak a body in here, place it in a drawer and have it go undetected?"

"I suppose it could happen, we have 60 cold drawers and we seldom see more than half of them filled."

"Could we check the drawers that are empty just to...?"

"You want me to open every empty drawer to see if a...Detective I have better things to do with my time."

Carrie stepped in front of the doctor, his towering six foot plus frame dwarfing Carrie's five foot two. Paul smiled to himself. "This is a matter of life and death, Doctor, so please quit griping and start opening the drawers. There is no time for discussion."

The doctor grunted and in anger turned back to the chart. "Then stand here and read me the numbers, the boxes without X's in them." Carrie planted herself before the large chart and began reading the numbers as instructed. Twenty minutes later all the drawers had been checked and all were empty.

Paul walked back to where Carrie was standing. "Doctor, is there any other area where we might look?"

"No. All of them come here."

"Where is Doctor Davenport?" Carrie asked.

"He's upstairs in a meeting."

"How about Doctor Samantha Perry?"

"Out on a call."

Paul and Carrie stepped to the door. "Dr. Jones, thank you for your cooperation and your time." The two detectives left the morgue.

"She's not here which means there's a better chance she's still alive."

"Then we must find her quickly."

"That's easier said than done, Paul."

"Damn it, there's a team out there looking for her. The posters went out this morning and the papers published her photo. We have every area covered. Let's hope something turns up."

▼▼▼▼▼ 4

It had only been three days since they had questioned Maitland when Paul received two disturbing pieces of information. The first came with a phone call.

"Salvatore."

"Detective, this is Don Redford with Surveillance Team Alpha." Team Alpha was posted at the front gate of Maitland's estate.

"Sure, Don, what's up?"

"I thought you should know that a white van from *'Perfect-Pile Carpet Cleaning Service'* has just entered Maitland Manor."

"What's so unusual about...what name did you say?"

"*Perfect-Pile Carpet Cleaning Service*. It's the same van that was seen leaving the hospital when..."

Paul sat up in his chair. "You sure it's the same company?"

"Same company and the exact same van."

"What do you mean the exact same van, Don?"

"When I viewed the security tapes last week, I noticed there was a light connector on the right side of the tow-hook assembly. This van has the same assembly." Paul relaxed a little.

"A million vans like that have tow hooks, Don."

"True but they don't have the same body damage."

"Are you certain?"

"Positive, Detective, I'd stake my reputation on it."

"Stay put. We're on our way." Paul hung up and looked at his watch. It was ten minutes to five. He called Gray.

"It appears our boy's making a move, Gray." Paul explained the situation. He was almost finished when his other line rang.

"Gray, hang on a second. I have another call...Salvatore."

"Paul, Mario. I have just received some interesting information. Some guy called here about five minutes ago, said he thought he saw someone loading a body into a white van in the parking lot behind the Merchandise Mart. I don't..." Paul was already moving. "Did they get his name and phone number?"

"Surprisingly, yes."

"Call the guy back, find out if there were any markings on the van, then meet me downstairs in five minutes." He switched lines. "Gray, you there?"

"Yeah, what's going on?"

"Meet me downstairs. It appears we might have a live one."

"What?"

"I'm leaving now. I'll explain when I see you."

"Are we going somewhere?"

"Maitland Manor."

"Oh...okay." Paul hung up as he dashed around his desk and out of his office. He then grabbed his cell phone and called Carrie.

"Carrie, find Yoshi and Mario and meet me downstairs. And ask Mario to pick up a search warrant for Maitland's place."

"What's up, Paul?"

"No time to explain, just find Yoshi and get that search warrant."

"Will do." He caught the elevator just as the doors were closing.

As the two vehicles raced toward the Gold Coast, Paul explained the situation to Gray.

"What are you expecting to find, Paul?"

"A body I hope, Gray. We have to catch this bastard red handed. This could be our chance."

"Right, and we could just as easily end up with egg on our faces when we find some guy laying new carpet."

"Possibly, but we can't let this go."

"I'm not saying to let it go Paul, but do you think converging on him like this is a wise idea?"

"Gray, we're not converging, we're investigating and if there is a body in that place, I want to find it."

"Do you think it's going to take five detectives to do that? I think you're sticking your neck out a little here."

"Not if our information is correct. A witness saw someone putting something into a white van. He also saw the same individual placing labels on that van. Twenty-five minutes later a white van, and not just any white van, one from the same carpet cleaning company seen at the hospital, entered Maitland's place. In my book that constitutes the need for action."

"The evidence is convincing, Paul, but be aware of what Maitland will do if you're wrong."

"I understand, Gray, but we can't lose this opportunity."

"I hope to God you're right."

"Since when have you been so cautious?"

"This is logic more than caution." They pulled up outside the Manor gates. Paul and Gray emerged from their car and Paul walked toward the gatehouse. "I'll have security open the gates." Gray, skeptical about the entire affair, went with him. As they approached the gatehouse, a guard appeared."

"Can I help you?"

Paul flashed his badge. "Detective Salvatore and Detective Farlon, CPD."

The River Styx

"What can I do for you, Detectives?"

"We need you to open the gates right now."

"But we can't..."

"I don't want to hear that. Get back in the gatehouse and open these gates. Am I making myself clear?"

"Quite, but..."

"You want me to arrest you for obstructing justice?"

"Okay, okay, you've made your point." The guard disappeared into the gatehouse and a few seconds later the gates began to swing open. Gray and Paul got back into the car and raced up the long asphalt driveway with Carrie hot on their bumper. The vehicles stopped in front of the large luxurious mansion. The five detectives got out of their cars and walked to the front door.

They stopped before the solid double wood doors with their ornate brass fittings. "Now what Paul?"

"Let's see what's inside."

"Do we knock or bust the door down?"

"Damn it, Gray, give me some credit." Paul rang the doorbell. A few moments later the maid opened the door.

"Yes?"

"We are here to see Mr. Maitland." Paul pushed past the maid who looked dumbfounded and very agitated.

"Excuse me, Sir, but Mr. Maitland is..." The rest of the group followed much to her dismay. As she closed the door, Maitland appeared at the top of the wide staircase.

"Well, I might have known. Don't you people ever knock?"

Paul pointed with his thumb. "We rang the doorbell."

"Would you mind explaining what you're doing in my home?"

"We want to know what you're doing with a van that was last seen at Memorial a few days ago. The same van, I might add, from the same company?"

Maitland descended the stairs. "Salvatore, are you accusing me of something? Because if that's the reason you're here, I would suggest you start updating your resume. I warned you the last time you forced your way into my home that if you did it again, I would have you busted."

"Where's the van, Maitland?"

"What van?"

"You know damned well what van. Carrie, Mario, Yoshi, search this place from attic to basement."

"You are doing no such thing! You have no right..."

Paul pulled the search warrant from his jacket and passed it to Maitland. "Wrong. This gives us the right." Maitland reluctantly took the document and glanced at it.

"What are you expecting to find, Detective?"

"I'm not sure, but we will find something."

"Oh, I have no doubt of that." The detectives proceeded to make a thorough search of the mansion. Half an hour later the five gathered in the lobby at the bottom of the stairs.

Paul looked at them in anticipation. "Anything?"

"That depends on what you mean by anything."

"What have you got, Yoshi?"

"I found this under the bed in the master bedroom." He handed Paul a ring in a plastic evidence bag. It was small, gold, with a blue stone in a simple setting. Its size told him it most likely belonged to a woman.

"You found it under the bed? Nothing else, no body or any indication one was ever here?"

"Nothing Paul, not even a hint of one," Carrie responded.

"I did find the van. It's parked in the back. It's clean. The driver said he had just returned a rug."

"Are you people satisfied now?" Maitland emerged from a door across the foyer. "Now that you know there is nothing here, would you all get out of my house."

"Not so fast, Maitland." Paul held up the bag containing the ring. "Is this yours?"

"I have been looking for that for days. Where did you find it?" Maitland's reaction was perfect, but Paul sensed an underlying hesitation and concern.

"When did you last have it?"

"About three weeks ago." He went to reach for it but Paul withdrew it and placed the bag in his pocket.

"Evidence."

"Hey, that's mine. You can't just take it."

"As I said, it's evidence. We will return it once we have it checked and it is cleared."

"Suit yourself. But you will find nothing unusual about it." Gray walked toward the front door.

"Paul, I think we're through here."

"Yes we are."

"Mr. Maitland, sorry for the inconvenience, but we will be in touch to return your ring," Gray said.

"Fine." Maitland followed them to the door and closed it behind them.

Carrie stepped in beside Gray. "Mind if I ride back with you two?"

"Not at all, Carrie." The detectives returned to their cars. The group left Maitland Manor. As they drove back to the city, Carrie revealed another discovery.

"A woman was in that master bedroom, Gray."

"Are you sure Carrie?"

"Yes. Her perfume was in the air, not strong but noticeable. I would say she was there no more than an hour or two before we arrived."

"But there was no other sign she had been there?" Paul asked.

"Apart from the impression on the bed, the perfume and that ring, no."

Gray half turned in his seat. "Did you notice that when Maitland was asked about the ring, he said it belonged to him?"

"You're right, but it wouldn't fit him."

Paul glanced at Carrie in the rear view mirror. "That's true, Carrie, but it could still belong to him."

"I suppose. But why would he want a ring he couldn't wear?"

"When Paul confronted him on it, he hesitated and there was panic in his eyes."

"You saw that, Gray?"

"Yes, Carrie, I did. Something's going on here and I intend to find out what it is."

"What do you think it is, Gray?"

"I don't know, Carrie, but I believe there is a great deal buried deeper than we're digging. If we are going to confirm or eliminate Maitland, we must dig it up and expose it."

▼▼▼▼▼ 5

It was dark. Not a sound except her breathing. Sally had no idea where she was. She was terrified and in pain. One or two of her wounds had not fully healed and were causing her far more than minor discomfort. She was sitting with her feet and hands bound. Her back was against what felt like cold stone. She tried to remember what had happened. It had all been a blur and then it all came floating back.

A doctor had entered her room. He pushed a needle into her arm. She woke immediately only to discover she was completely paralyzed. The policeman who spent his days outside her room was also there. Together he and the doctor had lifted her onto another, smaller bed. She was then rolled from her room. Someone closed her eyes. But they did not stay closed. Lights passed overhead. They stopped and the doctor spoke to a nurse. She was then taken into a small room and the doors closed. Again she tried to move but could not. She could not blink and her mouth, arms and legs were paralyzed.

The doors opened and she was moved into an area that looked as if it were still being built. Suddenly she realized this man was not a doctor. He removed his white coat and threw it aside. He then laid something heavy on her chest. That was when she passed out. Now she was in this place where she could not see or hear a sound.

Then came the horrific almost deafening sounds. Alien sounds, demons gnashing and grinding their teeth and roaring in anger in the darkness. Sally was horrified and barely able to breathe. She began to sob. What was about to happen to her? She had no idea, but she was sure death was upon her. The noise grew louder. The demons descended with screeching and wailing. Then silence took over once more.

Next came the rattling of chains and screeching sounds. Sally cowered, drawing her legs up and wrapping her arms around them. She tried to make herself smaller, yet how could she hide from something so demonic? Then a voice floated out of the blackness.

"Hello, Sally. It's good to see you again. I'm sorry you have been so uncomfortable, but we will take care of that right now." Footsteps approached. Sally shook uncontrollably. Then a hand was on her ankles untying the ropes that bound her.

"There," said the voice. "That has to be better. Now your hands." Two hands took hold of her, turned her around and released her wrists.

"Sit back and relax. That's better now, isn't it?" Sally was speechless. What was this creature's plan? "I want you to listen carefully now. If you don't do exactly as I say, you will die. Do you understand?" Sally tried to speak, but her voice was imprisoned deep in her throat. She nodded.

"Good. You're on a small ledge. To your left is a bathroom with all you'll need. Do not try to go anywhere else. Do you understand?" Sally finally found her voice.

"I understand. Who are you? What are you going to do with me?"

"You don't remember? You and I had a wonderful time together. Then you spoiled it all by running away. You look very much better now. The doctors put you back together. I will take care of that later."

"You are the one who hurt me?"

"Oh, you're quick. Yes, but you enjoyed it. You shouldn't have run, Sally; you should not have hurt me. Now I must make an example of you." Sally's courage was gradually returning.

"You are a monster. How could you do these terrible things?"

"Believe me Sally, it gave me great pleasure. You have such a beautiful body that I could not resist making it better." Sally could not believe her ears. This had to be the Devil or his helper.

"You are a very sick, evil person."

"No, Sally, I'm not evil. It is my responsibility to punish beautiful women who soil society so they are unable to continue their sinful deeds."

"I don't understand."

"Of course you do."

"I do not know about what you are speaking."

His voice changed, becoming sinister and malevolent. "You and your kind degrade society with your filth. I'm changing that. I'm making it better..." He stopped. "Enough talking. I will come for you later. You'll get food. I don't want you looking disheveled and starved when your turn comes." The footsteps moved away. What followed turned her blood ice cold.

She heard the voice again...terrifying, inhuman and filled with hate. He was speaking to someone. "I think you are ready to meet your public." The air erupted with earsplitting screams. To her horror Sally realized there was another woman in this place. She was suffering great pain at the hands of this hideous creature. The screams continued, and Sally could only imagine what was happening. Then silence. A moment or two passed and the voice came again.

"That's much better, isn't it? You didn't need all these other parts. They were the cause of all your troubles. Now you can rest knowing your sins have been forgiven. It is time to go." Once again the terrifying silence. Then Sally heard footsteps and the sound of something being dragged. She began to cry quietly knowing death had just passed her by.

The clanking of the chains, gnashing of teeth, a roar, the clawing and grumbling of the devil's servants as they departed. Sally was left trembling with fear and cold. The sounds from hell slowly faded until the deafening silence embraced her once more. In the darkness Sally shivered. What was to become of her?

▼▼▼▼▼ 6

It was Julia's day to present Gray with a surprise.

"Morning, Daddy, how are you?" She slipped her arm through his and they walked to the elevator.

"All the better for seeing you. What brings you by so early? I thought you were supposed to be on your way back to New York?"

"I'm not ready to go back yet. In fact I'm seriously considering staying."

Gray was stunned. "Really?"

"Don't get your hopes up, but, yes, I've been giving it some thought. I may approach the local papers and see what they can offer me."

"That would be wonderful, Julia."

"Enough of that. I have something for you."

"Have you been waiting long?"

"About 15 minutes. I was talking to Paul." They made their way to Gray's office.

"I need my cup of coffee. Would you like one?"

"No thanks, I've had three cups since I got up this morning. By the way I hear you have a lead on your killer?" Gray was in the middle of pouring his coffee. In shocked disbelief he stopped and stared at Julia.

"Where the hell did you hear that?"

Julia smiled. "So it's true?"

"Hell, you really are a damned reporter..." Gray poured his coffee and they walked the rest of the way to his office. "You guessed?"

"I had a feeling you were holding out on me." There was disappointment in her voice.

"Julia, I would love nothing more than to give you a story. I'm sorry, but there's too much at stake."

"You have to protect your witness."

Again Gray was stunned. "Where...how did you know?"

"I have my sources."

Gray was angry. They stepped into his office and sat down. Gray placed his coffee cup on the desk and looked at Julia. "Not good enough."

"Oh come on, Daddy. Don't get so up tight. I promise I will not print this story until you give me the word."

"That's not the point. Damn it, Julia! This case...that witness' life is at stake. She could also be the key that ends this whole mess. Who told you?"

"You leave too much laying about on your desk."

"Julia, would you quit snooping."

"Sorry, but it's my job."

Gray sat down. "Not in this office."

"All right, I know you have a witness."

"We had a witness..."

"Had! But then you lost her."

"We didn't lose her exactly. She was abducted."

"Abducted, lost, same thing. You no longer have her. She could be dead."

"We're pretty certain she's not."

"How long was she in the hospital?"

"Since January 29th."

Julia gasped. "January 29th! You've had her that long and no one knew about her?"

"Apart from a handful of us, no."

"What happened?"

"We're not sure, but we believe it was her attacker."

"What's her name?"

"Sally Mayfield."

"What's her story?"

"She doesn't have one."

"What do you mean?"

"I mean she doesn't have one."

"Come on, Daddy, tell me about her."

"I'm being honest. There is nothing to tell. She's suffering from acute amnesia."

"She remembers nothing?"

"Nothing. We have no idea who she is, where she's from, or if her name really is Sally Mayfield."

"That's scary."

"It's very disheartening."

"So what happened?" Julia listened intently as Gray explained Sally's story.

"She wants revenge. That was probably what kept her going."

"Revenge for what, Julia? She has no recollection of what happened. She fought to survive but not for revenge. The revenge part may come later when she regains her memory. Changing the subject, you said you had something for me."

Julia lifted her briefcase onto her lap and removed a large envelope. "The other day I was looking at your crime board and noticed those seven photos and followed a hunch. I contacted a friend in Philadelphia who owes me a few favors. Two years ago seven women disappeared from up and down the east coast. The police were baffled. There were no leads at all. This friend was on that case and sent me information on the victims." Julia opened the envelope and passed Gray a number of photos.

"This is what he sent me." As Gray studied the photos, an icy chill trickled down his spine. He was staring at seven women with shoulder length blond hair.

"This is a little eerie."

"I bet. Their physical description is on the back. The only common denominator was their last John. The name, address and phone number were false. Each call to the service for each hooker was the same...the client's name, the type of girl requested, hair color, everything. He paid handsomely and got what he wanted."

Gray turned the first photo over and read what was written on the reverse. He was stunned. It was the same thing all over again. The same physical description, the same four-day gap, and they were all high-class hookers. Gray could hardly believe it. The odd thing was that they were from different cities. Two were from Philadelphia, one from Baltimore, two from DC, one from Atlantic City, and the seventh from Boston, but all on the east coast and all in June and July of 2000.

"This is bizarre. This guy gets around. It doesn't say where or how they were found."

"They never were. And here's something else you're going to find even more unsettling. A case, very similar to that, occurred up and down the California coast in 2001. Twelve women vanished and were never seen again. The real eerie thing, they all had the same basic physical description."

Shocked, Gray looked up from the photos. "You're sure none have turned up?"

"Not one from either case," Julia said.

"This is unbelievable." Gray thought for a moment. "What the hell is going on? We have women disappearing who never show up either dead or alive. We have women show up dead who have, as far as we know so at this point, never disappeared. I wish I could put my finger on it. We have nothing and there are no connections. It's just unbelievable."

"It is. Here are the details on the east coast case." Julia handed Gray a tan folder. He took it, opened it and began to read. Then something caught his eye.

"Oh my God!" Gray stared at the paper in disbelief.

"What is it, Daddy?"

"Winslow. The John you referred to, used the name Winslow each time."

"What's so significant about that?"

"It's a name that keeps coming up."

"Who is this Winslow character?"

"We are not sure at the moment, Julia."

"The killer?"

"We don't know." Gray passed the photos and folder back to his daughter.

"Keep them, they're yours. You'll get him."

"I wish I could be that certain. Honey, I really appreciate this," Gray said holding up the photos.

Julia rose from her chair. "Daddy, I must go."

Gray felt his skin crawl, as he shivered. "My God what is this guy up to?"

"Whatever it is, you need to stop him."

"I wish I knew how Julia."

She smiled reassuringly. "You'll find a way."

Gray also stood. "See you for dinner?"

"Sure, where?"

"How about La Bohème?"

"Sounds very French…sounds expensive."

"It is one of the best French restaurants in the city."

"Great." Julia picked up her briefcase.

"I'll pick you up at seven."

"I'll take a cab."

"Nonsense, I'll pick you up." Gray walked around his desk.

She glared at him. "Not in that hearse of yours. I'll take a cab."

"Come on, Julia, don't be ridiculous…"

"Daddy! Don't you get it? I don't like your car. It's built to carry dead people. I'll take a cab."

"Okay, I'll be at your hotel at seven and we'll take the cab together."

"Fine, I'll see you then." Julia scooped up her coat and scarf, kissed Gray on the cheek and left.

▼▼▼▼▼ 7

As Gray watched Julia leave, he slipped the photos into the envelope and dropped them into the top drawer of his desk. He was a proud and happy man, the happiest he had been in a long while. Although he desperately wanted to give her a story, he knew he was doing the right thing. Eventually, of course, it would all come out, but they had to find Sally and get the killer before he killed again.

"Gray, do you have a moment?" Paul was standing in the doorway.

"Sure, Paul, come in and close the door."

Paul closed the door and sat. "My, we are being mysterious."

"Something's just come to my attention and let me say this. I was a damn sight more than shocked when I read it." Gray removed the envelope from his top drawer, pulled the report on the case and handed it to Paul. As Paul read, an expression of disbelief curtained his face. Finally he looked up and stared at Gray.

"Is this for real?"

"As real as it comes."

"Winslow?"

"Exactly. His damned name keeps turning up like a bad penny."

"Who the hell is this guy?"

"I wish I knew, Paul."

"Well, there appears to be a lot more to this guy than we have on him."

"Paul, this can't get out. Damn, talk about an upside down situation. We have seven victims, well six actually, that have no home and no ID. They just dropped out of nowhere. Then there are the seven women on the east coast who disappeared into thin air. Finally, there are those 12 women on the west coast."

"Sure it's the same killer?"

"If it isn't, then it's the biggest coincidence in history."

Paul waved the document in the air. "I hear you. Is this case still open?"

"Yes. Pass that on to the team, and impress on them it's for their eyes only."

"Sure."

Gray frowned. "If these cases are all connected, we are dealing with a crazed maniac who must be stopped at all costs."

"If it is, he's sure as hell been busy. How many more are there that we know nothing about?"

"I don't even want to think about that."

"Me neither." Gray's phone rang. Paul indicated he had to leave and stepped out of the office.

"Farlon."

"Detective, this is O'Malley."

"Yes, Patrick, what can I do for you?"

The young sergeant sounded agitated. "I have something you should see right away."

"Sounds urgent, Patrick, but can it wait until tomorrow?"

"I guess it could." He sounded disappointed.

"Good. Then why don't you meet us in the War Room at say *2:30* tomorrow afternoon."

"I'll be there."

▼▼▼▼▼ *8*

Gray called Rick Shelby at the Forensics lab.

"Rick, do you have anything for me on that ring?"

"Yes, it's nothing special, Gray. The band is 10 karat gold plated and the stone is blue quartz. Probably cost between 25 and 50 bucks."

"That's it?"

"Afraid so, why? What were you expecting?"

"I'm not sure, but more than that."

"Sorry, that's all I have."

Gray thought for a moment. Something didn't fit. For all Maitland's wealth, what would he be doing with a cheap ring? He must have known its value. He was uneasy when it was shown to him, so what was he hiding? Why was he reluctant to admit he owned it? Then Gray had an idea. He would use the information even though he knew it was a long shot, but something told him Maitland wasn't what he appeared to be.

"Okay, Rick, thanks anyway."

"Before you go, I do have something else. The pendant."

"What about it?"

"I told you we were unable to pinpoint a date. I believe we now have a good idea. It appears it might be about 80 years old and not 60 as we previously believed.".."

"Eighty...most likely an heirloom. What about the note paper?"

"Can't say. We're still unable to fix a date for that."

"Okay, keep trying, Rick. If you find anything, let me know."

"Sure will."

▼▼▼▼▼ **9**

With an idea running through his head, Gray dialed Paul's extension.

"Paul, we're going to pay Mr. Maitland another visit."

Paul's response was one of surprise. "We are? Why?"

"I have been through all the information Patrick gave me. I have learned a great deal more about our millionaire friend."

"I hope he understands, otherwise we'll all be looking for jobs."

"Oh, trust me, he'll understand. If you can find Carrie, ask her to join us."

Carrie, Paul and Gray drove to Maitland's mansion. Gray felt confident he was on to something.

"I thought I told you people, if I see..."

Gray stepped through the door, took Maitland by the arm and stepped further into the foyer. "Mr. Maitland, please give me a moment. We're not here to harass you. I would just like to ask you a few more questions."

Paul gave Gray a quizzical look. "We're not?"

"No, Paul, we're not."

Maitland looked skeptical. "Fine, but if you start with your accusations again, I'll have you thrown out."

The River Styx

"Agreed." Gray, Carrie and Paul were now standing in the center of the foyer.

"Carrie, Paul, please give me a moment with Mr. Maitland."

Paul looked perplexed. "No problem, Gray."

"Okay, Mr. Maitland, is there a place we can sit and talk?"

"The library, why?"

"We just need to talk." Gray followed Maitland down the hall into the large library.

"What's this all about?" Maitland said as he closed the door.

"Look, Maitland, I believe you're innocent of these crimes…"

"Well it's about time you came to your senses."

"Humor me a moment. I need you to be open with me. I want to know everything you can tell me then we'll get out of your hair."

"I have no idea what you're…"

"Damn it, quit fencing. We know your name is Dan Whitley…" Maitland's reaction was obvious; he was unable to hide it. Suddenly he looked like a man who had just had the weight of the world lifted from his shoulders. He wasn't even going to deny it.

"How did you know?"

"We have done a great deal of research, Dan. We know your girlfriend is Tammy Newton, cashier at the bank where you worked. You have been seeing her regularly unbeknownst to whomever you're working for. What's his name, Dan?"

"I have no idea. I have never seen the guy. All communications are done over the phone."

"No e-mail?"

"No e-mail, only the phone."

"And you have no idea who he is?"

"I'm sorry, Detective, if I did I couldn't tell you because he has so much hanging over me."

"He's blackmailing you?"

"It's far worse than that."

"Dan, you're a millionaire who came from nothing. How did that happen?"

"He made it happen. At first when I came into all that money, I was thrilled. Then when I realized I had all but sold my soul to the devil, it was too late and there was no way out. He had me boxed in and he owned my life. I wish I could be free of it all, but there is no way." As Gray listened to Maitland tell his tale, he watched as the man withered into a meek and terrified individual. "…then I shot the bank robber. I was not supposed to but he was going to kill Tammy and I could not let that happen."

"I understand. Okay, here's how it will work. What we have discussed must not go outside this room if you and Tammy are to remain safe. This nightmare is going to end, but for the moment hang in there. This guy will kill you and Tammy if he finds out you've double-crossed him."

"Yes. How much longer will it last, Detective?"

"I can't say. But you must keep up the act. Don't do anything to arouse suspicion." Gray rose from his seat and Maitland followed suit. As they walked to the door, Gray placed his hand on Maitland's shoulder.

"Don't get despondent, Dan. It will work out."

"Thanks for your help, Detective. You have no idea how much better I feel."

"Remember, we're watching you. If anything goes wrong, we'll be right there. One other question...the ring. We had it checked out. It's a cheap one, and I'm assuming it belonged to Tammy."

"It was a promise ring that I gave her. I asked her to marry me about three weeks before the bank heist. She shocked me when she said yes. I couldn't afford anything better at the time. Now I can."

"And the cosmetic surgery?"

"I told her it was because of the bank hold up. She accepted that."

"So you are still seeing her?"

"Yes."

"Be very careful. Don't take any chances, for both your sakes."

"We won't. Thanks again, Detective."

▼▼▼▼▼ 10

The cab rolled to a stop in front of Julia's hotel at 6:55. Gray asked the cabbie to wait while he went into the lobby to look for Julia. In the hotel as he crossed the lobby to the reception desk, he saw no sign of her. The receptionist looked up.

"Yes sir, may I help you?"

"Would you please call Julia Farlon's room to let her know her father's here."

"Yes, Mr. Farlon, but you can use the house phone just as easily." She pointed across the lobby.

"I'll do that, thanks." Gray walked to the table next to the stairs. He dialed Julia's room. It rang but there was no response. He hung up and waited. After five minutes he went up to her room on the fifth floor. She was not there. He returned to the lobby but she was still not there. Concerned, he went to the front desk.

The young woman stepped to the counter. "She has not come down?"

"No, and she is not in her room. Could you see if she left a message?" He wondered if she had decided to meet him at the restaurant.

"Certainly." The woman disappeared into the back room then reappeared moments later handing him a sealed envelope. She apologized. "I'm sorry, I should have checked."

The River Styx

Gray took the envelope and tore it open to find a single sheet of paper folded in half. As he unfolded it, his heart sank. The wind was sucked out of him and a hollow feeling hit his stomach.

He read the short, quickly scribbled note again and again in stunned disbelief, cursing himself for his incompetence.

> *Dear Daddy,*
> *I'm sorry. I can only say I am safe for now. You are to go to the phone in the hotel lobby and wait. At 7:30 you will receive a call. Please don't contact anyone, otherwise the man I'm with says he will kill me. Don't worry Daddy I'll be fine. Just do as he says.*
> *I love you, Julia*

"Is everything all right, Mr. Farlon?" The receptionist asked, as she noted Gray's concerned expression.

"Ah, yes. Yes, thanks." Barely able to control his emotions, he felt lightheaded but fought it off. When it was someone else, he could handle it, but this was his daughter – it was more than he could handle. He was in a state of panic. The bastard had his daughter and would kill her without remorse. Gray looked at his watch. It was *7:25*. Five minutes. This was the last thing he had expected; yet he knew it could happen. He knew if this maniac were going to get to him, he would try it in the most personal way.

Well you got about as personal as you could, you bastard. Now you are going to have to deal directly with me. You will have no peace from here on.

He paced the lobby glancing at his watch every few seconds. Five minutes never seemed so long. His mind worked overtime. He moved closer to the courtesy phone on a table beside the stairs, willing it to ring, yet terrified it would. Glancing at his watch again, it was *7:29*. Suddenly, like some giant bell tolling doom, the phone started to ring.

"That is for you, Mr. Farlon," the receptionist informed him, pointing to the phone.

He dropped into the chair next to the phone, scooped up the handset and pressed it to his ear. "Hello."

"Detective Farlon?" The voice was unfamiliar.

"This is Farlon. You hurt one hair on my daughter's head and so help me I will skin you alive..."

"Not a good start, Detective. Now cool your jets. Don't get so hot before you understand the procedure."

"You let my daughter go! Where is she? What do you want?"

The voice suddenly grew sinister. "Shut up and listen." The man snapped. "If you want your daughter back in one piece, you'll do exactly as I say. Screw up, and she's a corpse. Got that?"

Gray was sweating. "Harm her and I swear I'll kill you myself."

"You don't hear so well, Farlon. I said shut the hell up and listen. Besides you're in no position to make threats. Here's what you're going to do. First call off your bloodhounds. Secondly everyone else on this case, I want them off." As hard as he tried, Gray could not place the voice. "You get that?"

"Yes I've got it. You've got to be out of your mind, I can't..."

"If you want to see your daughter alive again, do it."

"How do I know she's not dead already? How do I know you'll keep your end of the deal?"

"Oh, there is no deal. Just do as I say."

"I can do my part, but my daughter could already be dead." Gray's heart sank and the hollowness in his stomach made him want to vomit.

"Do you think I'm stupid, Farlon? I have no need to kill her...yet."

"Then let me speak to her."

"All right, but no funny stuff. Try to send coded messages and her last breath will be a gurgle through this phone because I'll slit her throat, you got that?"

"Yes." There was silence. Then Julia's soft voice, full of fear, drifted through the phone. He felt the tears running down his cheeks.

"Daddy, are you there?"

"I'm here, Honey. Are you okay?"

"Yes, so far. Daddy, I'm scared."

"Yes, Honey, I know and so am I. Has he done anything to you? Where are you?"

"No, I'm tied up. I can't see anything. It's very dark."

"Do you know where you are?" There was sudden rustling and scraping sounds, then he heard Julia gasp.

"Okay, Farlon, enough. Now you know your little girl's fine. If you want to keep her that way, it's up to you."

"Be logical. How can I drop the...?"

"Enough talk. You have your instructions."

"What about the other woman?"

"What other woman?"

"The one from the hospital."

"She's not your concern."

"She is my concern..."

"Just you worry about your daughter. You've got 48 hours. If you have not complied with my wishes, I'll send your daughter back to you a piece at a time."

"If I comply, you let them both go."

"No deal. You get one or the other."

"Look, you sick bastard, you..." The line went dead. Gray slammed the phone down and resting his elbows on his knees, he put his head in his hands. Terrified. Empty. A feeling of complete helplessness swept over him. He knew this killer didn't make idle threats. He would kill Julia without a second thought.

The River Styx

As he pulled himself together, Gray stood, took his cell phone out of his pocket and called Paul. He'd made his decision, dangerous though it might be. Keep the bloodhounds, keep the 24-hour surveillance and keep everyone on the case. "Paul, we have a new development. He has Julia."

"Who has her?"

"The killer."

"Oh, God! Gray, I'm so sorry. Where are you?"

"At her hotel. Somehow he managed to get her out of here undetected. We have to get her back Paul."

"Of course."

"Then we get him."

"Right. But how do you know he has her, Gray?"

"He allowed her to leave a note. Then I talked to him and Julia on the phone."

"You talked to him? Where is he?"

"No idea. He also has Sally."

"What does he want?"

"He wants me off the case and surveillance stopped."

"He's got to be crazy."

"That's one hell of an understatement."

"Gray, does he really expect us..."

"He's not expecting it, Paul, he's demanding it. He kills both women, if we don't comply. I have news for him...we can't and we won't. Anyway, I do have an idea. It's going to be risky but it might just work. Can you meet me at the office as soon as possible? I'd like a plan of action before morning."

"Sure, I'll be there in half an hour. Gray, I'm sorry about Julia, but we'll get the bastard."

"Thanks, Paul." He hung up and called his office. Then he called Mario.

"Mario, Gray. We have a situation. Meet me and Paul at the office as soon as possible."

"I'll be there in about 20 minutes."

"That will be fine."

"What's happening Gray?"

"The killer abducted Julia from the hotel this evening."

"Oh shit! I'm so sorry, Gray. What are we going to do?"

"We'll figure that out when you get here."

"I'm on my way." Gray put his phone in his pocket. Within 15 minutes the hotel was swarming with police. As soon as he was satisfied that everything was under control, he had a squad car run him back to District. Mario was the first to arrive.

"Gray, how are you holding up?" he said as he walked into Farlon's office.

"I've been better, Mario."

"Okay, so what have we got?"

"It appears the killer abducted Julia sometime between six and seven this evening. He made her write a note before they left the hotel." Gray handed the note to Mario.

"Damn it, Gray, I'm so sorry. What does the bastard want?"

"He wants you guys off the case and the tails pulled."

"He knows that is impossible."

"He knows it, but I have an idea and that is why I called you both. There is something about this guy that bothers me."

"One thing bothers you, Gray? Hell, there are a hundred and one things about him that bother me!"

"No. That's not what I'm getting at. It's the way he talks, the expressions he uses. I don't know. I wish I could put my finger on it. At the moment this bastard has the upper hand holding both of these women. But it won't be that way for long. I told him he would not get away with it."

"You talked to him! For how long?"

"Barely a minute. He's a cocky bastard. The man's delusional so we must play it very carefully. We have to lead him into a trap; one we will spring in our own timing."

"The other thing is he has Sally. We must get to him before he kills either of them."

"How do you intend to do that, Gray?" Mario asked.

"How does he intend to do what, Mario?" Paul asked as he stepped into Gray's office. "I'm so sorry to hear about Julia, Gray."

"Thanks, it's good of you to come. I held off starting until you got here." Gray proceeded to lay out his plan for the two detectives. Although still in a state of agitation, by *2:00A.M.*, he'd explained all the details.

TERROR IN THE DARK

▼▼▼▼▼ 1

Paul walked into District 3 HQ at *8:15A.M.* his head fuzzy from two hours of sleep. He was concerned about Gray. He knew how he kept things to himself.

"Morning Mario, get much sleep last night?"

"Hardly."

"You seen Gray this morning?"

"No, but I've only been here a few minutes."

"He left here last night looking very depressed. Didn't even say good night and that's not like him."

"No, it's not." Carrie walked up to them.

"Morning Carrie."

"Paul, Mario. You two look like someone stole your lollipop."

"We have a major problem." Paul turned back to Mario. "Mario, did he say anything to you before he left?"

"Only that he needed to pay a visit to Shamus."

"Oh, shit." Paul panicked. Shamus was the name Gray had given to an Irish pub on the west side. He frequented it years ago.

"Problem Paul?" Carrie asked, as Paul made for the door. He paused and solemnly stared at the floor then looked up.

"Possibly Carrie. Look, do me a favor."

"Sure."

"I want you to stay put. I think all this culminated with Julia's abduction."

"My God, Gray's daughter was abducted?"

"Yes, early last evening. They were supposed to meet for dinner, but she never showed and left a note. The killer has her. Look, I've got to go. Mario will fill you in on the details."

Carrie gasped. "Oh dear God, no!"

"Carrie, I want you to stay here. I might need you."

"Let me go with you."

"No stay here. I'll call you later."

"Where are you going?"

"Not entirely sure, but if my hunch is correct, I think I know where Gray is."

"Who the hell is Shamus anyway?" Mario said.

"I'll explain later."

"Is there anything I can do, Paul?"

"Not now, Mario. Just bring Carrie and the others up to speed. If anything new materializes, call me."

"Right, Paul."

"It's all yours, I'm out of here." As he left the building, O'Malley intercepted him.

"Paul, you got a minute?"

"Not now Patrick. I'll get with you later."

"This could be very important..." O'Malley trailed after Paul as he hurried toward his car. Paul only had one thing on his mind.

"If it's that important, O'Malley, see Mario."

"But..."

"For crying out loud, didn't you hear me? I said later!" He shut O'Malley down immediately. He didn't mean to bite the Sergeant's head off, but at that moment he was stretched as tight as a drum. He got in his car and headed east then turned south. Although he knew roughly where he was going, he hoped he was wrong. He first headed for Farlon's apartment, then reluctantly changed his mind.

He turned onto Webster Avenue heading east again. He knew the tavern Gray had frequented in the old days, and if he had fallen off the wagon, that would be his destination. In the Lincoln Park area, Paul turned on to Clark Street heading south. Much to his disappointment, his hunch was correct. As he pulled into the parking lot behind The Shamrock Bar and Grill, he spotted Gray's white hearse.

Inside the tavern it was dark. The place was lit by a few low-hanging lamps in the booths and the light behind the bar. His eyes slowly grew accustomed to the gloom. He looked through the fog of cigarette smoke. There were only two people in the place that he could see. Neither was Gray. As he walked to the bar, he pulled out his badge and waved it at the bartender.

The bartender stopped what he was doing and stared at Paul. "Hey, I'm clean, friend."

"I'm not here to hassle you. A guy may have come here last night...five feet ten wearing a gray suit, blue shirt and black tie. He has long gray hair in a ponytail, a goatee and mustache. I'm assuming he hasn't left yet, since his car's still out back. Unless he took a cab." The bartender was drying glasses then hanging them.

"Yeah. Old fella?"

"Could be him, yes. He's still here?"

"In the booth at the back behind that partition. Said he wanted to be left alone, so I left him alone. Except for the odd drink he ordered, he hasn't said much."

"Okay, thanks." Paul found Farlon squeezed tightly into the corner of a booth with his head back and eyes closed. On the table in front of him was a half empty glass. Paul slipped into the booth across from Gray.

The River Styx

"Gray." He got no response. "Gray, what the hell have you done?" Still there was no response. "God damn it, Gray, you have gone and screwed it all up. What the hell did you have to come here for? What were you thinking?" Without opening his eyes he finally spoke. His words were slurred and disjointed.

"What do you care? Go...just leave me alone. What do you...hey, that you, Paul, have a drink. You finally found me...took you long...got the bastard yet? No...need me, huh? Need me to help you catch the son of a bitch. All my fault you know...all my fault. I let it happen...could have stopped it but let it...found him yet Paul?" Gray felt his head tumbling about like a ball in an empty clothes dryer. Why didn't they leave him alone? He just wanted to forget. It was not his problem in the first place. Why had he decided to climb back into the slime pit? But Julia, what to do about Julia? It was his problem now. It was his fault Julia was in the hands of this murdering madman.

"No Gray, we haven't found him yet."

"Told you, Paul, told you. You have to climb down into the pit. Crawl around in the filth and look into his mind to see for yourself what this bastard is thinking. Be a victim. You must be the killer. I saw, Paul...I saw it all and I hated what I saw..."

"What did you see, Gray?"

"What that monster did, the tormented monster. Horrible, Paul, it was so damn horrible." Gray still had not opened his eyes. He felt Paul's hand on his arm. "You're a good friend, Paul, a good friend. I promised her...I did promise...I would not...I made her a promise, Paul..." He began to cry. They were tears of grief and disgrace. He broke a promise. He knew he could not repair the damage. Not this time. Once again he had let Gwynne down. He also let Julia down all because of his pride. He despised pride but he was too proud to admit he had screwed it all up.

"Gray, don't do this, don't torture yourself like this! You are not to blame for what is happening. You have no cause..." Gray grabbed the sleeve of Paul's jacket, opening his eyes for the first time since Paul had arrived. They were tearful, tired and bloodshot.

"Don't you see, Paul? Don't you see? I broke a promise, I broke it and I can't take that back. I broke so many promises, Paul. Oh my God, Juanita is...she's dead Paul...dead and it's...oh shit, it's all my fault." His body shook as he sobbed even harder. He felt deep remorse and anger, anger at his own weakness. He had lost his will to stand against the demons. The monster eluded him, hiding in the shadows of his mind; refusing to step into the light. To solve this case he had to see his adversary. But he now knew the enemy.

"Promise? Gray, to whom did you break your promise?"

"I broke a promise I swore I would never break. Look, Paul, I broke a promise and...oh damn I will go to hell for it...I..." He could not control his emotions.

"Gray, nobody is going to hell except the killer. Damn it, Gray, would you get a hold of yourself! Look at you, you're a mess." He ignored Paul and continued to ramble.

"I'm going to hell, Paul. But first I've got to take a piss." He stood up. For a moment he thought he would collapse. The floor would not stay still. It rolled about and seemed to come up at him. Paul grabbed his arm to help steady him.

"I'm fine, Paul, but I have to go to the little boys room." He shook himself loose and staggered to the men's room. After taking care of nature's call, he slowly and painfully returned to his seat. His head would not stop rolling. It would not obey his instructions. "Now I can...boy that was a relief. Now I can go to hell relieved." He slid back into the booth and closed his eyes once more.

"Gray, let's get out of here. I'll take you home and you can sleep."

"No!" His voice seemed off in the distance. He felt strange, floating, not too sure of where he was. "I can't sleep, Paul, can't...I don't want to sleep. I see him in the shadows, but he's a coward Paul. The bastard is a... hell, he won't show his face. But I know who...he is...oh shit, Paul, he has Julia. I...no, no sleep...no sleep. I feel him when I sleep...he crawls into my head. No...no sleep...I must stay awake. There are too many ghosts Paul. They won't leave me...alone." He opened his eyes. Suddenly his head rolled backwards. Everything around him was becoming part of one giant, lazy vortex. He was unable to hold his head upright and everything went black. Paul got out of his seat and slipped in beside Gray.

"Okay, old timer, you've had plenty for one night. Let's get you out of here and back home where you can sleep it off." Paul's cell phone started to buzz.

"Salvatore."

"Paul, Carrie. I've been waiting for your call. Is everything okay? Is there anything I can do?"

"Hang tight, Carrie. I'm just wrapping things up and I'll be on my way. I'll call you. Please just stay put."

"Whatever you say. But would you mind telling me what the hell is going on? Where are you?"

"I'll call you back and give you the complete rundown." He hung up.

"Come on, Gray, let's get you home."

"No...I'm fine. I'm...I'm not going...anywhere. Need...another drink."

"No way in hell. That's the last thing you need. Give me a moment. I'll be right back."

"You...you got...to piss, too? Real bitch when...you put up all...that cash then just...piss it away."

"You're right." Paul tried to humor him. He got up and walked to the bar.

"Excuse me, do you have any coffee?"

The barman looked up. "Sure, probably damn strong. Been sitting most of the night, but it's hot."

"Great, may I have a large?"

"Only have one size."

"Then why don't you give me two." The barman poured two small styrofoam cups and handed them to Paul. "How much?"

"On the house. Don't charge for old coffee."

"How about the drinks he had? Did he pay you?"

"Yeah."

"Okay, thanks for the coffee."

"Anytime." Paul walked back to the booth, set the two cups down, then sat opposite Gray.

"Gray, before we go anyplace, I think you had better drink this."

"Great, another drink. Need to…wash away all the…filth of this job that's…swimming about in my…head." He lifted the cup and took a long gulp. Suddenly he sat bolt upright, sprayed the mouthful of coffee across the table almost hitting Paul, then stared at the cup. "What…what the hell is this…what's this sh…I…oh shit Paul." He was about to toss it away when Paul stopped him.

"No, no Gray, drink the damn stuff. I can't take you home like this, so get yourself sober. If Julia saw you now, she would not be a happy camper."

"Oh crap…damn it Paul you're…so right. You're good you know that? Taught you well, didn't I?"

"Yes you did Gray, now drink."

"This stuff tastes…tastes like shit."

"Maybe, but it will help to get you out of the state you're in my friend."

"Yeah, I'm in…deep trouble, aren't I?"

"You will be if you don't sober up." Gray drank and was slowly beginning to enjoy it.

"Damn!" He exclaimed staring at the cup in his hand. "Damn, this stuff is…strong stuff Paul. Must have been brew…oh hell it hasn't been…its been brewing all night. Has it?"

"Have no idea, but you're going to drink it all, then we can leave."

"Sure. Where are we…I drink all this I…oh crap I'm going to have to take another leak. Where are we going?"

"You're going home to sleep this off. I'm going back to work."

"Then I'm going with you. Need to…I must get to work, as well. Hell of a lot to…do you know…so much to do. Hey, I know, Paul, you know who the…who the killer is?"

"Yes, I know. And you're not going into the office today Gray, not today. Tomorrow will be fine. Today you rest. Clear your head."

"Look, Paul…Paul I'm fine…"

"The hell you are. Gray, what did you have to go and do this for? You said you were over it, that you had it under control. Now look at you, you're right back where you started. For God's sake, you're screwing up your life again Gray. You said you…"

"I'm sorry, Paul, I broke my...promise to her. I'm going straight to hell for that...you know that?"

"You won't go to hell if you get through this..."

"But Paul...I broke my promise to her."

"Julia will forgive you; of that I have no doubt."

"No...no, not Julia, well yes, her too. I broke my promise to Gwynne," he said angrily.

Momentarily Paul was confused then he understood. "To Gwynne? Oh, you promised Gwynne you would stay on the wagon."

"Yes and...I broke it."

"She will forgive you as well. She loves you very much, Gray. Of course she will forgive you."

"You think she will?"

"Of course she will. Now please finish the coffee then we can get going."

"What are we to do, Paul?"

"Gray, it will work out. We will find Julia. Count on it. Remember, it's always darkest before the dawn."

Twenty minutes later, Paul helped Gray out of the pub. He threw up in the parking lot. Despite the foul taste of bile, he felt a little better. When they arrived at Gray's apartment, Paul called Carrie and asked her to join them there. He did not give a reason. Half an hour later, Carrie arrived.

"What the hell is going on, Paul?"

"It's Gray..."

"Oh my God, is he hurt? What happened? Did he have a heart attack?" she said, a look of deep concern on her face.

"Carrie, it's okay, he's fine. A little under the weather, that's all." Both detectives walked into the bedroom. Gray was lying on the bed under the comforter. His ashen face was all that was visible.

"Will he be okay? He doesn't look good at all."

"He'll be fine after a good night of sleep. I managed to get two very strong cups of coffee down him which he duly threw up but it cleared his head."

"I had no idea he drank."

"He doesn't."

"So what the hell happened, Paul?"

"He had planned to have dinner with Julia last night. Anyway he took a taxi to her hotel..."

"Why didn't he drive?"

"Julia was adamant she would not ride in his hearse."

"Oh."

"Anyway, she was not there..."

"Mario told me what happened. She'd left..."

"Julia, is that you...?"

"No, Gray, it's Carrie. She came over to give me a hand," Paul said as he stepped to the bed.

"Oh. Hi, Carrie, forgive me for not standing up, but I seem to have lost my pants," he said without moving or opening his eyes.

"That's not a problem, Gray. You just stay where you are."

"Get some sleep, Gray." Carrie and Paul walked back into the living room. Carrie turned to Paul. "Okay, what do I do?"

"I would like you to stay with him this morning. I will relieve you at lunchtime. There are one or two things I must do right away. Don't worry about him; he'll be fine. Most likely he'll sleep for the rest of the day. I doubt he will throw up again; he has nothing left to dump."

"Great."

"You don't mind, Carrie?"

"Of course not. I only hope he's okay."

"Trust me, he's fine. A little embarrassed, so please don't mention this to him or anyone. He regrets what he did. He made a promise to his wife and he broke it. That bothers him the most."

"I thought his wife was dead."

"She is, but he's never gotten over that loss."

"Tough old bird."

"He is, and the best friend I've ever had. He taught me everything I know."

"Okay Paul, I'll stick around here. See you later."

▼▼▼▼▼ 2

Julia sat motionless, terrified, and barely breathing. Her feet were bound and her hands were tied behind her. She was not blindfolded but she could see absolutely nothing. The floor was cold and the air damp. A strong musty odor flooded her nostrils. She felt a little dizzy and sick to her stomach. As her mind slowly cleared, she tried to determine where she might be, but it was impossible. Her senses were dulled and her surroundings invisible.

An ominous silence enveloped her. Every now and again she heard a shuffling sound but was unable to identify it. She tried to move, but her bindings restricted her. Every joint and muscle in her body felt worn out, as if she had completed a grueling triathlon. Her eyes ached from staring into the blackness. The shuffling sound came again. Something moved. Panic swelled in her. Her first thought was rats. Silence. Then the sound came again.

"Who's there?" she said nervously.

A woman's weak voice floated back. "Who are you?"

"Julia Farlon. Who are you?"

"My name is Sally. I'm sorry you are here."

The statement surprised Julia. "Sorry? Why are you sorry?"

"Because you are going to die just like me." A sudden chill rushed over Julia.

"Why do you say that, Sally?"

"Because the one who brought you here is a killer. He tried to kill me but I was able to escape. He hurt me terribly. I was taken to hospital. But he came for me there and brought me here."

"That doesn't mean he's going to kill you or me, Sally."

"He will. He killed the other woman who was here."

"There was another woman?"

"Yes."

"When?"

"I am not certain how long ago it was."

"What happened to her?"

"I cannot say exactly. I do know he killed her, for she screamed so badly and he said terrible things to her."

"But Sally, that doesn't mean he killed her."

Her voice became agitated. "Yes, he did, he killed her. He told me so."

"I'm very sorry."

"When he took me from the hospital room, he told me he was going to kill me." It was then Julia realized who this woman was. It had to be Sally Mayfield.

"Sally...you are the one my father told me about. You were very badly hurt."

"Yes. Your father told you about me?"

"He is trying to catch the man who took you."

"Oh, he will never catch him. This is no man. He is the Devil himself, Julia. No one will ever find him."

"Don't be silly, Sally. He's not the Devil."

"He is, Julia!" she became hysterical.

"Sally, I'm sorry. It's not that you're silly, it's just that the Devil doesn't wander about like this."

"You will see, Julia. You will see when he comes. He needs no light. He can see in this blackness." Julia thought for a moment. *If Sally has been cooped up in this place for a period of time, she must be delirious.*

"Sally, how often does he come in here?"

"Not often. He comes only to bring food. Julia, how did you get here?"

"Someone came to my hotel room. He did not try to kill me, but the next thing I knew, here I was... wherever here is."

"I do not know where he took me first, but it was not here. It was a very strange experience. I thought I was flying, but I saw nothing but lights."

"He must have put you in a plane."

"Julia, you said your father told you about me?"

"Yes. My father is Detective Graham Farlon of the Chicago Police Department."

"I know him, a very kind and wonderful man. He is your father?"

"He is and I guarantee he's working this very moment trying to get us out of here. The man who brought me here told my father that as long as he does as he asks, you and I will be out of here soon." Julia lied but she felt obliged to try to keep Sally from panicking further.

"No!" Sally yelled. "He will not let us go. He finds pleasure in killing. He said he has killed many beautiful women because it gives him a great thrill to see them die." Suddenly the woman became hysterical.

"Sally, Sally, please stay calm. Look, I want you to think very carefully. Do you have any idea where we might be? It could be the basement of a building or possibly a warehouse. Have you seen this man? How long have you been here?" Julia slowed down as she realized she also was on the verge of panic.

"Julia, I do not know how long I have been here. He took me from the hospital and how much time has passed I do not know."

"I'm so glad he hasn't hurt you Sally. How do you feel at the moment?"

"I still experience some pain, otherwise I am very much better."

"That's wonderful."

"The people at the hospital told me I had amnesia. I only remembered my name when a doctor hypnotized me. I do not even know if it is my real name. I only wish I were able to remember who I truly am. It is so terrible not knowing, Julia." In the darkness, Julia could hear Sally crying.

"It must be but, don't worry, you will remember it all soon."

"Detective Farlon. Your father..."

"Yes, he is going to get us out of here."

"I hope so Julia. This monster calls himself Marshall, but he is not human, he is not. A human being would not do such terrible things."

"You're right Sally."

"I felt so safe in the hospital. I was beginning to accept I might never remember my past. I was prepared to begin again. Now I am back in this nightmare, not one second of which I remember."

"You still don't remember if it was this Marshall who tried to kill you?"

"No, yet he said so many things to me, which leads me to believe he is the one and he intends to finish what he started."

"My father will find us before that happens."

There was a long silence. Julia gave more thought to what Sally had said about her abductor. She wondered how he managed to come and go so easily. Sally broke the silence.

"Julia."

"Yes, Sally?"

"Marshall *is* the Devil and nothing can stop him. He took you from your hotel. He took me from the hospital. He came into my room and took me away..." Sally proceeded to relay her story as she recalled it. Julia let her speak hoping it might help to calm her. "...There was a strange red light then everything went dark. I woke up in this place." As Julia listened, she vaguely recalled seeing a red glow just prior to passing out.

"Someone brings you food?"

"Yes. A tray is placed on the floor then they leave. I feel like a bird in a cage. They never speak. But I am sure it is he because I smell the cologne. When he put me here he told me never to speak otherwise he would hurt me."

"How can anyone see to move about in this place without a light?"

"I told you, Julia, this is not a man. I saw his face, looked into those eyes; there is no life in those eyes, just black holes...empty...bottomless." Sally was crying again. Julia realized she had to try to keep this woman on the right side of sanity. She also knew she must find a way out of this place. But if she could not see a damn thing and had her hands and feet bound, how would she even take the first step?

Although not exceptionally tight, she was not sure she could free her hands, but it was worth a try. As she pushed herself away from the wall, Julia suddenly realized her feet were now hanging in space. Panic rattled through her once more. Trying to control it, she moved a little further away from the wall. She realized she was on a ledge about four feet wide. How much of a drop, she wondered.

"Sally, have you moved since you have been here?"

"Only to go to the bathroom."

Julia was shocked. "Bathroom? There's a bathroom?"

"Yes."

"How do you get to it if you are tied up?"

"Oh, I am not tied up, Julia. When I first came I was tied, then he removed my bindings. He knew I was not able to leave. To go to the bathroom I only move a short distance to my left. I do only as he instructed."

"Have you tried to move in any other direction?"

"No. He told me if I moved about I would die so I remain beside the wall."

"I believe I know why. There appears to be a hole in the floor. How long have I been here Sally?"

"I do not know."

"He must have drugged me."

"Your hands and feet are bound?"

"Yes, but I'm trying to get my hands out and then I will be able to check the floor."

"Julia, be very careful. If you upset this madman, he will kill you."

"Sally, believe me I have no intention of dying. I also have no intention of staying in this black hole." Julia struggled with the rope but was making little progress. Her right hand hurt as the cord bit into her flesh, but she was not ready to give up. She collapsed her hand as much as she could and pulled it back and forth twisting it slowly from side to side and tried to shut out the pain. It was working. Then her thumb was free.

"I think I'm getting there, Sally." The rope slipped over her fingers and her hands were free. Ignoring the pain in her wrist, she quickly untied her feet.

The River Styx

"Okay let's see what's around here." Julia got onto all fours and finding the edge of the floor, reached over. She couldn't feel a bottom. The ledge was solid as far down as she could reach.

"Julia, please be careful."

"Sally, don't worry. I'm just trying to get my bearings." Julia continued to carefully explore her surroundings. She discovered she was on a ledge with the bathroom to the right. In the bathroom she found a toilet and a sink. She returned to where she had been sitting, when a sharp clatter echoed through the building. The crash of steel, the whine of a motor and the scream of metal against metal cascaded from above.

"He's coming Julia," Sally said in a whisper. "He has his helpers with him; they make such terrible noises." Sally's imagination had gotten the better of her. Nevertheless, Julia wondered what menace was descending.

▼▼▼▼▼ 3

Gray tried to forget the events of the previous day. Although his head still hurt, he felt a great deal better. He had to concentrate on getting Julia back.

"What have we got, Paul?"

"Not much I'm afraid, Gray. We're scouring the city but we have no leads. Both Sally's and Julia's pictures are everywhere…newspapers, posters and TV. We have it all covered. All we can do now is wait and hope."

"I wish we had some idea where to start."

'I was thinking the same thing. I had…" Yoshi stuck his head through the door pointing to Gray's desk.

"Line 2, Gray. It's someone who claims to have seen Julia."

"You deal with it Yoshi, it's probably another dead end."

"No, Gray, this guy asked to speak to you personally." Gray picked up the phone.

"This is Detective Farlon, what…"

The voice that flowed from the earpiece sent a flood of chills through him. "You're not playing the game, Farlon. You are going to get both these women killed. You still have your bloodhounds on me and your team is still on the case…" Gray put his hand over the mouthpiece and whispered to Paul "It's him."

"The killer?" Paul whispered. Gray nodded.

"Keep him on the line and we'll try to get a trace." Paul dashed from the room.

"…Don't try to trace this call, Farlon; you're wasting your time. You've got 24 hours. Don't disappoint me…" The line went dead. Gray hung up just as Paul walked back into his office.

"Sorry Gray, no go."

"That's okay, Paul; we'll get him and we'll do it before he harms those women."

"I've pulled two of our guys off the case for now until we learn something. I am sure we..."

"Assign some others. Don't pull our team; we've got to find this guy fast. We also have to find Julia and Sally. But we have a commitment to the public to get this maniac off the streets before he kills again."

▼▼▼▼▼ 4

Bearings shrieked for lubrication as the elevator slowly descended. Like fingernails across a blackboard, the sounds sent chilling ripples through Julia's body. Air moved about her...a gentle breeze...a change in the environment. The sounds drew closer.

Julia waited with bated breath. Her eyes strained desperately searching the blackness. There wasn't a thread of light. She tried breathing slowly but nervous anticipation deprived her of that ability. What would come next? Was this the maniac who had abducted her? Was he bringing them something to eat or coming to impose more terror? Why was it so dark? How could this demented creature see in such blackness? As abruptly as it started, the noise ceased.

Silence reigned...then again the clatter of metal. Footsteps. Not loud, but distinguishable; someone moving about. Again silence, even the sound of breathing was indiscernible. Julia felt a presence. Strange, she thought to herself. When deprived of one sense, others become more acute. Someone was standing very close to her. Then she smelled it. The pungent cologne Sally had mentioned. It was not a cheap fragrance, but one that was probably found only in expensive shops. Then a voice shot out of the blackness directly in front of her. Julia recognized it.

"I see you have managed to get your hands free." *How the hell does he know that in this black hole,* Julia wondered? Then it dawned on her. He had to be wearing night vision goggles. He could see quite well.

"Well, never mind. I was going to untie you anyway. There's no place for you to run. As I have already told my other guest, leave the safety of the wall and you fall to your death. You might just as well be on an island in space. To your right Julia, you will find a..."

"Save your breath; I've already found everything."

"Good, then you know what I'm talking about. No doubt you have already met Sally. Make yourself at home but don't get too comfortable because you won't be here very long. Possibly a week or two, then we shall see. Sorry about the light, or the lack thereof. I didn't have the electric piped down this far. This is a fascinating room. Pity you can't see it. I had it modified for just such a purpose, to keep two or three beautiful women like yourselves here until I was ready for you.

"But there is no escape. The room is 100 feet high. You are halfway down. The walls are solid concrete, three feet thick and steel clad, so digging is impossible. But let's dispense with the details." Julia's senses were becoming more acute. She knew he was standing in front of her, but how close she could not tell.

"What are you going to do with us?"

"At the moment, my dear lady, nothing...at least not with you, Julia. Now Sally is another issue. She's caused me a lot of aggravation. She doesn't remember, but nevertheless she will have to be punished for her indiscretions. I will decide what I will do with her. I thought about depriving her of an arm to start, then possibly a leg. But because she is so beautiful, I will keep her head. The rest I might just send to the police as a keepsake." Though he spoke politely, his undertone was evil.

"You sick bastard..."

"Now that is no way to speak to your host."

"Jailor."

"That too. Sally is still a beautiful woman, Julia. Sorry you can't see her. Never mind. Before I started carving her up, she had a great looking body. You would have loved her body. But now, well, they have patched her up so I can do it all over again." He laughed, a demented cruel laugh. "She shouldn't have run. I would not have hurt her any more."

"Lies." Sally's voice ricocheted off the steel walls. "You were going to kill me. You were going to kill me from the very beginning."

"There, there, my dear woman; then why didn't you just leave the Nest? I would never have seen you again. You loved the pain and torment, didn't you? That's why you came back. You wanted me to hurt you again."

"I do not like pain. I cannot remember what happened but I do know you were going to kill me from the very beginning. You have taken everything from me. I have nothing left, not even my memories."

"Oh you still own one thing that I have not yet taken from you, but I intend to. I intend to take your life as my final act of revenge for what you did to me."

"You may take my life, but you will not get my soul. I will not give you that satisfaction. If I could get away from here, you would never find me."

The monotone, terrifying voice of their captor floated out of the darkness. "You would have nowhere to go. You have no idea where you are. Never mind, because your life is not worth saving at any time. If you feel like it, why don't you just jump over the edge?"

Julia exploded. "You sick son of a bitch! You lied to my father!" Julia's anger began to rise.

"Lied? No, I didn't lie, Julia. I just didn't tell the truth. I never said I would let you both go. I said I would let him have one of you, but he was greedy. He wanted both of you. Now you, I can understand; but Sally, she's just a whore, a slut, scum of the earth, no better than the rats that roam the sewers of this city."

"Whore! Who's the whore here? You're worse than a whore! Using people to satisfy your warped, twisted mind. You treat life as if it were a dirty rag to be used then thrown away..."

"Ah, you are a fiery bitch. Like a good fight, do you? Well I can give you one. I like women with spunk. When they fight hard it makes the performance so erotic and so exciting. Like Sally, she put up one hell of a fight." The sound of his voice gave Julia the chills.

"You're a whore and a liar! You have no intention of letting us go, do you?" Julia's anger boiled over.

"How could I? You see I could never let you go because if I did, you would tell the world about me and I would never have a moment's peace. I would have to leave and never return. That would be very inconvenient. I would have to stop this game I'm enjoying so much. No, I'll not do that. So neither of you will see the light of day again. Sorry."

"You are one sick bastard. You kill women and dump them in an irreverent fashion on a dirty street. You're an animal. In fact, there isn't an animal on this planet that would stoop to the depths you have. Bastard." Suddenly, two hands grabbed her by the shoulders and lifted her to her feet. She was then spun around. Terrified, unable to see, she felt death at her heels. Her heart raced. Perhaps she had pushed him too far. Would he just toss her over the edge and finish it right then? She almost screamed.

Although filled with anger, his voice was calm as he whispered in her ear. "Careful Julia, because I may let you go and you *will* die. I'm a patient man, but I don't like people scorning me. Don't try to make a fool out of me. I don't plan to do anything to you yet, but push me and I will take that enjoyment immediately." Julia shivered.

Sally remained silent through the entire event, fearful of what might transpire from Julia's badgering. Julia's invisible world exploded into violent action once more. The man spun her around and, like a rag doll, slammed her mercilessly against the wall knocking the wind out of her. Her feet barely touched the floor. One hand was now around her throat and the other on her left breast. She could scarcely scream. Then she felt his breath on her neck as he leaned close.

"Remember bitch, your life is mine. I can squeeze it out of you right now. But I wish to do it in my own time, so don't push me."

"I'll see you in hell first," Julia snapped.

"Of that I have no doubt." Then the hands were gone and he moved away. Julia almost collapsed. She breathed easily again.

"I'm leaving. Your food will be here in three hours. Sorry you have to eat it in the dark, but it's better than not eating at all, wouldn't you say?" He laughed an eerie, unsettling laugh. Then the screeching metallic sounds again ripped through the air as the elevator commenced its ascent.

"Julia, you must not do that."

The River Styx

"Do what, Sally?"

"Anger him so. When he comes back he will hurt you badly. He may even kill you."

The sinister voice floated down from above. "Listen to the little whore, Julia, she's right for once." Julia rested against the wall trying to calm herself. She shivered, still feeling those filthy hands on her.

The elevator stopped. Footsteps. A door slammed shut. Then silence. It was the silence of death. As she held her breath, the only other sound that reached her ears was that of her own heartbeat. Then the sound of Sally crying softly, drifted across to her.

"Sally, you've got to be strong. I don't intend to die here and I won't let it happen to you either. Somehow, we are going to escape. I have no idea how, but I'll think of something."

"No, Julia, do not try it. He will kill you. Please Julia, you must not provoke him, he..." She sniffled.

"Sally, hush. I know you're scared and so am I. But listen to me. If we stay quiet and give him everything he wants, he will kill us. If we cause a commotion and fight him, he will kill us. Either way, we're dead. We're not going to get out of here alive unless we do something. We must try. As long as we're breathing, we have a chance. Give me a little time and I'll think of something." Julia began running scenarios through her mind. Whatever she devised, she would need Sally's help. She knew she would not give in without a fight and she would not leave Sally behind.

▼▼▼▼▼ 5

Carrie accompanied Gray to his office. "Gray, are you sure you're up to this?"

"Carrie, I have enough problems with Paul mothering me. Don't you start."

"I'm sorry, it's just that I have..."

"I appreciate your concern, but I'm fine. Have a seat. What's on your mind?"

"I have been doing some research on Chinese history and mythology. The medallion came on the scene about 2,500 years ago, about 500 years after the Ivory Buddha, but it is a myth. The Buddha isn't. I have little information on the medallion; only that the two items are linked in some way."

"But, Carrie, if the medallion is a myth, how can there be a link?"

"I don't know, Gray. According to myth, it's supposed to possess some sort of power. There's another book that contains more details on the subject, but I'm unable to locate it."

"I'm sorry, Carrie, but this sounds like a lot of mythical nonsense to me."

"Well we know at least some of it is true."

"I must say it is fascinating. So what is this supposed connection between the two items?"

"That's just it, I don't know. That may just be fiction also."

"Maybe Mr. Yu could be of some help."

"That's an idea."

"Why don't we ask him?"

Taking the photos of the medallion, Gray and Carrie headed for Chinatown and Mr. Yu's shop. Gray believed that if anyone could help them, it would be the old Chinaman.

"It isn't enough that we have to deal with a mysterious connection between four individuals, now we have to deal with two damn trinkets 3,000 years old. I wish I knew what the hell was going on here and what we are getting into." Gray turned off Halsted Street toward Chinatown.

"The fact that the medallion is a myth takes much of the mystery away. Let's hope Mr. Yu can offer some explanation." Carrie sounded skeptical.

Twenty minutes after they'd left District, Gray and Carrie were standing in Mr. Yu's shop. They no sooner entered than a shadowy figure appeared, shuffling from the back of the dimly lit room.

"Sorry, we closed, must come back tomorrow." Yu emerged from the shadows. "Ha, my vely good friend Detective Farlon, you back, it good to see you again. You look much better. Come, come in please."

"Thanks to my friend Paul, I feel much better."

"This vely much a surprise. I not expect to see you for long time. Who this pretty lady?"

"Mr. Yu, this is Detective Carrie Simpson."

"Ah, woman detective, yes? Vely good see woman in high position in police. Why you here, Detective?" he asked shaking Carrie's hands.

"Just along for the ride," Carrie said.

"I think not. Woman detective never along just for ride, you both here for good reason. You come to talk about murders, yes?"

Gray then interrupted the small talk. "Mr. Yu, I would like you to take a look at a number of photos and give me your opinion." He walked over to the counter where the light was better and laid the photos on the glass. Mr. Yu moved in to examine them as he slid his frameless spectacles off the crown of his head onto his nose. He bent over the counter adjusting his glasses.

"I not sure what this is. I see it before but not familiar with Chinese history."

"You can't tell us anything about the medallion?"

"Cannot. I have relative in Los Angeles who might know. You are vely lucky...he arrive in Chicago day after tomorrow. I sure he must know something."

"If he can help us, Mr. Yu, that would be great. Would you let us know?"

"If relative can help, I call you." Gray and Carrie thanked Mr. Yu and left, a little disappointed.

6

There was a knock at the door. Gray looked up to see who was interrupting his reading.

"Afternoon, Patrick, come in."

O'Malley entered the office followed by Paul. "Excuse me, Gray, can we look at this now? You did say today."

Then Gray saw Yoshi and Carrie behind Paul. "Of course, have a seat. What's up?"

"I...that is Paul and I uncovered something very interesting."

An expression of anticipation crossed Gray's face. "This has got to be good to bring all of you here."

Patrick looked apologetic. "I wish it was news about Julia, Gray, but I'm afraid it's not. This is about our mystery man, Hal Moffitt."

"Gray, this sheds new light on the case," Paul said.

"It does?"

Patrick began. "We know Moffitt's background, most of it anyway. This reveals new evidence and it does get quite involved."

Gray smiled. "Try me."

Paul picked up the conversation. "You remember when Moffitt's wife was killed?"

"Yes, sometime in the mid '80s, during a bank heist, I believe."

"Right."

"But what does she have to do with this case?"

Paul glanced at Patrick. "Go ahead, Patrick, tell him."

"After that incident there were rumors that the shot that killed Moffitt's wife didn't come from any of the holdup weapons. Moffitt pushed hard for an investigation. He accused the department of stalling. Nevertheless, nothing could be proven. Suddenly he dropped all accusations and never mentioned it again. We now think we know why."

Gray frowned. "I'm listening"

"We believe Moffitt killed his wife."

Gray squinted at Patrick. "What? What led you to that idea?"

"Because..." Patrick paused. "May I?"

"Sure, go ahead."

Patrick spread a floor plan of the bank on the desk, and then went on enthusiastically. "...He was there that day."

"Who was?"

"Moffitt. He was in the bank during the holdup."

Gray stared at the floor plan of the bank. "Moffitt was in the bank during the holdup? Are you certain? I thought he arrived later."

"Positive, Gray. There was confusion as to how many customers were in the bank at the time. When the security guard was questioned, he said five people entered the bank that morning."

"I thought there were only four."

Paul picked up the story. "Everyone understood his statement to mean four plus Mrs. Moffitt. It wasn't until all the evidence was thoroughly reviewed that it was discovered there were actually six customers. The surveillance tapes show four men and a woman, the woman who was actually a guy dressed in drag, enter the bank after Mrs. Moffitt. The guard's answer was misinter- preted."

Gray glanced from Paul to Patrick. "Okay, so there were a number of discrepancies. I still don't see where this is leading."

"The body count was five, not six." Paul said.

"That's right, the four gang members and the Moffitt woman."

"Gray, there were six customers in the bank that morning. If all the gang members were killed along with the Moffitt woman, the body count would have been six. It wasn't. Someone was unaccounted for..."

"So who was it?"

"The last customer to enter was a guy in a gray suit and wearing a trilby hat and dark glasses. He was never connected to the holdup. The investigation determined he must have rushed from the bank when the shooting started. There were eight visible surveillance cameras." Patrick pointed at the floor plan. "...these five here, and these three. This one, the ninth, was hidden. Seven cameras were shot out, the eighth, this one, over the main entrance, was hit but remained operable. The tape from that camera shows ten seconds of static, possibly the result of the gunshot."

"All that sounds quite plausible."

"It does, Gray, but that's not how it happened."

"It's not?" Gray got out of his chair and paced his office, stretching his legs. "Excuse me, but old bones get stiff quickly. Go on, Patrick."

"The tape from the front entrance shows the customer in the gray suit entering. He acknowledged the guard with a casual salute, but did not look up. That salute showed a black onyx cufflink..."

Gray stopped pacing. "I'm sorry, Patrick, but if you're suggesting he didn't leave, where was he during the holdup?"

"That's what we've been trying to fathom and we think we have the answer. It's not conclusive, but it's a 99% certainty."

Paul jumped in. "I looked into all the evidence on the case, Gray, and found that Moffitt received a call on his cell phone soon after his wife was identified. He was in the bank less than a minute after that call."

Carrie raised her hands. "Wait, what's so strange about that? He was in the neighborhood."

"Oh, he was in the neighborhood all right," Paul said. "He was in the bank, but no one picked up on it."

Gray began pacing again. "So what about the two cameras?"

"The hidden camera, here, showed Moffitt just after the shooting started. He was against this outside wall. This is the hallway that leads to the manager's office; it was directly across from where he stood. His wife ran down this hall into the bank area and was shot here."

"So Moffitt's on film shooting his wife?"

"Not exactly, Gray. All that can be seen is a hand holding and firing a gun. But you can also see the same onyx cufflink."

Gray walked around his desk and rested his arms on the back of his chair. "That's hollow evidence. How does that prove Moffitt was the shooter?"

"Four reasons...first, the black onyx cufflinks. Second, the bullet removed from Moffitt's wife's skull didn't match weapons found at the scene. And a pair of gray, tear-away trousers found in a trashcan in the ladies room along with the hat. We surmised Moffitt was wearing a reversible jacket."

"That's three, what's the fourth reason?"

"Remember I mentioned Moffitt's first name is not Hal but William, and his second name is Bennett."

"His name isn't Moffitt?"

"Oh, it's Moffitt. His birth name is William Bennett Moffitt, which he never used."

Paul picked up the conversation. "Notes and documents belonging to the holdup gang, found after the holdup, had the noms de plume of the gang members Moe, Joe, Matt and Pat. There was only one variation. There were five names on the list. The fifth was only the initials WB. No one ever knew who WB was and there was no one left to question. It was concluded WB had to be the individual who masterminded the holdup. In effect, they were correct.

"Moffitt entered the bank for one purpose...to kill his wife. He then hid in the women's restroom. After he received the call, he emerged from the back of the bank. No one was the wiser...no one caught it because the place was in an uproar. Remember he was the detective on the case from the beginning."

"How do you know he went into the ladies room?"

Patrick pointed to the floor plan. "There were only two ways out of the bank, this rear emergency exit, or the main entrance. In either case this camera over the entrance would have caught him. It didn't, so we know he never left the building. He could only have gone into the women's restroom because the hidden camera covered the men's room here and this entire back portion of the bank. Also, the camera over the entrance never showed Moffitt entering the bank after he received the call. No one ever caught it."

Gray sat back and folded his arms, mulled over the information, then said. "Our friend was clever. This is very interesting, but where does it lead us?"

"To a number of important clues. I believe we can safely presume Moffitt shot his wife. Moffitt manipulated a cover-up; his position gave him that opportunity. Finally, the bank holdup was an inside job."

"How did you come up with that one?"

"Either Moffitt or the gang member they called Moe was acquainted with the bank security guard."

"What brings you to that conclusion?"

"Actually it's not a conclusion Gray, it's a theory. We have no concrete evidence to back that up."

"Then leave it alone. Unless you *can* back it up, I don't want to hear it. What else?"

"Only this, and it sort of throws the proverbial wrench into the works. We have irrefutable evidence that Maitland is not the killer. He can't be."

"How so?" Gray asked, already aware Maitland was in the clear.

"On the night of the stakeout, when the sixth victim turned up, he was in Washington attending a convention. Nine witnesses confirmed this. On the day Sally was abducted from the hospital, Maitland was in New York attending a luncheon."

"So you're saying that eliminates Maitland."

"There's one other piece of information that is the icing on the cake."

"And what might that be, Paul?"

"Miles Webber, Moffitt's twin brother…"

"What about him?"

"The investigation report claims you were the one who shot him."

"I'm aware of that Paul, so what's your point?"

"As close as Moffitt and Webber were, it would give Moffitt a good reason for revenge."

"That's nonsense. He may have held a grudge but to go this far, that's not Moffitt's style."

"Then why perpetrate this charade?"

"Let's find out before we start making further assumptions." Gray got out of his chair. "I believe we're through for today."

7

Spectral images continued to haunt his dreams. Gray didn't wish to escape them, but hoped to learn the identity of the killer and put a stop to his nightmares. Sleep was a menace; it brought no peace, for it came with constant torment and manipulation. He felt like a puppet with tangled strings, all his limbs being pulled in different directions. It was imperative he escape the clutches of this madman before he lost all semblance of sanity. The tables had to be turned if he were to gain the upper hand, but that did not appear to be in the stars.

Once again he lay in bed knowing he would wake exhausted and demoralized. His guide had been no help in revealing the identity of the killer, where Julia and Sally were or if they were still alive. He was desperate to know and more desperate to find them, but where were they?

The River Styx

"What do you want?"

"What do I want? What sort of a question is that? You know what I want; I want to know who killed those women. I want to see him without being seen. I want to know. I want satisfaction. I want closure. Damn it I want some peace."

"I am unable to help in that vein. Can you understand?"

"No I can't. Why can't you help?"

"I have told you, I am only able to guide you and advise you. I am unable to answer your questions or solve your mysteries."

"Then why do I need you?"

"Because I can be of help."

"Oh yes, in what way?"

"Any way you wish."

"Then answer my questions because that will help me."

"No, that would be doing for you what you must do yourself."

"I'm sorry but I don't understand."

"You have all the answers but you must find them. I am not able to give them to you."

"Would you quit talking in riddles?"

"Suit yourself."

"Hey I want answers and now."

"Then find them."

"Don't get smart with me."

"I am not getting smart. I am already beyond that."

"Oh hell, this is nuts. I'm sleeping holding a conversation with...am I sleeping?"

"That depends upon what you classify as sleep. Sleep is where the body is at rest, where you dream but your mind does not interact. Here your body is at rest but your mind and your spirit are very much alert."

"Who are you anyway?"

"I am your guide."

"I already know that, but who are you?"

"You already know the answer to that question."

"My conscience. Yeah well you aren't much help."

"Ask me a question."

"Like what?"

"Ask me a question."

"What the hell have I been doing the past...oh never mind."

"You must ask the right question."

"I get it, you can't answer directly, but if...so I must ask the right question.. Where can I find the killer?"

"I do not know."

"How can I find the killer?"

"That also I do not know."

"Oh come on. How do I get to the damn killer?"

"*You must pass the cauldron of death but do not follow the dark phantoms. Look for the red light and follow it.*"

"*Then will I see the killer?*"

"*That I do not know; first do as I say.*"

Gray was perplexed. He continually questioned himself whether this was a dream. Although he doubted, it all appeared too real. The scenery changed and he was walking in a field, but the grass was black and the sky was...green! Insanity was snapping at his heels. He knew he was on the brink. In an instant his surroundings changed once more. Blood curdling screams of agony struck his eardrums. He stood beside the cauldron once again. The stench was unbearable and the sight before him horrifying. He felt nauseated. He turned to look for the red light.

Phantoms cloaked in black floated into view. He tried to ignore them but like sirens in the storm they seemed to draw him to them. Their shrieking was painful to his ears but he could not raise his hands to cover them. He tried fighting against their magnetic forces. Then he saw the red light in the distance. He attempted to move toward it but failed. He was being drawn to the phantoms. It sounded so easy at first. Desperately he began to struggle and with sheer determination he pulled away. As he broke free, he leapt into the air and raced toward the light.

He was standing in the center of a baseball field, the bleachers filled with cheering people. They were jumping up and down in their seats and waving their arms. But when he looked closer he realized they were all dead, corpses in various stages of decay. In an effort to avoid this gruesome sight he searched for the red light, but it was nowhere to be seen. The grotesque crowd was all that was visible.

"*Okay, what am I doing here?*"

"*You are journeying to your destination.*"

"*Are you kidding? What kind of game are you playing?*"

"*Baseball.*"

"*Smart ass.*"

"*If you persist with that attitude I shall leave you here.*"

"*Okay, okay, I'm sorry it is just that I am getting a little frustrated with all this nonsense.*"

"*Apology accepted.*"

"*Take those dead people away. It is making me sick.*"

"*I am unable to do that. The red light is your path from this place.*"

"*So where is the red light?*"

"*Concentrate and it will come to you.*"

"*Hell, here we go again. Am I...*" Suddenly everything began to spin. The baseball stadium, the bleachers, the corpses all became a blur. "*...Damn! No! Don't do this; I'm not ready to leave. I must finish this journey. Wait, I can't leave. I have to see the killer. I must know the killer so I might stop his murderous acts.*"

The River Styx

"*I am sorry but your time is up. You must leave. You may come back another time to try again.*"

"Hey, this is not a carnival fun ride. This is a matter of life and death. You can't do this. Where are you? Don't leave, come back."

But there was only silence and the spinning continued. The colors blended then all turned black. There was only darkness. Gray was awake. He stared at the ceiling trying to make sense of what had just happened.

"*What did just happen? Damn it. Dreams, I hate them.*"

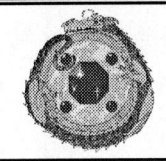

-EPISODE 4-

The River Styx

JOURNEY BACK

▼▼▼▼▼ *1*

In her search for additional information on the murders of 1865, Carrie uncovered something startling, another crime involving some disturbing events. At first she was unsure if the two crimes were related, but she soon found a link. It revealed an unbelievable story. Although it was getting late, Carrie had to tell Paul. Paul, being the cynic he was, dismissed the idea as preposterous. Carrie insisted.

"Oh, for crying out loud. All right you've convinced me we should pursue this but, I'm telling you, we're wasting our time."

"If it turns out that way, Paul, I owe you a dinner."

Paul shot her a cautious look. "And if you're right, what do I owe you?"

Carrie gave him a sly smile. "A weekend in Vegas."

"Are you out of your mind? I can't afford that."

"Worried?"

"Hell, no! I just don't want to chance it."

"You're worried." She smiled at him victoriously.

For four days, Carrie and Paul carried out intense research and slowly peeled back the pages of time. What they discovered led them to the town of Joliet, Illinois, and a small cottage located on the outskirts of the city.

They were seated in the comfortable but modestly furnished living room in the home of Alice Daugherty. She was an attractive woman who appeared to be in her mid-thirties though, if this were the person Carrie believed her to be, that could not be the case. What amazed both detectives was the likeness.

Alice Daugherty looked at her two visitors. "Why are you here, Detectives? Why have you come to see me? I've done nothing wrong."

"No, but we need to speak to you about something important, something that happened roughly 27 years ago. We don't wish to open old wounds, Ms. Daugherty, but we are looking for answers and we believe you may be able to help us," Carrie said.

"Please, call me Alice. Answers to what, Detective?"

Carrie hesitated. "About your baby."

Alice's reaction was one of stunned disbelief. "Oh my God! That was long ago. February of 1980 to be exact. My baby disappeared after I left her in St Pius Church. They never found her."

Paul coughed nervously. "We know, Alice, but we would like to know about the medallion."

"How do you know about the medallion? How do you know I had a daughter?"

"From the investigation reports."

Her eyes glistened but she did not cry. "Of course. It was such a mess. My parents went ballistic when they were told. They wanted to send me away. The police thought I had killed my baby but that was absurd. I could never have harmed her. She was so tiny, so fragile, so beautiful, and she meant the world to me. They learned the truth after they broke my heart and almost destroyed my life."

"What happened, Alice?"

"I suppose I was a foolish and rather rebellious child. I frequently disregarded my parent's rules. They were domineering and allowed me little freedom. Then about seven months after my 17th birthday, I met this man in a pub. I was wild in my teens...smoked, drank illegally, told everyone I was 22, even carried a false ID. This guy was so handsome. He thought I was 22 and I allowed him to believe it. We had an affair. He said he was from Indianapolis. I only saw him infrequently. When he came to town, we dined in fancy restaurants and occasionally went to the theater. I only slept with him twice, twice too many, but it was my fault because, basically, I seduced him.

"I was desperate for attention. I gave him what he wanted and he gave me all his attention. Then things turned bad when I found out he was married. I was scared and decided to break it off. But before I saw him again, I discovered I was pregnant. I was terrified because I knew if I told him he would be furious. That strengthened my conviction to end it. It was not easy; in fact, it was extremely hard."

"Why was that, Alice?"

"He had a violent temper. Never turned on me but I saw it with others. Broke a waiter's tooth in a restaurant one night; hit the guy with a plate."

"How did you break it off?"

"The next time he came to town, he called. He left five or six messages on my phone but I never returned his calls. He finally gave up."

"Did you ever see him again?" Paul asked.

"A few years later, I spotted him walking into a restaurant with a beautiful woman. I was not surprised since beautiful women were attracted to him. To this day I don't know what he saw in me."

Paul gave her a reassuring glance. "Don't put yourself down so easily, Alice."

"Anyway, there were actually two."

Carrie was confused. "Excuse me?"

"You mentioned a medallion. There were actually two; the second was a silver locket that belonged to my grandmother. It opened and you could place something inside. I placed a short note inside. But why do you need to know all this?"

The River Styx

Carrie leaned forward and rested her elbows on her knees. "We're involved in another case, Alice, and as we researched material, we learned of your old case. As I read through it, I became curious."

"About what?"

"Whether there might be a connection," Paul said.

"Is there?"

Carrie was cautious with her answer. "We are not sure, but it's possible."

"Oh..." She drifted off to another place in her mind with a faraway look in her eyes. Her gaze then fell on Carrie. "It was rather strange really..."

"What was, Alice?"

"Sally had a birthmark on her left thigh, looked rather like a crescent moon. I have a birthmark on my left thigh that looks very much like a star. Almost in the same spot...strange."

Carrie then asked. "Alice, may I show you something?"

"By all means." Carrie took the photo from her pocket and handed it to Alice. As the woman stared at it, the color drained from her face. For a long time she sat motionless and speechless. Finally she looked up.

"Where did you find this?"

"We haven't. That is the photo from the investigation."

"It was very precious to me. My grandmother left it to me, but I felt compelled to give it up for my baby. At least then my father could not benefit from it. It must have been very valuable. My grandmother told me all the stones were genuine. That ruby was just exquisite...but wait." She paused and looked closer at the photo. "Something's not right; this cannot be my medallion."

Carrie's heart skipped. "Why, Alice?"

"Because my medallion had a deep scratch across the dragon's leg."

"Are you certain? I mean, it's been a long time since that day, Alice," Paul said.

"Perhaps, but I distinctly remember there being a scratch." Alice drifted off again deep in thought.

Carrie hesitated then asked. "Alice, just one more thing. What was the man's name?"

"Man? Oh, the father of my child? He never told me his last name. His first name was a little unusual; it was Hal, spelt like the computer in the movie '2001'." Paul almost choked. He glanced at Carrie who also had a shocked expression on her face. Alice noticed.

"You know him?"

Paul quickly interjected. "No." The two detectives rose to their feet.

Carrie turned to Alice. "Thank you for your help, Alice. We appreciate your time. Sorry we had to dig up some painful memories."

"That's all right, Detective. I do have very fond memories of my daughter. I still miss her terribly. And I don't get many visitors except for my aunt who lives two blocks over."

"Your aunt lives here in Joliet?"

"Yes. She lives at 193 Ash Street. Has lived there with her husband for the last 15 years."

"Thank you again, Alice."

"You're quite welcome. Come back and visit any time."

Then Carrie had a thought. "One last question, Alice. Why Sally Mayfield?"

"I didn't want it to come back to me, so I named her after a distant cousin. I guess it didn't matter in the end, did it?"

"I suppose not." Paul and Carrie left the small home and headed for Ash Street.

"If that wasn't one hell of a bizarre story, Paul. This whole case has come full circle."

"Damn right. Moffitt, Sally's father...that's going to blow Gray's mind."

Carrie snapped her seatbelt. "Better believe it."

"Okay, let's see if the aunt is home. Hope it's not too late. Maybe she can add to this mess." They found the aunt's place and knocked on the door. An elderly woman cheerfully greeted them. They had a brief discussion; unfortunately, she was unable to add to Alice's story.

Carrie chuckled. "So was that Sally's mother?"

"You were right. That was Sally's mother." Paul sighed. "A trip to Vegas?"

Carrie laughed. "Dinner if you're free."

Paul looked at his watch. "You mean now?"

"Yes, now."

"Great. I'm starved. Where?"

▼▼▼▼▼ 2

Gray found it difficult to concentrate. Julia filled his mind and until she was safe he would not rest. Yet, he realized he could not let the team down again. He must remain focused. He was prepared to do anything to rescue Julia and Sally from that maniac. Lying in the dark he feared sleep for it brought nothing but pain and confusion. Then there were the other times when he was convinced he was not asleep for everything appeared so real. He dozed off.

"*I see you're back.*" The voice echoed in his head. He searched the darkness but saw no one.

"*Is that you?*"

"*Yes. Have you come in search of your daughter?*" The question took Gray by complete surprise.

"*Yes...well, no, not really, for I had no idea I could find her here...excuse me for saying this but this is nuts. I don't know who I'm speaking to; I have* no idea where I am and you keep asking me these crazy questions. Would you damn well tell me if this is a dream or not."

"Dreams, awake, conscious, unconscious, life, death...they are merely a state of mind. There are many avenues of life that take you into the unknown. This is but one. Is it important that you are either awake or within a dream?"

"Of course it is."

"How so?"

"Then I will know whether to believe or not."

"You must already believe."

"Why is that?"

"Because if you did not believe you would not be here."

"Then tell me where here is."

"Here is everywhere."

"Quit the double talk and speak in plain English!"

"I cannot be more plain than I have already been. I only speak the truth."

"Okay, enough. What am I doing here?"

"That should be my question, should it not?"

"Damn it, would you just answer me!"

"Very well, I shall answer for you. You seek what you have always sought...justice. You know where to find it, but an impenetrable force that you have been unable to overcome confronts you. To succeed, you must relinquish your anger and forgive before you are able to proceed."

"Forgive? Who am I supposed to forgive?"

"Your partner was not your fault. Neither does it merit malice on your part. You must first step away from the bitterness of that moment."

"I am supposed to forgive the bastard who shot him, the one who killed his daughter, the one who also ruined my life? Is that what you're asking me?"

"Yes."

"And if I do, will I be able to find my daughter? Will I be able to identify the killer?"

"Is that not for you to decide?"

"Damn it, I hate it when you do that!"

"Do what?"

"Answer a question with a question. Just answer my question!"

"I cannot, for it is only you who can answer that question."

"All right, I forgive the guy."

"That is not very convincing."

"Oh, for crying out loud, would you give me a break. I forgive the guy, I forgive him!"

Blinding lights exploded all around him. Gray felt the pressure in his ears. He was falling. There was darkness once again. Then he was standing on a cliff looking out over the ocean. He was...Gray could see a room. There was someone in the room but it was very dark. Then he saw another person. They were both only faint shadows almost without form.

"*Julia?*"

"*Daddy, daddy is that you? Where are you? I can't see you in the dark.*"

"*Julia, I will find you.*"

"*I know, I know.*"

He was floating. There was a house; no, it looked like a barn. A man emerged through a side door. Gray did not recognize him. He watched as the man walked to a white van, got in and drove away. Was that the killer, he wondered? If so, he had no idea who it was. He concentrated, trying to see him again, but nothing came. Gray knew how it worked. He went back. The man was in the barn. He was doing something, setting up some sort of display with figures. It was very dark in the barn and all Gray could see was the shadow of the man moving objects.

The man then walked out of the barn. Gray got closer but still he did not recognize him. He looked at the van – *Perfect Pile Carpet Cleaning Service.*

▼▼▼▼▼ **3**

On Monday morning Paul and Carrie found Gray in the cafeteria talking with Mario. "Morning, Gray; boy, do we have some great news for you. Doesn't solve the case but it sure as hell livens it up." Paul and Carrie sat down, both displaying a little more levity than usual for a Monday.

"We can use a little livening up at the moment. What have you got?"

"You are not going to believe this, Gray." They proceeded to relay the events of the preceding Friday, their trip to Joliet and their conversations with Alice Dougherty and Sally's aunt.

"You're saying this Alice Daugherty is Sally's mother and that Sally's father…this is spooky…is Hal Moffitt?"

"That's the way it's shaping up, Gray."

"My God, what a mish-mash of events. So you both believe that Sally is Alice Dougherty's daughter?"

"No doubt about it, Gray. They even look alike; short and slim, with those dark blue eyes and the blond hair. Side by side, they could be sisters. She's just as beautiful. She also confirmed the birthmark. That alone I would say is irrefutable evidence. What the aunt told us just confirmed everything we heard from Alice. Then there's the note Alice left in the church. She told us what she wrote. I believe we can safely say that the baby and Sally are one and the same."

"That may be so, Carrie, but let's not jump the gun. To be absolutely certain you should get a DNA test."

"Agreed. That will be the clincher."

"You said you spoke to the aunt?"

"Yes, Gray."

"Why did she give the baby up? Surely between her and Alice they could have kept the baby?"

"The aunt's health was failing. She said that had it not been for that, she would have adopted the baby. It was the aunt who suggested the church. Alice told us her aunt protected her from her domineering parents."

"This proves another point. There *are* two medallions."

"If the medallion Alice Daugherty had was not the one Maitland has, then where's Alice's?"

"We're not sure, Gray. Saint Pius Church burnt to the ground in '93 and was never rebuilt."

"Not so, Carrie. It was, but not on the same site. The diocese owned a piece of ground out in Oak Park. They built the new church out there."

"Do you know where it is, Mario?"

"Yes, Carrie. I attended a friend's wedding there about three years ago."

"Then let's visit this church."

"Good idea, Gray. I'd like to go along."

"I didn't know you were Catholic, Carrie."

Carrie gave Mario a stern look. "Very funny."

Gray raised his eyebrows and rolled his eyes in comic gesture. "Okay, you can tag along." Then as an afterthought he said. "I hope you didn't mention any of this to the Daugherty woman."

"Not a word, Gray. We only said we might be back."

"We tell her nothing. Nothing about the medallion or Sally."

"But Gray, doesn't she have the right to know her daughter's alive?"

"Yes she does Paul, but not until we find Sally. We also need that DNA match. As soon as we have that, we can breathe a little easier. We must be 100 percent certain of this."

"Gray, I don't think that..."

Gray raised his hand pointing a finger at Carrie. "Uh...uh."

"But Gray..."

"No...Carrie, this is not a debatable point. We go to the mother with this story only if Sally agrees to it, not before."

"Okay. I guess you're right."

"Good. Now let's go to church."

Carrie gave Gray a quizzical look. "Excuse me?"

"Church, let's go find the church."

▼▼▼▼▼ *4*

St. Pius Church was not quite what they had expected. It was very much 19th century. Set on a grassy knoll surrounded by large pin oaks and landscaped lawns; it was bordered on all sides by modern buildings and looked totally out of place. To the left of the church stood another building that Gray assumed was the rectory. They parked, got out and approached along a concrete path. The snow that had fallen the day before had been shoveled and plenty of salt was spread over the pathway.

"Now let's see if what we suspect is true."

"If it's here, Gray, how do you intend to get it?"

"It's evidence; therefore, we need it for our investigation. Let's see if it's here first." Gray pressed his finger on the door buzzer. Somewhere within the house, a dog barked. A few moments later the door opened and an elderly woman with a bright smile greeted them. She wore a dark blue dress with yellow flowers. The housekeeper introduced herself as May Grinnley.

"Good afternoon, I am Detective Farlon with the CPD. We would like to speak to the pastor."

"Yes, Detective, please come in." Motioning for them to proceed along the hall, May closed the door. She then ushered them into a spacious though sparsely furnished living room.

"Please wait here while I call Father." May disappeared through another door and returned a few minutes later followed by a priest.

"This is Father David. Father, these people are from the police."

"Yes, thank you, May." The old woman turned and shuffled from the room. Father David was in his late forties, short, rotund, bald and had a jovial rather ruddy face.

"Gentlemen and lady, please have a seat." There were only three armchairs in the room so Gray remained standing. So, what can I do for the Chicago Police Department?"

Gray introduced them. "Father, this is Detective Simpson, Detective Salvatore and I am Detective Farlon."

"Pleased to meet you." The priest shook each of their hands in turn.

"Father, we have a few questions about an incident that took place about 25 years ago."

"Oh my, I wasn't here then; neither was this church."

"We are aware that St. Pius formerly was located in the city. Despite the fact you weren't with the church at the time, perhaps you could still help us."

"I will see what I can do."

"Around that time a young woman gave birth to a baby girl. She decided the church should find the child a home and left her baby in the church."

"Yes, I recall hearing of the incident. If my memory serves me correctly, it resulted in a police investigation because the baby was never found. The woman was accused of murder."

"That's the case. Part of our investigation involves a medallion, one she apparently gave to the church as a token of her thanks." The priest appeared uneasy. "You remember the medallion?"

Father David hesitated. "I'm not sure that I do." Gray could see he was hedging.

"Father, we must find that medallion. It has a great bearing on the case and can possibly save a life."

The Father stared at his feet. "I'm not sure I should be talking to you about this."

Gray was surprised at the priest's reluctance. "Why not?"

"I know something happened at that time but...well I'm sorry, Detective, I'm not at liberty to say more."

"Then to whom should we be talking?"

"That would be our Pastor, Monsignor Capra."

"Then may we speak to Monsignor Capra?" Gray asked.

"If you'll excuse me for a moment, I will see if he's available." Father David, somewhat agitated, left the room.

"I think we hit a nerve, Gray."

"Possibly, Carrie."

"I for one have..." The door to the living room opened. Father David re-entered followed by another priest.

"Detective Farlon, this is Monsignor Capra." The two priests standing side by side looked rather like the religious version of Abbot and Costello. Unlike Father David, the Monsignor was tall and rather thin with thick graying hair. He appeared to be in his mid-sixties. He shook hands with Gray and the other two detectives.

"Detective Farlon, your reputation precedes you," he said as he eased into one of the armchairs.

"Is that good or bad?"

"Oh, it is good, very good. Please sit." Carrie sat down while he and Paul remained standing. "What may I do for you today?" Monsignor Capra's voice was soft and calming. *As if you don't already know*, Gray thought.

"As I mentioned to Father David, we are in the midst of an investigation and we need some information."

"You are talking about the incident involving the young woman?"

Gray pushed his hands into his pockets. "Indirectly, yes. But primarily, this involves a medallion."

Monsignor Capra looked up at him. "As I recall, the incident took place in February of 1980. The woman said she left the infant in the church. The police believed she had killed the child but, as it turned out, she had not. About one month after that an incident occurred in the church that could not be explained. Some say it was a miracle. All this took place before the fire. Miraculously, the medallion was not harmed in that fire.

"Two priests were in church preparing for early morning Mass. Suddenly they saw a red glow between the pews. Upon investigation they found an unusual looking piece of jewelry that had not been there moments earlier. How it came to be they had no idea, for all the doors were still locked. They immediately took it to Monsignor Laslow, the pastor at that time. He instructed them to say nothing of the incident. He then placed the medallion in a glass case and kept it in his office. When this church was built, a special room was constructed to house the medallion. We also had a similar case built for it."

Gray looked directly at the Monsignor "Where is it now?"

The Monsignor glanced at Gray. "Oh, it is still here, Detective."

Gray looked at Paul and winked. His heart jumped in anticipation. Had they found the second medallion?

"May we see it?"

The Monsignor raised his eyebrows. "I do not wish to appear rude, Detective, but for what reason do you make such a request?"

"Monsignor Capra, because a medallion, and it might be yours, is evidence in our investigation. We must determine if your medallion is authentic."

"If it is?"

"We will have to take it."

"For what purpose?"

We do like to play games don't we? Gray mused, "It is evidence."

"So you have said. But are you sure the medallion we have is the authentic one?"

"We cannot tell unless we see it."

"Rightly so. Then you should see it. If you will please follow me." He got up and walked from the room followed by the three detectives and Father David. The group left the rectory, taking a path that ran alongside the main church and entered through a side door.

"This way, Detective." They passed through an inner door, proceeded along a cavernous corridor, through another door and arrived in a small, almost darkened, room; the only light came from four candles on a single candelabrum in the corner. Monsignor Capra walked over to a case standing against the opposite wall.

"Father David, please turn on the lights." Moments later the room was bathed in brilliant light. "This is the medallion Detective," he said as he waved at the case. The three of them peered at the impressive display. The medallion lay on a raised section that was draped with purple velvet. It was certainly *the* medallion.

"It's been here since 1995, when this church was opened?" Carrie asked.

"That is correct."

Paul stepped closer to get a better look. "Who else knows it is here?"

"Many priests and nuns and now yourselves."

Gray peered at the Monsignor through the glass. "Are you certain no one else was aware the medallion showed up?"

"I'm afraid I can't answer that, Detective. Why? Is it important?"

Paul was studying the medallion closely. "We're not sure."

The Monsignor tapped the glass case. "So, Detective, is this the medallion for which you are looking?"

"I believe it is." Gray straightened and stretched his back.

"What do you intend to do with it Detective?"

"We must check for authenticity."

The Monsignor walked to the center of the room. "Will we get it back?"

"Of course. We only require it for the investigation, then it will be returned," Gray said.

"Very well. You may take it." Monsignor Capra nodded and Father David lifted a bunch of keys hanging from his belt, shuffled through them, found the one he sought and opened the case. "Please, Detective." Gray lifted the medallion and looked at it closely. It was heavier than he imagined. The priest relocked the case.

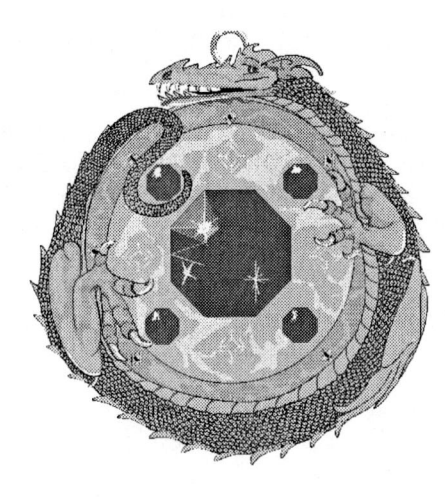

Eye Of The Spider

It has been said that the medallion, known as the 'Eye Of The Spider', was hidden somewhere in Northern India in the Himalayan Mountains in a town called Janakpur. Believed to be over 3000 years old it was, according to Chinese history, created by a monk named Mahindra. Some claim it is real and that it possesses great powers, while others say it is purely myth. Myth or not, this medallion is shrouded in great mystery. Many have tenaciously searched for this prize but none have ever located it. The big question remains, is it myth or is it real.

(Excerpt from 'Book of Shadows' written in the 1st century AD)

"Thank you, Monsignor, for your cooperation."

"You're quite welcome. You do realize, of course, there is something sacred about the medallion."

"No, I don't."

"Detective, you of all people should know full well things don't just materialize out of nowhere."

"Quite true."

"The priests who found it said one moment there was nothing and next moment there it was."

"A miracle, Monsignor," Carrie said.

"Yes, Detective. I do believe in miracles. They are part of my profession."

"But a medallion? This medallion? This is an odd sort of object to be related to a miracle, would you not agree, Monsignor?" Gray sounded surprised.

"Miracles come in many forms, Detective. I for one believe in this one as do most who know of it."

"That may be so, but for what purpose?"

"That, Detective, is something we may not know for years. God takes His time, He is never in a hurry and He doesn't always reveal His purpose."

Gray held up the medallion. "I see your point. I will personally return it to you."

Father David turned out the lights and the small group left the room. "That will be wonderful, thank you, Detective."

Carrie, Paul and Gray left St. Pius Church and returned to the city. With her curiosity almost at boiling point, Carrie could contain herself no longer.

"Gray, what do you intend to do with the medallion? I mean, there is no investigation and we really don't need it, so what's with this charade?"

"Carrie, I'm working on it. First we see if it's the same as the one our friend Maitland possesses."

"Oh, from the photos; I have no doubt it is the same one."

"We'll keep it for a while, give us time to study it further. Then we will return it. I am very intrigued to learn just what all the hullabaloo is about."

"Paul, there is one troubling thing about all this. If the church found the medallion, what happened to the baby?"

"I was wondering the same thing, Paul. The baby was never found. Alice Dougherty said she placed the medallion in the child's clothing. If someone took the baby, why would they return the medallion?"

"I don't believe they did, Carrie. I believe the medallion fell and rolled under a pew."

"It would have made one hell of a noise when it hit the floor."

"Possibly, but whoever took the baby may not have realized what had fallen or, they were in a hurry to get out of the church."

"That would explain it."

▼▼▼▼▼ 5

Alice Dougherty was surprised to see three people standing on her porch when she opened her door. Paul and Carrie along with Samantha Perry had returned to obtain a sample of Alice's blood for DNA testing.

Carrie smiled. "Hello Alice. May we come in for a moment?"

"Detective Simpson, what a surprise. It's good to see you again, and so soon. Please come in." She stepped aside as the three visitors entered. Alice closed the door and directed them into the living room.

"Have a seat. May I get you a cup of coffee or something cold?"

"No, Alice, thank you. We won't take up much of your time. The reason we're here is we would like a sample of your blood." Carrie hoped Alice would not object to the request.

She looked horrified. "A sample of my blood? Why?"

"Remember, on our last visit we mentioned a case that was possibly related to yours? Should we find your daughter, we could confirm her identity

The River Styx   183

with the DNA test. This is Dr. Samantha Perry. She'll draw the blood sample."

Alice Dougherty was agitated. "Oh, I see. Do you think you'll find my daughter?"

"We don't know, but it's possible," Paul said. "To confirm anything we'll need the blood sample. Would you mind?"

Alice hesitated as she looked from Paul to Carrie then to Sam. "If you think it will be of some help, I suppose it can't hurt."

"Don't worry Alice, it'll be fine. It's painless, believe me," Sam said trying to reassure the woman.

"Well, I suppose so. I have a confession; I don't remember ever having a shot. I've never given blood either."

"That's okay Alice, it's no big deal. Also, we promise, should we find your daughter we'll let you know right away," Paul said.

"Thank you, Detective. I feel so silly, a grown woman afraid of a needle."

"That's okay, Alice. I don't like them much either," Carrie said. Sam drew her sample and with her exquisite bedside manner managed to keep the woman calm though she did appear nervous throughout the procedure.

▼▼▼▼▼ 6

Gray walked into his office to find Assistant Medical Examiner Sam Perry waiting for him.

"Hello, Sam, solved the case yet?" The two shook hands.

She smiled. "I thought that was your department. Anyway, I have some more news for you regarding that blood condition we discussed the other day." She caught Gray's quizzical look. "The possible rapid aging condition."

"Oh, okay, I'm with you. Go on. I'm sorry, Sam, got a lot on my mind."

"You need a vacation, Gray. Your hospitalized patient…she's in bad shape."

"We know that, Sam, but she's recovering well." Gray kept Sally's abduction to himself. Not that he didn't trust Sam, he just felt it was better to keep it as quiet as possible for the moment.

"That's not what I'm driving at, Gray. Her body is aging rapidly. If our diagnosis is correct, she'll be dead within 12 years."

Gray was stunned. "What? Explain, Sam."

"Something has happened on the cellular level. What it is, at this point, we have no idea." Gray's thoughts turned to Julia. Had she been exposed to this terrible thing? Fear raced through him. All of a sudden his world was collapsing. Information poured in but none of it made much sense. "Is it reversible?"

"Gray, we have no idea what caused it, let alone how to stop it."

"Isn't there anything that can be done?"

"Without a cause, no. There's something else and, believe me, if you think everything you have heard to date is weird, this takes the cake." If you only knew, Gray thought to himself. "Each of the victims had been dead for about an hour when their hearts restarted."

"I'm sorry, repeat that. Heart restarted?"

"For some unexplainable reason, roughly an hour after each victim died, they revived only to die again."

"How long were they alive the second time?"

"At the most, five minutes. I have no explanation for you, Gray."

"Do me a favor, find one. I'm sick of mysteries, Sam. They give me a bellyache and at the moment, I'm suffering with a doozy. I want answers and I want them now. I want answers before we get buried so deep we won't be able to dig ourselves out."

"I'll do my best, Gray." Sam stood to leave.

▼▼▼▼▼ 7

Maitland did something completely unexpected. He donated the Ivory Buddha to the Museum of Natural History. This was an unprecedented move considering what he had faced to obtain it. During the elaborate ceremony, he made one request; the figure was never to be loaned to any organization or institution but was to remain in the museum.

Gray was highly skeptical. Despite the fact that Maitland was no longer a suspect, Gray believed there was an ulterior motive. He must determine what lay behind this sudden move. He knew if he pressed Maitland, he would get an answer if the man had one. He decided to take the chance. Gray made a phone call.

"Maitland, Farlon."

"Oh, yes, Detective, what can I do for you?"

"I need you to answer a question for me if you can."

"I'll do my best."

"I read the article in the Tribune this morning. Why has the Buddha been placed in the museum?"

"I can't answer that, Detective. All I can say is that three days ago I received instructions to do so."

"How did you get those instructions?"

"I was leaving a restaurant when a waiter passed me a note."

"And you were told what to do?"

"Yes."

"What else was in that note?"

"Nothing, Detective, only that I had to present the Buddha to the museum, and a set of instructions as to how I was to proceed."

"Do you still have the note?"

"Sorry, I gave it back to the waiter."
"As instructed?"
"Yes."
"Thanks, Maitland. That's all I need to know for the moment." Gray replaced the receiver.

▼▼▼▼▼ 8

Although there was a bathroom, Julia was unable to keep herself clean. In the beginning she had tried washing, but with only a hand towel and limited water it was almost impossible. Her skin had become slimy with sweat despite the coolness of the air and her body odor was repugnant to her. The clothes she wore clung to her like duct tape which added to her discomfort. She could not stand being with herself, how could this madman bear being close to her? A good night of sleep was unattainable; she only dozed for brief periods. Exhaustion plagued her and she struggled to remain focused. The pain in her back and legs was almost unbearable and the pain behind her eyes never subsided.

Time had become non-existent, but Julia did not submit to despondency. She spent every waking moment planning an escape. She paid close attention to everything their abductor did and said, relying entirely on all her senses. She was convinced the plan she had conjured in her head would work. It had to. Her main concerns were what would happen once they were outside, as she had no idea where they were. And would Sally cooperate at the right moment? She was also counting on their jailor believing they were too scared to attempt anything.

No matter how good her plan, Julia knew she had to do one thing first to make it work. Knowing the only way their jailor could see was by night vision goggles, she needed those goggles. They could then ride the elevator up and leave their jailor behind. But they had to get out, or they were both dead. Then came the now familiar screeching and grinding sound of the elevator. It was time.

"Sally, are you ready?" Julia whispered.

"I am not sure, Julia; I am so very frightened. What if we fail? He will..."

Julia tried to sound confident. "Sally, we won't fail if you help me. I cannot do this alone and I'll not leave you here because he will kill you. Once I start we must move quickly. Do exactly as I tell you. Don't worry; trust me and we'll make it." Julia stopped talking as the elevator drew closer then stopped. There was a long moment of empty silence. Julia knew their captor was observing them. Then the gate opened. Footsteps echoed on the hard surface. Julia waited. She was ready and as relaxed as she could be at that moment.

"You're both very quiet ladies. Are you asleep?" he questioned.

"Of course we're not. How could anyone sleep through that racket, you idiot?"

"Don't get your knickers in a knot. I know you've been cooped up down here for a time but it's almost over. You'll both be on your way soon." Julia's senses were now acute. He was moving toward her, but the distance between them was difficult to assess.

Julia kept him talking. "You're not going to let us go, are you?"

"You know, Julia, you're a very perceptive woman. You're right, I could never let you go; I've already told you that. You can understand, can't you? I am going to keep you here a while longer then..." He paused for a moment still moving closer to Julia. "Well, we'll see what's in store for the two of you. I think I will perform a masterpiece, a twosome. I will give this city something they will never forget. My 'pièce de résistance'...it will be an exhibit in art form, the likes of which has never been seen. You two will be celebrities, posthumously, but celebrities nonetheless. You will be front-page news. They may even make a movie about you. What more could you ask for?" Julia prepared herself.

"Now I would like you to stand up, Julia, if you wouldn't mind." Julia sensed he was immediately in front of her. She had been lying curled up facing the wall. It was now or never. In one swift flowing movement she straightened her legs and swept them in an arch rolling into a sitting position. Her legs struck the man's with considerable force just above his ankles. His legs were swept from under him. Pain shot up Julia's right calf.

She was unable to see her quarry flip in the air, grasping at emptiness, his hands flaying, his body contorted, trying to avoid falling into the pit. Julia judged roughly where his head would be when he hit the floor. Knowing her jailor was concentrating on saving himself, Julia was prepared to rip the night vision glasses from him. Immediately she would place them on her head. The advantage would then be hers.

Then came a dull thump, a loud gasp echoed about the room as the man had the wind knocked out of him. Cautious and aware of the precipitous drop only inches away, Julia, desperately controlling her emotions, groped in the blackness where his head should be. Her hand fell on a head of hair. She clutched it tightly and, with her other hand, found the goggles. Wrapping her fingers around them, she pulled. They were heavier than she expected. Before letting go of the man's hair, she lifted his head and slammed it against the concrete floor. He yelled in pain. Then juggling with the goggles, Julia hurriedly placed them on her head.

Immediately she could see. The man was struggling to get to his feet but he was severely winded, gasping for breath. He was now as blind as she had been. She didn't wait to congratulate herself. Julia leapt to her feet, and gave her captor a powerful kick in the gut. He gasped and began coughing. Then keeping her eye on him, Julia moved.

"You, you bitch, you...you filthy bitch!" He panted. "Shit, you...you honestly think you're going to get away. You think you can get...out of here.

You ride the elevator to the top...then where do you think you're going? You're trapped you...stupid bitch! You see I thought of...every possible contingency...that might occur and compensated for it. The chances of something like this happening...were so remote but I thought of it! Julia, you're an amazing woman. You surprise me. I didn't think...you would have been so audacious. You have made this a real challenge! Damn you, you bitch...you are going to pay for this!" Julia paused, her anger churning like boiling water. She turned and stepped to where the man was still panting.

"Just shut the hell up and challenge this you sick-minded bastard." Julia, now full of rage, kicked him as hard as she could, aiming for his groin but struck him in the stomach instead. He rolled over the edge into the abyss. To her surprise he did not make a sound save for a low agonizing groan. She stepped to the edge and looked down in shocked disbelief. Stretched across the pit about 20 feet below was a safety net. Their jailor was lying in the net, laughing and groaning in pain at the same time.

"Julia!" He called, "Julia, once...more you amaze me," he moaned. "Now what are...you going to do? On the other hand I...I'm going to climb up that ladder in the wall. Then I will deal with you."

"Suit yourself, you piece of shit, but don't think you're going to lay your grubby hands on Sally or me again! You're done! No matter what happens, your miserable life is now mine!" As she spoke she surveyed the walls and saw the ladder to which he was referring about four feet from the edge of the platform. It ran all the way to the top of the shaft. Sally sat huddled in shock, shaking and terrified. Julia moved quickly through the makeshift elevator to where the terrified woman cowered.

"Sally, it's me, Julia," she said taking her arm and helping her to her feet. "We have to go now." Sally was reluctant.

"Where are we to go Julia? You heard him say we cannot escape." She was almost paralyzed with fear. This had been Julia's concern.

"Sally, listen to me. We *can* escape and we will. He told us we would fall to our deaths, but there's a safety net down there. He lied then and he's lying now. Sally, please; let's get out of here. We have a fighting chance if we go now."

The man's voice floated up to them. "Julia, I'm coming. You had better hurry. Sally, if you stay where you are, I will spare your life. By the way, Sally, why don't you tell Julia who you really are, what you did for a living. She may be very interested." Julia ignored him; to escape was her only concern.

"Julia, you should be more than interested about your friend. She is a little whore, nothing more. Go on, tell her Sally, tell Julia where you come from, or don't you know? Have you not been told about all that has taken place over the past few weeks?"

Suddenly, Sally grabbed Julia's arm in panic and whispered. "We must leave now."

"Yes, good girl, let's go." The man's voice was beginning to grind on Julia.

"Sally," he warbled, his voice echoing up from below. "I will let you go free. I'll not harm you further if you stay where you are. Julia, you will not be so lucky. I'm sorry, but I will have to kill you. Only I will not do it quickly as I had planned but make you suffer as you have made me suffer." Julia guided Sally to the elevator, holding her around the shoulders, ignoring the voice.

"Don't listen to him, Sally, he's only trying to scare us." Julia closed the gate. As she looked around she found the controls and put the elevator into motion. It rose painfully slowly. Julia watched as their captor shrunk into the distance below. He was crawling across the net toward the ladder. She mused, shaking her head. *This is crazy. I feel I'm caught up in some bizarre Edgar Allen Poe plot.*

"Sally, are you all right?"

"Yes Julia, but what about him? How shall we get away?"

"We'll get away somehow. We'll get to the top. There has to be a way out."

"You do not sound very sure about that."

"Well, to be honest, I'm not, but we'll get out somehow, I promise."

The voice still drifted from below. "I'm coming, girls. Sally, did you stay as I told you?"

"I should have stayed and let you find a way out. He would have let me go." It was obvious to Julia that Sally was terrified listening to the ramblings of a madman, fearful of his reprisals.

"Sally, that's ridiculous. The man's a maniac. He would never let you go. He's a liar. Hell, the man has no heart. Remember, you hurt him and he won't ever forget that. He would kill without a second thought and he will smile at you while he does it. Besides, if you stayed, I would not have been able to leave because he would have used you to get me back. We're far better off together."

"But how shall we get away?"

"Leave that to me." The elevator was creeping to the top of the building. As she looked up, Julia could see a square hole in the ceiling through which the elevator was about to pass. There was also a rectangular opening off to her left where the steel rungs of the ladder passed.

The elevator slipped through the hole and stopped. Julia opened the gate and helped Sally out. It was still pitch dark. Julia checked around her. There was a door to her left, their only apparent means of escape. Holding onto Sally's hand she walked to where the ladder passed through the floor. Their captor was still over halfway down, struggling to climb as quickly as he could.

Turning away, Julia stepped to the door and inspected it closely. It was solid steel, constructed like a safe door but with no visible lock. Beside the door was a small pad. She cursed her arrogance, but it was far better to try and die than submit to this madman. As a child her father had told her, in the face of impossible odds, there was always a way out. She had never taken him seriously; now she prayed he was right. There had to be a way out and she was determined to find it. She looked around the room again but it was barren.

"Julia, how can you move around so well?" Sally asked.

"I stole the night glasses. He is now unable to see."

"Night glasses, what are they?

"They allow you to see in the dark." Julia looked down the shaft again. She was shocked. Their pursuer was nowhere to be seen. Julia was concerned.

"Where the hell are you?" Her voice echoed down the hundred foot well.

"Is he there?" Sally's voice quivered.

"I don't see him." Turning her attention back to the door, she tapped the pad cover. It flipped up exposing a calculator-type keypad. Knowing that punching them would serve no purpose, she tried anyway. The door remained sealed tight. The only way out was closed to them. She laughed.

"Why are you laughing, Julia?"

"Nothing, just considering our predicament."

"Then you see a way out?"

"Well – not exactly." Then Julia had an idea. She took Sally by the shoulders and guided her to the wall opposite the door.

"Sally, stay right here no matter what happens. Will you do that?"

"Yes. But why? What are you going to do?"

"Our friendly neighborhood killer is as helpless as you are in the dark, he can't see. When he comes through that hole in the floor, I will be waiting for him. I must immobilize him, then I will need your help. We need him to open that door. Between the two of us, we can certainly make him uncomfortable."

"Are you going to kill him?"

"As much as I would like to, no. He can take a life as easily as breathing, I can't. No matter how bad the man is, I'm not his judge. I will leave that to others. My father will take care of him, I have no doubt."

"Your father, is he also a judge?"

"No, Sally, only a detective."

"I thought he might also be a judge." Julia was looking down the shaft. There was still no sign of their pursuer. Suddenly the quiet was shattered when the voice echoed around them.

"Well, well, well, aren't we a cozy little troop. And where do you think you're going? No need to answer Julia because the only place you are going is back down the hole and then I will figure out what I'm going to do with both of you."

"All right, you bastard, where the hell are you?" Julia yelled.

"Julia, as I told you, I planned this place for a long time and was certain to take care of..."

"...of every contingency. Yes, yes so you keep saying. You sound like a broken record. So where are..."

"I'm right above you. I can see you very well though you can't see me even with those glasses." Julia looked up but could only see a brick ceiling; there was no window or opening of any kind. There were no cameras, so how could he see them?

"You cowardly bastard, why can't you be a man or are you just a wimp who has to hide behind all your gadgets? You're afraid a woman can whip your scrawny ass?" Julia had to get him in front of her. She needed one more opportunity.

"So you think you can beat me? You think you are better than I am?"

"Damn straight. I not only think it, I know it! I can take you with one hand tied behind my back! You're a sorry excuse for a man! Come on, I challenge you, you coward! Get in here and I'll whip you before you have time to spit!" She goaded him hoping he would rise to the challenge. But only silence permeated the room. Thinking quickly, Julia moved to where Sally was.

"Quick, Sally, come over here." She took Sally's arm as she urged her to her feet and guided her to the door.

"If that madman comes through this door, which I'm counting on, don't let it close behind him."

"How will I be able to do that Julia? I cannot see."

"I believe when the door opens, you'll be able to see. Now stay here and don't move. Stay out of his way." Julia positioned Sally beside the door. "Are you all right?" she asked removing the night goggles.

"Yes, I am all right."

"Good, now stay quiet and don't move." No sooner had Julia stepped back and the door swung open. The man was standing there, silhouetted against the light that poured into the room. For an instant she was scarcely able to make him out, but only for an instant. He also paused, unable to see into the dimness of the room. His hesitation gave Julia the edge. She leapt forward and struck him hard on his right shoulder with her left elbow. He grunted, spun around, lost his balance but recovered quickly. Without pausing, Julia kicked. The top of her foot struck the man square in the groin. Pain shot up her leg. Her victim slid slowly down the wall, slumped to the floor, his eyes as large as tennis balls. Then rolling on his side, he doubled into a tight fetal position as he moaned in agony, unable to move.

It was time to leave. Julia grabbed Sally's hand, jerked her to her feet and dashed from the room. The door slammed behind them. They were standing in a corridor that curved away to their left and right. Without thinking Julia went right.

"Come on, Sally, this way."

"Where are we going?"

"Out of here, I hope." As they rounded the bend in the corridor, Julia saw a flight of stairs. Pulling Sally along like a rag doll, she headed for them. "Then I must find my father. For now we have to put distance between us and that madman." As they hurried toward the stairs, Julia cursed herself for not having smashed the control panel alongside the door before they left.

9

Gray was still trying to fathom the reason Maitland was instructed to donate the Buddha to the museum. The move made little sense. His phone rang and startled him. "Farlon."

"Detective Farlon, this Mr. Yu." Gray was surprised.

"Mr. Yu, how are you?"

"Vely well. Detective, I would like you come to my shop now."

"You mean right away?"

"Yes, right away. I have something vely important. You come."

"I'll be there shortly." Gray hung up wondering what could be so urgent. He called Paul.

"Paul, I've just had a call from Mr. Yu. He wants to see me. If you're free, I'd like you to join me. Also, see if Carrie can join us." Gray hung up, opened the top drawer of his desk and removed an envelope. Slipping it into his jacket pocket, he left his office. He stepped into the elevator as Paul and Carrie appeared.

They slipped in just as the doors were sliding closed. "So Gray, what's this all about?"

"Not sure, Carrie."

"Answers to the medallion questions, maybe?"

"Could be, Paul."

Arriving at the old Chinaman's shop, Paul parked and they entered the small store.

"Ah, I see you bring pretty lady detective and partner. Good...we see what you think. First you wait here." He disappeared for a few moments and returned followed by another Chinaman. The second Chinaman was carrying a large book.

Mr. Yu made the introductions. "This my cousin, Mr. Lee. I told him about my friend, Detective Farlon wanting help. He think he can give you information."

"You think you can help us with some information, Mr. Lee?" Gray asked.

"This is not just information, Detective," Mr. Lee said matter-of-factly, his diction and English very precise. "This is very important. You told my cousin you have this medallion you speak of?"

"Well, not quite, Mr. Lee, we don't have the medallion, we have a photo of it. That's what I gave to Mr. Yu." Gray was reluctant to tell anyone they had the medallion.

"I see. That is good."

"Why's that?"

"The medallion, if it were real, could be very dangerous."

"Dangerous how?" Paul asked curiously.

"Detective, in Chinese mythology, this medallion is said to possess great powers. It can..." Mr. Lee paused and glanced down at the book. "Before I proceed maybe it would be prudent if I give you some background on the legend of that medallion."

Carrie interrupted Mr. Lee. "If I may ask, Mr. Lee, could you also explain about the Ivory Buddha of Janakpur?"

Mr. Lee raised his eyebrows in surprise. "Ah, you know the story of the Buddha?"

"A little, yes. I know that it and the medallion go together."

"A very interesting story, would you not agree?"

"I would. Especially since the Buddha is in a museum here in Chicago."

Mr. Lee gasped in shock. "Impossible. The Ivory Buddha is only a myth, a story. It was a figment of one man's imagination."

"I beg to differ with you, but you are quite welcome to go and see for yourself," Carrie said

Deep in thought, Lee rubbed his chin then looked at Carrie. "In a museum, you say? The real Buddha?"

"Yes."

"Here in the city?"

"Yes," Carrie reiterated. Lee looked dumbfounded. Slowly he placed the book on the counter beside him. He then turned and faced Gray, Carrie and Paul, concern written on his face.

"This is not possible. The stories in this book are mere fiction, mythology. Most were written thousands of years ago, developed from a storyteller's imagination."

"Well, your storyteller got his information from sources that were fact, because the Buddha does exist."

"My, oh my, this is incomprehensible." Lee was obviously stunned by the news.

"Mr. Lee, it's the truth. If you wish, I can take you to see for yourself. The man who found it recently donated it to the museum." Carrie could see Lee was not convinced.

In a skeptical tone he said to Carrie, "You say this medallion is also here in the city?"

Carrie proceeded cautiously. "Yes, but it, of course, is an imitation."

Lee shook his head in disbelief. "It is possible to purchase imitations just as you are able to purchase imitations of items such as the legendary sword Excalibur. The sword is purely myth but it does exist. I am certain the Buddha and the medallion you have are in this category."

"Not the Buddha, Mr. Lee, it has been tested and is over 3,000 years old."

"Oh, my. And the medallion?"

"That we cannot say. But I would say with certainty it is an imitation."

Mr. Lee turned and opened his book. "There is a drawing of the medallion made many centuries ago." Flipping through the pages, he searched until he found the page. "Here it is." He pushed the book along the counter. "This is your medallion." Gray, Carrie and Paul looked at the picture. It was definitely their medallion, intricately depicted in pen and ink.

"This is amazing. Yes, that's it." Carrie lifted the front section of the book to see the cover. "I have this book. I found it in the library."

"A book similar to this, Detective Simpson, but not the same."

"How come?"

"Because this is the only copy in existence. This is the Book of Shadows."

It was Carrie's turn to be shocked. "Oh my God. How did you come by it, Mr. Lee?"

"It belongs to my family."

Carrie gasped. "Someone in your family wrote this book?"

"Many of my ancestors wrote it over many centuries. The last entry was over 200 years ago."

Carrie turned back to the picture of the medallion. "This drawing is not in my book."

"That does not surprise me."

"Why not?"

"The book you have, Detective, is a copy made from another book that does not have this drawing. About 200 years A.D. a member of my family, who was in the business of absconding with others money, began to copy this book. He met his demise before he finished. The book fell into the hands of another. Unknowingly, they reproduced it as the original. The book you have stops here," Mr. Lee said turning back a few dozen pages.

Carrie looked at the pages to where Mr. Lee had the book open. "I see. But my book does have some history of the Buddha and medallion."

"True, but it is very brief."

Carrie paged excitedly through the text. "So it appears."

Mr. Lee could see Carrie's enthusiasm. "Nevertheless, the material is very informative and for the most part quite accurate. But it is all still a myth."

Carrie poured over the book, eagerly turning pages, scanning text and pausing every now and then. Gray was curious.

"What are you doing, Carrie?"

"I was reading some of this. It is fascinating. I..."

Again Mr. Lee was surprised. "You can read Mandarin, Detective?"

"Yes, Mr. Lee, but not very well. I have always been interested in Chinese history and culture. I studied Mandarin as a second language."

"That is wonderful, Detective. I am impressed."

Gray rubbed the back of his neck. "Me too."

Suddenly Carrie gasped. "Wow, listen to this." She began to read, loosely translating the text.

'Step through the portal of fire. Within the void the specters of evil await ready to plunder the spirit and steal the soul. Passage to the 'beforelife' is fraught with many dangers. Let the traveler beware; venture not upon this journey in jest for only death is the companion. To emerge unscathed is a falsehood. A tax is levied for each journey – surrender a measure of the soul. Once the portal is breached, death is inevitable – death is the victor. What is then done cannot be undone.

Such evil should never have been released upon humanity but must be left to sleep forever...'

Carrie looked up. "Et cetera."

"And what does it all mean, Carrie?"

"I'm not sure Gray, but I would suggest that, in some aspects, it may be similar to the Greek myth of the River Styx. In the Greek story the boatman, Charon, ferries dead souls across the River Styx for a fee. In the days of ancient Greece, coins were placed under the tongue of the corpse. This permitted them to pay the ferryman to row them across the river. If payment was not made, the souls were forced to wander the banks of the river for 100 years before they were then permitted to cross."

"So this is a similar story from China?"

"No. This is different, Paul."

"But you said that…"

"It's somewhat analogous. But as I look at it, there are many differences. This story suggests the traveler is still alive. There is no boat or any kind of ferryman. Also the traveler, in this case, must run a gauntlet of sorts, tormented by *'evil specters'*. I have no idea what *'to emerge unscathed is a falsehood'* means. I can only assume it has something to do with the traveler attempting to get through this void to emerge on the opposite side. After the journey they appear to be fine but they're not, for whatever reason. It also appears they forfeit a portion of themselves, their souls. Whatever it is, the traveler will, without a doubt, die."

Paul glanced over Carrie's shoulder. "Sounds like fun."

"Then, Carrie, the Buddha is of no concern to us?" Gray said.

"It would appear that it has nothing to do with our case, Gray."

Gray traced the sketch with his finger. "And this medallion?"

"The medallion is a myth."

"So everyone keeps telling me, Carrie, but…"

Mr. Lee closed the book. "The problem with myths, Detective, is that they do not always remain as such."

Carrie shot Lee a questioning glance. "What are you getting at, Mr. Lee? All the stories in that book are just stories, aren't they?"

"Maybe. When it was written, yes, but today it suddenly becomes a subject for debate." Gray felt it was time to hand Mr. Lee the document he'd brought with him.

Lee read it then handed it back. "Do you believe what is written there, Detective?"

"Of course not, it is just a lot of mythical nonsense."

"You surprise me, Detective."

Gray was a little curious. "Why is that?"

"Because you were able to solve every crime you were ever involved in. I am a scholar, Detective. When I knew I was to meet you, I learned all I could about you ahead of time."

"I'm honored as well as impressed, Mr. Lee."

As he pointed to the note, Lee continued. "That text is word for word what is written in this book."

"Do you know the meaning behind this passage?" Gray asked.

"Yes."

"That's it, just yes? No explanation, no interpretation?" Carrie quipped, wondering what she had missed.

Mr. Lee looked her straight in the eye. "I do not think you would like my interpretation, Detective."

"Try me."

"Have you read the text Detective Farlon showed me?"

"I have no idea what he showed you." Gray handed Carrie the two sheets of text. Finally she looked up with an expression of complete disbelief on her face.

"You don't honestly...come on, you're not serious." Paul took the text from Carrie and read it. As he handed it back to Gray he began to chuckle, then he laughed.

"I'm with Carrie. Tell me you don't believe this junk, Gray?"

Mr. Lee stepped in before Gray could answer. "I do not believe it either, but what is myth and what is fact, Detective? The world around us today is changing at a great pace. It is difficult to keep up, is it not? What is myth today may be fact tomorrow."

Gray waved the envelope. "Yes, but this could never be anything more than fiction."

"Is that not what was said of space travel 100 years ago?"

All three detectives looked at Lee in surprise. He had just said the text in the envelope was a myth, now he was arguing that it might not be. "True, but that was different."

"How so different, Detective?"

Gray hesitated. "Well it came to be."

"And that myth could not become a reality?"

"I don't know."

"Okay, Gray, time out here. Would you please tell me what it is we're talking about? Because if you are expecting me to believe what is written in that document, you're nuts."

Mr. Lee smiled. "Do you not think it might be possible in the future, just as space travel proved to be?"

Paul's brow wrinkled into a deep frown and a quizzical grin formed on his face. He stared at Gray and gasped in total disbelief. "Wait a second...you're not..." Paul shook his head. You're talking about *time travel*? You actually believe...are you nuts? You're implying this medallion is some sort of time machine?" He began to laugh again.

"No, Paul, but what Mr. Lee is saying is logical."

"Come on, guys. This is nonsense...pure nonsense; hell, it's impossible. There is no such thing."

It was Carrie's turn to laugh. "From your mouth to God's ears. Why not, Paul?"

"Because...well...well because science says it's impossible."

"As Mr. Lee has just pointed out, 100 years ago science said space travel was impossible, and traveling faster than the speed of sound would kill you, and forget the speed of light."

"Wait just a second. Gray, a few weeks ago you told me that you did not believe in the supernatural and all that sort of thing. Now you're going to..."

"Paul, this is not the same thing, this is science. Look, I'm no scientist, but Mr. Lee makes a very convincing argument."

"Well yes but...but...oh hell, this is nuts."

"Precisely."

"Damn it, Gray, don't you think you're getting just a little carried away here?"

"I am willing to be open minded."

Paul threw his arms up. "Open minded? Are you nuts?"

"Think for a moment, Paul. There are so many unknowns in this case. Add this into the equation and suddenly it begins to make sense."

"It does?" Paul paced to the front of the store and back.

"Yes. How did the killer get Julia out of the hotel or Sally out of the hospital, undetected? How does he manage to elude all surveillance? How can he arrive and depart a crime scene undetected? How about that red glow all of us have so adamantly dismissed? Shall I go on?"

"No, please don't. Look, I can't give you an answer, Gray, but I doubt any one of the team could either."

"That may have just changed."

"Then tell me, Gray, how is it you're now so willing to accept this, when earlier it was just as impossible?"

"Because I've been reading this and asking myself the questions I've just posed to you."

"I hope you're getting better answers than I am. I'm sorry, Gray, but this is just not possible."

"As it was with space travel 100 years ago?"

Paul submitted. "All right...all right I'll go along for now. Just say for a moment it is true, and I'm not agreeing with you, but say it is true, then what?"

"Quite honestly, Paul, I'm not sure. One thing of which I am sure is that we are then faced with a massive problem." It was at that moment Gray felt that icy chill gallop down his spine. His head spun. *Could it be? Could this really be the answer?*

Gray reached, shook hands with Mr. Lee, turned and headed for the door. "Mr. Lee, you have no idea how much we appreciate this information. We thank you for your time."

"My pleasure, Detective. I will, as you have suggested, pay a visit to the museum."

"Do that." Carrie encouraged. "What you will see is exquisite. That Ivory Buddha is something to behold. If you wish, it would be a pleasure to accompany you."

"I thank you for your generous offer, Detective, but I will let my cousin do the honors."

"Then Mr. Yu, we will take our leave, but we will be back. Mr. Lee, how long will you be in Chicago?"

"Two, possibly three weeks."

"Enjoy your visit and I will definitely be in touch. I may want to discuss the medallion further."

"It would be my pleasure, Detective." Carrie, Gray and Paul left the small shop.

Carrie caught up with Gray who was hurrying across the street. "Gray, would you wait a second. Where are you going in such a hurry?"

"Back to the office. There is something I must check."

"But we're not finished here," she said emphatically.

"Sure we are."

"Well I'm not. I wanted to learn more about this medallion."

Gray was troubled. "Later. For the moment there's something far more pressing."

Carrie stopped in her tracks. "There is?"

"Absolutely. Firstly there are two women we must find." But there was also something else niggling at the back of his mind and he felt an urgency to return to his office.

"I understand that. But what else is bothering you?"

"I would rather not say. But if my suspicions are correct, I will let you know."

▼▼▼▼▼ 10

Taking the steps two at a time, Julia encouraged Sally to keep up. They turned the corner and entered a large open area with windows set high in the walls. The room was bathed in sunlight. Julia made a quick survey and then ran to the door on the opposite side. As her shoulder crashed against it, the door flew open, swung and crashed against the outside wall. A scream exploded from her lungs. Julia hung in space, the ground far below.

With all her strength she gripped the panic bar and prayed. Fortunately Sally had not been right behind her otherwise both would have fallen to certain death. Julia's shoulder and elbow were in agony from the collision with the door. Terror set in as she slowly lost her grip on the bar.

"Damn!" she cursed. "Sally, quick, take my hand." Sally planted her right arm firmly against the wall just inside the door and stretched out her left. Terrified, Julia released one hand and reached for Sally's. With her left hand slowly slipping from the bar, Julia desperately grasped Sally's hand. She locked her fingers around Sally's wrist. Then Sally, using all her strength, pulled Julia from the precipitous drop.

Julia stood up and caught her breath. She looked at the ground far below. Her heart pounded in her chest. "Thanks, Sally. Wow! That was close." Julia's body shook and her head pounded. She stood for a moment and tried to quiet her racing heart. Gradually she managed to calm herself. Aware that time was against them Julia made a move. "Okay, let's try that door. It has to be an exit." Sally remained silent and followed Julia, hoping she knew what she was doing.

Julia approached the second door with a little less gusto, pushed the panic bar and the door swung open. Steps led to a lower, smaller room that was in semi-darkness with the light from one small window. She stepped through the door and Sally followed. Julia descended the steps. There was only one other door in the room.

As Julia approached it, she had a terrible thought. She turned as Sally released the door through which they had just entered.

Julia yelled. "Sally! Don't let that door close!" Sally reacted immediately, spun and caught the door just before it could slam shut. "Good. Okay, let's see if we can get out this way." Julia reached and opened the second door. She was instantly struck by a blast of frigid air.

Outside was a small, badly rusted steel plate landing. From that, a very narrow, dilapidated steel staircase disappeared around the side of the building. Julia pondered its condition. Neither was equipped with a railing and neither looked safe. Julia stared at the stairs then at the ground some 50 feet below them. Not wanting to face the maniac who pursued them, she cast caution to the wind.

"Let's get out of here, Sally. You can let that door go." Sally ran down the stairs and across the room. The two women stepped into the bitter cold. With their backs pressed against the wall, they began their descent. With each step Julia became more concerned. In addition to missing treads, sections of the stairway had become detached from the wall.

Sally stayed close to Julia and stepped exactly where she stepped. The icy wind snapped and tore at them, chilling them to the marrow. Julia wore only a pair of slacks, a long sleeve blouse and low-heeled shoes. Sally was in a flimsy summer dress and a pair of sandals. But there wasn't time to worry about the lack of clothing. They must escape this chamber of horrors.

Suddenly there was a thunderous crash and a portion of the wall behind them burst open. Their jailor appeared and almost staggered off the edge of the stairway. Sally screamed.

"I'm going to kill you both! Wait till I get my hands on you!" He grabbed for Sally but she was just beyond his reach. Julia picked up the pace. Sally tripped and stumbled, but managed to regain her balance. In seconds, their pursuer was upon her. He had Sally by the arm and attempted to throw her from the stairs. They were now only about 30 feet from the ground, but still too high to jump. The stairs began to sway violently.

Julia, as she tried desperately to keep her balance, was unable to help Sally. Then Sally retaliated. In a burst of violent anger, she turned on the man. Taken by surprise by the vicious onslaught, he tried to back away but the stairway was too narrow. He had no place to go. As he fought to protect his face, he released Sally and lost his balance.

He teetered momentarily on the edge of the staircase. In desperation he reached for Sally but missed, then he fell. Julia did not wait.

"Sally, stay close and let's keep moving." Sally needed little encouragement. When they reached the bottom, they turned and ran from the building. Julia glanced over her shoulder but saw no sign of their pursuer.

Their goal now was to get as far away from this place as quickly as possible. Julia looked around trying to orient herself. They stood in a large staging area for city vehicles. To their left was a line of yellow snowplows. Not far from the plows was a building that stored salt. Railway tracks cut diagonally across the property a few yards ahead of them. In the distance, she could see the Chicago skyline. As Julia began to hurry, she heard Sally moan. She turned to see the young woman's face contorted in pain.

"Sally, what's wrong?" She did not respond. "Sally, what's the matter? You don't look at all well." Then Sally collapsed to her knees. Julia caught her as she fell.

"Sally, what's the matter?" She stared at Julia, obviously in great pain.

Then she spoke for the first time since they left the building. "Pain, Julia, there is so much pain."

"Where is the pain?" Julia asked greatly concerned.

"My head. I...cannot see...Julia. What is happening to me?"

"I don't know, Sally, but we must get out of this cold." Then Sally became delirious. She mumbled incoherently and finally passed out. Julia panicked. It was still some distance to the street. As petite as Sally was, Julia wasn't sure she could carry her. Her own head pounded. Her arms and legs were growing numb. The bitter cold was taking its toll. If they were outside much longer, neither of them would survive. They had to move.

Julia lifted Sally into her arms. After ten yards or so she was exhausted, but she knew if she put the woman down she would not be able to pick her up again. She paused, took a deep breath and continued. Julia moved slower as she tried to conserve energy. She approached the fence at the edge of the property and walked along it. There had to be an opening.

She came to a spot where a section of the heavy wire had been cut away. She held onto Sally and squeezed through the opening. Now on the sidewalk, Julia surveyed her surroundings. *Where the hell's a cab when you need one?* She began to walk along the sidewalk, but Sally's weight rapidly drained her strength.

Then Sally stirred. "What has...where am I?"

"Sally, you scared the hell out of me. How do you feel?"

"My head...terrible pain."

Julia helped Sally to her feet. "Can you stand?"

"I believe so. I will try."

"Good girl." The young woman stood unsteadily.

"Julia, I remember! I lived in a big house on a large estate. I was in the employ of the Baxter family, and was a personal maid to Mrs. Victoria Baxter."

"You remembered that just now?"

"Yes. I remember more. My best friend Jenny was there with me. I..." She doubled in pain once more.

"Sally, are you sure you can walk?"

"I will try." The sun had retreated and it was starting to snow.

"We have to get out of this deep freeze before we both freeze to death." Julia wrapped her arm around Sally's waist and helped her to walk. Suddenly Sally screamed, grabbed her head and slipped to the pavement. Julia was unable to hold her.

"It is my head. There is so much pain, Julia." Then without warning Sally began to thrash and fight. She kicked vigorously and threw her arms in every direction as if battling an invisible assailant.

"Sally, calm down. It's me Julia. It's okay, you're safe." But Sally continued to fight. Julia was stunned. She did not know how to handle the situation. Finally, she did the only thing she thought would help. She slapped Sally sharply across the face. It worked. The fighting stopped. Julia held Sally tight. She wondered what kind of mental hell this woman was experiencing.

"Sally, are you all right?"

Then another ear-piercing scream erupted from her throat. "Julia!"

Julia knelt on the icy pavement, held onto Sally and rocked her gently as Sally began to cry. "More memories?"

"Yes. Terrible things and so much pain. He tried to kill me but I got away. I fooled him. He came after me, I ran in the snow but he caught me and...oh Julia, it was awful. He tried to kill me and I do not know why." She continued to cry.

"I'm listening to you, Sally, but we must walk."

"Very well..." She helped Sally to her feet and held her firmly around the waist. They started down the sidewalk once more. "I was in the employ of Madam Francine. She had many girls working there," Sally said softly.

"Where, Sally?"

"The Feathered Nest on Payton Street." Assaulted by the severe weather, the two women moved as quickly as they could. Sally held on to Julia in a desperate effort to remain on her feet. She looked up at Julia.

"That man in the building was Claude Marshall. He was the one trying to kill me." Julia was now desperate to find a cab. Snow flurries danced on the wind and with each passing second the storm became more intense. Julia cursed under her breath, as the air grew colder.

April 20, 2006

▼▼▼▼▼ *1*

11:04 A.M.

What churned in Gray's mind was something highly improbable, yet it could not be ignored. Upon returning to District 3 he went directly to the War Room. His gut felt it had been dropped into a dough mixer. He was sweating profusely. Paul had badgered him all the way back but he was not ready to discuss it. In the War Room Gray closed the door. He did not want to be interrupted.

He stepped to the crime board and methodically scanned every piece of paper, note, map and photo. He was searching for that fleeting wisp of terror that slithered across his mind while talking to Mr. Lee. Here on this board was the clue to solving the crime. He searched, his eyes repeatedly returning to the set of seven photos of the victims from 1865. Why had they been pinned on the crime board in the first place? What possible significance could they have? Yet for some unknown reason here they were. Finally he focused on the seven photos; he stared at them until his eyes almost hurt. Mesmerized, he glanced from one picture to the next, over and over. Their familiarity haunted him. He tore at his memory like a child at Christmas wrappings, but he couldn't find the surprise inside. He couldn't fathom why these seven photos, the photos Carrie and Paul had recovered from the archives, looked so eerily familiar.

Then again came that icy chill. The hairs on his arms and the nape of his neck stood erect. Like a thunderbolt from the heavens, the terrifying realization of what was before him slammed into him, and then he remembered. Yet he doubted. Despite what he had just said to Paul, this was beyond his comprehension. Was he delusional? Had he finally lost all his marbles? He had to confirm it. He must be absolutely certain. But it was that confirmation he feared most of all. Could he believe it? Did he want to believe it? If it were true, if it was happening, what would it mean for him, for the task force, for everyone? Could they deal with such events? How do you confront such power?

Gray turned slowly from the crime board, left the War Room and made for his office. Each step was a step toward a possible terrifying climax. It could send the investigation spiraling out of control. It could turn the whole world upside down. He stepped out of the elevator and took the final few steps to his office. He walked to his desk, paused and pondered a moment. His next move could change humanity. His mind raced across the planes of

The River Styx

time, stumbling over all those great inventions and discoveries that had been turned into objects of destruction. Was he prepared to expose this, something that had a greater power of destruction than an atomic bomb? Was he willing to take that chance?

Gray reached for the top drawer. Again he paused. Was this the right thing to do? Should he turn away and forget he ever saw the photos? If he never said a word, no one would ever know. He could destroy them, ending it right here. No, despite the implications, he knew he had to do it. It had come too far and he knew too much. He could not turn away now. Pandora's Box had been cracked open. He had the opportunity to slam it shut.

He pulled the drawer open and stared at the envelope Julia had given him. Reluctantly, almost unconsciously, he reached for it. He tried to tell himself he was mistaken, that his mind was just playing tricks on him again. He picked it up, looked at it once more, then opened the clip and lifted the flap. Reaching into the envelope, he removed the stack of photos.

In an almost hypnotic trance, he stared at the photo on top. His stomach rolled. His vision blurred. His heart raced. The world around him went into slow motion. He lifted the photo and stared at it. Maybe. It was hard to tell. The quality of those on the crime board was poor. He looked at the second but still it was hard to tell. The third. The fourth and he still wasn't sure. It was time to make that final comparison. Gray turned and retraced his steps to the War Room.

Once there he held the first photo up against those pinned on the corkboard. His blood chilled. As impossible as it seemed, reality stared back at him. Time stopped. From one photo to the next the truth tore at him. He studied each photo meticulously, again and again. The answer was the same. There was no doubt.

With a trembling hand he reached for the phone and dialed Paul's office. He remained transfixed, unable to tear his eyes from the photos. The phone rang once, twice, it ricocheted through his head like a bearing in a pinball game, three, four...

"Salvatore."

"Paul..." He felt as if he were suspended in molasses. "This is Gray...I think...you had better come to the War Room...right away...and you'd better bring everyone with you..."

"Gray, are you okay? You sound a little frazzled. Haven't been back to the tavern?"

"That's not even funny. Get everyone up here."

"Okay, we're on our way." Gray hung up, his eyes still locked on the photos. Then he heard voices in his head but paid little attention. He did not want to break his concentration.

"...Gray...hello Gray. Paul to Gray, are you receiving me? What the hell is the matter with you?" Gray quickly came to his senses. Tearing his eyes from the board for the first time in over five minutes, he turned and faced the team.

"Sit," he instructed, motioning to the chairs around the table.

"Gray, are you sure you're okay? You don't look so good."

"I'm fine, Paul. Okay, folks, here's what we have." He paused as he looked at the faces around the table. He took a deep breath and continued. "Actually, to be quite honest, I'm not sure what we have..." He sat down feeling totally exhausted.

He looked from one team member to the next, swallowed hard, then got up and went to the water cooler and filled a paper cup. He returned to his seat.

Paul watched him. "Gray, what the hell is wrong with you?"

Gary raised his hand for silence then went on. "I'm not quite sure where to start or even how to put this into words so that it will sound rational, let alone believable. Paul and Carrie are aware of what we discussed while at Mr. Yu's."

Paul, who was still standing, slipped into a chair. "You mean about the medallion?"

"Yes. Look, instead of me going through it all again, why don't you see for yourselves?" Gray stood again. Nervously, he paced the length of the room with his hands clasped behind his back as he tightly clutched the photos.

Carrie looked up at him. "See what, Gray? Damn it Gray, what's wrong? What's going on?"

"I want you all to take a good look at the photos of those seven women who were murdered in 1865." There was a groan from the group.

Paul squirmed in his chair. "Come on, Gray, we know what they look like. Carrie and I put them up there for crying out loud. Besides they have nothing to do with our case, and what's more we've looked at them a thousand times."

"Then look at them once more and give me your comments. Paul, would you just do as I am asking you." Everyone lethargically got out of their chairs and stepped to the crime board. "I want you to look at them very closely. Remember them. Burn them into your memory." They all obliged reluctantly. When they were through, they returned to their seats.

"Now I want you to look at these photos that Julia gave me some weeks ago." He passed the small stack to Paul. "Don't only look at the photos, read what's on the back." The photos passed from one team member to the next. In silence, each picture was studied. Like a flash of lightning the grin on Paul's face vanished. He turned pale...almost sickly. He twisted in his chair, looked at the photos on the crime board, back at the photo in his hand, then at Gray. All four team members were now staring at him, open-mouthed, in shocked disbelief.

There was a hint of a smile on Gray's face. "So?" The silence was smothering.

Yoshi spoke first. "When did you...my God, when did...?"

"I had an inkling while talking with Mr. Lee in Yu's shop. But I wasn't sure."

The River Styx

"What made you compare them?"

Gray picked up the photos. "I'm not sure, Carrie. I knew I had seen them before but couldn't remember where. Then it hit me. Julia gave me this pack but I had since forgotten about them."

"Gray, but this is...this is utterly impossible."

"My sentiments exactly, Yoshi. At least that's how I felt before we spoke to Lee. For the last 15 minutes I have argued with myself. I lost. Why? This is why," Gray said waving the photos in the air. "You cannot dispute these. Argue as much as you like about logic, this is irrefutable evidence." He dropped the photos on the table.

"But it all just seems so..."

"Impossible, Mario? Yes it does. But if you're looking for an explanation, I'm not your man. Not in this case. Believe me, I can't comprehend it myself, but there it is folks. These photos confirm what Lee told us. The seven missing women from the east coast are the seven victims in those photos up there. Don't ask me to explain it because I can't."

"This is the power the killer was referring to?"

"What do you think, Yoshi?"

"At this point, I'm afraid to."

"I would say without a doubt that...never mind, let's for a moment look at what we have. Believe me when I say I don't want to go where I'm afraid this seems to be leading us."

"It appears we have little choice," Carrie said. In confused apprehension everyone stared at Gray expecting he had all the answers.

"But Gray, how do you explain it? This is nuts. Things have become so twisted."

"Possibly, but how would you like to explain it, Carrie?"

"I wouldn't."

"That's exactly how I feel," Yoshi said.

"So how do we deal with it?"

Gray shrugged. "I'm not sure Paul."

"I hate to be the one to ask, but are we really talking about...?"

"Time travel, Mario. Yes."

"It's impossible! It would change all the rules of physics. It would change everything as we know it."

"Exactly." Gray realized they were skating on thin ice. The information held in their hands was as volatile as an atomic bomb. His dilemma was how to move beyond it. Yoshi interrupted his thoughts.

"You're suggesting this is why we have been unable to identify *our* victims?"

"I believe so. They all come...hell I really don't want to say this. They're all from some place in the past."

"But how do we solve a case where the...this is crazy." Paul buried his head in his hands.

Yoshi got up and stepped to the crime board. He stabbed his finger at a piece of paper that had only a profile on it labeled 'The Killer'. "Gray, what about this guy? Where is he from?"

"No idea. From here, from the past...hell, I have no idea, Yoshi." Gray suddenly realized the staggering implications. "Any suggestions?"

"I'm sorry, Gray, but what's to suggest? For something like this there are no suggestions."

Carrie leaned forward and placed her chin in her hands. "Paul's right, Gray. How do you deal with this?"

"We deal with it. Whatever it takes, like it or not, we deal with it."

"This is the craziest conversation I have ever had. My God, what kind of crime are we dealing with?" Mario stammered.

Carrie picked up one of the photos and looked at it. "One that by all accounts is going to cause us an even greater headache from here on."

"So this means the nurse at the hospital did see the medallion vanish?"

"I suppose she did, Yoshi."

"I hate to throw cold water on this enlightening conversation, but this is nonsense. We are all sensible adults deep in a discussion on science fiction...time travel...bodies from the past...bodies in the past from the future...a killer going back and forth in time like he's making business trips. This is enough to drive one insane."

"Yoshi, calm down."

"Calm down, calm down? How the hell can I calm down? We can't catch a killer because he can slip back to 1865 or wherever the hell he goes. Do I sound insane to you because I sure as hell sound insane to me."

"Yoshi, take it easy. I realize what we are dealing with but no matter what we have to face, we must do it calmly and with level heads."

"Excuse me, Gray, but we're not equipped to handle this. This is for a bunch of cone heads."

"True, Carrie, so this does not go beyond this room."

"We're not to say anything...to anyone?"

"Absolutely not. This stays right here. Think about it for a moment. What would be the first response if you spilled something like this to, say, a reporter or the Mayor?"

"Free food and lodging in a padded cell and a straight jacket for the rest of our lives? Plus how do you bring the guy to justice without evidence?"

"Precisely Paul. And that's the big one. How do you bring this guy to justice? This has to remain our secret. No one breathes a word. Understood?" All heads nodded in agreement.

"This killer of ours certainly gave himself an appropriate name...Charon," Carrie said.

"Sharon...right, you mean Charon with a capital 'C', the ferryman who transported the souls of the dead across the River Styx," O'Malley added.

"Exactly. The killer is transporting his victims across a river of time."

"You're right, Carrie."

"You know guys, this is getting very creepy."

"Getting, Carrie?"

"Come on Carrie, where's your sense of adventure?"

"This is not adventure, Mario, this is…I'm not sure what it is but it's certainly no adventure. Gray, with this capability, how do we catch our killer?"

"We'll catch him, Carrie, but it will be impossible to hold him. Our big advantage now is that we know his secret, but he doesn't know that we know and he must never know."

"Without this knowledge this case would have been unsolvable."

"But is it fact, Paul? Is it the truth?"

Gray dropped his head. "I hate to say this, but it appears to be. But this case is not yet solved."

O'Malley interrupted them. "Excuse me, Gray, there's also his note. The one that reads, *'in death they go two by two, as twin sisters hand in hand. A mirror of the fate to come, repeated, in time again.'* It now makes sense. He was sending a message through time."

"Maybe, but there is no way in hell we would have ever figured that one. But I agree with you Patrick, it makes perfect sense now," Paul said.

"It does?"

"Sure Carrie. The first part, *'in death they go two by two, as twin sisters hand in hand.'* One died in the past and one dies here. They were twins so to speak because their physical characteristics were almost identical and they died on the same date only in a different century. The second part, *'A mirror of the fate to come, repeated, in time again.'* Both deaths were executed in the same fashion, one in the past and one in the present, or to be exact one in the present, 1865, and one in the future 2006."

"Okay, now I see it. How about the other one, the note he left on our victims?"

Gray looked up. "That one still eludes me. *'I'm not what I used to be.'* The killer changed his identity. That is all I can think of."

Yoshi placed his head in his hands in frustration. "Oh, my God."

"What's the problem, Yoshi?"

"What Paul said earlier is true. We can never convict this guy."

"Why not?" everyone echoed.

Then Carrie explained. "Yoshi's right. First, how do you prove it? Second, who's going to stand up and tell a jury he killed seven women in the 1800's and brought them here dumping them on our streets? Or for that matter killing women here and taking…you know. Hell, this whole thing *is* insane. We have bodies without ID's. We can't even go to the FBI on the east coast and tell them we've found their missing women. That would go over real well."

Paul snickered. "You think?"

"Then there's the murder weapon, or rather the lack thereof. Finally, there's absolutely nothing to implicate the killer, whomever he might be.

We're unable to prove anything unless we want to look like a bunch of deranged, raving lunatics. He's free as a bird."

"Right, and he's fully aware of that fact."

Yoshi waved the photos. "That's not quite true regarding the evidence, Gray. We have these."

"Yoshi, I hate to burst your bubble, but they're worthless."

He looked shocked. "How so?"

"Because of the reasons we have just stated."

"True, but Forensics can prove these photos are from 1865. We could then use that as evidence."

Carrie interjected. "Damn it, Yoshi, then what? What would you do with it? Would you be willing to go to court with it? Would you risk losing the killer just on those photos? To say nothing of what would happen to all of our futures?

Gray shook his head addressed Yoshi. "Say we were to take this to court, our chances of getting a conviction is an even zero. We would be laughed out of the courtroom. The killer would walk. They would put a moratorium on all our activities. We'd be the laughing stock of the entire investigative world. Hell, if some late night talk show host got hold of this we'd be toast. Forget all those celebrities who make the headlines, we'd be the main topic of conversation for months, hell years. No, Yoshi, the killer would be the victim; he'd be the celebrity and we would look like the horse's ass. Trust me, it's best to let it rest."

"Our killer is then free to kill again."

"I guess you're right, Carrie, but what can we do?"

"*We* find a way to stop him."

Mario looked surprised. "How, Carrie? He can leave whenever he wishes."

"Carrie's right, Mario, *we* stop him," Gray said.

Paul stared at Gray, a grim expression on his face. "Are you saying what I think you're saying? We take him out?"

"Only as a last resort, Paul. Can you think of any other way?"

"Gray, you're suggesting we be judge, jury and executioner? I don't like the implications."

"Neither do I Carrie, but if you or anyone else can come up with a better solution, I'm willing to listen." There was a long silence as they all looked nervously at one another. Finally, Paul looked at Gray.

"Gray, this is not your style."

"It's not, but desperate times call for desperate measures. I believe this qualifies unquestionably." Gray looked at the faces around him. No one spoke. "Don't look so morbid, guys, we're not in that predicament yet. There's still time to work this through to a palatable conclusion."

"I think we all understand Gray, but how do we explain it all in the end?"

The River Styx

"If we play our cards right, Mario, it won't be necessary. Finally, everything related to this case must be destroyed, everything except the simple and explainable stuff. There must be no paper trail."

"But, Gray, you can't keep something like this hushed up. It's not possible."

"Watch me, Mario, just watch me. Think for a moment the negative impact this would have. We're already dealing with one possibility. I could throw out a few dozen more. Do you have any idea the devastating impact this could have in the wrong hands? No, this stays with us and only us."

"How are we going to do that? It's an almost insurmountable task."

"Almost, but not impossible, Yoshi. We start right away to clean it up, then we move on." Suddenly Gray had a sickening thought.

"What is it, Gray?" Paul asked.

Gray hardly heard. He stared at the far wall yet saw nothing. His mind was only on Julia.

"Gray."

Finally he responded. "What if the killer is holding Julia and Sally in 1865 or some other place in the past?"

Carrie looked up in shock. "God, Gray...we'll...we'll never find them."

"Precisely. Remember, he said he had them where we would never find them. I am afraid that's where he has them."

"Then we're going to have to find a way to get to them. If there is nothing else we do with this case, we get those women away from that demented maniac," Paul said.

Gray nodded his head. "I'm with you, Paul."

"We have the second medallion, Gray."

"Carrie, don't even suggest it."

▼▼▼▼▼ 2

11:07A.M.

The two women continued their slow walk along the street, Julia supporting Sally and encouraging her to continue moving.

"Come on, Sally, you're doing great. It's not much further and we should be able to find a cab. How do you feel? You still don't look good."

"I feel a little light headed, but better. It is the cold, I believe, that is bothering me. I am also very hungry."

"Not long and we'll sit and have a good meal. First we'll go to my hotel so we can shower and freshen up."

"I would like that," Sally said, her voice trailing off.

"Or you can soak in a bath. I prefer showers, myself." Suddenly Sally's legs buckled and she collapsed in a faint once again.

"Sally, Sally, please stay awake." She grabbed Sally under her arms to prevent her from falling. Julia slowly sat and leaned against the fence so that Sally's weight rested against her. Julia was exhausted and deeply concerned. This was the third time Sally had passed out, and she was thinking the worst.

"Sally, please don't die on me. You can make it; we don't have far to go. Just down this street." Sally stirred and started to struggle.

"Sally, it's okay, Sally, it's me Julia."

"Jenny...what is happening? So much pain."

"Sally, it's me, Julia." Julia rose to her feet and helped Sally to stand. Sally turned to face her. Her face was expressionless and her eyes glazed.

"Sally, are you all right?"

"Where are we?"

"We're on our way to my hotel. What happened?"

"Julia, oh God Julia, my head!" she screamed. She clawed at her head with both hands as if trying to tear the pain from it.

"Sally, it's okay, everything's okay. I'm here." Julia recalled the name her father mentioned as their murder suspect. "We escaped from Maitland. Now we're safe. As soon as we get to my hotel, we will be warm, then we can eat."

"Not Maitland, Marshall. Claude Marshall. That is his name. He killed Victoria. Julia, I must tell someone. He tried to kill me and...Julia, he is a very dangerous man."

"We know Sally, we know. The police will get him. In the meantime we must keep moving."

"He killed Victoria. I thought Baxter did it but it was Marshall. Baxter killed Jenny. Oh, God I remember...Julia!" Sally screamed. "There is so much pain in my head." Again Sally convulsed, her body contorted, her eyes rolled upward and she was unconscious once again.

Julia was in a state of panic as she held Sally, not knowing what was happening. Was she going to die? Julia lifted Sally into her arms and she began to walk. Half a block and they should be out of the woods. It was snowing heavily which made it slippery underfoot. As Julia approached the corner, Sally stirred.

"Julia..."

Julia stopped. "Sally you're not at all well. I must get you out of this weather."

"Where...where are we?"

"On the way to my hotel."

"I must get...Julia I have to get home."

"You will, you will, but not right now."

"Julia, you may put me down."

"Are you sure? You're sure you can walk?"

"I will be all right. You cannot keep carrying me. I will try to walk."

"Very well." Julia eased Sally's feet to the ground. She was gratefully relieved though Sally was not heavy. Holding on to Julia, Sally slowly balanced herself.

"Are you okay?"

"I believe I am able to stand."

"If you can walk, it's just around the corner."

"I can walk. It is my head. Every now and again there is so much pain." Julia was amazed at the strength and determination of this petite, frail woman. She would not relent. They rounded the corner just as a cab was approaching from the opposite direction. Julia raised her arm and yelled. The approaching cab made a U-turn and pulled up to the curb. Julia grabbed the door handle, opened the door and carefully helped Sally into the cab. She climbed in after her then shut the door. The sudden warmth of the cab was almost intoxicating. A lightheaded feeling came over her. She looked at Sally who was slumped back in the seat with her eyes closed.

"Where to, ladies?" Julia wasn't sure. She wondered if she should take Sally straight to the hospital.

"Memorial Hospital."

"No!" Sally barked. "Not the hospital. Julia, please. I do not wish to return to the hospital."

The driver twisted round and glanced at Julia. "Look lady, it's your money but make up your mind."

"Shut up and just wait a second," Julia yelled at him. "Sally, I think you need..."

"No, I will be fine once I am warm."

"Are you certain?"

"Yes."

"What about the pain in your head?"

"It only lasts for short periods. I will be all right. Please, Julia, do not worry."

"Okay, driver, take us to the Downtown Sheraton. And do me a favor, step on it."

"No problem, lady." As the cab leapt from the curb, Sally let out an ear splitting scream.

"Sally, it's okay, we're on our way. Sit back and relax."

"Pain. Julia, I have that terrible pain again in my head. It is so bad." She doubled over and clasped her hands to her head. Julia put her arm around Sally's shoulders and tried to comfort her. The woman shook violently.

"What the hell's the matter with her? She don't look so good. Been on the bottle?"

"Look, buster, shut up and just drive."

"Okay, okay, lady." Julia turned her attention to Sally who'd dug her nails into Julia's leg. The grimace on her face indicated her level of pain.

"Sally, it's okay, we'll be there soon. Are you sure you don't want to go to the hospital?"

"Nnnn...no, Julia. Please, it will pass. Once I am warm and have some food, I know it will pass."

Julia doubted it. Sally looked terrible...her ashen skin, bloodshot eyes and the continual head pain caused Julia grave concern. Her sudden bouts of pain were occurring more frequently. But Sally was adamant that she did not want to go to the hospital.

"Sally, I'm very worried about you."

"Julia, it is kind of you to worry about me, but I shall be much better soon."

"All right but if you pass out on me again, I *will* take you to the hospital." Sally was silent. As the cab rolled, jerked and raced through the city, Julia tried to warm Sally by holding her close to her.

Then Sally lifted her head, looked at Julia and forced a weak smile. "I feel better."

Julia hugged her. "That's good. We'll be at my hotel soon."

"Julia."

"Yes, what is it, Sally?"

"I am remembering more of my past."

"So I noticed. That's great. But you seem to pay a price each time."

"I do not think it is so good. What I remember is terrible. There is so much torment and death, and the pain. Julia, there is one thing that is troubling me."

"What's that?"

"Where am I? This is not Chicago."

"Yes, it is, Sally. Your memories will not return in order. Pieces will be missing."

"I did not grow up here. Chicago is a small city. This must be New York for it is a very big city."

"It is, but this isn't New York, it's Chicago."

Sally changed the subject. "I work at the Feathered Nest."

"So you said earlier. You were a waitress?"

"Oh, no."

"A bartender?"

"No, I live at the Nest. I entertain men and women."

"Excuse me, you entertain men and...okay, Sally, I understand. You don't have to explain."

"Payton Street is down by the river. I used to walk..." Her voice dwindled to silence and she stared out the window.

"Something you remembered?"

"Yes, my best friend Jenny. One day a week we were free and we would go to town. In the summertime we walked along the river. It was so peaceful with just the sound of the river racing to the lake. Sometimes we kicked off our shoes, sat on the bank and splashed our feet in the cool water. Then that bastard Baxter killed her." Julia was a little shocked for she had not heard Sally swear.

"Driver, do you know a place called The Feathered Nest on Payton Street? It's not far from the river."

"Don't know it, and I have been driving a cab in this city for over ten years. No Payton Street either."

"You're sure?"

"Sure, I'm sure."

"Sally, I think your memory is still in a state of confusion. The driver says there is no such place or street."

"No, I know there is such a place; there has to be. I remember it quite clearly." Sally became agitated.

Julia attempted to calm her. "Sally, when we get back to the hotel we will look up the address. Then we will know exactly where it is. But it might not be in Chicago."

"Thank you, Julia. I should let Madam Francine know where I am."

"We can do that."

"I still find it very difficult to believe this is Chicago."

▼▼▼▼▼ 3

12:10P.M.

For Gray, April 20th had, so far, been a day full of surprises. It began with that most improbable information from Mr. Lee. Next came the unnerving realization of the implications behind that news. Then Samantha Perry presented her disturbing news. Gray felt sick to his stomach. But things were about to get even more unsettling.

He had just finished a phone conversation with Karen Pulaski, an old board member who relayed news about Hal Moffitt, a subject on everyone's mind. *Could Moffitt be Winslow?* Finally O'Malley was about to present the most devastating piece of evidence that would reinforce the theory on time travel. It would confirm Winslow's death.

"Okay, Patrick, talk while we walk," Gray said as he, Carrie and Paul were on their way to lunch.

"Hal Moffitt called me." Gray was surprised. Things were definitely growing more complex.

This case is turning into a briar patch. If it becomes more complex we'll never escape it. "When?"

"The last time was just over a week ago."

Gray was even more surprised. "What do you mean, the last time?"

"He has been calling regularly over the last six to eight weeks."

Paul glanced at Gray. "What for?"

O'Malley looked nervous. "He was interested in our progress."

"And you gave him the rundown?"

O'Malley was on the defensive. "I was never told not to speak to board members, current or past."

Gray put him at ease. "Relax son, you did the right thing. So what did you tell him?"

"That things were going well and we had some interesting leads but if he wanted more details he would have to speak to someone else."

"That's all?"

"I did tell him we had a reporter from New York covering the case."

"How did you know it was Moffitt?"

"He told me. I had no cause to doubt the man."

Gray stopped and stared at O'Malley. "It might not have been Moffitt. I just received a call from Karen Pulaski. Moffitt called her from Nassau. Apparently he knew nothing about the case. She suggested he call us directly. He told her he didn't want to do that." The small group stood in the center of the lobby and continued their conversation.

"Then if it wasn't Moffitt, who was it?"

"I've been giving that some serious thought, Paul."

"Gray, let me interject a moment. I believe that although we have ruled out Maitland, I believe he is still involved."

"I agree, Carrie," Paul said.

"Okay, folks. Let's clear one thing up here and now. Apart from his being linked to the medallion and the Buddha, Maitland's in the clear. I had a long talk with him. Our mysterious killer is manipulating him, but he is not involved in any other way. There's no doubt about one thing, the man is scared to death."

Carrie snapped her fingers. "I knew it, I knew he was no killer. Didn't I say he was no killer?"

"Yes you did Carrie. You have something else for us, Patrick?"

Patrick glanced at the envelope in his hand. "Yes I do. We found Winslow."

Gray was stunned. "You found him? Where?"

Paul smiled. "We thought you might be interested."

Gray was eager for the answer. "Interested? You bet. Where?"

"You're going to love this." Patrick pulled a photo from the envelope and handed it to Gray. "That's a photo of Winslow's body…taken in 1865."

"You're kidding!" Gray's heart leapt to his throat. "Dear God alive. So Moffitt *did* kill Winslow in his apartment that night!" Gray gasped.

"Winslow was shot once in the head. Apparently the coroner was somewhat dumbfounded when he extracted a copper clad bullet. In his report he stated it was a type of bullet he had never seen."

"What's going on here? Three former board members directly or indirectly have their hand in this case. Why? For what reason?"

"Three, Gray?" Paul said.

"Yes. Moffitt, Griffith and now Pulaski."

"But Pulaski only called to get an update."

"Nevertheless she has suddenly come into the picture. So the mystery deepens."

"Then who is our killer, Gray?

"I'm not certain, Carrie, but I'm leaning more and more toward Moffitt. He has motive and the money."

"Yes, but he has never been to Hong Kong."

"We don't know that. We need to do some more digging, folks."

"Why not Griffith?"

"My God, Paul, Griffith didn't have the brains to concoct such a plan. Besides he wouldn't have the guts. Griffith was a born coward."

"As it stands, there are more questions than answers."

"Let's get a low down on Moffitt. His full background, who his friends are, what he eats for dinner, how many times he goes to the bathroom. I want to know everything down to the number of fillings in his mouth. Also, see if we can nail down a solid connection between Moffitt and Griffith." As the four left the building, Gray relayed the news about Sally's condition.

"That sounds bad."

Gray shook his head. "It's worse than bad; it's devastating, Paul. Sally is under a death sentence; either from some outrageous affliction or a mindless killer."

"Mind if I change the subject for a moment?"

"Go right ahead, Carrie."

"I don't really want to bring this up, Gray, but I feel we should look at it despite its outrageous implications."

"With everything that's taken place today Carrie, I doubt we can get more outrageous."

"I paid Mr. Lee another visit. I wanted to find out more on the medallion and what else was in his book. What I learned was not only amazing, but, should it be true, it's quite terrifying. This medallion has tremendous power. Its ability to open a portal to the past is only one of its functions."

"It can do other things?"

"Yes, but we should only concern ourselves with the aspect of time travel. As I read the book, two things became apparent. Only one person at a time can pass through the portal. Secondly, and we are already aware of this, the more those passing through the portal use the medallion, the faster they will age..."

"Wait a second, Carrie. You said only one person at a time can pass through this portal?"

"According to what I read, yes."

"Then how did our killer manage to get the bodies through?"

"They were dead, inanimate objects. Another point, the medallion has a sort of built in homing device. When used, if the settings are not disengaged, the medallion returns to its point of origin...hence the medallion showing up in St. Pius Church. The unsettling fact is that frequent use of the medallion can be fatal."

"Carrie, the book is wrong."

"Hey, Gray, I don't believe in this stuff either. Besides, I didn't write it."

"That's not what I'm driving at. Think about what we now know. Sally is rapidly dying. The other victims would have died anyway. Time travel is a killer whether you make one trip or ten."

"My God, Gray, you're right." There was an ominous silence.

Then Paul spoke. "That's bad news."

"It's disastrous, Paul. Everyone exposed to that thing is condemned to death. That includes Sally and, very possibly, Julia. Sally for certain because we have the results of her blood work. Damn it, we have to find those two women quickly and we must get Julia's blood tested." Gray felt a tightness in his chest and a helpless emptiness in his gut.

"Gray, maybe Julia wasn't exposed."

"Then how the hell was she taken from the hotel unseen, Paul?"

"I get your point."

"We'll deal with that when we find Julia and Sally. Go on, Carrie."

"The function of the medallion is complex and precise. There are very specific steps that must be followed to activate it..."

"I have just had a thought," Paul suddenly blurted out. "The young girl, Sally's mother, left Sally at the church. Patrick, didn't you say that there was an orphanage in that general area?"

Carrie interjected. "That's it. Paul, you're right."

Paul raised his eyebrows in surprise. "I am?"

"Yes. The baby was transported into the past. This is fantastic. No wonder they accused Sally's mother of killing her baby..."

Gray interrupted Carrie. "Not only is it fantastic, it may be the answer to a terrible sequence of almost fatal events. Sally was condemned to grow up in an alien world only to encounter some crazed maniac who sent her back into another alien world. This is unbelievable." The stunning implications were impossible to comprehend.

"Then that crazed maniac followed her here to finish what he started," Paul said.

Carrie looked at Gray. "That has to be it. Then it is irrefutable, Gray, that Sally is from the present. The birthmark clinches it."

"Hey, I've just had an idea. We can use the second medallion to send a message."

"What are you talking about, Paul?"

"We use the medallion to send a message back to 1865. If..."

Gray interrupted. "To whom?"

"The police. Send them a pile of evidence and tell them who the killer is."

"Paul, we have no evidence and we don't know the identity of the killer."

"That doesn't matter. Look, how do you bring a time-traveling killer to justice? We can't, but if we fabricate sound evidence for the police in 1865, they can deal with him and put a stop to his rampage."

"If it didn't sound so outrageous, Paul, it might be a good idea."

"This is an entirely new playing field and the game has changed. It also means we have the advantage."

"We do?"

"Yes, Carrie, because we know the killer's main weapon, and he doesn't know that we know."

▼▼▼▼▼ 4

1:20P.M.

Back in his office Gray called the Operations Room. "Sergeant, any news on my daughter?"

"Nothing yet, Detective."

"Keep me posted. I know you guys are doing your best but I…"

"We're on top of it, Detective; we'll get your daughter back for you. Could you hold a second, Detective?" Gray was put on hold for a moment, then the Sergeant was back.

"Detective, I have just had one of my guys come in with something that could be a lead. There is a warehouse on the north side that's been abandoned for about 15 years. My guy informed me that there has been activity on that property recently."

"What sort of activity?"

"Vehicles going in and out, mostly late at night."

"Maybe somebody bought the place."

"No, it has not been sold."

"Then we'll check it out, Sergeant. Thanks for your help."

"Any time, Detective." Gray immediately called Paul.

The warehouse was a mile west of the expressway on Church Street. The name on the marquee beside the gate, though barely legible, read 'Zell's Grain & Feed – Established 1895'. The building, that had seen better days, was set back from the road behind a high wire security fence. The gate was bent, old and rusted and secured with a heavy chain and large padlock that were new. Despite the chain and lock, there was a large gap between the double gates. Access to the property was certainly not a problem.

"Let's go take a look." Gray squeezed through the gap. Yoshi, Carrie and Paul followed suit. The many tire tracks confirmed recent activity.

"There's definitely been traffic through here. And not too long ago either."

The four crossed the abandoned yard and approached the building. The wind, now warmer, scurried across the open ground, picked up old leaves and trash and like some skillful juggler tossed them about then gently laid them down, only to begin all over again. The spring thaw was taking place and the ground under foot had become a slushy mess.

"We have access, Gray," Yoshi said and stepped through the opening into the building. The other three followed. Inside it was dark, quite warm and silent. The four stood for a moment while their eyes grew accustomed to the gloom. The wood floor was covered with a thick layer of old straw. The air was heavy and rich with a musty odor that irritated the nostrils.

"Strange! Unlike outside, it doesn't appear that there's been recent activity," Yoshi commented.

Gray glanced about him. "Scout around, see what you can find. Be careful, don't go falling into pits or over old pieces of machinery." The four broke out flashlights. High in the rafters the flapping of wings could be heard.

Carrie's voice trickled out of the gloom. "Hope that's not bats."

"Not bats, Carrie, pigeons. You won't hear bats."

"Oh great, that's comforting."

They had been scrambling about the building for 15 minutes when, from deep within the structure, Paul shouted.

"Up here...second floor." Carrie, Gray and Yoshi hurriedly found the stairs and climbed.

"Where are you, Paul?" Gray called.

"Follow the corridor until it ends." The three Detectives moved along the corridor until they saw Paul's flashlight.

Carrie, Gray and Yoshi stepped around a collapsing partition. "What have you got?"

"See for yourselves." They crossed the room. He raised his flashlight and the three Detectives gasped in shock as they stared at the macabre scene before them.

Yoshi drew in a quick breath. "What the hell is that?"

Carrie stepped closer to get a better look. "It's a mannequin."

"I can see that, Carrie, but it's also someone's idea of a sick joke."

Gray also stepped closer. "Hell, I don't believe it. It's the same outfit right down to the shoes."

"Not only that, Gray, there's this," Paul said handing Gray a slip of folded paper.

"Down to the note as well?"

"Well, not quite. Read it." Gray unfolded the paper and read it... *'Sunday, March 10, 1974 Got you fooled, haven't I?'* was all it said. Gray raised his flashlight and played the beam on the face of the mannequin that stood before them. The shoulder length blond wig, the crimson evening gown with gold trim, the long black opera gloves, the black high-heeled shoes; everything was as it should be, as it had been in every murder, save one. Gray shivered. He dropped the beam of light to the floor and saw a rug lying at the mannequin's feet.

"This is weird," he said.

"This is sick," Carrie added.

"Why?" Yoshi asked.

The River Styx

Gray walked around the display. "I told you…he's playing with us. He's letting us know he can do this over and over again and we can't catch him."

Carrie shivered. "Perverted son-of-a-bitch."

"Thank God it's not another victim."

"Amen Yoshi, but why would he do this?"

"What the hell does Sunday, March 10, 1974 have to do with all this, Gray? It was 28 years ago."

Gray was silent. He was certain he knew the significance of the date but his mind was riddled with so many thoughts he was having a hard time focusing. Then it came to him. The shock rumbled through his brain like thunder. *Could that be the answer?*

"Did you say something Gray?"

"No, just thinking out loud." Because there were more pressing issues he pushed the thought aside.

Carrie interrupted his train of thought. "Gray."

Gray looked over to where she was crouched. "What is it, Carrie?"

"This straw is fresh. It was placed here quite recently, and lots of it."

"Yeah, and a great way to destroy and avoid footprints," Mario commented.

"Paul, let's get Forensics in here. They may not find much, but it's worth a try." The four left the old warehouse.

As they climbed back into Paul's car, Carrie asked. "What do you think the date meant, Gray?"

Once again Gray's thoughts turned to that day that now seemed so long ago. His mind drifted back to the nightclub. How, because of ignorance and sheer incompetence his partner had been killed. It all seemed like yesterday.

"Thirty-two years ago I was a cop on the beat. My partner was Juan Rodriguez, the only policeman I trusted with my life. We were on the graveyard shift about ready to call it a night when a call came in. There was a disturbance at a nightclub down on South Michigan Avenue. It was an all-night jazz joint, called the *'Keynote Club'*; a pretty high-class place. Anyway, we responded to the call. When we arrived we found some guy hold up in the place with five hostages. When we went inside we found an utter shambles, tables and chairs thrown everywhere.

"The guy was a disgruntled citizen who had been evicted from his place and tossed out on the street. He was looking for restitution and figured this was the best way to get it. He sat on the bar swigging on a bottle of whisky. Anger and booze never mix. He was jumpy and threatened to shoot hostages if he didn't get what he wanted. Between Juan and I we managed to talk him into putting his gun down. We also managed to have him start to release his hostages.

"Things were going fine until Griffith walked in. He was also a cop on the beat, but he was a loose cannon and never followed the rules. He was the last person I needed at that moment in that situation. The first thing he did was to pull his weapon and aimed it at the guy at the bar. It was all over. The guy lifted his gun and fired at Griffith hitting him in the arm. The club was now in chaos. Hostages were screaming and gunfire filling the air.

"When it was over, the guy was dead and so was my partner. It was a mess. There was, of course, a full investigation. As it turned out, and based on Griffith's testimony, it was my gun that killed the hostage taker as well as my partner. I was immediately suspended and the investigation proceeded. I knew full well I did not fire those shots because when we entered the club the suspect insisted I place my gun on a table before he would let me approach the bar. When Griffith was shot, he lost his weapon. He saw mine; picked it up and using his left hand proceeded to fire.

"Griffith thought he was Hollywood hero cop. He always wore dark glasses; he also wore gloves though he didn't carry a 44 magnum. It was the gloves that caused all the trouble. There was no way to prove he had fired the shots. I lost my partner and although I was eventually exonerated, it was never the same. The rest of the story, I suspect, you all know."

"You're saying Griffith sold you out, Gray?"

"He did more than that Carrie. Griffith moved up the ranks as I did. We never got along, and that was no secret. In the end he was able to take my job from me. It was partially my fault. I began to falter in my work after my wife died and Julia left. He used that against me and I was forced to retire early. It was a long battle but he won and I lost."

"But, Gray, what about the hostages? Didn't any of them see what happened?"

"They were no help, Yoshi. None of them were even looking; they were all crouched down in a booth. All I could do was plead my case but it didn't help. Without his prints on my gun there was no proof."

"What a snake."

"He was Carrie. He could never be trusted under any circumstances."

"But why has that date surfaced now? We now know the significance of it, but what does it mean?"

"I would guess that our killer has just confirmed why he's doing this."

"He has?"

"Yes, Yoshi. It's revenge, definitely revenge."

"But hasn't Griffith had his revenge, Gray?"

"This is not Griffith, Carrie. This is someone else and I'm not sure who at the moment, but I have my suspicions."

"Care to share them with us?"

"Not yet, Paul."

5

12:16 P.M.

The cab glided to a halt at the entrance to the Sheraton. The cabbie turned to collect his fare. It was then Julia suddenly realized she had no money.

"Would you mind coming in with me? I will ask the manager to pay you." The driver frowned, then decided if he wanted the fare, he would have to follow Julia. Julia helped Sally and together they walked into the lobby. People stared at them, and Julia realized she and Sally must have looked a sight in torn and dirty clothing, not to mention that Sally was wearing only a summer dress and sandals.

Julia walked over to the reception desk. "Hello, I'm Julia Farlon," The clerk looked up and stared at the two decrepit looking women before her with a shocked expression on her face. Julia ignored her. "I have a room here, 514." The clerk referred to the guest list then turned to Julia.

"You said the name is Farlon?"

"Yes."

"I'm sorry Ms. Farlon, but that room is not registered in your name. When did you book the room?" Julia realized she had been away for at least two weeks and they must have removed her belongings.

"Let me speak to the Manager and I think we can clear this up." The woman disappeared and returned a few moments later with the Manager.

"Ms. Farlon, I'm John Wise, the Manager. How may I help?"

"You will no doubt recall activity in your hotel not too long ago. I'm not sure of the date but a woman was abducted from her room."

"Oh my God, it's you! You're *the* Ms. Julia Farlon. That was just over two weeks ago, Ms. Farlon."

Julia smiled. "Yes it's me, and we have only just escaped from the son of a bitch who abducted me. Two weeks…that long…wow. Could you oblige me? My friend and I are in need of a room so we can shower and clean up."

"Yes, of course. Also I believe your belongings are still here. Your father, Detective Farlon, was to come by to pick them up but has not yet done so."

"Oh great. Look, could you give me a room and send them up. All I need immediately is my briefcase. I must pay the cab driver."

"That will be unnecessary, Ms. Farlon. We will take care of the cab for you." He selected a room and handed Julia the key card.

"Just my briefcase, please."

"Surely." He went through the door and returned with Julia's case. "Anything else I can do for you, Ms. Farlon?"

"We would like to order some food. Neither of us has eaten for the last…well a few days."

"I will have a meal sent to your room and the hotel will cover it. We will also take care of your room for the next few days."

"Thanks very much, Mr. Wise, that's very generous. Oh, one other thing. I don't want anything said about my return. The character that caused us this agony may still be out there and if he is, we never want to see him again."

"I understand, Ms. Farlon. Everything will be handled discreetly."

"Thanks, I appreciate everything you have done, Mr. Wise."

"It's our pleasure, Ms. Farlon." Julia took Sally by the arm and led her toward the elevator. Then without warning, Sally staggered and fell onto her knees. Julia took hold and tried to keep her on her feet, but she had passed out once more. An inquisitive crowd quickly gathered and the Manager was immediately at her side.

"Shall I call an ambulance, Ms. Farlon?"

"That won't be necessary; she'll be fine. She just needs a little food. I can handle it if everyone can move back...she also needs air."

"Sure." The crowd moved away as Sally slowly regained consciousness.

"Sally, you must stop doing this to me. You're scaring me," Julia whispered. "I am going to have to take you to the hospital if this continues." Sally grabbed Julia's arm and squeezed it.

"No, Julia, please. I will be all right. I promise."

"Okay, but you must rest as soon as we get to the room."

"I am very tired. I would like to sleep a while."

"Me too." Julia put her arm around the woman's waist and helped her to her feet. They continued to the elevator. Once inside their room and away from prying eyes, they relaxed.

"Okay, here we are. Sally, why don't you shower first? I'll wait for the bellboy to bring my cases and see if someone arrives with food." Sally walked over to one of the queen-sized beds and stood staring at it for a while. She turned to Julia.

Then almost childishly, she said, "May I?"

"Of course, go ahead." Sally sat down cautiously.

"It feels so good to sit on something soft after that hard stone floor."

Julia sat beside her. "You're absolutely right."

"Julia, I must thank you for everything you have done for me."

"Nonsense, you don't have to thank me; you would have done the same for me."

"I am not sure that I have your courage, Julia...the killer, Marshall."

"What was that?"

"The killer...do you believe he is dead?"

"No idea. All I wanted to do was get the hell away from that place. I didn't bother trying to see if he was dead or not."

"I hope so."

"Me too."

"He used a long knife; he tried to kill me. He cut me badly, but I stood up to him. I defied him. He thought he could make me scream but I did not. I continued to defy him and he grew very angry. Then I ran..." She paused in thought. "He chased me. I ran from the Nest into the cold and snow. He tried to kill me, but I fought him. I pushed him and he fell on his blade. Then came a strong gust of wind, the snow was very thick and I could no longer see him. I ran. All I could think about was escaping. I must have fallen unconscious, for when I awoke I was in hospital. I do not know what happened to Marshall but I do not doubt he returned to Madam Francine's. He will tell her lies. She will believe him. He is a very rich man."

"You were very lucky, also very brave. You stood up to him, just as I did."

"Julia, I am truly beginning to remember. But..."

"But what, Sally?"

"My head is filled with so many things that I am unable to see it all. It frightens me."

"Scares the hell out of me also Sally, and it's something I'm sure should not happen."

"That may be true, Julia. Nevertheless, if I remember my past, it is good. I am remembering my past, am I not?"

Julia had some reservation for she feared for Sally's health. "Yes, you are, and that's wonderful."

"That murdering tyrant. I serviced him five times and all the time he was planning to kill me. It makes my skin crawl. I should have seen it coming. I should have known. I know men and how they are with women..." Sally paused, her mind wandering once again to another place, another time.

"Sally, you said the name of the man who attacked you was Marshall."

"Yes, Claude Marshall. I believe he is a banker. He also owns the most luxurious and exclusive men's club in the city."

"Well you're safe now, so why don't you try to sleep a while."

"If you do not mind, I think I would like that very much."

"Go ahead. Once you're rested, we will have something to eat." Sally lay back on the bed and Julia covered her with the comforter. She fell asleep instantly. Julia tried to call her father at District 3 Police Headquarters. Having received no reply after two attempts, she decided to try later. She glanced at the clock on the nightstand. It was *1:35P.M.* Julia wanted to surprise him so she did not leave a message. She lay on the bed and was soon asleep.

At *3:40* Julia woke with a start. It took her a moment to realize where she was. As she got up, she saw Sally was still sleeping. Julia went into the bathroom and splashed cold water on her face. When she returned to the room, Sally was stirring.

"Well, hello. You slept well."

Sally raised herself on one elbow. "I feel very much better."

"Good. How about that nice hot shower?" Julia suggested. Sally sat up and swung her feet to the floor. There was a knock at the door. Julia nervously went over and looked through the peephole. She saw the bellboy standing in the hall with a clothes trolley.

"Yes, what do you want?" she asked through the door.

"I have brought your suitcases and clothes, Ms. Farlon." Julia opened the door and allowed him to enter.

"Just leave it there. I will empty it and put the trolley in the hall." He caught sight of Sally sitting on the bed and paused.

"...That will be fine," he stuttered.

Closing the door behind him, she turned back to the room. "Okay, Sally, let's get cleaned up. Then we'll see what I have that you can wear." Julia opened the bathroom door. "There you go." Sally stood staring into the room with a perplexed look on her face.

Julia glanced at her. "You do remember how all that works, don't you?"

"No, I'm afraid not." Julia showed her. She handed Sally a towel, soap and shampoo and told her to relax for as long as she wished. Julia left the room and pulled the door behind her. Before it closed, the handle was snatched from her grip. Sally was standing in wide-eyed panic.

"Please Julia, may I leave this open? I am afraid to be alone behind a closed door."

"Sure, Sally, I'm sorry. I wasn't thinking."

Then Julia discovered modesty was not one of Sally's strong points. Before Julia realized it, Sally was standing quite naked before her handing Julia her old clothing. Julia could not help but stare at the small, shapely, but terribly mutilated body of this young woman.

She was covered with numerous vicious-looking scars and bruises. Some scars were small, others large. The worst ran from her right shoulder down to her navel and had sliced through the nipple of her right breast. The grotesque image of Frankenstein's monster rushed through Julia's head. She shuddered. Julia felt sick at the sight of what had been done to this poor woman. No doubt it was a tremendous ordeal for Sally, suffering at the hands of this monster. Her body was a scarred map of insanity, but she had the doctors to thank for a magnificent job. Suddenly Julia realized she was staring.

"Sally, I'm so sorry. I did not mean to stare but..."

"Do I look so very ugly Julia?" Julia could see she was crying.

"Oh Sally no, you look fine. You're going to be just fine. The doctors have done an excellent job."

"The scars, they look so ugly. Men will not want me any more." Tears ran down her cheeks.

"Sally, it's okay. When they have all healed properly, you will hardly see them."

"Are you sure?"

"Of course, I'm sure. You will be as beautiful as always, you'll see. You'll still be able to wear that bikini."

"Bikini?"

"Yes. Tell you what, why don't you shower, and then we'll talk about bikinis. Are you okay? Some of those wounds still look bad. I still think you should see a doctor."

The River Styx

"No, Julia, please, I don't want to go back to that hospital. I wish to remain with you."

"Why Sally? Did they treat you badly there?"

"Oh, no! No, not at all, they were very kind. It is the thought of what happened there. I do not feel safe there any longer. I do not wish to return."

"Okay, have your shower, then we'll talk. I will have a first aid kit sent up also." Julia wondered if Sally should even get the wounds wet. She stepped closer to check them. As Julia ran her finger over the longest scar, Sally flinched.

"Oh, I'm sorry, does that hurt Sally?"

"No, it is only sensitive." Julia checked the rest and for the most part they appeared to be healing well. While Sally showered, Julia first called the front desk and asked for a first aid kit to be sent with their meal. She then tried calling her father again, but he still did not answer. A few minutes later there was another knock at the door. Julia looked through the peephole to see their food had arrived. She opened the door.

"Your dinner, Ms. Farlon, compliments of the Manager." He pushed the food trolley into the room. "There is a first aid kit on the bottom shelf," he said.

Julia was awestruck. "Wow! That looks like an awful lot of food."

"Enjoy your meal," the young bellboy said as he left. Julia stood for a moment staring at all the dishes on the trolley. She peeked under each one to find fish, steak, vegetables and desserts. On the lower shelf there was coffee and a bottle of chilled champagne with two glasses, and the first aid kit.

While Sally was still in the shower, Julia began to move her clothes into the closet. At the same time she looked for something suitable for Sally.

Once Sally and Julia had finished showering, Julia took care of Sally's wounds. Then they sat, dressed in white hotel robes, and attacked their meal.

After consuming steak, fish, vegetables, dessert, a full bottle of champagne and coffee, Julia outfitted Sally with clothes. When she handed Sally a bra, she received a look of total confusion. Julia was surprised. She realized this woman had lost her memory, but surely not to that degree. But what did she know about memory loss? Julia suggested that Sally watch her dress then follow suit. Finally came the high-heeled shoes. Through the entire process both women were laughing so hard they were barely able to continue dressing. After all the instruction, manipulating, tugging and stretching, Sally was dressed. Julia looked her over.

Her long hair, now washed and brushed, hung to her shoulders, glistening like a field of golden wheat. It framed an exquisite, oval face, accented by high cheekbones. The most alluring feature was her almond-shaped eyes that were deep pools of dark blue. She was wearing a gray skirt and white blouse. A pair of dark stockings and black high-heeled shoes completed the outfit. Sally looked fresh as a spring flower. There was no doubt as to her stunning beauty.

Sally caught Julia smiling. "You are smiling, Julia. Why?"

"I was thinking how strange it is that you are wearing my clothes looking so very beautiful and we met in that dark, dank, terrible place."

"It is strange, but also terrifying. Julia, you have been wonderful. You have saved me from that demon, allowed me to bathe and given me your clothes to wear. You are a very special friend. I had a very good friend whose name was Jenny. We were very close. The man we worked for, Mr. Baxter, killed her." Julia noticed Sally was repeating herself periodically.

"Oh, Sally, that is terrible. I'm so sorry. Did he go to prison?"

"No, he was a very wealthy and powerful man and people feared him. He made two of his workers bury Jenny somewhere then told them if they said anything he would report that they had killed her. He has now been judged and received his punishment for he is dead." The faraway look returned as Sally stared off into space. "I still miss Jenny so very much."

"I'm sorry. That's so sad."

"But I have much to be thankful for, Julia. I managed to escape that killer and that is a great blessing to me for I want to see him suffer as he made me suffer. I also have you as a friend and I feel very happy."

"You may have the opportunity to see the man suffer a little."

"You have never told me what you do. What is your work? You speak about working with your father."

"I don't work with my father. I'm a Journalist. I work for a New York City newspaper. I'm here in Chicago to cover the Mannequin Murders. I was born here and grew up in this city. My Dad has always been with the police force."

"I can see that you love your father very much."

"Yes, I do."

"Where is your mother?"

"She died some years ago."

"I am very sorry. You loved her very much also."

"Oh, yes. She and I were joined at the hip. We did everything together."

"Was that not painful?" Sally asked innocently.

"Painful?" Julia started to laugh. "No, Sally, that's an expression. It means we were very close. I'm sorry, I am not laughing at you. It just sounds funny to explain it."

"That is a funny expression. Joined at the hip..." Sally repeated it and chuckled. "I never knew my mother or father. I was placed in an orphanage when I was very young." As the hours passed, Sally's memory improved and her fainting spells seemed to subside.

"I think I should try to call my father again and plan to meet him. He will..." At that moment the phone on the nightstand rang. Julia hesitated then picked it up.

"Hello."

"Hello, Julia." That unforgettable voice slithered down her auditory canal, struck her eardrum and sent ripples of fear up and down her spine.

Julia froze and broke into a cold sweat. Her skin crawled as panic exploded in her mind. She almost dropped the phone.

"I've missed you," came the eerie, mesmerizing voice. "It wasn't very nice of you to turn down my hospitality and run away like that. You've made me very angry and you hurt me badly."

"My heart bleeds for you, you demented creep."

"Don't speak to me like that, Julia. I will have my revenge. I will hurt you and that bitch friend of yours." Julia's heart almost stopped. As she pulled herself together, she responded.

"Look, you bastard, don't even think about it. If I see your face once more I'll rip it off and shove it down your throat. Someone should do to you what you did to this poor woman, you sick son of a bitch!"

The tone of his voice became ice-cold. "Mind your tongue, Julia, no woman speaks to me like that and gets away with it. I do things to women that would make your skin crawl. When I get my hands on you and that little whore with you, I will carve you like a Christmas turkey. Then I will feed you to the dogs in the neighborhood. Exciting isn't it..."

"Go to hell you sick psycho." Julia slammed down the phone but was panic stricken. She took a deep breath. How had this madman found them so quickly?

"Who was that?" Sally asked nervously.

"Our friend." Terror flashed across Sally's face. "Damn...Sally, we have to leave now." Julia picked up the phone. She was about to dial District 3 again when she remembered her father's cell number. She dialed; it rang twice, three times, four. She sat on the edge of the bed, nervously drumming her fingers on the tabletop.

"Daddy, please answer." Julia hated phones. "...Come on, Daddy, damn it, where are you? Please answer."

▼▼▼▼▼ **6**

4:53 P.M.

"Gray, I have a question about our earlier discussion."

"And what's that, Yoshi?" The team had returned from the warehouse and was seated in the cafeteria.

"There's one thing troubling me about the time travel scenario."

"Only one?"

"According to what you said, Carrie, anyone who travels through that portal dies a rapid death."

"Yes, that's what we know so far. Why?"

"Because if Sally, as a baby, was sent back in time, she should not have survived as long as she has."

Carrie put her coffee down. "You're right, Yoshi. Why is she still alive?"

"That is one of the many things about this that has been bothering me. Maybe this would be a good time to get with Sam. There's a possibility she might be able to shed further light on this mess. It would be great to have some sort of an answer," Gray said.

"Good idea."

"But, Gray, the tests on her blood indicate she is dying. That suggests that no matter what happened in the past, something occurred to change her condition."

"That's possible, Yoshi, but I certainly can't explain it. I would say Gray is right; we must speak with Sam," Carrie said.

"Either there's a flaw in the explanation or it's being interpreted incorrectly."

"That's possible," Carrie said. "Bear in mind that the book is written in an ancient language, and we're relying on Mr. Lee's interpretation, as well as my limited knowledge of the language. There could quite possibly be discrepancies in the translation."

"It appears all we can do for Sally is wait and see."

"That's about it, Mario."

"By the way, Carrie, has anything come back on the DNA tests?"

"Oh yes, Gray. With everything else going on I almost forgot. It was a match. There is no doubt that Sally is Alice Daugherty's child. Of course, whether Hal Moffitt is the father or not is another story. We need his DNA for that."

"That's good news, Carrie."

"Are we going to let Sally and her mother know, Gray?"

"Not at the moment. It would be premature considering we have no idea where Sally and Julia are."

"Will you tell them later?"

"That decision will be up to Sally. Our immediate concern is to find the two women and find them fast. I don't care how we do it. I want your full concentration on this task and this task alone."

"What about our investigation, Gray?"

"Our priority, Mario, is to find the women, then the killer."

"Finding them is not going to be that easy if..."

"I don't want to hear that, Yoshi. All I want is to get Sally and Julia away from that maniac. You got that?"

"Right, we'll get right on it, Gray. We'll find them."

"Good, then let's go find them. I'm going to pick up a few things in my office then I'm heading home. I'll see you all in the morning." As they filed out of the cafeteria, a cell phone started ringing. Everyone went for theirs.

"It's mine. I'll talk to you guys later." Gray stopped to answer the call.

7

5:30 P.M.

The phone rang five times...six, still she hung on and listened to the monotonous sound. She prayed for her father to answer. As she continued to tap on the tabletop, she grew more agitated with each ring. Ten, eleven, and was about to hang up when she heard the line open and a familiar voice.

"...Hello." Julia pushed the phone to her ear.

"Daddy? Is that you?"

"Julia! My God, Julia, what...where...how are you...where are you?" A floodgate opened and released all his emotions.

"We're in my hotel room but we must get out of here..."

Gray almost shouted into the phone. "We...who we? How did you get away?"

"Daddy, calm down for a moment and listen. We don't have a lot of time. I will explain everything to you when I see you. That maniac Maitland was just on the phone..."

"It's not Maitland."

"What?"

"The madman who abducted you is not Maitland."

"Never mind that for now. Daddy, Sally and I must get out of here. Where's the best place to meet you?"

"Sally? Sally's with you?"

Julia grew more agitated. "Would you please..."

"Okay, go to the lobby and wait there. He may be deranged but he's not stupid. Paul, Carrie and I are leaving now. Julia, don't take any chances. Don't let that bastard get close. He's cunning, crafty and deadly."

"Oh, I know, Daddy. I won't let him touch either of us."

"How's Sally?"

"She's fine. Still in some pain, but fine. She was hurt really bad."

"Yes, yes I know. I'll see you in about 15 minutes. Julia, it's good to hear your voice again."

"Likewise, Daddy." Julia hung up.

8

5:33 P.M.

"Sally...we've got to move." Julia hurried to the closet and removed her winter coat and a lined raincoat. She handed the winter coat to Sally. They left the room and quickly walked down the hall.

Suddenly Sally said to Julia. "You curse a lot."

Julia was a little stunned. "Excuse me?"

"You use a lot of bad words, bad language."

"I'm sorry, but it's the way everyone talks. I know it doesn't take intelligence to swear. I'll try not to do it so often."

"As I remember, men swear but not in front of women. Educated women do not use bad language either. Many street women do, but even then, not as bad as you do. Women should always be very dignified when in public. In private it can be different.

"Women are very sensual and enjoy that bonding with men. We find it is the one time we are able to control men in very powerful ways. Men are so weak when it comes to sex. They would lose their souls to a woman just to be able to bed with her. It is all they ever think of. They think they invented the game." As Sally spoke, Julia became more fascinated. She wondered where this woman came from. By the way she spoke, it was not Chicago, though Sally was adamant that it was.

"You are so right. Men's minds are constantly in their pants. I agree."

"Men are the same everywhere Julia. I used to say to Jenny that if a man's penis was his brain, he would be the most powerful thing in the universe." The two women burst into laughter.

"That's the best description I've heard." Instead of immediately taking the elevator, they walked the stairwell down two floors then called the elevator. Once in the lobby, Julia felt safer. Seated in a secluded corner with a clear view of the entrance, they waited.

▼▼▼▼▼ **9**

5:34 P.M.

Gray, filled with excitement, relief and agitation, hurried to catch up with the others. "Hey guys, wait up."

"What's up, Gray?"

"That was Julia on the phone. She..." He began with guarded jubilance.

"Julia? Where is she?" Carrie asked, a look of stunned disbelief on her face.

"Sounds like she and Sally managed to get away from our killer."

The group felt Gray's relief. "That's great news, Gray. Where are they?"

"The Sheraton Downtown. I'm on my way there. Apparently he found out where they had gone. He called Julia at the hotel. I told her we would meet her in the lobby."

Paul looked confused. "Who called her, Gray?"

"The killer."

"The madman that kidnapped them called them at the hotel?"

"Apparently so, Mario."

The River Styx

Carrie strode down the hall. "Then why the hell are we standing around? Let's go!" The rest followed her.

"Gray, Mario and I have to make a number of calls. We'll see you later."

"No problem, Yoshi." Paul, Carrie and Gray went quickly to the garage.

"Gray, this is great. Did Julia say how they managed to get away?"

"She was too panic stricken to say much Paul." When they reached the garage, they all got into Gray's car.

"I wonder where he was holding them." Carrie said closing her door.

Gray started the engine and headed for the street. "We'll know that soon enough, Carrie."

"Gray, I was thinking about our discussion earlier. What if the Buddha is a decoy?"

"What's your point, Paul?"

"Placing it in the museum was an unprecedented move."

"It was a surprise move, I grant you but..."

"No Gray, Paul could have a point. Every move this guy's made has been meticulous, but more so, everything he does has a reason. He made sure all the focus was on someone else. Maitland. What if..."

"But, Carrie, giving the Buddha to the museum does not constitute an outrageous act."

"I agree but there must be a sound reason behind that action and it certainly wasn't generosity."

"Go on."

Carrie rested her arms on the back of the front seat. "We know Maitland is the fall guy. What we have to do is use that to our advantage."

"How?"

"I'm not sure. It would be simpler if we knew why the killer placed the Buddha in the museum."

"This guy is leading us by the nose, Gray," Paul said.

"Maitland doesn't know who the killer is?"

"He has no idea, Carrie. He's never seen him.

"Hell, what a mess. Maitland, who was Whitely, a bank guard, is now a multi-millionaire. Moffitt, who we're assuming is behind this whole fiasco, is now whom?"

"We can't be certain but I would say Winslow. He had to get to that money somehow."

"But why would he then place so much money in Maitland's hands and give him all that power? Why didn't he just carry out his mad scheme on his own?"

"Good question, Carrie. I wish I could answer that. He controls Maitland, who fears him enough to remain loyal. But there is one thing he's overlooked. People reach a breaking point and are forced to make a decision. Maitland chose to let it out when I confronted him that morning at his place."

"So we've gained an ally."

"Not that it will do us much good. Maitland is scared to death and he's also afraid for his girlfriend. No, we will have to proceed without his help."

"Pity. We might have been able to draw the killer out by using Maitland."

"Possibly, Paul, but I believe our man is too cautious to be trapped that way," Gray said as they approached the Sheraton.

▼▼▼▼▼ 10

6:09P.M.

It was an anxious 20 minutes before Julia saw her father walk through the revolving doors. She and Sally stood and raced toward the three Detectives.

"Daddy!" Julia exclaimed as she extended her arms and approached them. Farlon embraced his daughter, elated to see her alive and well. Tears rolled down his cheeks as he kissed her on her forehead and held her to him not wanting to let her go. Finally, they separated. A very happy Farlon stepped back and looked at his daughter.

"Julia, how did you get here?"

"It's a long story, Daddy, can we talk on the way? I just want to get the hell out of here. Daddy, this, of course, is Sally." Julia looked at Paul, who, she noticed, was staring at the young woman. Everyone was staring at her amazed at the transformation. "Paul, put your eyes back in your head and let's move." She looked at Sally and winked. Sally smiled.

"I believe you all came to know Sally over the last months. She, of course, knows all of you."

Paul was almost drooling. "But she never looked like that."

"Paul, stop, you're embarrassing the poor girl," Julia said. "Last time you saw her she was lying in a hospital bed. That's no place to look like a beauty queen."

"You look wonderful, Sally, if I might say so." Sally glanced at Julia and they both laughed.

Paul frowned. "Am I missing something?"

Julia looked at him and smiled. "It's a private joke."

Gray turned toward the entrance. "If you're all ready, I think we should move." The five walked out of the lobby into the chilly evening air. Gray turned and took Julia aside.

"Has she said anything? Does she know?"

"Does she know what, Daddy?"

"Does she remember where she's from?"

"Yes, she says she lives here in Chicago, but swears this is not the city where she grew up. Her memory is gradually returning. At times I'm convinced she's from another planet by the way she speaks."

"She's definitely from Chicago, but her Chicago, not ours."

"What kind of double talk is that?"

"Julia, you had better brace yourself because you're not going to believe this. Sally is from the past."

"Past what?"

"Long past, Julia, 1865 to be exact."

Julia began to laugh. "You're pulling my leg. Be serious."

"This is serious, Julia. I gather she has no inkling?"

She saw the expression on her father's face and realized this was no joke. "Come on Daddy pull…" She stared at her father. "My God, you're serious?"

"Never more so."

In shocked disbelief, Julia stared at Gray then over at Sally. "But how?"

"It's extremely complicated, and we need to talk about it."

Julia paused for a moment, deep in thought, and then turned to her father and whispered. "It would definitely account for all the strange things she keeps saying and simple things she should know, but doesn't. But Daddy, it can't be; time travel is impossible."

"I thought so too, until now."

"Damn! You're telling me that Sally…you're putting me on. Sally is over 150 years old?"

"I know it sounds a little crazy, but yes and no."

"A little? You have no idea!" Julia stopped dead in her stride and stared at Gray. "What do you mean, yes and no?"

"We've discovered Sally was actually born in Chicago in 1979. Then, by some freaky coincidence, at six months old she was thrown back to 1841 where she grew up. Look, let's talk about all this later."

"Your father's correct, Julia. Sally's from 1865…well, she is really from…it is complicated. The killer has been able to elude us all this time by using the medallion."

A crooked smile formed on Julia's face. "Come on guys, this is a joke right?"

"Would you keep your voices down. We learned of this during the last few days."

Julia gave a cautious side-glance to Sally. "Damn, that poor woman."

"What simple things?" Gray asked his daughter.

"What?"

"You said she didn't know simple things. Like what?"

"Women's underwear for one. She had no idea what a bra was. She was shocked when she saw brief panties and pantyhose. She did not know her way around a bathroom."

"I guess that would get you thinking."

"You bet it did but, hell, not in a million years would I have put it down to this. You swear you are not putting me on?"

"I wish we were, Julia, but it's quite true." Julia shook her head in disbelief. Looking at the petite woman standing alone on the sidewalk, she suddenly felt her loneliness.

"She has no idea? How in the name of hell are you going to explain that one to her?"

"I'm not."

"You're not going to tell her?"

"No, you are."

"Come on, Daddy, why me? Do you have any idea what this might do to her? Hell it could send her over the edge. Damn it, she's almost there now."

"That's why I want you to do it, Julia. She has come to know and trust you. You will have a far better chance to ease her into the idea." At the curb was the large white hearse. Julia stopped and stared at her father.

"Didn't you get rid of this damn thing? Daddy, it's an eyesore. I hate it."

"My sentiments exactly." Paul chimed in, but he immediately realized it was the wrong thing to say.

"If you two don't like my car, walk. Besides, it's roomy, comfortable, smooth riding and seats all of us."

"But, Daddy, it's...well it's a hearse for God's sake, for dead people, not us living folk." Julia felt a hand grip her arm. She turned to see a look of panic on Sally's face.

"This is a vehicle for dead people?" she asked with terror in her voice.

"Sally, it's okay. We all joke about riding in my father's car. Actually it really isn't that bad."

"Sally, don't you pay any attention to them. It's a great car." They all got in and Sally gripped Julia's hand for comfort.

Gray, anxious to hear their story, prompted Julia. "Julia, what happened? How did you manage to escape?"

"It wasn't easy. The place was a fortress. I think it's an old silo on the northwest side. He converted it into a sort of Pit and Pendulum madhouse of horrors. Sally and I were placed on narrow ledges halfway down inside the structure. The place was pitch dark all the time. That maniac brought us food now and again. My stomach constantly felt that my throat had been cut. By the way, Sally knows him as Marshall not Maitland." Julia proceeded to explain how they escaped.

▼▼▼▼▼ *11*

6:33P.M.

Immediately after returning to District 3 with Julia and Sally, Gray took Julia aside and brought her completely up-to-date. Then they all gathered in the War Room where Julia and Sally finished their story.

Julia went to the large map of the city. "I believe we were being held...here, in this area." She stabbed her finger at a spot on the map.

Gray rose from his chair and stood beside Julia. "You said there was a large open area?"

"Yes."

"Were there railroad tracks?"

"Yes, two or three, as I recall."

"How about vehicles? Trucks, heavy equipment?"

"I don't remember seeing...yes, there were city snow plows. I'm sorry, I did not pay a lot of attention. All we wanted to do was get out of there as fast as we could. Sally was not well either. She passed out on me three or four times. I wanted to get her to a hospital, but she said no."

"You took a cab to the hotel?"

"Yes, a Blue Light Cab. We walked a fair distance before that."

Gray turned to Paul. "Paul, let's get a lead on the cab that picked them up. I think I know where Julia and Sally were."

"Right on it, Gray," Paul said and left the room.

"It sounds as if you were very lucky to get away."

"Believe me, we were. I certainly caused the creep some pain. Kicked him so hard in the groin he probably thought he'd had a sex change."

"Way to go, Julia. Pity you didn't kill the bastard," Carrie said enthusiastically.

"Right, a pity."

"This character was certain you were both going to die. Did he speak freely about himself or anything he had done or was about to do?"

"He didn't allude to anything we didn't already know, but the man's cautious as well as clever. He always wore rubber gloves."

"How did you know that if it was dark?"

"One time he grabbed me by the throat. Also, when he gave us our food he guided our hand to the tray."

"Maybe to ensure he never left fingerprints," Carrie said.

"That's possible, Carrie."

"Whatever the reason, the guy gave me the creeps."

"Nothing else?"

"Oh, there was something else but I'm not sure if it's important. I don't think he was well."

"What do you mean?"

"It's hard to describe, but he was continually stopping to catch his breath. He sort of wheezed. The guy sounded sick. Hope whatever he has kills the bastard."

"From what we now know, Julia, it will. Is there anything else?" Gray asked.

"Nothing more on our jailor, but there's Sally."

"What about her?"

Paul walked back into the War Room and sat down. "We should have the information on that cab in about half an hour, Gray."

"Great. Thanks, Paul. Sorry, Julia, go on, what about Sally?"

"I told you she wasn't well. She suffers from tremendous headaches."

"She has the bug."

"The what?"

"We'll go into that later. How do you feel at the moment, Sally?"

"I am well, thank you. A little weak but very much better."

"No headaches or feeling faint?"

"No."

"Good. Let us know if you do."

"I shall."

"What else, Julia?"

"Each time she has one of her fainting spells, she remembers more of her past."

"She does?" They all looked at the young woman seated in silence at the end of the table as she held tightly onto Julia's hand.

"What do you remember, Sally?" She hesitated and looked at Julia.

"It's okay, Sally, we're all friends here. Tell them," Julia encouraged her.

Quietly, almost in a whisper she told them. "I remembered when I was working for the Baxter's. I was personal maid to Mistress Baxter. They lived in a big house just outside of town, a place called Riley Estate. It is a very large place..." Gray was shocked as he listened to Sally relay her story. He looked at Paul who appeared just as surprised.

"...when Victoria, I mean Mrs. Baxter disappeared it was the Master, Mr. Baxter who sent me to the Feathered Nest..."

Paul responded with curiosity. "Feathered Nest? What was that?"

"It is Madam Francine's place, a bordello on Payton Street..." Sally was trying to recount her past as accurately as possible but she was definitely not aware of the time difference. In her mind it all happened yesterday.

"...I had worked there a few months when I first met Claude Marshall. It was the worst day of my life. Not a month later he tried to kill me. I ran from the Feathered Nest into the snow. He followed me and continued to cut me with that long knife of his. I do not remember any more. When I awoke, I was in the hospital." By the time she'd finished, everyone was sitting in stunned silence, eyes fixed on this beautiful blond, blue-eyed young woman who had survived the most horrific and excruciating ordeal. It was necessary for Gray to clarify one thing. He got up and went over to the crime board. Removing the photo of Maitland, he laid it in front of Sally.

"Do you recognize this man?"

She looked at the photo then at Gray. "I do not know him."

"You're sure you've never seen him before?"

"I am sure." Gray picked up the photo and placed it back on the crime board. He returned to his chair.

"Sally, you have experienced a great deal and we are pleased to see you have recovered so well. It's now time for you to learn a little more. We are going to leave you and Julia alone for a while. She will explain everything to you." Gray ignored Julia's silent objections.

"Julia, when you are ready, call my extension and we'll come back." The three detectives left, leaving Julia with a situation for which she was unprepared. She looked at Sally, wondering what the outcome to the incomprehensible news would be.

Julia took a deep breath then began. "Sally, I need to ask you a question and it may sound rather silly."

"Do not worry, Julia, I will answer whatever you wish to know."

"I only wish that were so. Anyway this is a kind of test to be certain you have not suffered serious injury. The question is, do you recall the date and the year before you were abducted from the hospital?"

"I was in that prison for a long time and therefore I no longer have knowledge of the exact date. The year is 1865. I believe the month is January or February; I am not certain. I remember a Christmas tree at the Nest."

"Good, let's move on. You said you live and work on Payton Street in a place called The Feathered Nest?"

"That is correct, and it is run by Madam Francine."

"Sally, what I'm about to tell you is going to come as a great shock. All I can do is say it plain. The date today is April 20..."

Sally gasped. "That demon had me locked away for that long?"

"In a manner of speaking, yes. But this is April 20, in the year 2006..." An expression of horror spread across Sally's face and she turned a ghostly shade of pale. Tears formed and ran down her cheeks. She looked as though she might pass out again. Sitting in silence, crying, she stared at Julia.

"There's more Sally. Although you lived in 1865, you were born here in Chicago on September 12, 1979. You are 26 years old. You were given up for adoption at six months. Then something happened and you were sent back to 1841." Julia looked down at her clasped hands, waiting to go on but fearful of the damage that might already have been done.

Then Sally spoke in a hushed voice. "I do not understand. How can this be?"

Julia looked into those dark blue eyes. "Quite honestly, Sally, I don't understand it either. It is very complicated and I cannot explain it."

"Julia, you said I am from the past, yet I am also from this time?"

"Something like that, yes. Sally, let me call my father to have him come and explain it to you." Julia called Gray's office.

"Daddy, I think you'd better come and explain all the details to Sally."

"We'll be right there." Julia hung up.

"Julia, what am I to do? If, as you say, I am not from this time, how am I to return home? I do not like it here, Julia."

"Sally, I am so sorry but I cannot answer that. Perhaps my father can." Gray, Carrie and Paul walked into the War Room.

"Daddy, Sally, understandably, has a lot of questions, questions I'm unable to answer."

"All right, Sally, what do you wish to know?"

"I do not understand. Julia says this is the year 2006."

"That is correct."

"How could this happen?"

"It was the work of the madman you call Claude Marshall. He has the ability to move from one time to another. I won't complicate things by trying to explain how he does it."

"This is just not possible, how can I be here...?" It was evident Sally was unable to grasp the magnitude of her situation.

"May I go home? Am I able to go home?" she asked with tears streaming down her cheeks. This was the one question Gray feared for he did not know the answer.

"We're not sure, Sally. I'm being very honest. If there is a way we can send you home, we will, if that is what you wish. But, there are some things you should know before you make that decision."

"What should I know?"

"We are doing everything we can to determine how to send you home, then the decision will be yours. I think it might be a good idea if we start from the beginning. When you were a baby, only about six months old, your mother left you in a church. A piece of jewelry was left with you. We believe that instrument was responsible for sending you back in time.

"You then had the terrible misfortune of crossing paths with this Marshall fellow. That unfortunate encounter sent you back to the present."

"I am sorry but this is too much. I am not able to continue...I feel very tired."

"I understand, Sally. You have absorbed a great deal over the last few hours. Why don't we get something to eat then call it a night? Paul, could you do these two girls a great favor?"

"Sure. Anything. What?"

"Let them use your apartment for tonight until we have a chance to make other arrangements. I only have one single bed and that uncomfortable pullout so you can bunk with me."

"Sure, Gray, I don't mind."

"That's settled then. Julia, there are a few things the team must clear up before we leave. We won't be long."

"Go ahead, Sally and I will wait here."

▼▼▼▼▼ *12*

7:45P.M.
Sally stood before the large picture window and stared at the city. For a long time she was silent, still, and deep in thought.

Finally she turned away. "They are so big."

Julia was seated at the table. She looked up. "What's that?"

"The buildings, they are so big, so tall. I never dreamed of buildings that tall. This is Chicago?"

The River Styx

"Yes Sally, Chicago 2006, and a very big city compared to the Chicago you know."

"There is a war going on."

"A war? Oh of course, the Civil War. Did you see any of it?"

"Not really. There were soldiers in town quite often."

Julia tried to lighten the atmosphere a little. "Sally, do you realize that, in theory, you are over 150 years old? You are the oldest person on this entire planet."

"How can that be? I am only 26. Oh, I understand, because I come from 1865."

"Precisely. You are younger than me but...well never mind. Sally, I would like us to be good friends. If there is anything you need, just say so and I'll do what I can. Also, the people here will help you."

"Detective Paul, he is not married?"

"Yes, I mean no, he's not. You like him don't you?"

"He is a very attractive man."

"Yes, he is." Julia felt a little uncomfortable with the conversation.

Sally went on. "You like him very much."

Julia smiled. "Yes, I do."

"I am sorry I speak so freely. He is your beau?"

"Not really, well sort of. We have been out a few times to dinner but that's about it."

"He has not bedded you?"

Sally's terminology and bluntness caught Julia off guard. "No."

"Yet I see you have very strong feelings for him?"

Julia stiffened. She didn't quite know how to respond. She wasn't accustomed to discussing her intimate private life with a stranger. "Yes, in all honesty, I suppose I do."

Sally smiled. "Good, for I can see he is a good man."

"Yes, he is." Julia changed the subject quickly. "Sally, would you like a cup of coffee?"

"I do not drink coffee. I do like tea."

"Then why don't I get us both something to drink?" Sally stepped away from the window. As she walked by the crime board, she glanced at it, then suddenly stopped and stared.

Julia stepped to her side. "What is it Sally?"

"This picture...this woman...this is Victoria."

"Victoria? Sally, who is Victoria?"

"Victoria Baxter." Immediately, Julia realized to whom she was referring.

Julia snatched the photo from the board "Sally, come with me." They hurried toward the elevator.

"Where are we going Julia?"

"To see my father."

13

8:10 P.M.

Carrie and Paul were seated in Gray's office. Gray was pacing, his hands buried deep in his pockets. Then pausing, he pondered a moment and sat down.

"Carrie, could you please arrange to have Julia's things picked up from her hotel?"

"Sure, Gray. Where do you want them taken?"

"To Paul's place, where the girls will stay for a few days. With Paul bunking at my place, we can keep a close eye on them."

"Quite honestly, I doubt they will be going anywhere soon, not after what they've just been through," Paul said.

"If I had the room, they could have stayed with me," Carrie offered.

"That's real nice of..." Suddenly the office door flew open. Julia and Sally rushed into the room.

"Excuse me for busting in, but you had better hear this." Julia thrust the photo of the woman at Gray.

He glanced at it and looked up. "We've seen it, Julia, what about it?"

"Tell them, Sally."

Sally looked shyly at the faces around the room. "That is Victoria Baxter, my first employer's wife, the people I told you about. But why do you have her picture, Detective?" Sally asked with an echo of fear woven into her obvious curiosity.

"It appears, Sally, that Mrs. Baxter, Victoria, was Marshall's last victim before you."

"But why would Marshall kill Mrs. Baxter? She was a wonderful woman, kind, beautiful and so young. She was my age but her husband was much older. He traveled a great deal. But when he was home, he did not trust her out of his sight. Look at her. You can understand why. On many occasions, when Mr. Baxter went away, Mrs. Baxter would slip out of the house and go into the town to join a party or possibly meet a friend. She…loves…loved to…dance." Sally stopped and stared at the photo.

"What's the problem, Sally?" Julia asked.

"It was he," she stated emphatically in an unusually strong tone. "She was seeing Marshall." She paused then took a deep breath and proceeded. "One day when I was in my room, the bell rang. I went to tend to her needs. There was a bell in my room for each of the main rooms in the house so I would know where she was when she called for me.

"She was in her boudoir. I was about to enter when I heard Mr. Baxter shouting. He was extremely angry, shouting so loud all in the house could hear. He was calling Mrs. Baxter a harlot, a whore, all sorts of horrible names. He then burst from the room and stormed downstairs. Victoria was crying. There were many times she would tell me she wanted to leave that house. When she knew she could trust me, she would talk about a great many things." Gray interrupted her.

"Excuse me Sally. You're saying this Marshall mingled with the elite?"

"He is a very wealthy man," Sally whispered. "Before I worked at the Nest I did not know of him. It was only after I had been at the Nest for about a year he came there."

"Excuse me Sally...the Nest?" Gray asked.

"The Feathered Nest is operated by Madam Francine. It is on Payton Street..."

Gray snapped his fingers. "That's where I know that street. That name has bothered me from day one. I knew it was not in this Chicago. Now I remember it was located roughly where North Kingsbury Street is today. Sorry Sally. So Marshall was that wealthy?"

"Yes and he must have deceived Victoria."

"That poor woman had no idea what was coming. She was dead before she crossed the threshold." Then Gray had an idea, an answer to their prayers, but he decided to wait to mention it. "Please go on Sally."

"I knew Victoria was seeing someone, she did not say whom, but she was very happy. She began spending nights away from the house. It was very dangerous. If the Master had returned, he would have killed her. Then she disappeared and was never found. At first it was thought Mr. Baxter harmed her, but that proved to be incorrect. Although he killed my friend, he did not kill Victoria." Sally stopped.

"Did either of you get a good look at the guy who was holding you?"

"Are you kidding, Daddy, all we wanted to do was get away from the maniac."

Gray then pushed a photo across to Sally. "Is this the man who killed your friend Mrs. Baxter, and who tried to kill you?" Sally picked up the picture of Hal Moffitt.

"No, this is not Claude Marshall."

"Are you sure Sally?"

"Yes, quite sure."

Gray was not surprised. If Moffitt had taken Winslow's identity, he should show Sally a picture of Winslow, which he did. To his utter disbelief the answer was the same. So the question remained, who was Claude Marshall? He decided to put his idea to the group.

"Folks, I believe we have the sprat to catch a mackerel."

"A what?" Paul asked.

"Never mind. Let's move back to the War Room where it'll be more comfortable." Everyone trooped from the office back upstairs.

"Okay. We are going to nail this guy. Mrs. Baxter is going to help us."

Paul spun around and stared at Gray in amazement. "She is? And how do you propose she's going to do that? She's dead, for crying out loud. How can a dead woman help us?"

"Here's how. We send Mrs. Baxter back..."

"We what? For what purpose Gray?"

"Paul, shut up and hear me out. We send Mrs. Baxter back but we add a few things. We use a handkerchief with Marshall's initials on it. We write a letter from Victoria Baxter to Marshall. We set the scene and hope the plan works. We hope the cops in 1865 find her body."

"It sounds feasible, Gray, but how do we ensure the body is found?" Carrie said.

"That's the chance we'll have to take."

"Sounds viable. It'll certainly be an excellent trap," Mario said.

"But, Gray, this is not like running over to Cleveland or New York or even Paris and placing a body. In this case, we'll be flying totally blind. We won't even know if the body gets...wait a second, you're not thinking of sending one of us with her?"

"Good God, no, Carrie! We do it with Sally's help and old city maps. We should get close enough."

"What if our killer doesn't go back when we want him to?"

"He *will* go back and that's what counts Yoshi. When he does...bam... they get him," Gray said slamming his fist on the table.

"Sally, where did Marshall spend most of his time?" Paul asked.

"He travels a great deal but when he is in town he spends most of his time at 'The Eastern', his gentleman's club."

Gray rested back in his chair. "Wow, our man was a busy little beaver. He even had time to get involved in business ventures."

"He too, is very wealthy, Detective. He owns many businesses, a bank, a hotel, and two restaurants, in addition to the men's club."

"Well guess who is going to crash and burn on this one? Paul, first thing in the morning get over to the ME's office. Have them prepare the body. I will explain it to Justin when I see him. Carrie, get with Yoshi, and gather all the evidence you can to link Marshall and Mrs. Baxter. Keep in mind they are years behind us so draw them a big picture, if you get my drift."

Gray leaned close to Julia and spoke into her ear. "Julia, I need you to do one more thing for me. Actually it's for Sally, more than any of us. We know who her mother is and...."

"You do? When did you find this out?"

"Keep it down...a few days ago. DNA has confirmed it. We now need to know if Sally intends to remain here or return to 1865. Depending on her first decision, would she want to meet her mother?"

"You want me to tell her she can meet her mother?"

"Yes."

"How do you think she'll deal with that?"

"Julia, I have no idea but she needs to know now."

"Yes, but, my God, Daddy, this woman is facing something no other human being has ever faced."

"I understand. That is why you must be sensitive to her situation."

"Being sensitive has little to do with it. Once we tell her, she's got to deal with it. That could be the last straw. She still doesn't comprehend the magnitude of what we have already told her."

"I know, but she must know. I'm asking you to tell her."

Julia looked at her father. "Damn, this is a tough one."

"I know it is, Honey, but will you do it?"

"Yes. I only hope it doesn't break her."

"She's a tough kid."

"You'll get no argument there, but she's had about all she can handle."

"Just break it to her gently."

"I will, trust me."

"Thanks, Julia. Find the right moment to tell her."

"I will."

"Good girl." Gray kissed Julia on her forehead then straightened. "It's so good to have you back. I was never so terrified in all my life. I thought I would never see you again."

"I'm glad to be back."

He squeezed her arm. "I don't ever want to lose you again."

"You won't Daddy, I promise."

"Okay, folks, we all know what must be done. If there's nothing else to discuss, let's break up this little party and get something to eat. I'm starving."

▼▼▼▼▼ 14

10:34P.M.

After a quiet dinner, Paul drove Sally and Julia to his apartment.

"Your dad asked Carrie to arrange to have your clothes picked up from the hotel."

"That's okay, Paul, I can do that, thanks anyway."

"No, Julia, your father doesn't want you going anywhere near that place. In fact it's better if you and Sally keep a low profile for a while. No running off to the mall."

"Okay, I understand."

"Carrie will come by in about an hour. If there is anything you ladies need, just let her know. Remember, this is a single man's apartment," Paul said as they emerged from the elevator and walked down the hallway.

Julia smiled to herself. "What are you trying to tell us Paul...it's a mess?"

"Not at all. It's just that...well it's not set up for women."

"Okay, I'm with you."

"Thank you for opening your home to us. You are so very kind, Detective."

Paul stopped before his apartment, unlocked the door and ushered the women in. "Sally, if we are going to be friends, please call me Paul. And thank you for those kind words."

"Very well, Paul," Sally said with a smile as she stood on her toes and kissed him on the cheek.

They were standing in the living room. Paul waved his arm in a semi-circle. "This is the place."

Julia glanced around. "Doesn't look so bad, Paul. It is tidy at least. But you're right, it is a man's apartment."

"Thanks. Okay, please treat the place as if it were yours. Good night, sleep well and I'll see you both in the morning." He turned, stepped back through the door, closed it and was gone. A day that had been a nightmare for all involved had come to an end. For most, it would pass into history uneventfully but for this select few it would never be forgotten.

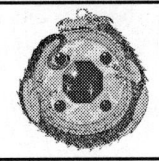

-Episode 5-

Tragedy Strikes

SMALL FISH BIG FISH

▼▼▼▼▼ *1*

Two weeks had lapsed since Julia and Sally's escape. Although Sally was showing signs of adjusting to her new environment, she had not yet reached a decision as to whether she would remain or return home. Gray and his staff thought perhaps she would be encouraged to stay if she knew of her mother, but Julia was still waiting for the right opportunity to tell Sally.

To the delight of Julia and Gray, Julia's blood test results revealed she had not traveled back in time. What it indicated was that the medallion was also capable of teleporting an individual from one place to another in the present. This posed a greater challenge for it gave the killer more latitude, one on which they hadn't counted. It also answered a number of long-standing questions. Their two remaining tasks were almost complete but they were struggling with the second. After numerous visits to the morgue Gray and Paul were still attempting to convince Justin Davenport to honor their request.

Paul rested his hands on the desk. "...Justin, this is not body-snatching for crying out loud. We're sending her home."

"Guys, it's not that simple."

"Why not? Justin, her body doesn't belong here, it belongs in..."

"So you keep telling me. But you know what...I can't accept that! You have continually tried to convince me that this woman comes from 1865. Do you know how ridiculous that sounds?"

"It may sound ridiculous, but that's not the issue."

"Damn right it's the issue! That's what this is all about!"

Gray angrily stabbed his finger in the direction of the cooler drawers. "Wrong! This is about stopping a killer and, at the moment, she's our only hope of accomplishing that."

"I'm sorry, Gray, but I can't see it. You want to send this woman's body back in the hopes it will be found by the police in 1865 so they can nab...this is nuts, you two are nuts! Killers traveling back and forth in time, bringing bodies with them like extra baggage. Dear God, listen to yourselves. You're both certifiably insane!"

Paul strode toward the door. "I told you we shouldn't have told him, Gray, I told you."

"Paul, shut up, we need him for this. Justin, calm down. We realize this all sounds far fetched..."

The ME stared blank-faced at the two detectives. "Far fetched...you have no idea!"

"Justin, we're not shooting you a line. We *are* dealing with facts, like it or not."

"And you want me to release a...oh boy, a 150 year old body?" He began to laugh. "If nothing else, this would make a good movie."

Paul walked back to the desk. "Justin, would you stop! Yes, we want you to release her damn body."

"Then what do I tell my people when it's not returned?"

"Tell them anything, make up something...use your imagination."

"Hell, I don't have to do that, you guys are doing more than your share." There was a long, nervous silence. Davenport got up and paced the morgue with his hands buried in his lab coat pockets as he stared at the floor. Paul and Gray watched him in anticipation. Finally he stopped, turned and faced them.

"You realize what you're asking me to do? I have to account for that body. I have to fake all the damn paperwork, I have to lie then have my people lie so you can..." He paced some more then stopped in front of Gray. He wasn't smiling. "Damn you. All right, I'll do it. But this is insane. If someone hears about this, I could lose my job."

"Justin, no one is going to find out. That's why I told you to destroy all paperwork related to this case and send me every original."

"Gray, our friendship goes back a long way but do you have any idea what you're asking? I'll do it, but you owe me big time. Now get out of my hair as I have work to do. One other thing, Gray, this will take some time to arrange and prepare."

"How long?"

"I'll need about two weeks to avoid any suspicion."

"Two weeks...to do what?"

"Paul would you just drop it. Fair enough, Justin, take whatever time you need. Look, my friend, if there were another way to do this we would, believe me, but I'm afraid there isn't. Sorry to put this on you, but it's the only course..."

"All right, all right, enough said. I'll call you as soon as the arrangements have been made."

"Good man. Justin, I don't know how to thank you."

He still wasn't smiling. "I'll think of something."

"We appreciate your understanding."

"Understanding hell! Gray, if it were anyone else, well...."

"Then thanks again. And remember I still need all your records. Also, as I mentioned to you before, this is strictly confidential."

"Are you kidding, who the hell would I tell, no one would believe me. And as for those documents...I'm busy, but I'll get to it. Now get the hell out of my morgue and leave me in peace...1865, damn, you people are crazy." Davenport was still mumbling to himself as the two detectives left.

"You think he's okay? It sounds like he's about to go off the deep end. Anyway why does he need two weeks?"

"He knows what he's doing Paul. Besides, he'll be fine, maybe we pushed him a little hard."

"You think this is going to work, Gray?"

"Who the hell knows, but it's worth a try. If it does, our killer won't suspect a thing."

▼▼▼▼▼ 2

It was Mario who presented them with a solution as to how they might corral their killer. It came in a box the size of a briefcase.

"Gray, remember the incident at the hospital when Sally was abducted? We noticed a burp on all the computers and security cameras in the building?"

"Yes."

"I believe it was when our notorious friend used the medallion. Which means we have a way to detect his presence."

"Are you saying we can pinpoint where he will arrive?"

"Roughly where, but definitely when. It picks up the energy signature of the medallion."

"And you have a device that can do that?"

"Yes. You also said you were sure there was a reason behind the donation of the Buddha to the Natural History Museum. I may have an answer for you on that also."

"You do?"

Mario hesitated. "Yes, and we believe it makes sense."

Gray raised his eyebrows. "We?"

"Yoshi and I."

"So what's this theory?"

"We believe the killer doesn't just want the Buddha. Yoshi believes his plan is to lure you into the museum so he can deal with you one on one."

"You've got a point. It is obvious the guy has an unbridled hatred for me, otherwise he wouldn't have gone this far."

"He also despises the law, Gray. He wants to belittle law enforcement, make us look like bumbling idiots, but most of all he wants to see you crawl. If we don't bring him down, he'll succeed."

"You think we can corner him, with this device of yours, before he's aware we have him?"

Mario smiled triumphantly. "Yes, something like that. The only drawback is that the equipment has a limited range. It will have to be mounted in close proximity to the Buddha."

"I doubt that will be a problem."

"I can arrange for you to visit the company."

"Not necessary, Mario, you go ahead and take care of it. If you believe it will work, set it up."

"You want me to make the decision on this?"

"Yes."

"Okay, Gray, consider it done."

"Keep me informed."

▼▼▼▼▼ 3

As the days passed, Sally became more morose. Julia tried to keep her in good spirits but with little success. She was still waiting for the right time to talk to Sally, but would there ever be a right time?

One evening while Sally and Julia were watching TV, Julia decided she could wait no longer. She switched the TV off and turned to Sally. "Sally, there is one last thing I must tell you."

Sally looked dejected. Her shoulders drooped; the spark of her joviality had faded. "What is it, Julia?"

"Before I tell you, it is important you understand that no matter what you decide, we are all with you."

"I understand." Her voice echoed her feelings.

Julia took her hands. "I'm hoping this news will make you very happy."

"Then please tell me, Julia."

"We have found your mother." The expression on Sally's face immediately changed to one of shocked excitement. She neither moved nor spoke.

"Did you hear what I said Sally?" Sally remained unresponsive. "I understand this is a great shock but I have…"

Then she spoke. "Is it possible? You have found my mother?"

Julia smiled with relief. "Yes, Sally, we found her."

Sally smiled, something she had not done in days. "How did you find her?"

"Remember the other day we were talking about the medallion and sending Mrs. Baxter's body home?"

"Yes."

"That medallion belonged to your mother."

"I cannot believe…you found my mother?" Sally was beside herself. Riding the emotional roller coaster, she laughed, then cried.

"Yes, we have."

"What am I…what? I have a mother. I really have a mother. She is alive?" Julia nodded.

Sally bubbled with excitement. She got out of her chair, approached Julia and threw her arms around her. Hanging on as if meeting a long lost sister, her head buried in Julia's neck, Sally wept.

"We will arrange a meeting when you feel you're ready. There is also the decision as to whether you wish to stay or return home." Sally stiffened and fell silent. She cried and continued to hold onto Julia. After a time she dropped her arms and stepped back. Her eyes were red and her face streaked with mascara. Julia handed her a tissue.

"Does this...mean I will...not have to return home?"

"That is entirely up to you."

"I find it very difficult here."

"I'm not surprised. I find it difficult at times myself and I was raised here. I can't imagine how you feel."

"Everything happens so fast. Your world is very complicated. It is noisy and people are rude and inconsiderate. I am not speaking of you or your friends. They have been wonderfully kind. Those outside are to whom I refer."

"I understand, and I agree with you."

"I am not sure I will be happy."

"Sally, it is not necessary to make an immediate decision."

"How long should I take?"

"That's entirely up to you. I can't help you. You alone must make this decision."

"I understand. Does my mother know I am here?"

"No."

"If I decide to return home, she would not know I was here?"

"Right, she would never know."

"If I meet her, then I will feel obligated to remain."

"Not necessarily."

"Yes, it must be so. I could not break a woman's heart because of my selfishness. It would also break my heart to leave once we are reunited."

"Sally, I'm very sorry but I can't advise you."

"Julia, please do not be concerned." Deep in thought, Sally got a far away look in her eye. Then she lifted her head and looked at Julia. "I always dreamed I would someday meet my mother. I knew then precisely what I would say. Now I have no idea. It is no longer a dream; my life has become a nightmare." She began to sob. Julia tried to comfort her.

"Sally, we will help you in any way we can."

"I know."

▼▼▼▼▼ *4*

Justin Davenport had been true to his word. In a little less than two weeks Victoria Baxter's body lay in somber repose on the autopsy table. The Chief Medical Examiner had prepared the body himself, and she had enough evidence with her to ensure that Claude Marshall would be put away for the rest of his life. The group gathered in the morgue consisted of Carrie, Paul, Sally, Gray, Julia, Mario and Yoshi, along with Justin. They stood beside the dead woman in silence. Victoria Baxter was ready to return home. The medallion had been placed in her hands, which were clasped together across her stomach. Sally stood staring at her dead mistress, tears running down her cheeks. Lately it was evident that Sally's despondency was becoming more prevalent and this concerned everyone.

Gray scanned the group. "Are we all ready?" They nodded in unison. "Carrie, are you ready?"

"I guess so, Gray." Then Carrie, following the instructions given to her by Mr. Lee, systematically touched the different stones. After a few uncertain seconds, it was done.

"All I have to do now is tap the large ruby."

"Will the medallion return to this spot?"

"As far as I know Paul, but we won't know until we send it."

"Then send her home, Carrie." Almost reluctantly, Carrie tapped the stone. For a few seconds nothing happened. Then the medallion began to glow a dull red. The air became charged with static. The intensity of the light from the ruby grew; it pulsated and, just as had been described to all of them on three separate occasions, sparkled.

What happened next was astonishing. Mrs. Baxter's body began to glow faintly. It then grew lighter until it appeared transparent. The pulsating glow faded and finally vanished with Mrs. Baxter. The entire event lasted a mere five seconds. They all stood dumbfounded and breathless. The group just stood and stared at the spot where the woman's body laid a moment earlier. Silence invaded the room like a choking fog. The next instant, they all jumped as the glow reappeared on the floor beneath the table. When it faded, the medallion appeared.

It was Gray who broke the silence. "My God! If I had not experienced it, I would never have believed it."

"What just happened?" Justin was standing open-mouthed and stunned by the event.

"We sent Mrs. Baxter home, but how?"

"Don't ask me Mario...ask Carrie."

"That was...unbelievable. Carrie, how was that possible?"

"Quite honestly, Justin, I can't explain it. All I did was follow the instructions."

"Fantastic! Like Gray, had I not seen it, I would never have believed it."

"Now, friends, I think you can understand why this must never become common knowledge."

"I agree 100 percent, Gray."

"One other thing. Carrie, I want you to contact Mr. Lee. Arrange for him to send us the best replication of the medallion he can find." Gray stooped and picked up the medallion. "This one's going to disappear."

"You intend to replace it with a fake?"

"I do, Carrie. Because of its unprecedented power, I consider it to be the only thing to do."

"What if the Monsignor discovers it is not the original one?"

"That's why the reproduction must be perfect."

"I understand."

"Justin, thanks for your help."

"Thank you, Gray, for allowing me to witness this extraordinary event."

Gray stared at the empty slab. *The trap is set. Hell, I only hope it works. But I suppose we'll never know.*

▼▼▼▼▼ 5

The Field Museum of Natural History is a large gray, majestic stone structure standing on the edge of the city overlooking the vast body of water that is Lake Michigan. Within this massive granite edifice, one of the largest museums of its kind, can be found exhibits from all corners of the globe. Ancient cultures are displayed in all their magnificence to enthrall, mesmerize, challenge and encourage the imagination. But only one species breathes life into these grand halls where thousands of others presented in silent, sightless, timeless, and motionless activity prowl, crawl, fly, swim, sleep and feed.

Locked in eternal sleep rest the creatures that had been, mindless of those that are. They rest behind walls of clear crystal, safe forever from the most tenacious hunter killer in all of earth's history. In the cavernous central vestibule called Stanley Field Hall, towering over her awestruck audience, a striking figure of ancient earth is the great and mysterious skeletal remains of the T'Rex, Sue. Frozen in time, this Mesozoic monster poses in silent challenge. Her mummified roar of hunger is only a dream in the imagination of man as she searches eternally for her next meal.

Paul and Gray stood looking at the Jurassic Queen in all her glory.

"That's quite a smile. Sure would make a Hollywood mogul squirm."

"Hey, that smile led that Hollywood mogul to the bank."

"Good house pet."

"Um...she looks hungry."

"Yeah, one helluva meat bill."

"Glad she's on our side."

"Either a dentist's nightmare or his biggest dream."

"A dental floss dream house."

The two men chuckled and fearlessly turned their backs on this colossus of creation.

"Let's get to work and see if everything is as it should be."

Paul and Gray spent three hours inspecting the new and highly sophisticated security system installed in and around the hall displaying the

Buddha. Mario's magic box was housed in the room directly above the display room. A contingency of Chicago police had been added temporarily to the security staff. Police dogs also patrolled the building since their senses were more attuned to environmental and atmospheric changes than their human counterparts. By the end of the day an army of contractors and police personnel working diligently had everything in its place. It was time to sit back and wait.

"Now we see if all our efforts pay off. If I know this guy, it won't be long before he realizes how much he wants this piece and he *will* come for it." The two men stood in front of the brightly lit display case and stared at the object they hoped would lure the killer.

"I will say this, not even a renegade flea from one of our canine crew could get to this case without being caught. When our guy arrives, we've got him. It will be a rock-solid event."

"Nothing is rock-solid, Paul. Not until he's lying at our feet breathing his last breath or sitting behind bars in some dingy prison 150 years in the past. Then and only then can we call it rock solid." From the cafeteria they each picked up a cup of coffee, then made their way to the squad car to begin their first night's surveillance. Parked at the far corner of the lot, Gray and Paul sat in silence, each caught up in the events of the last few days. They sipped at the hot coffee and waited.

Gray glanced at the museum building bathed in moonlight and lit intermittently by floodlights. He hoped this was the beginning of the end. This would be a six-hour surveillance stint. It was not to catch Moffitt going into the building for they knew he would not get in that way. It was to be on hand when he made his move. Gray was a trifle agitated. He knew this could be their last chance to grab the killer and he was not prepared to lose the opportunity. Not now. If Moffitt escaped, he was well aware of the consequences.

"Are we going to do this every night?"

"Not every night, Paul, I just want to be on hand when he shows up."

"Good, Gray, because I can think of far better things to be doing than sitting in this car waiting for a damn killer to show his face."

"I don't like it any more than you do."

"Let's hope it's all worth the effort."

"We'll soon know." So began a vigil that was to last more than six weeks.

▼▼▼▼▼ 6

Almost seven weeks had slipped by since the new security system had been implemented and, aside from one false alarm and a power failure, nothing eventful had occurred.

"We have seen neither hide nor hair of the killer, Gray. It's as if he's fallen off the face of the earth. Do you honestly think he'll show up?"

"Paul, have patience. Trust me, he'll be here. I told you he would play this cool. He's waiting for the right moment, however long that might be. I think that false alarm a week ago could have been him."

"What? But that was in the middle of the night and nothing happened. If it was him, why didn't he just take the Buddha?"

"Because he's playing with us...testing our defenses."

"But if he slips through this noose, we'll lose him for good."

"That's possible, Paul, and we'll have to chalk it up to experience."

"I don't like that idea."

"Neither do I. But remember, we have two traps."

"Granted, but if we miss him here, we don't get to savor the other one."

Gray glanced at his watch. "Let's get out of here. I'm tired and need some sleep."

"Good idea. I would like to get a good night sleep myself," Paul said starting the car.

▼▼▼▼▼ 7

"I'm sorry, Gray, but her doctors believe they have done all they can for her," Rashid said from the other end of the phone.

"Ben, I understand, but is there no other solution?" Gray had just received the disturbing news that Sally's condition had further deteriorated forcing her doctors to admit her to hospital.

"Gray, she has closed all doors. She has shut herself away in her mind and no one is able to reach her. Her doctors say she has a ten percent chance of recovery."

"That's it? We're just going to lock her up and forget she ever existed?"

"Come on, Gray, you know better than that. They have done everything they possibly can for her, but she's not responding."

"She has a life. She deserves better. For God's sake, Ben, we can't lock her up and let her just waste away."

"She won't waste away. Gray, she will still receive intensive therapy."

"So what now?"

"She will be moved to Glenmoore..."

"My God, that's the home for the insane. Sally's not insane, Ben."

"Damn it, Gray, I know that as well as you do, but she will receive the best treatment there."

Gray felt deeply concerned and bitter. "Right, but will she ever come out?"

Ben Rashid let out a long sigh. "We don't know that. Only time will tell, Gray."

▼▼▼▼▼ 8

It was the beginning of the ninth week. Nerves were strained but Gray kept everyone focused. Paul and Gray were keeping vigil across the street from the Museum. At three in the morning Gray called it quits.

"Okay, let's go home. Our relief will be here in a few minutes."

Paul sighed deeply. "Thank God. I was wondering if you were going to sit here all night." He started the car and pulled onto Lakeshore Drive. At that moment the police radio crackled to life notifying them of a security breach in the museum.

Gray slammed his hand on the dash, "Told you he would show up sooner or later. Turn this heap around and let's get back there." He looked at the clock on the dash. It was *3:06A.M.*

"It could just be another false alarm, Gray," Paul said as he turned and raced toward the museum. The tires screamed as they resisted the abuse. Paul did not spare the speed as he pushed his foot to the floor. Gray knew he was just as anxious to see the man who had eluded them for so long, brought to his knees. They tore into the parking lot and screeched to a halt at the main entrance. Gray and Paul burst from the car. Paul sprinted up the steps. Gray watched as he trailed behind fighting to breathe.

"Come on, old man, am I going to have to spend the rest of your life waiting for you to catch up?"

"Screw you, my friend, I may be getting on in body, but the mind and spirit still work better than yours." As they approached the entrance, one of the doors opened, and an officer in plain clothes appeared.

"What have we got, Frank?" Gray asked the police officer at the door.

"I think you had better see for yourself, Detective. Never seen anything like it. Strangest damn thing you ever did see." They rushed across the main hall, through a set of double doors into a short corridor. As they approached the display room, a thunderous roar reached their ears. They also noticed a dull pulsating red glow. As they entered, they stood dumbfounded and confronted an unearthly vision before them. Neither man believed his eyes. Paul placed his hands over his ears.

"Told you it was strange, Detective," the officer shouted.

"What the hell is going on, Gray?" Before them was a wall of boiling reddish orange mist, churning in the fury of a tornado cloud. It glowed bright then faded then brightened again and pulsated rhythmically. At the center of this vortex was a black disk that vibrated in rapid motion sending forth an almost deafening roar. The three men watched in awe. The black area then became transparent, a window to a place out of time. Suddenly, it blinked to the edge of insanity; evil flowed into the room and seemed to seep through all living and inanimate objects.

Paul leaned close to Gray and shouted in his ear. "I don't like this, Gray."

"Me neither. We had better be prepared."

"For what, Gray?"

Gray shouted back. "How the hell should I know, but I would guess the portal has been left open for a reason."

"Why?"

"Beats me."

"Maybe Moffitt's planning a reception."

Gray stepped close to the officer. "Frank, I want this place locked down tight. No one gets in or out without my authorization, got that?"

"Yes, Sir." The officer continued to stare.

"Now, Frank, not next week!" Gray shouted.

"Yes, Sir, I'm right on it." He hurried from the room.

"Where the hell's Moffitt? If the portal is still open, he has to be here or..." Gray hesitated. Something was very wrong. The words Lee had spoken echoed in his head, *'...if the portal remains open too long a terror of unthinkable proportions shall crawl from the abyss and infest the earth for centuries to come..."* The portal had to be closed immediately.

▼▼▼▼▼ *9*

There was a sudden shift in activity. A blinding red flash burst from the center of the vortex. Transparent shadows appeared, dancing like puppets on a red screen. The vortex pulsated faster. As the brilliance increased, the cloud slowly shrank. The shadows swelled and contorted, melded, and then instantly flew apart. There was a deafening report and the room vibrated violently.

Paul glanced at Gray and yelled above the din. "This is not good."

Gray didn't move but yelled back. "We have to close that damned thing, now!"

"I agree, but where the hell's Moffitt? Where's the medallion?"

Gray looked around as he searched for answers. "Someone turn on the lights!" At that moment there were two muffled explosions. The swirling vortex rapidly shrank and the glow faded. Then without warning, a body was vomited from the boiling mass, and landed in a heap like a discarded rag doll. The vortex swallowed the churning cloud, then blinked out. Darkness and a deathly silence filled the room. For now it was over.

Paul started across the room but noticed Gray was not moving. He looked at the old man who was staring blankly at him.

"Gray, are you okay?" There was no response.

A strange feeling passed over Gray. The strength in his legs slipped away and he slowly sank to the floor. He felt a slight pain in the right side of his chest. Paul tried to stop him from falling.

"Gray!" Paul yelled, "Gray, what the hell is the matter?" Gray looked up from where he had collapsed and saw Paul's blurred outline.

"I don't know, Paul, it's a pain in my side." Salvatore looked at him in horror.

"Okay Gray, just lay there and I will get an ambulance. You could be having a heart attack."

Gray responded adamantly. "Bullshit. No damn ambulance, I'll be fine. Just let me rest a moment."

Paul ignored the old man. "Not a chance. We get an ambulance." Gray grabbed Paul's jacket as a deep stabbing pain shot down his right side.

"Just help me up I...want to see that body." Paul knew it was futile to argue with Gray so he reached to help him up. He withdrew his hand in shock.

"Someone turn on the damn lights!" he yelled. "Hang on, Gray, I want to take a look." Paul gently rolled Gray onto his left side. He noticed a dark patch forming in the center of Gray's right shoulder blade. Carefully, he lay Gray back on the floor.

"Damn it, Paul, I...don't want to lay here...I want to..." Paul ignored Gray and opened his jacket. He saw a small dark patch on the right side of his chest.

"Gray, it's not a heart attack, you..."

Gray waved his hand impatiently. "Whatever. Just get me on my..."

Paul placed his hands on Gray's shoulders. "Gray, listen to me, you're not going anywhere; you've been shot."

"Shot? What the hell are you talking about? How could I have been shot? You're out of your mind," he stammered.

"I have no idea, but you have been shot." Gray suddenly went cold, and then he chuckled.

"Paul, quit messing around, I want to see that body. Come on, help me up." He tried to get up but his legs weren't there. Adrenalin rushed through him. What was happening? Why was he not able to walk?

"This is ridiculous, I think..."

"Damn it, Gray, you've been shot, for crying out loud, stay put."

Gray was confused. "But Paul, who could have shot me?"

"No idea, but we'll find out. For the moment just lay still. Somebody turn on the fricking lights, and get a damned ambulance here now!" Paul screamed in desperation.

Suddenly the room was bathed in brilliance. Gray saw the blood on Paul's hand. He seldom panicked, but he was on the verge of it at that moment. His first thought was Julia. He had plans; he couldn't die now. He would not be cheated out of them. He looked up at Paul.

"Hey, guy, why do you look so damned scared? I'm the one who's been shot. I'm not going to die, not yet anyway." But Paul's expression didn't change. "How bad is it? I'm a big boy. I can take it."

"It doesn't look good, Gray."

The River Styx

With broken speech, he stared at Paul. "You're one damn... depressing... guy...you know that." Pain shot through his chest. He flinched.

"Gray, what is it?"

"Just a tweak of pain. Nothing to worry about." At that moment the officer returned.

"Excuse me, Detective, we have secured the building...my God what happened? Where did that one come from?" Paul was short on an answer for a second then replied.

"He was here all the time hidden behind that podium."

"What the hell happened to Detective Farlon?"

"He's been shot. Get a damned ambulance here now!"

"Yes Sir." The officer grabbed his radio. "Officer down...officer down... requesting back up."

"Damn it, Frank, we don't need back up. Half the Force is already here. Just move your ass and get that ambulance. This man's bleeding to death." Gray closed his eyes for a moment, the pain making itself known. Frank left the room then returned a few minutes later.

"The ambulance will be here in a few minutes, Detective."

"Thanks. Gray, are you still with us?"

He gave a weak smile. "What kind of dumb question is that? Of course I'm still with you. Where in the name of hell do you think I'm going?"

"Well, I was worried that..."

"You worry too damn much, my friend. Anyone ever tell you that? You're going to have a heart attack one of these days, Paul, with all that worrying. I'm fine and not ready to die. Not yet anyway." He winced.

"Gray, just shut up and lay still."

"Are you telling me to shut up?"

"Yes, I am. You talk too damn much when you're worried."

He winced again as pain shot down his side. "Worried? Who's worried?"

"You are."

"I'm not...I...would you quit it."

"You were the one who..." Gray grabbed at Paul's jacket as another wave of pain snatched his breath away.

"Look, Paul, just quit all this nonsense and tell me who the hell is lying over there." Paul removed his jacket, rolled it up and placed it under Gray's head, then stood up.

"Okay, damn you, if it will make you less grumpy. Anyone ever tell you that you're a pain in the ass?" He walked over to the body lying in the middle of the room, and crouched down to examine it. Gray turned his head and watched with deep interest.

"Can't tell, Gray, it could be anybody."

"Anybody! What the hell do you mean, anybody? Get me up...Damn it, Frank...get me up..."

"Don't you listen to him, Frank. Gray, you're staying right where you are until the medics get here."

'That's bullshit. I want to see for myself. I have to see." He would not be told what he could or could not do. He made a desperate effort to get up but nothing seemed to work. He had another idea. "Paul, bring him over here."

"What?"

"Why do I have to keep repeating myself? I'm shot and you suddenly go deaf? Just bring the damn body here."

"I can't do that Gray, it's not..."

"I don't give a damn about the rules. Let me get a look at the guy. Hell, Paul, are you weak as well as deaf?"

"Oh boy, you are one pig headed old...okay but it's your head. Plus it's not a body, the guy's still alive."

"Oh, good, get him here and I'll wring his scrawny neck. I'll hang the bastard by his balls." Paul and Frank dragged the man to Gray's side. Gray watched in eager anticipation but his breathing grew weaker.

"I guess this was the guy who shot you, Gray, his gun is lying next to the wall. Also in his eagerness to shoot you, it looks as if he also shot himself in the leg."

▼▼▼▼▼ 10

Gray's breathing was more labored and his vision blurred, but he was not giving up. He had come this far and had his prey within his grasp. He would not let it slip away. He stared at the dark figure beside him.

"He only has a leg wound but he's in real bad shape," Paul commented.

"Turn his head to me; let me see him." Paul obliged. "What the hell happened to his face?"

"It looks burnt," Paul said going through the man's pockets. He found a card. As he stared at it, he could barely believe his eyes. The name on the card was Claude Marshall.

At that moment the man mumbled something. "I...I so..."

"What the hell is he trying to say?" Gray said.

Paul got down and put his ear close to the man's mouth. "I'm so...sorry...but I'm not..."

"What are you trying to say? What are you sorry about?"

"I did...didn't mean for this...it was not supp..." The man passed out. Gray stared at that scorched, contorted visage. His eyes did not deviate but watched as the muscles writhed beneath the blackened epidermal layers as if trying to tear themselves from the skull. It was apparent the man was in agony. As Gray watched, it appeared the bone structure of the skull was in a state of flux. But as he observed the grotesque contortions, he knew he was staring into the face of his adversary, the one he swore he would bring to his knees, Hal Moffitt.

He drew in a deep breath, as deep as he could, and ignoring the pain, Gray spoke. "Moffitt, you son of a bitch...don't you die on me...not before I fry your sorry ass. You thought you could get away. Well, let me..." Another wave of pain; only this time it was not just a pain. His whole body felt it was on fire then turned to ice.

Maybe I won't get the chance to talk to Julia. Don't you damn well talk like that. You will get to see and talk to her. You're not going to die. You hear me! You're not going to die!

His eyes were closed but he sensed a bustle of activity around him. His jacket was being removed and the front of his shirt ripped open. What in the world was going on? He forced his eyes open. Medics surrounded him and busied themselves. They prodded and poked at him mainly on his right side.

"I hope you guys know what the hell you're doing." He gasped.

"Detective, please lay still and refrain from talking. You *have* been shot and we must get you stabilized." He looked up and saw Paul.

"Gray, its Marshall."

"Marshall...Moffitt...they're the same murdering...hey watch what you're doing with that needle."

"Gray, would you just let these guys do their job. We'll get him to hospital then you'll get the chance to see him behind bars..."

"No!" Gray coughed. Another spasm of pain followed.

One of the medics chastised him. "Detective, you must stop talking."

"Look son...I..." Gray coughed again.

"I'm sorry, Detective, but we must go."

"Go...go where...damn it...I'm not going anywhere. I have a killer to take to prison. I want to see that bastard behind bars. I..." He was now gasping for each lung full of air. Getting the words out was a great effort. At that moment he felt fear creep into his soul. Death was not a stranger to him but he had never been this close. He refused to shake hands with it.

He was not yet ready or prepared to leave this world. He would not be deprived of the opportunity to fulfill the promises he had made.

'I have made a commitment and you'll not deprive me. Do you hear me? I have not been given the sign that I should be crossing the river yet. So until I get that sign, I refuse to climb aboard your damned boat. You will have to wait for a few more years yet. My daughter has priority. She put her name down before you did so she has first dibs on my time. So, Death, take a number and get in line like everyone else.'

'Gray, I'm waiting for you.'

'Gwynne! Gwynne is that you?'

'Yes Gray, it's me.'

'Gwynne, oh Gwynne, I've missed you so very much. Since you left life has not been the same, it has been so empty. I have been so alone then Julia came back. My life...'

Gray began to cry as he saw his beloved Gwynne standing in front of him as beautiful as she was the very first day they met. His sorrow was so painful he could not breathe. His chest swelled and burned with pride. He reached out to her but she was too far away.

'It's all right, Gray. Don't cry. Everything is going to be just fine.'

'But, Gwynne, I can't leave now. I have so much to do with Julia. Gwynne, I made her promises. I must keep those promises. I must Gwynne'

Tears ran in torrents down his cheeks.

'Gray, everything will be fine. It has all been arranged. You will find peace now. You have sought peace for so long, Gray, and you deserve it, now you will have it.'

He watched as Gwynne slowly faded.

'No Gwynne, please don't go. I must talk to you. Please don't leave me. Gwynne please...come...come back...Gwynne.'

'Soon, Gray, we will be together, soon. Be at peace now.'

The world around him was transformed to a misty gray. Gwynne was gone and he was alone in a cold empty place.

'Gwynne come back. Please Gwynne, come back. I love you so much and I need your strength. Please come back, Gwynne.'

Only silence pervaded the mists about him. He strained to catch a glimpse of his beloved Gwynne. To see her once more as she had been, her grace and beauty, her warm comforting smile. Her eyes said all she needed to say without an utterance. How he missed her...more than he ever realized. Then the mist began to clear and a bright light appeared. Voices surrounded him. Was Gwynne among those who spoke unseen? Was she coming back to him?

'Gwynne, I'm not ready. I have things to attend to. I still have important work to do...'

The mist had dispersed but there was nothing, no one, in its place. The voices continued and he could hear them clearly.

"...Detective, I'm afraid you will have to wait for that. At the moment you are in no fit state to go anywhere." The medic continued to attempt to stop the bleeding. Another medic took his arm, pulled it straight, searched for a vein then smartly inserted an IV needle. He then secured it with a strip of tape.

He was back, but for how long? Would he be with Gwynne? She said soon and if so, when would that be? He felt a wave of nausea and fear, a fear of lost opportunities. He had planned to show Julia just how much she meant to him. Juanita's killer had to be brought to justice and he was the one to do it. He had to do it. He could not leave now. He had to stay.

Paul stood looking on. He was greatly concerned for his best friend. He stepped up to one of the medics who had just finished setting up the IV.

"What's the prognosis?"

"I can't say for certain, but there is internal bleeding. We must get him to hospital immediately." The world around Gray was going into slow motion. He tried to speak but nothing happened.

"Well, get moving and you make sure you save his ass, otherwise I'm telling you, he will come back in his second life and beat the crap out of you guys." The medics laughed.

"Don't laugh, it's the truth. He does not stand for failure and to let him die would be considered nothing less." As Paul spoke to them, Gray felt himself being lifted onto a gurney. They then raised it and began wheeling him from the room.

Gray tried to speak again. "Paul...you there?"

"I'm here, Gray."

Gray staggered verbally through what he was trying to say. "Make sure...you get...that son of a bitch to hospital. Make certain...don't let...the bastard die."

"No problem, Gray, I'll take care of it. You just cooperate with these guys."

"I'm serious...about this Paul. I want to be there...to see...I have to see that demented monster...swing for what he's done."

"I know you're serious Gray. I will take care of it. You just take care of yourself. I'll see you at the hospital."

"Make sure you see...that Julia does not get...the idea...don't let her think...that I could buy it okay. Because...I'm not ready...yet..."

"You're not going to die, you old war horse. But I'll tell her, Boss."

"We must go now, Detective." Paul stepped aside as the medic pushed the gurney into the back of the ambulance and climbed in after it. Gray lifted his head to see a forlorn and worried-looking Paul. Paul raised his hand and waved but he couldn't respond. The doors closed. The ambulance started to roll, its sirens screaming into the early morning darkness as it sped up Lakeshore Drive.

TWIST OF FATE

▼▼▼▼▼ *1*

July 27, 2006

Paul stood and watched the ambulance disappear into the darkness. The only sound filling the early morning air was the haunting wail of its siren. He felt despondent and helpless. A cold foreboding emptiness passed over him. He shivered and reached for his cell phone.

"Hello," a weary voice answered.

"Julia, this is Paul..."

"O God, Paul, what has happened? It's Daddy?"

"I'm afraid so, Julia. He has been shot but we have no idea how bad it is. He's on his way to Memorial."

"I'll see you there."

"I'll be there as soon as I get things wrapped up here." Paul then called Yoshi. "Yoshi, Paul. Gray's been shot. Medics are taking him to Memorial as we speak."

"How bad?"

"Can't say. He took a hit in the right side of his chest. We'll have to wait for the prognosis. I need you down here with me. How quickly can you get here?"

"The Museum?"

"Yes."

"I'll be there in 20minutes." Paul put his phone away and walked back into the building just as the second ambulance pulled up. As he walked through the main entrance hall, Officer Frank Parks approached.

"The medics are having a tough time with that guy, Detective."

"I'll see what's happening." As he entered the room, it appeared Moffitt had tried to get to his gun. The medics were trying to restrain him. Paul watched.

One of the medics approached Paul. "Detective, this guy is in bad shape. His pulse is almost undetectable. We have done all we can. We must get him to the hospital."

"Hell, he was only shot in the leg for crying out loud!"

"He also has severe burns on his face. The guy is barely hanging on."

"Fine, but don't you let that bastard die." The paramedic returned to the patient.

The River Styx

With a gloved hand, Paul carefully picked up the gun. He left the room and headed for his car. As he reached the entrance, he heard someone call him.

"Detective Salvatore, you may want to see this." Paul stopped and turned to see one of the security police hurrying toward him.

"What is it, Sergeant?"

"I found this lying behind the door on the other side of the room. Thought it might be of some importance." The officer opened his hand and Paul stared in disbelief. The light splashed off the red stone in bursts of brilliant shards and scattered in all directions. He looked up at the policeman then back at the medallion.

"Thank you." Paul lifted it by the silver chain and continued to his car. Moffitt was going nowhere. He opened the passenger side door and retrieved two plastic bags from the glove compartment. The gun he placed in one and the medallion in the other. There were footsteps behind him. It was Yoshi.

"Paul, how is Gray doing?"

"Not so good, I'm afraid. We've had one hell of a night." Paul proceeded to explain.

"What about the guy who came through the portal?"

"Moffitt? It doesn't look too good for him either. If he kicks, Gray will not be a happy camper."

"If he was in such bad shape, how did he manage to shoot Gray?"

"Damned if I know. Determination I guess...or just dumb luck; certainly unlucky for Gray. Moffitt did not look as if he stepped out of the portal with guns blazing; he all but flew out of it."

"Sounds like dumb luck."

"But that's not the amazing part of all this. This is what's amazing, unbelievable in fact," Paul said holding up the plastic bag containing the medallion."

"Holy crap! Is that what I think it is?"

"Yes."

"Where?"

"In the display room."

"But how?"

"No idea, Yoshi."

"This means Moffitt is stuck here."

"Yes and he's now flat on his back. A card he was carrying identified him as Claude Marshall."

"Well I'll be."

Paul held up the medallion. "If he pulls through, he'll want this really bad and will no doubt do anything to get it. Take this back to the office and lock it in the safe. Do it before you do anything else." Paul handed Yoshi the small evidence bag.

"I got you. Claude Marshall, Moffitt, how about that," Yoshi said shaking his head

"And, Yoshi, remember, keep this under wraps. Also call Carrie and Mario."

"Right away. Where are you headed?"

"The hospital. Hope that I can talk to Gray."

▼▼▼▼▼ 2

The situation grew tense for everyone. Gray's condition was not improving and Julia was devastated. The four detectives did all they could to comfort her. The hours passed painfully slowly but the news of Gray's condition didn't improve. Early the following morning, Paul sat with Julia in the visitor's lounge trying to make small talk but most of the time there was an uncomfortable silence. When Carrie arrived at 9:15, Paul excused himself and returned to District HQ. He told Carrie to call him immediately if there was any change. No sooner had he entered his office than the phone rang. Paul quickly reached for it.

"Salvatore."

"Detective, this is Doctor Wenfield at Memorial. I have some news." Salvatore prayed. He first wanted to be sure Gray was okay, then to know if they had saved Moffitt.

"What have you got Doctor?"

"The patient, your prisoner, is still alive but I'm afraid his condition is critical. There is a possibility he might have suffered brain damage from the poison. It was in his system for some time and almost killed him but we were able..." The doctor now had Paul's complete attention.

"Wait, wait, wait a second, Doctor. Poison? What poison? Are you telling me he was poisoned?"

"Yes, Detective. He had a large dose in his system. Luckily we detected it quickly and took counter-measures. But whether we caught it in time has yet to be determined. As you know, he is also suffering from bad burns to his face and hands. We have no idea what caused them. You say this might be your killer?"

"Yes. He had plastic surgery to elude us once; he won't get that chance again. When anyone tends to him, one of our people must accompany them. Don't take any chances, do you understand Doctor?"

"I understand. But Detective, I'm a little confused."

"Why's that?"

"You said this man underwent cosmetic surgery?"

"That's correct, why?"

"No work like that was performed." It was like a punch in the gut. Paul quickly recovered.

"Doctor, we have proof that he underwent extensive surgical procedures to change his identity. Both on his face and his hands."

"That may be Detective, but not this patient. Although he was badly burned, I can assure you this man never had plastic surgery." Paul's heart fell. He could taste bile. Sweat poured from his body like the dew from a car on a cold foggy morning. This could not be happening. Gray swore it was Moffitt. The ID card said it was Claude Marshall, one and the same; he had no doubt about it.

"Doctor, I want a thorough examination. Have your best plastic surgeon examine him. I must know right away. In the meantime I will have someone there to get his prints."

"We don't need to go through all that. I..."

"Doctor, I am not asking you, I'm telling you. I want an examination performed. I must know the identity of that man. Do you hear me? I want concrete confirmation. You understand, Doctor?"

"Yes I understand Detective but I don't..." Salvatore was no longer in a calm frame of mind. If Moffitt had managed to elude them again, he doubted he would be able to stand the disappointment. He knew for certain Gray Farlon wouldn't.

"Damn it, Doctor, do you not understand plain English? Cut the crap and do the job. I'm not making a damn request. I want to know who the hell he is and I want to know within the next 12 hours. Am I making myself clear? I don't want excuses, just make it happen." He slammed the phone down, got out of his seat and left his office.

▼▼▼▼▼ *3*

After lunch, on his way to the parking garage, Paul ran into Yoshi and Mario as they emerged from the cafeteria.

"Hey Paul, where are you going?" Yoshi said.

"The hospital."

"Mind if we tag along?"

"Not at all. What about Carrie?"

"She went over to have lunch with Julia. We just received a piece of bad news. Moffitt is not Moffitt after all."

"Not Moffitt? Then who the hell is he?" Yoshi asked.

"No idea, Yoshi. Doctors are checking him thoroughly. I've also asked them to take a set of prints. That should give us an answer quickly."

"Damn, that's a hell of a blow. Good thing Gray's not aware of it."

Mario looked concerned. "What is his condition, Paul?"

"Can't say. Doctors have been working on him and they're doing all they can. Although he's a fighter, it doesn't look good."

When the three detectives arrived at the hospital, Carrie and Julia were seated in the visitors lounge. Julia looked exhausted.

"Hi Julia, how's he doing?" They each gave Julia a reassuring hug then took a seat around a small oval table. Julia picked up the conversation.

"He didn't have a good night. They had to take him back into surgery two hours ago. He started hemorrhaging again. They are trying to stop it but he's in bad shape Paul. The bullet passed through his left side damaging the heart and arteries. His age is against him, and with that amount of damage they're only giving him a 20 percent chance of pulling through." Julia was managing to maintain her composure though everyone could see how much of a strain it was on her.

"Julia, I'm so very sorry this happened."

"Paul, please, don't beat yourself up over it. It wasn't your fault. My father has a will and determination of his own. He does what he thinks he should and that is commendable. I am very surprised it has taken this long for a bullet to catch up with him."

"He's a tough old bird and has the constitution of an ox. He'll make it through, Julia," Carrie said with as much encouragement as she could manage.

"Time will tell, Carrie. But he won't rest...you all know that. Before they took him into the OR he wanted to know if we had heard anything about Moffitt. Damn he's a stubborn man. Why didn't he just quit and be done with it? Why did he have to pick it up and start all over again?"

"Julia, you can't blame him. Police work has been his life; it's in his blood. He is and always will be the best. His work gave him life especially after you left. When your mom died he still had you. Then he had nothing but his work. When they took that away from him, his life went to pieces."

"I'd no idea until he told me everything."

"Julia, even if you had been here, there was nothing you could have done. He had to work it out for himself. He had to realize he still had a life."

"Yes, but you gave him the opportunity Paul."

"No, I only offered him an alternate path. He could have quite easily walked the other way but he didn't. It was only because of you he made the effort. Julia, you gave him the drive; you gave him hope."

"How long will we have to wait for results?" Mario asked.

"The doctor said it could be three to four hours. I was speaking to him just before you arrived."

"Then I guess we have a long wait. We also have news that's not so good. Moffitt is..." Paul's cell phone started to buzz. He pulled it from his pocket.

"Salvatore."

"Detective, this is Steve."

"Yes Steve, what have you got for me?"

"I'm not so sure you want to hear this."

"Nevertheless, lay it on me."

"Your prisoner, victim or whatever you wish to call him is definitely not who you think he is."

"So I have been told. Then who the hell is he?"

"David Griffith." Paul was thunderstruck.

"Griffith! But...that's impossible. We thought Griffith...are you certain?"

"There is no question, Paul. It's Griffith." Paul rose from his chair and began to pace.

"Then Moffitt...okay. Steve, thanks for the call." In almost hypnotic slow motion Paul placed the cell phone back in his pocket.

"What's up, Paul?" Mario asked but received no response. Paul shook his head and then focused.

"That was Steve. He's confirmed we don't have Moffitt. We have Griffith."

"Griffith! How the hell did he get into the act?"

"No idea, Carrie. The problem now is, where is Moffitt?"

"That's if Moffitt is the one we're really after."

"Bite your tongue, Yoshi. We have enough on our plate without having the waters all muddied again."

"I hate to tell you, Paul, but they're already muddied. Griffith just did that."

"Whoever our killer is, he's pretty damn clever and cunning."

"We can't let our guard down for a second."

Paul sat down. "You're right, Carrie, we cannot." For the remainder of the day the detectives came and went from the lounge. The atmosphere was somber and each silently prayed for the best though they feared the worst. By 5:30 Julia was growing nervous having had no news about her father. She now only sat barely participating in conversation. Early in the evening as they all sat talking quietly over the new developments, the doctor walked up.

"Julia, may I have a word?" Julia looked up with panic written on her face. She got up and walked with the doctor. They disappeared through the double doors at the far side of the room.

"That doesn't look good."

"No, Yoshi, it doesn't."

"She's a wonderful person. Such a pity she has to suffer like this. She loves her father dearly," Carrie said.

"Yes, and she finally realized Gray was everything she needed in a father. I only hope it's not bad news."

"I hope it's..." Mario's voice trailed off into silence. Time seemed to be on hold as the four detectives sat staring into space, each saying a silent prayer. Paul glanced up at the clock on the far wall. Almost half an hour had passed since Julia left with the doctor. The anxiety of waiting and the unknown was tearing at them all.

Paul rose and began to pace again. Yoshi walked over to the wall of glass, stood and stared out into the night. Only the ghostly reflection of his face stared back at him. Carrie and Mario continued to sit in silence.

▼▼▼▼▼ 4

The doctor guided Julia into a small waiting room and the two sat. She hoped for good news but realized it was not to be. Her heart was heavy. The doctor was talking to her but she hardly heard him. Her mind was focused on the man who had just come back into her life only to possibly be snatched away again. She drifted from one memory to another, pictures of the past raced through her mind. Those times of joy and times of heartache all piled into her head at once. Then the doctor's voice, like a distant echo, intruded on her thoughts.

"...he's holding on, Julia, how we don't know. But we must be honest...we don't hold much hope. The bullet caused a great deal of damage. I'm so very sorry to be the one to give you this news."

Julia cleared her head. "Please, doctor, I understand. Is he able to talk?" she said, forcing back the tears.

"Yes. You may go in and see him." Julia stood. The doctor ushered Julia through a door, into a room with one bed surrounded by three nurses and two other doctors. She stopped and looked at the frail form of her father, almost invisible in the large bed. He looked so small lying there; a man once powerful and healthy, now weak, frail, so pale, his life slipping away.

"You may stay as long as you wish, Julia. We'll leave you. If you need anything, please call."

"Thank you, Doctor," Julia said softly as the five left the room. The doctor squeezed her arm, tried a reassuring smile, then left. Slowly, and with great effort, Gray turned his head and stared at his daughter.

"Don't stand so far away, Honey, come closer." His voice sounded so distant, just a whisper on the wind. He was dying, he knew it but he would not let that get in the way of talking to his daughter. He spoke slowly but forcefully. "Sit and let's talk." Julia pulled a chair close to the bed and sat. Taking her father's hand, she rested her arms on the bed. Tears filled her eyes.

"Why, Daddy? Why did you have to do this?"

"Let's not talk about this mess, Honey. Let's talk about you."

"But, Daddy..." Gray raised his hand to quiet her.

"Ssssh...relax. Just be calm. Listen to me for a moment..."

"But Daddy you should not be talking so much. You need to rest and get..."

"Julia, where I'm going I'll get plenty of rest. For now humor me please. Listen to me for once." He paused, took a shallow breath and continued slowly. "You were the most wonderful thing that happened in our lives. I..." Gray paused trying to gather his strength. He looked up at Julia who was crying quietly, tears dripping off her chin and falling onto the bed covers. "I was never more proud of anything than I was of you. When your mother died..." He stopped again, as pain shot through him, not a pain of agony but

The River Styx

one of remorse. He cried. He looked at Julia, "You look so much like her. But when you left that day my life ended. I had nowhere to go, Julia; I was lost...lost without you...lost without your mother..." Tears rolled down his cheeks onto the sheets. Julia was sobbing as she watched her father slowly fade before her.

"Daddy, please don't, you have to..."

"Julia, don't interrupt me while I'm talking." He smiled weakly. "Now, where was I? Oh yes...when I lost my job that was the final blow..." Again he paused. He squeezed Julia's hand. "I lost what I had worked all my life to build, but far worse than that I lost the two most precious and important people in my life. You know that I'm not the kind of person to give in, but at that moment I was ready to..." The strain was getting to him, he found it harder to breathe, and he was losing his ability to focus on Julia. He could see the tears falling from her chin; he reached up, his hand shaking and wiped them away. "No more, Honey...no more tears." His voice was now barely a whisper. "It's time for me to move on. I want you to be strong." It was becoming difficult for Gray to catch a breath.

"Follow your heart, don't...don't let trivialities get in the way. You...only go around once, Honey; don't mess it up like I did. And don't you let him get away." He stopped again, his breathing very shallow.

"I don't understand."

Panting, he went on. "Paul. He loves you. I think you know that, but he's afraid you won't let him in...give him a chance."

Julia rested her hand on his arm. "I will Daddy. But it's time for you to rest."

"Hush, child, there's no need...your mother's waiting..." He knew his strength was rushing from him like water through a breached dam. He gasped for more air. "Go get that Pulitzer, show them you can do it. I'm proud of you Honey...so very proud to have you as my daughter...I love you so much, Julia, and..." His eyes grew misty with that far away empty stare. A tear trickled down his cheek. His last breath escaped from his lungs as he departed this life. Julia buried her head in the crook of his neck and cried.

"No, Daddy, why...why..." She did not move for a while unwilling to let her father go. She had lost him once more but this time for good. Why had God done this to her? He had given him back only to take him away again. It wasn't fair. It was not supposed to be like this. A terrible anger filled her momentarily then faded. She knew he would not want her to be angry.

Julia lifted her head and looked at her father once more. "Goodbye, Daddy, I love you too..." she whispered as she reached and closed his eyes, the tears falling more freely now that it was over. She stood, leaned over, kissed him on the forehead and quietly left the room.

▼▼▼▼▼ 5

Chicago said goodbye to the man whose life's mission had been to clean up her streets. Graham Farlon's funeral was a memorable event of pomp and ceremony. The Mayor, numerous other dignitaries and a large contingency from Chicago's finest attended. Julia held her composure through it all feeling great pride as each tribute was made in honor of the man she had never really known. It was a sunny day on that 1st day of August. The haunting tune of 'Amazing Grace' from the bagpipes echoed mournfully across the cemetery as if beckoning all the dead to join the ceremony. It was a grand day to send a true Irishman to meet his creator and the woman he loved so deeply. Julia knew he was happy because he was with her mother now for eternity. That alone gave her comfort.

It was time to gather her thoughts and move on. What did the future hold? What should she do? Where should she go? As she stood and looked over the city her father loved so passionately, she felt cheated. She must return to New York and at the very least finish what she had started. After that, who knew. Yet as she looked at her life, all that she had in New York held little meaning for her now. Julia finally realized she loved this city almost as much as her father had. Then there was Paul.

As she walked away from the gravesite surrounded by all those who had been so close to her father, she was at peace. Then her thoughts turned to Sally. Poor Sally, a prisoner of her mind, who had only three days earlier been shut away in a 10x10 world, a world as alien to her as another planet. Even if she recovered, could she find peace and contentment in a place she despised? Julia felt compassion flood her heart for this woman and was determined to do everything she could to help her.

Julia had lost her father in death...Sally Mayfield lost her life without death. Should she recover, there was no way home. There would never be that familiar welcome and the warm comforting hugs from those who loved and missed her. She deserved a life so much better than the one in which she had been unwittingly thrust. Julia walked to the car accompanied by five of her father's closest friends.

▼▼▼▼▼ 6

Griffith had been unconscious the day he was admitted to hospital and had remained that way until August 3rd, one week after the museum incident. Paul then received startling news. A doctor from the hospital notified him that Griffith had regained consciousness sufficiently to talk. He immediately sent Mario to see what could be gleaned from the man. The conversation was very much one sided. Griffith wanted to tell his story and

The River Styx

for 20 minutes Mario said very little. Soon after that Griffith slipped into a coma. What he told Mario shed some startling light on the events of the last seven years. On this morning the investigating team was gathered in the War Room, the chair where Gray always sat, empty.

"Now what, Paul?" Carrie said.

"We proceed with our investigation."

"What about Griffith?"

"What about him, Mario?"

"What if he recovers?"

"I was about to cover that. Griffith and Maitland are little fish. It's the big fish we must concern ourselves with…namely Moffitt. As far as Griffith recovering, we'll cross that bridge when we get to it. At the moment his doctors hold very little hope of that happening."

"But that doesn't answer the question, Paul. If he recovers, we have a case with no possible solution."

"Before we go on, let me tell you what Gray and I discussed a week or so before he passed away. We had no idea, at the time, that Griffith was part of the big picture, but nevertheless that's still applicable. Griffith dies…he's our killer. It ends with him and the case is closed. There is no alternative. It was Gray's intention to never let the killer get away, whomever he might have been."

"I'm not sure I like the implications, Paul."

"I'm not implying anything, Carrie; only that Griffith is the scapegoat."

"We'll still be looking under rocks."

"No, Yoshi, it ends there with no further questions."

"I still don't like this, Paul. You make it sound as if Griffith is dead already."

"Carrie, with his doctors giving him a thousand to one chance, yes he might as well be dead. The poison caused irreversible brain damage. They were more than surprised when he was able to talk to Mario"

"But I hope I'm not hearing what I think I am." Paul knew what Carrie was driving at as she pressed on. "Gray said he had no intention to let the killer get away, that we would do whatever it took to close this case. It was a troubling statement."

"Yes it was, but it was a mutual decision. We agreed the killer had to be stopped. We needed a way out. Griffith may just be our salvation."

"I'm not comfortable with it, Paul. You're saying he's our ticket out of this case regardless of the truth?"

"I'm afraid that's about it, Carrie."

"Of course, there may be a simple solution to all this."

"And what might that be, Carrie?"

"Moffitt could kick from the disease he contracted using the medallion. Julia did say he was ill."

"That's a good point, only we can't sit around waiting for that to happen."

"Then everything now hinges on Griffith?"

"Yes, Yoshi. He's become the main part of the equation. But we can't discount Moffitt, the one who can solve this entire case for us," Paul said.

Mario locked his hands behind his head. "So we still have to find Moffitt?"

Carrie then remembered a brief conversation she had had with Patrick. "That may not be necessary Mario. Paul, I think you should get O'Malley in here."

"Why is that, Carrie?"

"Just prior to Gray passing away, O'Malley dug up something very interesting, but I'll let him tell you about it. He was so excited he could barely contain himself. I convinced him he should wait for a more appropriate time."

"Then let's get him in here!"

Five minutes later O'Malley was seated at the table.

"I understand you have something of interest for us, Patrick."

"Yes. I'm sure this is going to come as one hell of a shock" Although enthusiastic, Patrick appeared a little subdued.

Paul folded his arms. "Then go ahead."

Patrick hesitated for a moment glancing at the chair at the end of the table; empty, silent. As he gathered his thoughts, he looked at the faces around him. He knew what he was about to say could be a critical part of closing the case.

▼▼▼▼▼ 7

Julia stared at the young woman seated in a chair before the large window. She looked so frail, her pale face showed no sign of expression or recognition. The silence that enveloped the room was one of sorrow, tragic loss and terrible defeat. Sally had retreated into a place deep within her mind; unreachable and imprisoned by her own fears. So much had been lost to this tragic event. Here was a woman in the prime of her life, living but not alive. She existed in the present, her mind in another place; maybe home, where it longed to be.

Tears of deep sadness ran down Julia's cheeks. Sally had become a dear and valued friend. She had been confident Sally's life was going to be a good one and that she would eventually adapt and settle down. Now she sat in this empty room, but in another place. Friends and doctors had tried everything humanly possible to turn Sally away from the abyss but had failed miserably; she had plummeted to the bottom. It was no one's fault; it was just the way things turned out, a terrible unavoidable tragedy. But Julia was not ready to give up.

For one hour every evening Julia sat and quietly spoke to this young woman. She believed her presence was an obvious sign to Sally that she was not alone. But no matter what Julia did or said, the young woman never stirred. She continued, hour after hour, to stare through the window, her face expressionless, not hearing or see, but Julia believed differently. Julia stood, walked to the chair and rested her hands on the silent woman's shoulders.

"Goodbye, Sally. Take care of yourself. I'll be back tomorrow." As she kissed Sally goodbye, something wonderful happened. A single tear trickled from the corner of Sally's eye. Julia said a silent prayer of hope.

▼▼▼▼▼ *8*

Patrick took a deep breath. "I'll start with the letter that arrived the day after...Detective Farlon died. It's from the killer."

Paul gasped. "From the killer?"

"Yes. Shall I read it?"

"Good idea. Go ahead." O'Malley proceeded.

Friends,

By the time you receive this you will have arrived at one conclusion. I am unstoppable. That is the heart of it all, don't you think? At the moment you are racking your brains trying to figure out who I am and how you can trap me. You're just wasting your time. I am unstoppable. You have no idea what you're dealing with and by the time you do find out, if you find out, I will be gone forever and you will be left with the biggest unsolved crime of the millennia.

You are all so dense and naive you couldn't find what you were looking for even if it were right under your noses. I am not only unstoppable and even if you did catch me, you would not be able to hold me, because I'm far more superior. Ah yes, how did you all like my charade at the museum? I thought it was rather well done though I say so myself. Thought you had me worried didn't you? Well, I'm sorry to disappoint you all but I'm still quite well and oh yes...free. Sorry about Griffith, but he was expendable.

Hope we can chat again soon. How did you like that little added piece with the gun? Hope Detective Farlon is feeling better.

Until next time, yours cordially,

Charon

P. S. Maybe you should check your valuables.

The group sat in stunned silence. O'Malley passed the letter to Paul.

"Friends! Who the hell does he think...damn that arrogant son of a bitch." The bitterness in Carrie's voice echoed everyone's feelings.

Paul reread it, horrified by its implications. Reading between the lines, he could see this killer was far from finished. An empty foreboding formed in the pit of his stomach. He finished and looked at the group with an expression of anger on his face as he waved the sheet of paper in the air.

"You all heard it."

"I don't believe the blatant impertinence of the bastard," Carrie said.

"Do you think he knows Gray is dead?"

"By now, Yoshi, yes, but not when he wrote this." They fell silent.

Then Mario spoke. "Paul, we can't stop this guy? And what did he mean about checking our valuables?"

Paul did not answer immediately, as he was deep in thought. The statement about valuables troubled him. Then suddenly he realized the implications.

"Excuse me, Paul, but I..." O'Malley tried to interrupt.

Paul cut him off. "Not now, Patrick."

"The medallion. Yoshi, where's the medallion?"

"Right where you told me to put it. In the safe upstairs."

Carrie was confused. "Wait, wait, wait. Wait a second, we have Moffitt's medallion, Paul?"

Patrick tried again. "Excuse me, but may..."

"Please Patrick, not now. We'll hear your comments in a moment." Paul turned to Carrie. "Yes Carrie, I believe we do, but now I'm not so sure. Until a moment ago I had all but forgotten about it. We believe the killer dropped it during the commotion in the museum, but...Yoshi, would you mind getting it?"

Carrie was still confused "Moffitt left the medallion behind?"

"Yes. It was found in the room where the Buddha was on display."

"But why would he leave it?"

"I wondered the same thing, Carrie, now I'm beginning to understand." Yoshi returned and handed Paul the envelope. He removed the medallion. Everyone stared at it and pondered its powers. As if hypnotized by its presence, all eyes followed it as it rotated lazily at the end of the silver chain. Then without saying a word, Paul drew his automatic from under his jacket. He placed the pendant on the old oak table. As he turned the gun around, he gripped it by the barrel. Suddenly he brought the butt crashing down on the pendant.

"Paul, I don't think that's such a good idea."

"Why is that, Carrie?"

"Because you'll only damage your gun. I'm no gem expert, but I believe rubies are the hardest natural stones next to diamonds." Paul ignored Carrie, raised his gun again and brought it down square on the medallion. The outcome shocked everyone. The large red stone shattered.

Carrie gasped. "That's not possible."

"It's quite possible. You see...he switched medallions," Paul said with a grin.

"He left a fake one in the museum?"

"No, Mario. The one he left was genuine. He did it to show us his abilities. He switched it right out of my cabinet."

"But how? Why?"

Paul held up the broken medallion. "No idea, Yoshi, but this proves he did. And the reason he did it was to prove he has the power and we can't touch him." Paul re-holstered his gun and dropped the smashed medallion in the trash.

O'Malley interrupted. "Excuse me, Detective, but I..."

"Oh for crying out loud, what is it, Patrick? This is not the time to ask questions."

"I don't wish to ask a question, Paul."

Paul was somewhat agitated. "Then what?" Just then the phone rang. The room fell silent as Carrie answered. She turned and handed it to Paul.

"It's for you."

"Salvatore."

"Detective, this is Dr. Medfield."

"Yes, Doctor?"

"I'm sorry to inform you, but Mr. Griffith passed away about 15 minutes ago." Paul did not quite know how to react. He was sorry that Griffith had died, but he was elated knowing they could now close the case without recourse. "I'm sorry to hear that, Doctor. Did he wake before he passed?"

"No, Detective, he never regained consciousness again."

"Thank you for calling, Doctor. I will have someone come up there as soon as possible. In the meantime I will have the officer there return to normal duties."

"Very good."

Paul handed the phone back to Carrie. "Griffith just died."

"That's convenient for us," Carrie said.

"True. Now we close the book on this case. And from the media's standpoint, Griffith was the killer. Does everyone understand that?"

"Understood, Paul."

"Paul, I have one question. What about Moffitt? What if he decides to begin again?"

"We'll call it a copycat."

At that moment Paul's attention returned to Patrick "Okay, Patrick, ask your question."

"I don't have a question Paul. I have this." As Patrick waved an envelope in the air, he was about to drop his bombshell.

"And what is that?"

▼▼▼▼▼ 9

The morning sun streamed through the window warming the small room. Julia was visiting Sally, but on this day she was saying goodbye as she was preparing to return to New York. She intended to return to Chicago, the question was when.

"I have to leave, Sally. I will ask Carrie if she will visit as often as she can. I'll be back, but not for a while. I want you to keep trying, Sally. Please, try to come back. You can do it. I know you can. You're strong. Please don't let this thing beat you." Julia reached out to grasp Sally's hands. As she squeezed them, she looked into the eyes of this troubled woman. There was no recognition; Sally only stared ahead at the world beyond her room, oblivious to its existence.

Remorse swept over Julia. What would happen to Sally? Would she wither away in this room, never knowing those who had fought so hard to save her, those who loved her so dearly? It seemed so futile, such a waste of a precious life. So many weeks had passed and there had been no sign of change. As she released Sally's hands, Julia stepped to the window and looked over the lush grounds of the sanitarium.

"It's such a beautiful day, Sally. I wish we could walk in the garden and enjoy it together. Maybe when I return we'll do that." Julia thought of her father and how she had been cheated of her time with him. She longed to hear his voice again, to sit and talk to him. Sadness filled her heart, not for herself but for Sally and so many like her who lived but were nevertheless deprived of a life.

It was time to leave. She hated to go because she knew so much time would elapse before she would return. A tightness formed in her throat. Julia turned from the window, crouched and held Sally's hands again and said goodbye. "I promise that I will be back. But I want to see you well by then. Look after yourself and I will see you soon." Julia kissed her on the forehead, then stood and walked to the door. As she opened it, she looked back at the lonely, pathetic figure. "Bye, Sally." She pulled the door closed and paused for she thought she heard a voice, but Julia knew it must have been the wind.

▼▼▼▼▼ 10

Patrick opened the envelope and removed a sheet of paper. "This is a clipping from an old Chicago news-paper dated August 23, 1866." He passed it to Paul who began to read it. His face slowly lit up with a broad grin. Everyone watched closely and became more curious. Finally Paul burst out laughing.

"What's so hilarious, Paul?"

He then erupted in a burst of joviality. "Hot damn! We're in the clear, Carrie. Now we can close this case and walk away from it. Moffitt's dead." The atmosphere in the room immediately turned electric. Everyone started talking at once.

"Where Paul?"

"Here, in Chicago, in 1866; he apparently suffered a massive heart attack and dropped dead. There is a picture of him at his wake." Paul passed the clipping.

"I don't know if you noticed, Paul, he had his medallion buried with him."

Carrie stopped reading and studied the photo closely. "My God, Patrick's right." The news charged the War Room with a jubilant atmosphere. The clipping was passed to all at the table, and then Patrick added the icing on the cake.

"I think we need to look at the remainder of this story, if I may?"

"Sure, Patrick, go ahead." Patrick proceeded to explain the connections between Moffitt, Winslow, Maitland, Whitley and Griffith. The group listened intently, finally learning how it all fell into place; why Moffitt had gone on a killing rampage as revenge against Gray for having killed his twin brother and against the law for letting him down. How he planned the entire operation; how he used Griffith, Winslow and Whitley for his own gratification. How he avoided being caught. Patrick laid it all out for them much to their amazement and curiosity. When he finished, he was bombarded with questions.

"Where did you find all this information?"

"Partly from this, Mario," Patrick said waving the clipping in the air. "There is a lot of information in this article. I found one section particularly interesting. Marshall wrote a book called, of all things, 'Charon', which he published in 1845." A murmur rippled through the team.

"1845? My God, he did get around."

"Apparently so, Carrie. I learned a great deal on his background from his book. He was not adverse to spilling everything, feeling confident there was no way he would ever get caught." Patrick picked up the book and showed it to everyone, then passed it around the table. "This is the book he wrote. I went digging in the library and found it in the old book section. He published it under his full name, William Bennet Moffitt."

Paul paused from studying the book. "You mean the murdering bastard recorded his escapades for posterity?"

Patrick nodded his head positively. "Exactly. Everything is in there, in graphic detail."

Carrie shook her head. "This is unbelievable. He thought he could cheat death, but it caught up with him. He also thought he could outwit us, but he was outwitted by his own cleverness."

"He *almost* outwitted us, Carrie. If it hadn't been for all your efforts, this case would have remained an unsolved mystery and our killer never brought to justice."

"But he won't be brought to justice, Paul."

"Not in a court of law, Yoshi, but he has been given a name, be it the wrong one, a name nonetheless."

"You're referring to Griffith?" Mario said.

"Yes. With him this case ends."

Patrick interjected. "Moffitt was totally off his rocker, and possibly for good reason. At the age of ten, his father committed suicide. Young Moffitt discovered the body. The father had shot himself in the head. From that moment Hal Moffitt was never the same."

"I can understand why. That's enough to drive adults nuts. I wish Gray had been here to see the outcome."

"I do too, Carrie, I do too."

"Now we know Moffitt definitely changed his identity and became Winslow. He then set himself up in the 1860's as Claude Marshall and by traveling back and forth in time was able to pull off what could have become the crime of the century, but his arrogance was his downfall. If he had left Griffith out of the equation, it would have ended differently. Instead, we now have a crime that will only go down as another event in the annuls of crime solving history."

"Paul, what happens to the second medallion?"

"Yoshi, if everything has been taken care of as Gray wished, it's quite safe." Paul looked at Carrie. "Carrie?"

"It was taken care of exactly as Gray wanted. The medallion now resides at the bottom of the lake."

"You threw it in the lake?"

"We did, Yoshi. Mario and I took a trip on a friend's boat. A few miles offshore we discreetly dropped it over the side."

"And the fake one?"

"At St. Pius Church Patrick, and no one is the wiser. Of course, if our friend Moffitt lived up to his sly reputation, it would not surprise me if he left some gag trump card behind to cause us future heartburn." Paul stood. "I believe this wraps the case up except for all the paperwork." The team congratulated each other as they slowly filed from the War Room. While staring at the crime board, Paul recalled the haunting, macabre events they had encountered over the last months.

With everyone gone, a strange sort of hush fell on the room. It was one of victory, yet one of poignancy. They had won the war but at great expense, for the victory was bittersweet. Paul glanced up at the ceiling.

"Say, old friend, I know you're up there. I'm going to miss you. You were not only a good friend Gray, but a great mentor and teacher as well. As they said at your memorial service, all those who knew you loved you. We all wish you could have been here to celebrate the solving and closing of another crime. Hope you're happy the way it turned out. Well, goodbye, old friend. See you around and Godspeed."

Paul walked over to the phone and called Julia in New York.

"Hi, Honey."

"Paul! What a surprise. It's so good to hear your voice. I can't wait to get back. I'm getting ready to wrap up here. The writing is all but complete. I should have it together by next week."

"That's great. Good luck with it. You'll get that Pulitzer because your Dad was behind you."

"True, but it's no longer that important. What's up?"

"The killer is dead."

"Fantastic! Congratulations, Paul. How?"

"Electrocuted, trying to break into the Field Museum." He lied, although he knew he would tell her eventually.

"Bummer."

"Right, but it's finally over."

"That's great. I'm so glad for you."

"When are you coming back?"

"In about two weeks."

"I miss you."

"Yes me too." There was a long nervous silence.

"You all right Julia?"

"Yes. It's just that I miss him so much, Paul."

"I miss him too. Look, hurry back, will you?"

"I will. I'll see you in two weeks. Love you."

"Love you, too." The line went dead. Paul replaced the receiver, turned out the lights and left the War Room, as he closed the door quietly behind him.

EPILOGUE

Reflections

▼▼▼▼▼ *1*

Chicago – September 1, 2006

Eight months to the day and it was all over, yet the haunting memories remained. They would never leave. Even on those bright, warm, sunny days it cast a cold shadow, sending a winter chill through those involved in a most evil encounter. They would not forget, although with time the stark sharpness of it would become frayed and weathered. No matter how much time passed, the phantoms would always be there, creeping into their dreams. The evidence of those eight months had been buried as deep as the Mariana Trench never to be seen or heard of again. It was better that way. Better for those who lived the experience, better for all humanity. But as much as those involved wished it, they weren't forgotten.

Julia leaned against the stone wall and gazed over the calm dark waters of Lake Michigan. It was a tranquil evening invaded only by ghosts. The gentle lapping of the waves against the concrete and stone pier and the distant rumbling of traffic were the only sounds interrupting the stillness of the evening. It was a time out of time. The lights from boats anchored in the bay danced and shimmered on the surface of the water. August had been a warm and peaceful month, an opportunity to reminisce over old times, happier times. It was a time of healing, adjusting, planning for the years ahead and remembering old friends.

Julia missed her father terribly. She missed him because she had finally begun to know him. Missed him because they had been apart for so long and had lost so much. Her world had been turned upside down. Nothing would ever be the same. She would never look at a clock as she had in the past. Time had taken on a completely new concept. They had buried her father with great pomp and ceremony, but his spirit still walked the streets of this city.

As she turned, Julia leaned her back against the wall and rested her elbows on the ledge. She gazed at the dark, cloudless sky lit only by a billon stars. Light that was thousands of millions of years old. What stories could they tell, she wondered? Were they mysterious and unknown messages out of the past that might never be understood? Time for her suddenly became a monster that had finally revealed itself. The mystery had been comforting. The knowing was terrifying. She tried to shake the thoughts from her mind but they were caught, trapped like a fly in a spider's web.

What became of the medallion, she wondered? Had it truly been buried with Moffitt, as they all hoped? The second one, found in April, now lay at the bottom of the lake. Moffitt was dead and he had taken his medallion with him, but it still retained its powers. Would it some day be exhumed and fall into another's hands? Would they become twisted, perverted, and corrupted by its power and use it for mindless, demonic purposes? Or would its secrets remain buried for eternity? That, she hoped, is how it would be.

Julia was happy its companion was also unreachable; happy it could not be used again. It could no longer cause needless pain and suffering. She knew they had done the right thing by casting it into the depths of the lake. There it would remain, hidden for eternity, if humanity were lucky. Yet, there would always be a nagging doubt that its secret might be rediscovered.

Time was interminable and best left alone. Let it run its natural course. The river of sand had stopped, the hourglass cracked; but time had not escaped. They had seen to that. The past should remain in the past. Dabbling had proved disastrous. It was trespassing on forbidden ground. People died and that was unacceptable. The city had, at last, returned to normal. The Mannequin Murders were to most just a memory overshadowed by other more pressing events. But for those who had been involved in its web of terror and intrigue, it had been a journey through hell. Not everything was as it should be. Hundreds of questions still remained, emerging from the darkness like fireflies on a summer evening. They came then vanished, unresolved.

The one person who had given so much meaning to her life was gone. He had promised her the Pulitzer, it might be forthcoming, but it would have little meaning for her now. The father she loved so dearly would be unable to share her excitement. She still cried each time she thought of him. How he had worried about her. How he had worked so hard to rebuild their lives, trying to make up for all the shortcomings. In the end, did it really matter? He had told her forgiveness was the cure for all ills, the remedy for happiness. They had enjoyed the brief but precious time spent together, but she could not accept the loss and would never forgive the one who took her father from her. Tears trickled from her eyes once again. Remedy or not, she just couldn't bring herself to forgive. So many things were wrong at that moment, things that could not be ignored. Maybe with time that would change, but the pain would not leave, no matter how hard she tried.

Julia's thoughts drifted to the victims, and to one in particular. Sally was still in limbo. She existed somewhere between the present and the past. Seeded in one and thrust mercilessly into the other, then by tragic fate snatched back. But she was alien to both. She was the only surviving victim of a heinous crime, yet she had no home. No matter where she stood she was out of place. Without a past, Sally had been condemned to a life she despised from the moment she was thrown, bleeding and dying, into it. She was the proverbial fish out of water. The fear was that she would finally suffocate. She was used to a simpler life, more space, and a slower pace.

Julia knew that if Sally was unable to adapt it could be her demise. The knowledge of whom and what she was terrified her and had driven her to the brink of insanity. Could Sally Mayfield survive in the 21st century, or would she remain that fish out of water? Though a product of the 21st century, maybe Sally Mayfield should never have remembered. She had come through her therapy, but not unscathed. Then she was discharged from the sanitarium and was now making a bold attempt to adjust to a new life in an alien world. Would she? Could she adjust and accept the change? She continued to view the world about her with skepticism and trepidation, something that concerned Julia.

Julia shivered. Paul noticed and put his arm around her and pulled her close to him. She snuggled closer seeking comfort.

"Cold?"

"Not really. Just footsteps on a lonely grave, chills from alien thoughts."

"Better stay away from those."

"Difficult."

"I know."

"Things have become really screwed up Paul, haven't they?"

"They were, but I believe it's looking better."

"True, but what's done cannot be undone. There is no way it can be corrected…ever."

"No it can't Julia, time won't allow it."

"Time…there's that ominous word again. It is our biggest enemy. We spend such a short period on this earth; we are but fleeting shadows that pass unnoticed. We can heal our wounds but time will not erase the terrible memories."

"But don't forget the good memories. As for passing unnoticed, I doubt that. Your Dad made his mark on this city. He certainly did not go unnoticed and he won't be forgotten. You made your mark in the world of Journalism and you won't be forgotten. We are, for the most part, just little fish swimming around in a great big pond, but we can make a difference."

"I suppose you're right, Paul. But it's so unfair that someone like Sally is afflicted with such a devastating and debilitating condition through no fault of her own."

"That's a terrible tragedy, but as the saying goes, life is unfair and it's that way so often."

"Isn't that the truth. At least she regained her memories even though they were full of so much pain and terror. But her doctor did say confronting them will help make her a stronger person."

"I hope so. You really like her, don't you?"

"I have grown to love her like my own sister. I believe it was that bond that gave her reason to fight her way back. You have no idea how happy I was when she spoke for the first time."

"Then things haven't turned out so bad."

"I only wish we could be sure the horror of it all was truly over."

"Honey, there are never any guarantees, only reality."

"Where are we to go from here?"

"I have no idea Julia. As Mr. Lee would say, Confucius say road of life is short and unknown; rest often and enjoy the solitude."

"I guess he would say something like that. But it's so true."

"Anyway if Confucius didn't say it, guaranteed Mr. Lee would have. He comes up with many of them, some having no practical meaning whatsoever." They laughed.

"I'll tell you where I wish to go from here."

"Where?"

"Marry me."

Julia pushed herself away from the wall, turned and faced Paul. "Marry...are you serious?"

He reached out and pulled her to him. Julia did not resist. She wrapped her arms around his waist and rested her head on his shoulder relishing the security.

He kissed the top of her head. "I've never been more so."

To her surprise Julia felt the butterflies of excitement flitter in her stomach. "But...Paul I'm not sure. We have never really talked about it."

"Tell me you haven't thought about it."

She looked up at him. "Well, yes I suppose I have but...well I'm not sure I'm ready to take such a big step."

"I love you. I guess I always have. Your father knew it and tried to get it out of me but I never told him."

"Why?"

"He was afraid."

"Afraid? Daddy was never afraid. What was he afraid of?"

"He thought you were a devout Journalist, that it would get in the way of a good relationship. He feared you would end up breaking someone's heart."

"I can see why he thought that I suppose, but it's not that way. I could never put my work before the one I love, and I do love you Paul, but marriage...give me a little time, will you?"

"Take whatever time you need. I'm going nowhere."

"Thanks Paul." They stepped away from the wall. With arms locked around each other, they walked toward the parking lot. Each was caught up in their own thoughts, wondering where the road would lead, carrying their burden of terrifying, haunting secrets. Julia paused, turned and for a moment stared over the darkened waters. The chill of knowing what lay beneath the waves would forever trouble her. Could she find peace in the days ahead? She turned and they continued to walk.

Suddenly she said. "I hate that word."

"What word's that?"

"Time."

▼▼▼▼▼ 2

Chicago – February 2, 2007

The TV was playing to itself as Julia relaxed on the sofa with her eyes closed, a glass of red wine in her hand. She was half listening to the 6:00P.M. news when suddenly she sat bolt upright. The glass of wine slipped from her fingers and shattered on the parquet. She was stunned, terrified, her whole body shook, she was not breathing as she stared in horror at the screen. Then she gasped for a lung full of air and yelled at the top of her voice.

"Paul, come quickly!"

Paul, who was busy in the kitchen, responded with mild interest. "What is it, Honey?"

Julia, still on the verge of hysterics, yelled. "Would you just get in here...hurry!"

Paul, realizing something was amiss, raced into the living room. Julia was perched on the edge of the sofa with her eyes locked on the TV. She didn't turn or acknowledge his presence as he sat beside her. The newscaster was introducing a field reporter in LA.

> *"...to bring us up to date on the situation we go to Shannon O'Donnell in Los Angeles...What can you tell us about this case so far Shannon?"*
>
> *"Well, Tom, here in downtown Los Angeles the body of a young woman was discovered on the street behind me at about 5:30 this morning. She was dressed in eveningwear and had been wrapped in a rug. I have spoken to a number of people working this case, but there is not a lot of information available at the moment. I did speak to Detective Alvarez, the detective on the case, but he would only say that she was Caucasian, had been dead for about three to four hours and was between 20 and*

> *25 years old, with shoulder length blond hair and blue eyes.*
>
> *Now the strange thing about this case, Tom, is its similarity to a series of murders that took place in Chicago in January of 2006. I was told that..."*

Julia turned to Paul, terror written on her face. "Dear God, Paul, what the hell's going on? It can't be happening all over again?"

"Julia, calm down."

"Calm down! How can you say calm down? Paul, this brings back too many terrible, haunting memories."

"I know, Julia, but there's no need for panic." Paul placed his arm around her shoulders. "It's a copycat. There's no doubt about it. Some lunatic has decided he would like to try to duplicate the crime we dealt with and solved a year ago. He probably wants to see if he can get away with it."

Julia shivered. "It gives me the creeps, Paul. But what if it's..."

"Julia, don't even think that. You know full well that what you think may be happening is not only improbable but absolutely impossible."

"Like time travel?"

"Oh for crying out loud, Moffitt is dead. We confirmed that to be 100 percent fact. We dealt with time travel and got through it unscathed. We are not looking at resurrection here so you best forget it."

"It's just that I have this uneasy feeling."

"If it will make you feel any better, I will call LA in the morning and speak to the Chief Medical Examiner and see what they can tell me."

"Paul, you know they are not going to give you any information."

"If I tell them I was on the case out here, you bet your life they will. Besides we could be of great help to them."

"You may be right."

"Of course I'm right. Now turn the TV off and let's get to bed."

Julia suddenly froze. "What's the date?"

"Um, February 2, I believe, yes it's February 2. Why?"

"One year and four days since he tried to kill Sally."

Printed in the United States
62496LVS00002B/415-474